About the Author

Traci Harding, bestselling author of *the Ancient Future* series, has published 22 books through HarperCollins/Voyager Australia, Brio Books, Bolinda Audio and Dragon Circle Publishing. Her work blends fantasy, fact, esoteric theory, time travel and quantum physics, into adventurous romps through history, alternative dimensions, universes and states of consciousness. Her books have been published in several languages throughout the world.

To find out more about Traci and her books, visit her website at:
traciharding.com

For autographed copies of Traci's books, visit her store at:
allthingstraci.com.au

Get Exclusive Content at Patreon:
https://www.patreon.com/user?u=20034469

Find Traci on Facebook at: Traci Harding Fans - All Things Traci Store - Trazling & the "Mastering Your Reality with Traci Harding" Group

Traci is also on:
Twitter: @tracharding
Instagram: traciharding_author
YouTube: youtube.com/@TraciHardingChannel
& Redbubble: redbubble.com/people/traciharding/shop?asc=u

Books by TRACI HARDING

THE ANCIENT FUTURE TRILOGY
The Ancient Future (1)
An Echo In Time (2)
Masters of Reality (3)

THE CELESTIAL TRIAD
Chronicle of Ages (1)
Tablet of Destinies (2)
The Cosmic Logos (3)

THE TRIAD OF BEING
Being of the Field (1)
The Universe Parallel (2)
The Light-field (3)

THE TIMEKEEPERS
Dreaming of Zhou Gong (1)
The Eternity Gate (2)
A.W.O.L. (3)

THE MYSTIQUE TRILOGY
Gene of Isis (1)
The Dragon Queens (2)
The Black Madonna (3)

THE STAND ALONE NOVELS
The Alchemist's Key
Ghostwriting
Book of Dreams
The Storyteller's Muse
The Immortal Bind
This Present Past
The Twelve Chapters of the Infinite Night

The
Twelve Chapters
of the
Infinite Night

Traci
Harding

Character Art by Rei Harding

Dragon Circle Publishing

ISBN : 978-0-6456141-0-7

First Published by Dragon Circle Publishing in 2022

More information : http://www.allthingstraci.com.au

Cover design by Traci Harding
Character Design and Art by Rei Harding
Dragon design by Ben Ferguson
Logo design by Traci Harding
Author Photo by Kathy Luu
Title Text Typeset Khiara Script 48/30
Typeset in Goudy Old Style 11/14

Dedication

This book is dedicated to
my lovely Patreons
past and present

Cassandra - Lindsay - Carmel - Erica
Kristen - Gyrid - Erin
Nanci & Zanthe
Dean & Noella
Alison - Kylie - Hael - Tess
Rebekah - Acrah - Sarah W
Paula - Sarah M - Talie - Jenni - Janine
Brinley - Chelsea - Laura - Miranda - Leah
Anastasia - Kass - Nicole - Linda
Niki - Nomes - Katherine - Sandy
Jennifer - Jemma - Sophie
& Nicole

Many blessings for all your support and
encouragement while I wrote this.

I hope you enjoy finally hanging out with the
characters you've heard so much about
and that the tale exceeds expectations!

Acknowledgements

First of all, I have to give thanks and praise to my Dragon Circle Team, starting with my wonderful editor, Sue Moran, without whom no one would be able to decipher my tales. You are a legend, an angel, and the best BFF EVER! My deep appreciation to Rei Harding for the fantastic character artwork - you put in an amazing effort to get finished by our deadline. Thanks also to my wonderful proofreaders, Cheryl Hesketh and Becken Fuggle, who save me the worry of spelling mistakes, which is the greatest horror for a dyslexic person like me. And an extra dose of gratitude to Chez for keeping my store and website in such excellent working order.

I owe so much to the wonderful guidance and help of the very talented and generous, Kylie Chan, who has been such a patient and helpful guide throughout my journey to publishing this novel - definitely my sister from another Mister. Love you!

I am really grateful to my agent, Selwa, and Drew at Selwa Anthony Author Management for their lovely feedback.

A hat tip also to Ben Ferguson for the beautiful dragons for our logo.

Thanks to all my wonderful Patreons - listed in the dedication - for your support, encouragement and belief in me. You've really kept me going and I appreciate every single one of you!

Big love and gratitude also to all my readers who support me through my store, All Things Traci, and through your follows, likes and shares on Facebook, Instagram, YouTube, Twitter, Redbubble, etc. Most of all, I appreciate your recommendations to friends and family, and your wonderful reviews - you are all awesome!

The Twelve Chapters of the Infinite Night

Other Characters of the Infinite Night

The Inter-dweller aka : Id - Onderwyser - Làoshi - the Ancestor - Api

The Archons aka : the Naga - Naga Raja - The Demiurge

Kambuja
Surface Earth - 262-261 BCE

Mother of Tamous and Bào - Chenda Satura
Granddaughter of Chenda - Luye
Brother of Soma - Kosal
Anik's bondsman - Hamza
Anik's wife - Rhaiyche
Anik's horse - Vasky
Emperor - Ashoka
Emperor's brother - Tissa
Emperor's Viceroy - Saras

Khmeri
Surface Earth - 2081-2082 AD

Zhi Sumati's 2IC - Arun
Zhi Sumati's husband (deceased) - Chamroeun
Amari's tour manager - Rodney
Chief of State - Chief Li

Other Characters of the Infinite Night

Khmeri - Cont'd
Surface Earth - 2081-2082 AD

The Family of Xi Ching
Wife (deceased) - Lanying
Eldest son - Tian
Younger son - Wei
Eldest daughter - Heng
Sweet daughter - Annchi
Rebel daughter - Chyou

Agartha
Inner Earth - 4105-4133 AD

The Council of Sophia
Lord of Agartha - Thrasceon
Lady of Agartha - Zili
Representative of the Whites - Saegoi
Pleiadian Ambassador - Ormodon Sonas
The Titan - Magnar Yeddais
Thrasceon's Transhuman Advisor - Achiever

Ormodon's son - Jeroke Sonas
Jeroke's companion - Gozin
Shankara's student - Adahn
Naga Raja - Shesha
Inner Earth Central Sun - Sophia

 # The Ancient World

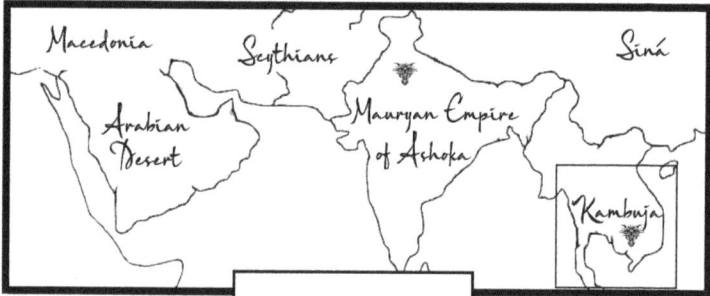

Macedonia

Scythians

Siná

Arabian
Desert

Mauryan Empire
of Ashoka

Kambuja

262 BCE

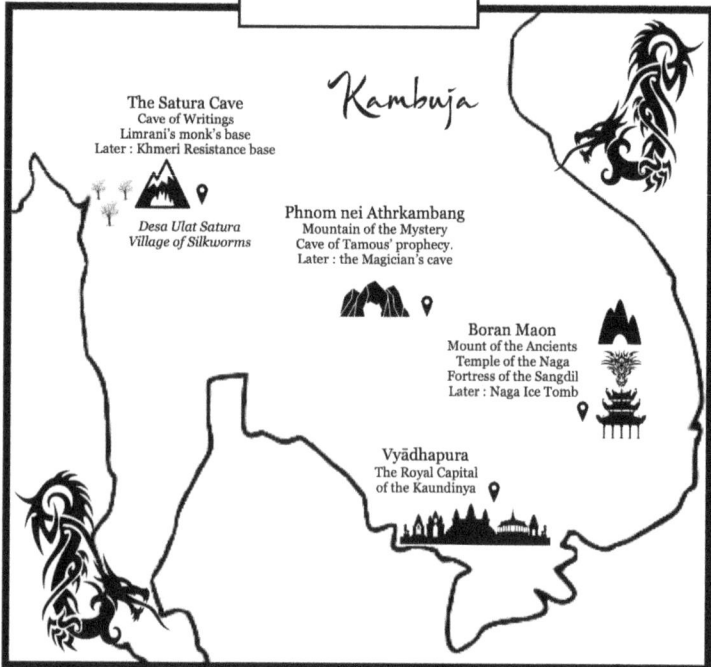

Kambuja

The Satura Cave
Cave of Writings
Limrani's monk's base
Later : Khmeri Resistance base

Desa Ulat Satura
Village of Silkworms

Phnom nei Athrkambang
Mountain of the Mystery
Cave of Tamous' prophecy.
Later : the Magician's cave

Boran Maon
Mount of the Ancients
Temple of the Naga
Fortress of the Sangdil
Later : Naga Ice Tomb

Vyādhapura
The Royal Capital
of the Kaundinya

Prologue
The Inter-dweller

We are that beyond I am, yet to realise the potential of those transcended, formless ones who dwell in the primordial light realms of creation. Just as a human form is composed of atoms, so is our form composed of the human soul minds currently embroiled in the physical reincarnation loop unfolding within the earth plane. We dwell on the threshold between heavenly realms and the material world, and within the chapters of our Akashic library, every aspect of the human condition has its place.

We too have endured individual manifestations through karmic cycles of time, life, death and rebirth. We have been pure of heart, abandoned, caring, and warlike. We have explored the depths of our feelings, our own destructive natures, and sought answers to the great mysteries that ignited our imagination. We have coveted absolute power and knowledge, worked miracles, and relinquished all we once held dear. Through this seemingly endless process, we, as individuals, came to understand that time and space are merely forms of ideas that express our cyclic activity. That which seemed an endless process was only an instant, broken down through time for our observation, growth and understanding. Our commitment not to contribute to this delusion liberated us from the illusion of separateness, and we therefore ceased to create karma in the three worlds of our physical, mental and emotional being. The physical temple we had so carefully constructed around ourselves vanished and in shedding all material matters, I merged with spirit to assume the calling of an Inter-dweller.

Attraction is the modus operandi of human beings, for they command the atomic structure of the matter required for form building in their material world. The modus operandi of the Inter-dweller is synthesis with the human incarnations to whom we are a spiritual conduit home. We are their channel for inspiration,

1

imagination, willpower and conscience. In times of darkness, we are to be found within. We are their means to exert influence over the material world for the benefit of the whole.

We move along a similar path to those we seek to guide, only on one higher turn of the spiral, one higher octave in the grand symphony of creation. As our Inter-dweller before us, we are the torch that leads soul-minds out of karmic darkness. In mutual meditation with our human kindred, we draw them into the vacuum of our slipstream, leading towards a greater awareness of oneness. Once the units of our being resonate in harmonious frequency, spirit and matter will sound the same note, and infinite light will illume the infinite night.

Chapter 1
Kambuja 262 BCE
Tamous – The Innocent

The gushing of a cascading stream intermingles with the morning buzz of living creatures, drawing my awareness into a singular present moment - from oneness with all there is, into one that is.

My sense of smell awakens me to the sweet scent of the fresh, cool earth beneath me. I roll over, casting off my crisp blanket of leaves, and open my eyes to behold a clear blue sky beyond the canopy. Red and gold leaves fall in long, slow spiraling motions all around. The tree branches and ground are swathed with leaves - nature's blanket has thickened overnight. A gentle wind sets branches above dancing, allowing shafts of sunlight to pierce through the canopy and warm my face. My eyes close once more in reverence to the splendour.

In this instant, between the unconscious sleep connection to spirit and the physical waking state of one of its many forms, consciousness provides all the information this manifestation needs to feel secure in this present moment.

I am the eldest of twin boys, born into a family of weavers in the village of Desa Ulat Satura 'the Village of Silkworms'. The silkworm and the white mulberry trees on which they thrive were the gift of my family to this, our adopted homeland. The trees not only provided silk and trade, but food for our animals, tea, medicines, and wood for carving out the tools of our trade. With little tending and no irrigation, the mulberry trees created industry, and where my ancestors had once settled in peaceful isolation, an entire village sprang up. My family, famed for our silk-cottons, had been named the Satura by the local people, as this was their word for the yarn. Our fabrics were lighter than the pure silks of the northern Sinàese, less expensive, and more suitable for the peoples of these warmer southern climes. I was the third generation of the Satura dynasty born into this lush southern land, which in the Shauraseni dialect of the western Hindustani traders was called Kambuja.

My earliest memories of tending herds of pig and buffalo with all the males of my family, and harvesting berries, silk cocoons and cotton with the women were joyous! I would watch in wonder as the precious fibres were spun like magic and transformed into yarn for dyeing. Like a spirit taking mortal form, I saw it woven into fabric on the looms of our womenfolk. It was a time rich with colour, laughter, and a freedom my people took for granted. That illusion was obliterated in the Spring that marked my sixth year upon this earth, when the Sangdil warriors of Anik Bodi cast their odious shadow over our land.

Sangdil is a Shauraseni term that implies soulless, cruel and unforgiving - this is the creed to which the invaders adhere; this is what they strive to embody. They came from the far north-western region of the Mauryan Empire. But unlike all the Westerners that had come before them, the Sangdil had no interest in peaceful trade. The sanctity of family and the worship of ancestors and nature was abhorrent to them and banned. Those they conquered lived only to serve the Warlord Anik Bodi, his Emperor Ashoka, and the Naga Raja that resided within the temple at the heart of the Sangdil fortress. Their ranks were swollen with once loving fathers and sons, who sold their souls and relinquished their scruples to Anik Bodi to protect their families from the wrath of their own comrades in arms. They recruited the strongest males in every family. My father and the other young married men of our clan were easily conscripted after my uncle challenged the invaders' authority. My aunt and cousins were all defiled before us and slain, and my uncle lived only long enough to bear witness to the consequence of his resistance. My father's attachment to us ensured his compliance. Our livelihood became a business of the state, which the remaining family were left to run on the invaders' behalf.

This instantaneous, brutal eclipse of our kin and culture shattered the sensibilities of all who bore witness. All hope for the return of a happy, peaceful life was scattered to the four winds as we watched the death pyre of our loved ones burn.

Inside my tiny being, the waves of shock shot ever deeper, fracturing my core with fear for the future. In self preservation, I withdrew from my horrendous new reality to stand outside my form and simply observe. Within this deep state of shock, my eyes remained wide open, but my body became lifeless and despondent. Not the pleas and tears of my mother, nor the anger and disgust of my twin brother, could persuade me to come back to the land of the living; this numbness was infinitely better than the trauma that awaited upon my return to my body.

For days my awareness resided in an otherworldly place - grey, barren, and shrouded by mist. In the nothingness of this isolation, there was peace and safety. My spirit form dwelt upon a rocky outcrop, attention focused on the surface of a still dark pool. I desired nothing more than to remain in this void, believing here, nothing and no one could touch me. For a short time my delusion proved sound.

You cannot stay here, young Tamous. The inner whisper stirred my mind into movement, but I was strongly resistant to gathering my wits. I kept my focus on the pool, but beneath the water's surface the face of an old soul took form. I could not tell if it was male or female, for it appeared the perfect blend of both.

You will die. It said without moving its lips.

The voice in my mind sounded two-fold - a man and a woman speaking in perfect unison. I believed the being was an ancestor, as it knew me by name.

I do not fear death, I fear life. I replied.

If you no longer fear death, Tamous, then you have nothing to fear in living.

I did not agree. *The Sangdil will come for me. I cannot be as they are, not even to save my family.*

The ancestor rose out the water into full form, assuming a more masculine appearance and voice. *If that is what you believe, then sadly there is no avoiding it. However...* He came to sit alongside me, not a drop of moisture on him or his robes. *If you wish to never be Sangdil, imagine some other more appealing outcome.*

I don't understand? I observed a man, hair white with age and wrinkles inset in his face, yet he radiated with vitality and his movements were subtle and fluid. This is why I came to regard him as 'the old boy'. Yet his eyes were not dark like those of my kin, they were a pale mauve. I could not help but be fascinated by them, for they were the only colour in this otherwise monotone landscape.

You are using your imagination to draw a destiny in the ranks of the Sangdil to you. But surely you can envision a better life ... not just for you, but for every living being.

Of course I can, but how would I bring it into being?

Ah, that's the beauty of co-creation. It's your job to do the imagining, and it's creation's job to bring about the means to realise your aspiration. So you don't have to worry about how you achieve your goal, just follow every step that creation puts before you to lead you closer to it.

I was only six years old and due to my recent trauma, I already found it difficult to believe life could be so simple.

You think me a foolish old man, he smiled, amused. *But, take this place...* He referred to our surrounds. *It's so grey and dismal. If you must escape, why not choose somewhere that is beautiful and alive?*

This place is in my mind. I was completely aware that I was preventing myself from returning to consciousness.

That is where everything begins. What is in your mind will manifest in your life. The modus operandi of human beings is form building. How do you think Anik Bodi built his army and came to conquer so many lands? He posed.

I shrugged. *He made war and won?*

Yes, he allowed. *But first he had to imagine the possibility and believe he was capable of achieving it. His will and vision is greater than those who oppose him. Be vigilant of allowing anyone to suggest what your truth is, for what you believe determines what's possible in your future.*

When I observed the wasteland around me, the fear of bringing this sad reality into being compelled me to envisage the most beautiful, colourful, and life-filled forest that I could possibly conceive of. With awe and delight, I watched as it exploded into being all around me.

Now, some twenty years later, I reside in that paradise. Through stillness and deep concentration, I continue to commune with the old boy, my Inter-dweller, whom I have come to call Làoshi - a title given by my ancestors to any wise teacher of skill. When I am in the company of Làoshi, I do not waste away, but rather I am filled with vitality. Through him, I have learned how to ground my earthly vehicle through fluid exercise and concentrated breath, to draw upon the underlying life force of nature - undetectable to the naked eye, yet evidenced in abundance when perceived through the eye of the spirit body. This vital life source is the primordial light of creation, existent before the sun, moon, and stars. It nourishes, strengthens, and warms the soul and all its bodies, and is freely available to all who would attune to it. My grandfather, in his writings, referred to this vital life force as *qi*. He claimed that all matter, including his own form, was composed of tightly knit units of this vital life force. Qi, in an energetic dance of entanglement, creates the illusion of solid form - like water and air when they create a typhoon, or when drops of water combine into a raging river powerful enough to cut through the hardest rock. The path to realisation lay in disentangling from the illusion of physical form in order to see it - something I do on a regular basis. Once my consciousness had stepped outside of my physical transport, I understood that I extended far beyond the one tiny expression of manifestation that is Tamous Satura. Once qi is realised and the channelling of it mastered, one can employ what my Làoshi calls constructive interference, which is harmonic resonance. This principle may manifest as a miracle healing, a change in the weather, or exerting influence over others or events in your sphere.

Since that first encounter with Làoshi, I have striven to discover a better way of being, and in this pursuit I now realise the interconnectedness of all things. It was my attachment to the self and all its material world desires that was at the root of my suffering as attachment equates to suffering. Once I let go of everything, the delusion of separateness fell away and therein I found true euphoria. I now know there is only one being in existence, so the premise of seeking the approval, love, and acceptance of another is an absurd notion. There is no 'other', there is no 'me', all are one. Làoshi is not one of my ancestors as first suspected, but a means for this particular aspect of source to link back to itself. This manifestation greatly aspires to return to spirit, and although I have ceased to create karma in this life and have entertained only pure thoughts for many years now, a karmic residue from the past still remains - along with a reluctant yen to share this awareness with all sentient life to end their suffering. A previous attempt to share this knowledge ended in disaster and resulted in me seeking isolation. To impose the way was not the way, for there are as many paths back to source as there are beings upon this earth and all must find their own way - that is the entire point of life of the material world. Should that path lead a willing student into my sphere, then that is in flow with the way.

Seated now, legs crossed, eyes closed, attention focused on the mid-point between my eyebrows, I see Làoshi smiling at me. He advises me to be in the flow with the 'as-it-isness' and fades from my mind's eye.

A vision of a young man, semi-transparent and fairer of complexion than anyone I have encountered in my life, appears in Làoshi's stead. His hair is paler than raw silk and his eyes, the colour of a clear post-dawn sky, gaze right through me. *Your brother is coming for you,* he informs, without shifting a single muscle of his deathly serious expression. He communicates directly with my mind, as the Inter-dweller does. *You predicted this event unfolding on the same day that the leader of the Mauryan Empire kneels before a holy man.*

Ashoka kneels? I am shocked because Ashoka is the emperor who holds Anik Bodi's leash. I do not doubt the honesty of the vision, although such premonitions are usually delivered via Làoshi and are always accurate. But this fair youngster is obviously another expression of my Inter-dweller and therefore just as trustworthy.

The lad in my vision nods to confirm. *Ashoka seeks spiritual redemption.* The image fades back into the darkness of my mind's eye as I detect a human presence entering my energy field - my only pupil is early today.

Limrani has come a long way since first we crossed paths, but she cannot resist trying to sneak up on me every time she visits. This rather speaks to my failing as a teacher, but I have to admire her persistence.

'Good morning, warrior.' I call her out of hiding.

'*Argh.*' Her footsteps become perceivable to the ear as she stomps into the clearing.

She employs the deportment of a man, dressing as a warrior with a staff in her hand and a sword holstered on her hip - the latter of which she stole from a bandit who intended to attack her. Her long dark hair is unbound today, but when it is strung up on her head, she could be mistaken for a man; her height aids this disguise. 'You astonish me, monk.'

'I have told you many times, I feel your presence.'

'With your spirit.' She regurgitates the explanation I've given her before. 'Your spirit must be very large to detect me all the way over there.' She points back in the direction she has come from.

'Spirit is limitless. When you pursue a connection to the Inter-dweller, you will understand.'

Limrani sucks in her cheeks and shakes her head in such a way that it is almost undetectable. 'Although I envy you this skill, your inner path exercises put me to sleep. Best that I just stick to learning to master your way of fighting.' She seems eager to begin the day's lesson in the external method, yet it is the internal method that she needs to master.

'The postures I practice are not for fighting or self-defence, they are for my own good health and connection with the infinite.'

'That didn't stop you whooping me when first we met.' Limrani poses, indignantly.

'I did nothing but stand there and deflect your own force back at you. It was you who whooped yourself. I only observed.'

She musters a smile. 'My point is, the external method works a treat when the occasion demands.'

'The internal method leads to mastery of the self, which is the only true form of self-defence.'

'Half as good as you will be good enough.'

'Have no enemy and you will never need to defend yourself.'

'I have a need and well you know it.' Her glare implies that my suggestion is preposterous. 'I had the need in the past and I *will* have it in future.'

'Then you allow your life to be ruled by fear. Give evil nothing to oppose and it will disappear all by itself.'

'Anik Bodi and his Sangdil are not going to simply disappear.'

If my prediction is correct, she is wrong about that.

She nears, going down on one knee before me. 'But one day they *will* fear me. On *that* day I will be safe and *free*.'

'You are safe now.' I point out. 'You are free *now*. Kill Anik Bodi and you will become the twisted soul he now is, a slave to your own misdeeds. And quite probably you'll be jailed and executed, who will that serve?'

'Then *so be it*.' The determination in her words and expression pain my heart.

The Sangdil wounded her deeply, but it is Limrani herself that has kept the wound open and has allowed the injury to fester and disease her soul.

'You might be prepared to sit meditating on a mountain while the people of this land suffer, but I am not.' The warrior withdraws to stand. 'You have infinitely more skill with any weapon than I. You could defeat Anik Bodi without even raising a sweat! Just because you have been fortunate enough to avoid his wrath, doesn't mean you should turn a blind eye to his insatiable ambition and cruelty.'

'I have felt his venom many times.' I never mention this, as I have no desire to antagonise those sleeping dragons.

Limrani gasps. 'You never said.' She comes to sit cross-legged in front of me, eager to delve into my shadowy past, as we had delved into hers.

It seems only fair that I share my experience with her, then perhaps she will better understand the way of my teaching.

'Anik Bodi tore my family apart.' I begin by filling my heart with compassion and love for my enemy, so as not to be affected by the recollection - a gentle stoke for my inner dragons to bring them to a calm awakening. 'They took our menfolk, my father included, and killed those who opposed them. The proceeds of our livelihood were handed over to the state, and every month they sent my father and a large force of Sangdil to collect their spoils. If our family didn't deliver as much as expected, my father was forced to beat us - the threat of a massacre ever hanging over his head. Father pushed us hard and we survived. For six long, horrible years this continued, until news came of my father's death. It was never made clear whether he died of natural causes, by his own hand, or at the hands of others. The only thing that was clear was that the Sangdil had come for his eldest son ... me.'

Up to this point, the most terrifying day of my life was the day the Sangdil took my father. The deep trance state into which I retreated thereafter lasted four days. My mother was overjoyed when I returned to consciousness, but my younger twin, Bào resented how mother fussed over me, for it was clear to all that I had been touched by the divine ancestors. Through my association with Làoshi, I sprouted wisdom beyond my years and my mother recognised much of the terminology as being aligned to the philosophical tradition of our ancestral home. Mother believed I was Fangshi, as her grandfather had been. I learned how he had once produced works of great literary merit to adorn the shelves of the universities of the mighty northern empires of Sinà, and was highly prized for his prophetic skill. But the warring dynasties were more interested in the quest for immortality than spiritual enlightenment, unable to see that these quests were the same. The rival kings grew evermore dissolute and incapable of valuing virtue, so my grandfather packed up his family, his saplings, seed and silkworm, and travelled south beyond the borders of any established kingdom. Here, in the byway lands that lay between Sinà and the western empires of Maurya, Scythia and Macedonia, were a far more hospitable people, residing in self-governed and self-sufficient mandalas.

Fangshi in my ancestral tongue of the Sinàese meant 'method, recipe, formula master'. The term encompassed all manner of highly trained technical specialists; the alchemist, immortalist, astrologer, diviner, geomancer, necromancer, doctor, monk, mystic, psychic, prophet, technologist, thaumaturge, wizard! Although Fangshi usually only specialise in one or two of these fields, they are all scholars who read, write, and leave records. These skills had passed down to my mother, for she was the accountant in our household, and although she conversed in many different dialects, she still wrote in the old tongue.

The Sangdil insisted Mother switch to the Shauraseni script of the Hindu's - with which they were familiar - for her record-keeping purposes. With all nature and ancestor worship also forbidden, they hoped to repress the spirit and the culture of my people. However, I was quietly forging a new path of individual connection to the divine within that could be practised in silence, anywhere at any time, no ritual worship involved. This practice of coming into alignment with the Inter-dweller, I came to call the Way. For it was the way back to source, the way of nature, the way of mastery over the self and the mundane world. The Way had an inner and outer path to bring balance into being. I would sit and discourse on my revelations to the womenfolk as they worked, lifting their spirits and, as a side effect, heightening productivity. Other people from nearby villages got word of my awakening and came to hear me speak also. Even the village elders agreed that my knowledge was extraordinary and divine in nature. Unbeknownst to me, my mother began to transcribe some of my discourses, despite the fact that writing was forbidden beyond noting accounts and figures.

The day the Sangdil came for me, I was in the fields tending to the feeding of our flocks with my brother. My mother was more distraught than ever I had seen her as she ran towards us. 'Your father is dead!' She howled and fell to her knees, unable to stand the weight of her bereavement. 'The Sangdil have come for his son.'

The shock of her words shot through my body, heating my core with such trepidation that I could no longer feel the morning chill. 'How can this be? Làoshi said I would never be one of the Sangdil.'

'And you never shall.' Mother gathered her sensibilities and looked to my brother. 'I am sending you, Bào, in your brother's stead.'

'What?' His expression turned from mild delight to betrayal, and as his gaze shifted my way I saw pure hatred in his eyes. 'He is the one they have come for.'

'Your brother will never survive the Sangdil conditioning.' Mother rose and grabbed hold of my brother to reason with him. 'You are a warrior by nature, Bào, you are our best and only hope of survival.' She appealed to his ego, but he saw right through her.

'You just want to keep your precious little prophet safe!' he recoiled from her. 'You have always favoured him over me!'

'No,' she shook her head.

'So good with words and advice.' Bào eyed me over like an insect he meant to squash. 'If you are so in tune with the spirits, then you go confront the Sangdil and save us all!'

'Of course ... you are right.' It was time for me to put my faith in source to the test. I put down my shepherd's staff and began my walk back towards our little village for perhaps the last time.

'No, Tamous!' Mother appealed to me and then my brother. 'The villagers will not allow the Sangdil to take him without a fight.' This was her true fear.

'You encouraged this!' Bào exploited her guilt.

'I know!' She sobbed. 'But we all needed someone to believe in.'

'You backed the wrong son!' My brother said spitefully.

'I love and believe in you both.' My mother moved to come after me, but Bào overtook her.

'Idiot!' He grabbed hold of me, swung me around and punched me fair in the face. 'You'll get us all killed.'

I hit the ground, delirious.

'Tamous,' Mother was on her knees beside me, caressing my throbbing face as I observed my brother stride away to assume my place among the Sangdil.

No! I wanted to stop him, but my mind and body were not connecting.

'Bào, my son, wait!' She left me to pursue my raging brother.

'You are my mother no longer!' He turned about to roar. 'From this day forward, I have no kin.' He threw his staff away and walked on.

'Your brother is Sangdil?' Limrani's mouth hangs open in shock.

'Anik Bodi's right-hand.' I feel the discontent of my inner dragons as long dormant recollections fill my heart with pain. 'He killed our mother for recording my insights, and attacked our village when no one would disclose my whereabouts. These acts earned Bào his dubious honour.'

In meditation I have seen my mother, smiling at me, telling me that I did the right thing. I have asked the Inter-dweller many times whether this is her generous spirit assuring me from beyond the grave, or my wishful imagination attempting to ease my guilt? Làoshi would say, *it is all an illusion of my own creation.* These days I have learned to accept all as it is, knowing it is not for me to judge the will of creation. In my soul I feel that my mother is in a happier place now, and that knowingness brings me peace.

'You have as much reason to hate the Sangdil as I do. How can you be so complacent? Why have you not sought justice?'

'It is as it is. I follow the way. When creation wills that I confront the Sangdil, they will cross my path.'

'Out here in the wilderness? Not likely.' She doesn't have to call me a coward, the accusation is conveyed in her expression.

Her opinion is of no bother to me; I am no longer moved by the views of those who do not understand the oneness of all things. 'I have foreseen the event.'

'When?' She is so eager to confront the Sangdil.

'I have told you, when–'

'Creation wills it!' She finishes my sentence, her dissatisfaction with the answer made plain by her abrupt response.

I smile. 'Today we focus on breath. The one constant that remains with us all through this illusion we call life. In stressful situations, it is the breath that changes. Learn to control it and you...' Over my student's shoulder, I spy an entity.

At first glance, I believe it is a ghost, as I can see the woodland right through him, and yet he does not lack colour. A bolt of shock permeates through my being as I recognise the fair young man from my vision this morning. He is dressed very strangely, with all manner of oddity upon his person.

'Monk?' Limrani queries as I rise up and move past her.

'Who are you?' I ask, and the mysterious visitor is astonished.

You should not be able to see me. He backs away, fearful of my advance.

I halt, not wishing to alarm him into departing. 'I see you quite clearly, and understand you very well.' Just as in my vision, his mouth does not move when he speaks; he converses directly with my mind.

'Who are you talking to?' Limrani pursues me, curious about the breach in her lesson.

She cannot see me. The visitor seems relieved to observe.

'You cannot see him?' I look at my student.

She looks to the place of my distraction, eyes glazed in nil recognition. 'Are you toying with me? There is no one else here.'

I look back to the visitor to find he has fled, foliage swaying in the wake of his swift departure.

'I stand corrected.' Limrani draws her weapon and pursues the anomaly through the woodland.

I follow, confident that if the entity can be trapped. Limrani will

15

see to it.

I join my student at the mouth of a large cave that has served as a shelter during many a wet season.

Limrani stands poised, sword raised and ready to strike, her eyes darting from one side of the cave opening to the other. 'The spirit is in here somewhere.' She states confidently, indicating the low lying foliage across the entrance that would be disturbed if the entity tried to backtrack past her. 'Can you see it?'

'No. He must be further within.' The gap in the rock narrows into a natural corridor, then widens into a large inner cavern. I lead her through the crevice.

Our target is inside. He notes our entry, but is preoccupied inspecting the cave wall. *This place is known to us. Why haven't you written your teachings upon the walls here?'*

'My teachings have a way of getting people killed.'

'Very encouraging.' Limrani trails me, unsure as to whether I am addressing her, the spirit, or Làoshi.

'When written down,' I clarify for all those listening.

'I cannot write or read.' My student is happy to be ignorant and immune.

You don't understand. The teaching that led me here, is not here! So how then can I be here?

I stare back at the fair lad blankly, at a loss for a response.

The piece you carved into this wall. He motions to the smooth stone rock face next to him. *You know .... why man and woman? Why a dualistic universe, blah, blah, blah...* He scours the wall with a strange glowing stick, as if expecting words to suddenly appear - what a curious being he is.

The visitor exhibits such distress that I endeavour to impart my understanding. 'I imagine the dualism of man and woman, or any being apart from the self, is the opportunity to love that which is not the self.'

Yes! He clicks his fingers at me. *That was part of it.*

'You see him?' Limrani assumes.

I nod, my attention fixed on the ghostly figure. 'He believes that one of my teachings should be recorded upon this wall. But I think who he is, and why he is here is a more pressing concern.'

He ceases his fruitless inspection of the wall and turns his attention fully my way. *I am Herodotus, a Seeker sent to find you, as your teachings are pivotal to future generations.*

My shadow-side is flattered, yet easily bypassed by curiosity. 'Is this prophecy, or are you implying that you hail from a future time?' This would explain his mysterious attire, appearance, and tools.

'Are you crazy, monk?' Limrani lowers her weapon. 'Or is this a test to gauge how gullible I am?'

Master Tamous, you have to believe me. The visitor is too impatient to allow me to indulge my student's insecurities. *If you don't write that piece on duality on the wall here and now, we'll never know you were here, or about the prophecy.*

'The prophecy that you relayed to me during my merge with Làoshi this morning?'

I did? Herodotus frowns. *Who ... is Làoshi?*

I am stunned he does not know. 'The Inter-dweller who binds all of us together.'

'So you keep saying.' Limrani is sceptical of all aspects of the inner path, including our spirit guide.

The visitor is baffled, and now it is he who stares at me blankly. *So you know your brother is coming for you? You predicted this event unfolding on the same day that the leader of the Mauryan Empire kneels before a holy man.*

'Ashoka kneels.' I nod, as this confirms the premonition I had earlier.

Herodotus moves closer to assure me. *Ashoka seeks spiritual redemption for all the killing done in his name ... his conversion is a well-documented event that has been accurately dated in my time.*

'What do you mean Ashoka kneels? Before whom?' Limrani's interest is struck in the conversation that - it must appear - I am having with no one. She moves around in front of me to collide with Herodotus and, startling each other, they both back up a few paces. 'Your ghost has mass.' Limrani's weapon is on guard again.

Please tell her that I mean neither of you harm. Herodotus holds up his hands in truce. *In order to be in resonance with your three-dimensional world, my form needs to be of the same vibrational frequency. Thus I can be physically harmed, so I'd really appreciate it if your novice would cease swinging that huge, razor sharp shard of metal about.*

I motion with my hand for Limrani to back down. 'You will not need the sword, we are in no danger.'

Limrani replaces the weapon in its sheath, frowning all the while.

Thank you. Herodotus relaxes.

'So, my friend, I feel quite sure that you've not come all the way from the future just to warn me that my brother is coming for me today.'

'Today!' Limrani is horrified and appeased in equal measure. 'He will not take you. We can fight him together.'

She must not be here when the Sangdil arrive. Herodotus warns. *Your student is the channel for your legacy.*

I look back to Limrani, so suddenly that I alarm her.

'What did it say about me?'

'You must leave-'

'No. I've waited too long to confront the Sangdil.'

'You are not ready.' I am sorry to say it, but it is the truth. As hardened as Limrani is, I can see my opinion cuts her deeply. 'It is my fault, I should have taught you the inner path sooner. I should have insisted! Now we are out of time.'

Something bites into my neck and reaching back I find the mite gone. Only a small bloody puncture wound remains, as evidenced by the tiny drop of blood on my fingertips.

'You're wrong, monk.' Limrani counters. 'We can win this fight.'

'I will not fight.'

Jaw clenched, my student glares at me in disbelief. 'You cannot just let them take you.'

Especially not before you write on this wall. Herodotus' panic is telling.

'I do not expect to survive custody.' I advise Limrani, and as Herodotus makes no attempt to correct me, I assume I am correct.

'I do not understand you, monk.' She tries to cover her hurt with anger, but her voice cracks to betray her dismay.

'One day, you will.' I glance to the Seeker, who nods. 'Conflict will never lead to inner peace.' My attention reverts to my student. 'Loving the self ... true self care, means not creating anymore catastrophes in this life. I trust the path being presented before me, because I know better than to question the way.' Limrani opens her mouth to argue, but not knowing enough about the inner path, she cannot debate me. I turn my attention to the Seeker. 'Even if I was aware of the teaching to which you refer, it would take months to inscribe this stone.'

Herodotus pulls from his multifaceted suit a small, slim object. *This will engrave this stone as easily as ink marks papyrus.* Moving back to the wall, the Seeker taps one end of the tool and the opposite end turns fiery blue. He crouches down and with the illuminated end, begins carving a foreign text into the wall.

As symbols appear in the stone, Limrani is awestruck. 'What does it mean?' She looks to me for answers, but I can only shrug.

Tamous Satura was here. Herodotus enlightens me, then stands and offers me the tool. *Don't touch the shiny end.*

My interest exceeds my fear in this instance and I take possession of the item.

To Limrani, the shiny slender object magically appears out of thin air and she gasps at the oddity.

I write upon the stone in the text of my grandfather's people. It is immensely nostalgic to have a writing implement in my hand; it has been far too long. This tool is a delight to wield and in only moments I document the first two lines of the piece just as Herodotus conveyed it. I pause to dwell on the question, whereupon I consider that my earlier response was not complete.

The sound of numerous horses rumbling towards us snatches our attention.

'Sangdil.' Limrani looks beyond the crevice through which only men in single file can pass. 'This shall be easy with you as bait.' She unsheathes her sword, knowing that only Sangdil have horses in these parts anymore.

I hand back the amazing tool to Herodotus and when it vanishes into his possession, I realise. 'You can get her out undetected.'

Herodotus holds his hands up and backs away. *I'm not supposed to get involved or change anything. You are not even meant to know that I am here.*

'There are no accidents, Seeker.'

'If your Seeker friend comes anywhere near me, I'll kill him along with the Sangdil.' Limrani whirls her sword in a figure eight motion around her body to prevent anyone getting close. When horses are heard entering the outer cave, she moves to one side of the inner crevice and raises her weapon, ready to smite anyone who enters. Herodotus holds out the stone writing device to me once more. *Please finish, I can tell you exactly what to write.*

'Coward!' My brother's voice is heard in the entry passage. 'I know you are in here, I've had trackers following you.'

I see Bào entering through the crevice, his weapon already drawn. Despite my signal to Limrani to back down and take cover, she will not budge from her ambush position. 'Stay where you are, brother.'

I attempt to ward off the confrontation.

Bào laughs as he enters the inner cave, eyes fixed on me. 'You will not harm me.'

As Limrani brings down her sword, Bào senses the movement and deftly blocks her blade with his own weapon. 'But I will.' She grins.

They thrust apart, each viewing the other as prey.

'A woman!' Bào jeers. 'Why am I not surprised that you need a little girl to defend you?'

'Who are you calling little, short man?'

It is true, Limrani is taller and lankier then either my brother or myself.

Bào ignores the taunt. 'It is against the law for a woman to possess a sword.'

'Then why do you have one?' Limrani baits, using Bào's massive outpouring of angst to deflect him backwards - it is gratifying to see my instruction in motion. 'Do you think I care about the laws of the Sangdil?'

The warrior in my brother is quietly impressed by her skill and defiance, I can tell. 'You do know I have an entire battalion with me? Whatever happens, you leave this place my prisoner.'

'You are all walking corpses,' Limrani baits him again, 'and you will pay with your lives for serving the oppressors of our people.'

Bào's sights shift my way a moment. 'I find being the oppressor preferable to the oppressed.'

Again there is a clash of swords, and as the sound echoes through the cavern, more Sangdil begin to head down through the passage.

I look to Herodotus for aid. Finally accepting that his verse is not going to be written, he turns the writing tool off and tucks it away in his attire. He pulls out another small object that he pushes onto his finger like a large upside-down ring.

'You will pay the price for your crimes against the innocent.' My student threatens Bào as Herodotus sneaks up behind her, and with a touch of his strange ring, Limrani turns invisible and falls unconscious into the Seeker's arms.

Her sudden disappearance disturbs my brother, who swings his sword about in a frustrated search. 'What trickery is this?'

Herodotus struggles to carry Limrani's unconscious form out of harm's way, and is forced to duck around Bào's free-wielding blade, which grazes the luggage that the Seeker carries on his back. *Agh ... damn it.*

'I believe you came for me.' I draw my brother's focus.

The Seeker lays my student down and is forced to duck down himself. He presses Limrani hard against a wall behind him, and breathes in to avoid being stepped on.

'No one threatens me and gets away with it.' Bào continues slashing about.

'Circumstance disputes that.' My observation compels my brother to swing the tip of his blade to my throat.

'Who is she?' Bào demands to know as a battalion of Sangdil come to stand at his back.

'A victim of Anik's hostile takeover, just like the rest of us.'

'Lie.' The steel tip of the sword pierces my skin. 'Ordinary folk don't just vanish. Is she one of your evil spirits?'

A warm trickle of blood runs down my neck and pools in my collarbone. 'I do not know any evil spirits.'

'Sure you do ... I've seen you pull a really good vanishing act before today.' Bào grips me around the neck. 'But not this time.' His forehead smashes against mine and I make no attempt to block him or protect myself - karma is at work and must be served.

The pain penetrates deep into my skull and is so intense that my vision blurs. Head throbbing, I fall to my knees. I could withdraw into my subtle form and feel nothing, but I would lose control of my physical form in the process. I could rebel and reclaim control of my fate by using my knowledge of vital life force to deflect the aggressive energy back at my attacker. But the test is to remain in flow and not resist what is. This is my brother, who took on the life of a monster to spare me that horror and allow me a life of idyllic self-examination. If he still wants to kill me for our trade of fates, I would consider that a fair thing, but first we do have some final business to attend to.

'Now I get to finish you.'

'I have some vital news for you about your warlord.' The comment stalls a fatal blow from Bào's blade. 'I shall tell, but only you.'

'You don't make demands.' Bào clutches my throat, squeezing the air from my windpipe.

'You can kill me, but my news will change everything!' I force out the words.

Bào reluctantly loosens his grip, and shoving me backward, I draw breath. 'If you have something to say about my warlord, then you say it in front of him.'

Bào waves a finger in my direction and moving out of the way, men from the battalion grab hold of me. As they drag me towards the crevice - some in front and several behind - my sights drift to Herodotus, bewildered on the floor. I would have liked to speak with him of the future, but I knew as much as I needed to. 'Oh to be home in our little village Desa Ulat Satura.'

Herodotus frowns, curious about my parting words, but he holds up a hand to bid me farewell as I am hauled away.

'All you would find there now is forest.' Bào assures me.

I guarantee grandfather's mulberry trees and silkworms still thrive. A thought best kept to myself. Some unsuspecting locals would stumble onto a very profitable business there one day. I hope Herodotus will see Limrani there. If any of my people survived my brother's revenge, my student will find herself a safe haven and be welcomed as family.

Bào backs into the passage to guard the flank on the way out. 'I don't trust this place.'

I feel certain my long-lost sibling would like to drag me behind his horse all the way to our destination. Instead, my hands are bound and I am slung over the mount of one of his soldiers - arms one side of the horse, feet the other - to be stomach hammered by the horse's pounding movements for the entire journey. I would have been surprised to be provided the luxury of a transport, but I am not the only man taken captive by the Sangdil this day; two other men are bound and slung over horses in this fashion. I suspect my sibling is very eager to have the obstacle to killing me resolved.

Most of the journey I spend in a meditative state, listening to the reassurances of Làoshi, who tells me that it is good that I follow my own instinct; intuition is the compass to seek the divine. I no longer fear my mortality, seek safety or peace - these are just concepts created by humans to aid us in the exploration of this material construct. I do not fear abandonment for I have found solace in my own company; and as all are one, who is there to miss? I have nothing to hold me in this existence, nothing to protect; I do not claim ownership of anything in this world or beyond. I am honoured to have been able to learn and co-create in this existence, but there are many other expressions of being in creation that are equally amazing. So I am ready to detach from here and now, to experience, explore, and learn from other existences. Every being who ever lived and would ever live has a unique experience to contribute to the one great being of which we are all part, and I await my new assignment with great expectation.

By dusk we reach the capital of the Sangdil at Boran Maon - 'the Mount of the Ancients'. I wonder whether it is coincidence or quite deliberate that Anik Bodi chose to base himself here, as our people have long considered this place to be an abode of evil. Like attracts like, and thus the warlord would no doubt be attracted to the resonant frequency of this place.

I emerge from my trance state. The ache from the battered trauma I have sustained down the front of my body seeps into my conscious awareness. So intense is the pain that I almost retreat back into my incorporeal state. The other prisoners endeavour to repress their moans of pain as their Sangdil captors beat them every time they release a sound. Instinctually, I soften my breaths. I focus my qi on the afflicted area and my suffering eases.

It was in my fourteenth year that Bào and the Sangdil destroyed our home and I fled into the wilderness, and so it has been over half my lifetime since I visited a village. It is plain that civilisation has degenerated since the Sangdil came to power. Bào and I used to accompany our father to the local marketplaces in our youth. The once vibrant, jovial, thriving trade market I remember is no more. The dilapidated streets and dwellings are now littered with starving children, old and sick people, and young women carrying Sangdil offspring. The forced recruitment of our menfolk had come at the cost of the collapse of our family life and business that had been driving our culture and commerce.

All able-bodied people flee to hide as the Sangdil enter the main thoroughfare leading to the elevated, walled sandstone fortress where Anik Bodi bases himself. The streets reek of excrement - both human and animal - rotting food, fear, and death. The squalor and oppression here is surreal to me - do the people not realise that they have but to walk away from this place and into the forest to obtain a far greater quality of life? Have they been so brainwashed that they feel they have no choice but to stay in this misery? Several of the unfortunates, too debilitated to flee, are randomly lashed with Sangdil whips as we pass. All hope is gone from their eyes; they are just awaiting death now, like me.

Upon arrival in the fortress courtyard, the Sangdil dismount. The two other prisoners are pulled from their mounts and immediately collapse to the ground in agony, only to be whipped then dragged back to their feet.

'Take them to the temple.'

I wonder about Bào's instruction, for I assumed that prisoners would be incarcerated or executed; however, it dawns on me that my fellow captives are to be sacrificed to the Sangdil god of death, the one they call the Naga Raja. Was this to be my fate too?

My brother approaches, drags me off the horse, and appears surprised when I land solidly on my feet without complaint. 'Bring him.' He strides into the fortress complex.

I am gripped from either side around the tops of my arms and hauled along behind Bào.

My mind drifts back to the first time I met Làoshi, when he claimed that Anik won wars because his will was stronger than those he opposed. This was a perfect example of constructive interference at work. Anik Bodi's interference is more destructive, but the warlord gets what he wants by enforcing his will. Anik has aged since last we met. How strong will his will be when he discovers he no longer has his emperor's leave to make war? If Ashoka seeks absolution for those killed in his name, he will surely order the Sangdil to withdraw and stop adding to his karma. Both the Hindu and Buddhist faiths will expect this. The question is, will Anik obey? And if the Sangdil do depart, what will Bào do in that power vacuum? Will he continue the cycle of oppression or cut a new path for our people?

The repressive atmosphere increases as we progress deeper into the fortress. I am dragged before Anik Bodi in his war room. The chair upon which the warlord sits is elevated on a platform at one end of the chamber. The seat of power is not ornate enough to be called a throne, but it does give that imposing impression. In one hand, he holds a metal staff with daggers at each tip. It is bejewelled with polished black stones between the blades and the central hand grips. There is an ominous epicentre of shadow hovering around him, yet it is his weapon that seems to be the source.

The sleeping dragons within me stir at the sight of the man who destroyed my family and the lives of everyone I've ever known. I could assert myself and take my revenge, yet the only thing that will alter is my chance of joining with the Inter-dweller.

'So this is the good twin. I am surprised you have brought him before me alive.' Anik remarks.

Bào slams his fist into his open palm, gives a rigid bow, then addresses his superior directly. 'He claims to have vital news regarding you, lord, that he would tell only me.'

The warlord grins. 'Now you can share with the group.' Anik refers to the Sangdil all around him.

'Are you sure you want an audience to know your emperor's business?' I ask.

'Say your peace and die ... or just die.' Anik's deep, gravelly voice conveys his indifference perfectly.

'Your emperor will bow down before a holy man before this day is done. Ashoka seeks absolution and will recall all his armies. Your time in our land is at an end.'

The destroyer doesn't even blink. Either Anik doesn't believe me, or he is expecting this event. 'And that is the problem with prophecy, it's open to interpretation and thus filled with half-truths.' The warlord explains to my brother and the other Sangdil present. 'Yes, Ashoka will kneel, *to appease his wife*, who is a Buddhist. And yes, I have been called back to serve my emperor to secure his expanded kingdom, but ... my time ruling this land is far from over, little monk.'

He glares at me in challenge. I am certain he is wrong, but I cannot determine if he has convinced himself that his claims are true or whether he is just lying outright. I lower my sights, submissive.

'I leave a battalion of my personal Sangdil guard here in my right-hand's charge.' Anik motions for Bào to approach, and my brother moves past me to ascend the stairs towards Anik's council chair. When he reaches the plateau it occupies, he kneels before Anik.

My inner dragons writhe in protest, yet I make no sound or movement. I am not here to judge how Bào survived Sangdil conditioning. I want to believe he had no choice but to kill our mother and destroy our village, yet given the same choice I would lay down my life first. But then, as Bào predicted upon our parting all that time ago, I may have just got us all killed and the outcome would be no different.

'You will take charge in my absence.' Anik presents Bào with his shadowy staff; if he was hostile to me before, I fear he will be doubly so with this weapon in his possession. 'I am glad you left your brother alive, he will make a fine sacrifice. Take him and present him to my priest. He will be pleased by your offering, and your sacrifice in foregoing the pleasure of killing the last of the family who betrayed you.'

I am shocked to realise Bào must have told them about swapping places with me.

'I will see to it personally.' My brother rises and stands the staff upright. 'But does my lord not wish to have the honour.'

'I have only delayed my departure to advise you of your orders. The sooner I depart, the sooner I shall return.' Anik rises. 'When that day comes, I know my territories shall be just as I left them.'

'I swear, upon my life.' Bào vows.

'Yes, you do, Satura ... yes, you do.' Anik takes his leave through the doors at the back of the chamber and most of the Sangdil within follow him.

My sibling strides back to me, and pointing one of the bladed ends of his new staff towards the door through which we entered, he instructs me to 'move!'

Through a courtyard filled with Sangdil preparing horses to depart, I am herded towards a temple. The oppressive atmosphere I felt earlier pales in comparison to the malevolent energy we approach now. This ethos of depravity seems to penetrate the entire structure with a repulsive undercurrent that repels and yet compels at once, stirring dis-ease and conflict.

'You told them about us trading fates, is that why they had you destroy our village?'

'It was the writings we came to destroy! Your nonsense got everybody killed.'

It was as I feared, and my inner dragons began to eat away at my insides. In my mind's eye, I see Làoshi shaking his head. I know that my brother must have told the Sangdil about the scripture, but I am equally to blame as I knew writing was banned. Had I not inspired my mother and other elders in our village to write, then there would have been no crime to find. 'So I am to be sacrificed to their god. What is the Naga Raja?'

'King of the Nagas.'

'Who are the Nagas?'

'We are about to find out.'

Clearly, Bào has not been granted access to the unholy mysteries of the Sangdil priests before today.

'What if your warlord never comes back? The fate of our land and people is in your hands. You could restore our land to its former glory.'

'If you'd not been so gutless and accepted your place among the

Sangdil, you'd be in my shoes and have some say in the matter.' Bào goads. 'But you chose to run away and save your own skin, so don't pretend now that you care about the welfare of our people.'

I understand why he feels as he does about my choices and see no point in arguing the matter.

Inside the temple, carved snakes wind their way up the pillars supporting the roof of the central chamber. Here a dark priest awaits us, carrying a staff adorned with the same black shadowy crystal as the one presented to Bào. He greets my brother, accepts his offering, and then dismisses him.

'No. I am under orders to witness the demise of this prisoner. This is my brother, and I have been left in charge.' Bào raises the staff to emphasise this point.

I didn't recall any order to this effect.

'Hold onto that, very tightly.' The priest warns as the horrified screams from the men led down here before me emanate from within. 'There is no delight the Naga find more attractive than brother against brother.' He leads us towards a stairwell that descends into the structure.

My skin prickles, sensing the dangerous, debased energy ahead; however, my dread of death left me years ago, hence there is nothing more to fear. My soul longs to take flight to again be at one with my cosmic ancestor.

At the bottom of the stairs, we come to an observation balcony that overlooks a huge underground chamber. There are larger, grander columns in here, depicting half-humans with serpent tails. Central in the torch-lit cavity is a pool of thick, undulating, black liquid, and it is the epicentre of foulness I sensed all the way from the outskirts of the city. I suspect that the black jewels on my brother's and the priest's staff are composed of the same putrid stuff hardened into solid form.

As we follow the priest down a set of stairs open to the sacrificial chamber, we observe a dead body being dragged away from the poolside by the servants of the temple, and a live prisoner is then chained up in the corpse's stead.

'What happened to him?' The prisoner asks his captors as they bind him.

I wonder why the man asks, when he'd been close by and must have witnessed the last prisoner's demise. I see no blood on the dead man to indicate how he might have met his end.

The man to be sacrificed looks to the pool with trepidation, and his eyes widen as a stressful expression manifests on his face and he begins to scream.

The sight is so distressing that both myself and my captor stop in our tracks to bear witness.

Clearly the prisoner wants to look away, but is unable.

What I see with my spirit sight is the man's life force being sucked towards the dark slime in the pool, and his screams are his physical form desperately trying to hang on to his subtle bodies. At length he loses the struggle whereby his spirit-form is sucked into the pool and his physical vessel falls down dead. To everyone else in the room, it must appear as though he simply died of fright. Now I understand why this fellow had wondered at the cause of death of the man sacrificed before him. Fear begins to niggle at my consciousness. I do not fear death, that is true, as the spirit goes on. I have never considered that the eternal part of me might be destroyed though and it is difficult not to find that notion utterly terrifying.

Shadow retreats in the presence of light.

Làoshi's quiet wisdom fortifies my resolve. I look to Bào, who appears baffled by what he has witnessed. 'It ate his spirit. I can only pray that this is not how our father met his end.'

Bào's jaw clenches. 'Shut your mouth.' He shoves me forward with the crossbar of his staff. 'You shall not be missed.'

The dead body is dragged away and replaced with my body.

As I am tied up before the pool, I close my eyes to meditate upon the green heart centre of my subtle body, emanating light like a celestial flower. In time, I hear a bubbling sound within the pit before me and the panicked chants of its priests. A screech, like a huge bird of prey, demands my attention. My eyelids part to behold the huge head and body of a snake, formed from the black gooey liquid rising out of the pool. The high priest holds up his staff toward the abomination, mumbling incantations. There is no doubt in my mind now that these staffs - at least the black stones on them - identify the carrier as a faithful servant, rather than soul-food for the creature. My brother mimics the priest's gesture to avoid falling prey.

The Naga Raja rears up, hoping to elicit horror, but it shall have no such satisfaction from me - my breath remains as calm and quiet as an infant drifting into sleep. From what I have just observed, I understand that this presence is far more of a threat to our people and our homeland than Anik Bodi could ever be, and may well be the driving force behind his reign of horror. This creature must be understood. My whole life and all the choices I have made up until this point suddenly make perfect sense. This is what Tamous Satura was put on this earth to do. The monster opens wide its jaws and staring down the black abyss of its throat, I understand that it intends to swallow me whole. I fill my heart with love for all existence and embrace my destiny as it is.

Chapter 2
Agartha 4125 AD
Dilan – The Lover

Why man and woman?
Why a dualistic universe?
Attraction and repulsion, from the microcosm to the macrocosm.
Spirits unite to fire,
by heated friction,
a solar flare.
Creating an opportunity to love that which is objective
- the non-self -
and ultimately use,
with wisdom,
the form.

Looming in the twilight between a meditative state and wakefulness, this recently discovered verse is foremost in my mind, and my attachment to the piece draws me back to a singular conscious perspective.

Attributed to Tamous the Innocent, this text was discovered in a cave on surface earth, and awards but a small glimpse into the psyche of my thesis subject. Yet it also gives me hope that there are more of Tamous' musings, scratched upon an ancient, long-buried cavern wall elsewhere, laying in wait to be uncovered. Previous exponents of the Master's wisdom claimed that there was such a place. If found, I would dedicate my entire existence to transcribing the ancient wisdom. I telepathically convey the piece to Herodotus, who has propped up his half of our meditation bed and is now seated alongside me.

That's the most polite way of describing mating that I have ever heard. Which seems rather odd, coming from a man who was purportedly celibate. Hero's eyes remain firmly fixed on the smooth, white curved wall of our dwelling - he is mind-scanning research for his final assessment.

I repress the urge to roll my eyes, sure that he is aware that sex is not the crux of this text, and look up to the green leafy foliage beyond our open roof dwelling. The canopy is abuzz with colourful creatures, flowers, and fruits. The sight is so glorious that I can overlook my lover's cynicism. I understand he has far greater concerns at present than the subject of my thesis. I roll onto my side to observe his beautiful being. *If you would just take a moment to meditate, perhaps the answer will present itself?*

All the truly great luminaries of history have been sought already. Herodotus stands to pace out his frustration, and I now have his full attention. *I'm going to lose my chance if I don't come up with a feasible target soon.*

He isn't exaggerating. His will be one of many proposals submitted to the Creator for consideration. Of these submissions only one, if any, will be considered worthy to execute. Herodotus' chances of being chosen to participate in a DNA retrieval program are slim - a fact that has been of quiet comfort to me ever since Hero and I became involved. *The history of humanity on surface earth spans hundreds of thousands of years, and if all the prime targets had been exhausted already, then both your vocation and mine would be redundant.*

But we are now dealing with periods and people in history so obscure, they are little more than myth and legend. Your beloved monk is a prime example-

There is no evidence that Tamous was a monk. He pursued a solitary existence, but he was never part of an established religious order.

Hero ticks his head to one side to grant that I have a point. *Well, being that his only student was female, maybe-*

There is no evidence to indicate they were lovers, if that's what you're suggesting.

Hero holds up his hands in truce. *Only a fool would attempt to argue the subject of your thesis with you ... all I am saying is that Tamous would have been targeted long ago if any of his work had been accurately dated. His DNA is the MOST desired by the Creator.*

Well, Tamous' teachings did inspire generations, for thousands of years after his death. The mediation bed on which I recline rises and transforms into a lounge, in line with my mental vision and my partner's seat.

If his twenty-first century devotees had not been divided, they might have overcome their oppressors ... then maybe we would have a more intricate account of Tamous' life.

Then what would I have to aspire to? I grin, briefly. But clearly Hero is not in the mood for me being cute. *I assume you refer to the Khmeri revolution against the Republic?*

Hero shrugs and gives a single nod, as if this goes without saying.

But as leader of the resistance, how could Zhi Sumati possibly risk trusting the word of a drug addict, who claimed to have accidentally stumbled upon the holy site that the rebels were using as a base? Of course, she had to ensure his silence on the matter.

Have him killed, you mean?

Hero's comment makes me smile, not because it is accurate, but because the story of the Sage and the Magician, is one of the few stories and time periods associated with my research that really intrigues my partner.

Yet somehow he survived! Hero delights in the karma of it all. *To become a mighty Magician that could have saved Zhi Sumati from persecution later in her campaign and together they probably could have won that revolution.*

I know you admire the Magician-

Taylay Zeya was so far ahead of his time. He justifies. *More like us, then the humans of his own time.*

I had to agree, as Zeya's purported mastery over the elements and third-dimensional matter did seem to indicate that he was functioning more from a fifth-dimensional state of being then the other physicals of his day and age. *But trust during such times must have been a very tall ask.* I feel it is easy for us to sit in judgement of our ancient ancestors having never experienced their trials. *At least Tamous' birth place has now been established as being north of what would become the Funan Empire.* I telepathically share a map with Hero and highlight the area for his information. *In Sanskrit, this place was called Kambujadeśa - the land of Kambuja. The text I recited when I first woke was recently discovered in the north western mountains, inside a cave. I have a picture captured at the site.* With a thought, I also share this image with my companion.

Hero quietly focuses inward on the information.

We had hoped that other text found in this cave might mention the name of the village where Tamous was born, as legend has it that his pupil, Limrani, fled there and established a secret underground order of warrior monks. If a cave full of his teachings does exist, the village of his birth would be the prime place to look. But so far that location remains elusive.

So this text is what ... Sanskrit?

Actually it's very ancient Sinàese, confirming that Tamous' family did migrate from there before his birth.

Has it been dated?

To a few centuries before the common era. I know the answer is disappointing, as very exact dates are needed for Hero's proposed venture.

Why is part of this picture to the lower right side blurred out?

I knew he would ask about that. *Professor Royden advised it was some modern graffiti, and not important.*

How could there be modern graffiti at a site they have only just rediscovered?

35

There were thousands upon thousands of years between Tamous' lifetime and the demise of human habitation on the surface of the planet.

Aren't you curious about what it says?

Not really. I lie, as his excitement is making me feel ill at ease.

Perhaps there is some clue-

I'm sure it's meaningless, or my professor would have us study it also.

Where will I find the unedited copy of this picture?

Oh no. If he thinks I am going to request said copy from my professor, which is tantamount to doubting my superior's word, he's very much mistaken. *If you want it, you ask.*

But you know what professors are like. Hero comes to kneel on his haunches before me, his large grey-blue eyes gazing up at me in the hope of swaying me to his cause. *If I am not part of that course of study, my request will be denied.*

You're clutching at straws with this, Hero, and putting me in a really awkward position-

He knelt up to be closer to me. *I know I am, but I'm all out of ideas and you know how hard I've worked to even qualify to apply for this program.*

I resist, not because I don't care, but because I care deeply. *We can explore the entire universe from here, in complete safety-*

No, observing from inside a transport, or in an astral projection, is not the same as experiencing firsthand! And maybe we don't travel at all, and are only experiencing the perceptions of others, or some fantasy the Agarthans dreamt up for us.

I could see his point, but it was moot. *A human body, even as subtle as the fifth-dimensional forms we employ, is going to find the forty million tonnes of pressure and fifty thousand degree temperatures needed to form the liquid diamond ice fields of Neptune and Uranus uncomfortable. But we can witness these kinds of wonders that our outer-world forebears could only dream about. Why can't you be content with that?*

Herodotus stands and backs up a few paces. *Our entire existence is dreamlike, Dilan. Everything here is so cerebral! We even make love, just by thinking about it.*

Well, of course. We abandoned our dense physical forms before puberty. I for one don't miss feeling ill, being subject to time and the elements, having to speak to be heard, eat our plant and animal friends to survive, and all those bodily functions and fluids ... AUGH ... no thank you. Not to mention an etheric being is the best form of birth control ever. The last thing either of us need is a child to look after at this stage of our studies.

I do desire to have children one day. At that time, I will lower my vibrational frequency and take on a full physical form once again in order to conceive, give birth, and raise the child to the point where they too can assume a fifth-dimensional state of being. Even as we are, our surroundings feel solid to us, as they have fifth-dimensional resonance also, but they are more malleable and respond to our mental bidding instantly - reality manifests as fast as we conceive of it. Unless another stronger will is working against you - like that of my professor, withholding the image Hero wishes to access.

I want to go somewhere where every place, being, and experience is not completely perfect, safe and predictable.

It hurt that our life together was not enough for him; I personally could not stand the thought of leaving Agartha, losing this wonderful existence, or him! *History is the only truly dangerous destination you could have chosen.*

You knew this was my aspiration when you met me. Our mutual fascination with history is what brought us together. The hurt in his tone and expression appear to match my own as he sweeps the long silvery fringe back off his face.

If you are sent back in time, you will be invisible to the surface world inhabitants, yes ... but you will have to take physical form in order to carry out the DNA extraction. You won't be protected from natural disasters, sickness, or equipment malfunction. There are a million variables that could go wrong, many Seekers never return. You may never return. My voice breaks over the true reason behind my opposition.

Hero's stance and expression soften. *Isn't Tamous' teaching all about following the as-it-isness? And that negativity is just a resistance to the way things are? That the value of anything is in the void, the not knowingness?*

You are the one resisting the way things are. I am content. I point out.

Hero turns away, momentarily frustrated, but after a thought he confronts me. *If I was sent back, I could discover where Tamous was born and investigate the claims about the cave containing all his teachings.*

I cannot hide how appealing that notion is, which only excites and encourages him further.

If you are refused the photo upon request, then I'll drop the subject and all aspiration to time travel as it will be clear that my aspiration is not meant to be.

I groan, persuaded but still opposed. *Very well then. Here goes.* I submit a mental request to my professor to be supplied with an unedited copy of the image in question, explaining that my partner is interested in the original for his own project research. *Done.*

Hero's smile fills my heart with joy, and I receive a telepathic kiss for my efforts.

I am surprised to receive a response to my request almost immediately, and not from my professor either, but my partner's. I look at Herodotus and we both gasp and advise at once.

Shankara is requesting an audience with us.

For a brief second, I am as excited as Herodotus. Then my heart sinks, as I fear I may have helped my love get one step closer to his dangerous aspiration.

Master Shankara is known as the Creator because the Gate of Days - a means to traverse time - was her brainchild. A resident of the inner earth colonies since the demise of Atlantis, Shankara, like the other inhabitants of the etheric city of Agartha and its sister city in the physical realms, Shamballa, had only had very limited contact with the surface of this planet since that time. She is the curator of the DNA retrieval program and the commissioner of the Seekers - that elite group that Herodotus aspires to join the ranks of. I've had very little association with the Creator myself, and I am puzzled as to why this esteemed master has requested to meet with me also. Obviously it has something to do with my request to Professor Royden.

As Hero and I await our scheduled meeting with the Creator in the foyer cum waiting room of the Department of Time, I can only hope that we have not caused offence. I have worked extremely hard on my thesis in the hope of securing a position in the Surface Earth Antiquity Department here at Agartha's Ancient Mystery School - displeasing my superiors will not bode well for that aspiration. I glance aside at my love, whom I have never felt to be so nervous and excited. His surging emotions are quite disturbing, yet I cannot help but be amused by the childish exuberance. *Calm yourself.*

Am I not?

I shake my head slowly, grinning all the while.

Apologies. Hero closes his eyes to steady his emotions, whereby I feel the lingering erratic energy begin to dissipate.

My attention drifts to the large image moving slowly across the curved walls of the foyer. It is an animated fly-through reconstruction of a foregone surface earth city as studied and re-created from the minds of the scholars and Seekers at this institution. The school had produced many such animations for students in other departments to study. At present, I am being flown around inside of an early Roman villa. I find these magnificent glimpses into the past utterly mesmerising and fascinating; and although I do not have the mettle for time travel, I can appreciate why Herodotus desires to explore such places - dangerous as they are.

Many apologies for the delay. A gentle, calm voice advises as a doorway appears in the wall, ahead of the barrier within the elaborate framework vanishing. *Please enter.*

Herodotus gazes at me, wide-eyed and overcome with expectation as we proceed into the chambers of his superior.

Our attention is immediately drawn to the far wall where an enormous arched opening frames our beautiful blue, rotating sun, sparkling over the lake and forest. On the balcony admiring the breathtaking view is the Creator, who, shockingly, is bidding farewell to my professor.

Professor Royden?

My heart begins pounding in my throat as he silently waves to acknowledge me on his way past. *Dilan.*

The entryway vanishes upon his departure.

Master Shankara, we are honoured by this audience. Herodotus bows his head respectfully.

Although we are a little puzzled by it? I smile and bow also. *I hope our query has not caused you any inconvenience.*

Not at all, quite the contrary, we are overjoyed. She smiles in a fashion that seems equally genuine and forced. Shankara's complexion is as pale as any of our kind, and her white hair is cropped shorter than Hero's. The Creator's androgynous attire is practical, simple, and ensures that she is white from her head to bare toes. *We've been expecting you ... well, expecting someone.* Her pale mauve eyes drift back to Hero. *But I had a hunch about you two.*

You expected us to ask about the picture? Herodotus frowns, perplexed.

We expected someone to ask, yes. Shankara motions with a finger for Herodotus to follow her to her desk. *How is your handwriting?*

Ah... Hero considers the question while the Creator's back is to him. *Not too bad?* He trails her. *I've had little need for it since childhood. Had I known it was a requirement of the program, I would have brushed up a little.*

A little will suffice. She glances at him and Hero rousts a reassuring smile.

On her long desk, around which are several chairs, a sizeable stone tablet is propped up on a wooden easel. The Creator motions Herodotus to the seat in front of it and once he has complied, she hands him a laser carver.

I want you to write, Tamous Satura was here. She instructs.

On the stone? Herodotus warily questions the instruction. *Wouldn't a simple pen and paper be easier?*

I wonder the same thing.

Seekers ask questions, do they? Shankara raises an eyebrow. *I was under the impression that they do exactly as instructed.*

Of course. Hero activates the tool and begins to engrave the said words on the tablet.

The Creator leaves Hero to his work. She motions towards the balcony and I accompany her outside.

I welcome the opportunity to admire the university grounds and gardens surrounding the lake below, as I have never seen them from this vantage point before. The garden is exactly as it appears - one large, breathtakingly colourful, intricately intertwined being in perfect balance and harmony with every aspect of itself. For no one person designed this city, it grew according to the best intentions of the occupants.

You've done wonderful work compiling the information and history on Tamous the Innocent. Shankara's praise is unexpected, and my ego does a quiet little dance.

Thank you.

You must admire his teachings very much.

I do. How I wish my response was more engaging, but I am utterly flabbergasted that this magnificent being even knows of my existence - let alone my work.

We love him too. She assures with a smile, and shifts her gaze to the horizon. *There is no tomorrow, only today. The present is stable, only consciousness unfolds.*

I realise that Shankara is quoting Tamous from some of his teachings passed down to us through the late twenty-first century revolutionary and sage, Zhi Samati.

The past and future curve toward each other to encircle the present. When we give attention to past regrets or future worries, we waste the only true time in which we have any power to affect change. This is why the great plan unfolds so slowly.

To be present, I chime in, *is to wake in the place from which you*

40

departed. I had memorised all of Tamous' teachings unearthed to date, but even with all my study, I couldn't claim to understand them all; for I am, after all, more of an analyst than a sage.

So ahead of his time. She concludes, having infinitely more insight than I.

I nod so as not to appear ignorant; although Shankara is, mostly likely, completely aware of what I do and do not understand.

His parents must have been very proud.

It is said that his mother adored him, I'm not sure his father ever knew about his awakening. I share what I understand from my research.

I am done. Herodotus joins us to announce.

Splendid. Show me. Shankara accompanies him back to the stone tablet and I follow, curious to see the purpose of this impromptu exam.

The Creator appears very pleased as she views the tablet.

An image of the unedited picture we requested from my professor earlier presents itself in my mind. As Herodotus' gasps along with me, he's obviously seeing what I am seeing.

The handwriting on this stone before us and the modern graffiti in the photograph are identical. There is an additional line of text that in our modern tongue reads 'The day Ashoka kneels.' This is an event that we have an exact date for. Also on the picture, two words have been inserted into the first sentence between was and here; those words were 'taken from'.

Tamous Satura was taken from here the day Ashoka kneels. Herodotus recites and concludes with a gasp.

I am fascinated, as it is written that the holy man was arrested by his own brother. Was this the incident referred to here?

This can mean only one thing. Hero pulls my attention back to the present. *I go!* Waves of shock are pulsing through his system, much to the disturbance of everything around him.

Shankara winks to confirm this. *You'd best go prep.*

Now shock is pulsing through my system. *But won't he need special training?*

What do you think I've been learning all these years? Hero looks back to Shankara. *Right now?*

Right now. She is happy to confirm.

Now? I panic, not yet ready to face the prospect of him not coming back.

Hero backs up towards the exit door that reappears in the wall.

41

I'll see you before I go, and be back before you even miss me.

Actually, Dilan will be in your ear the entire time. Shankara's announcement quells some of my anxiety, yet raises a multitude of questions. *Your partner knows more about this target and era than just about anyone in Shamballa or Agartha.*

Fantastic! Hero smiles pleased as I quietly handle my distress.

I'm sure you have questions. My bemused expression doesn't escape Shankara's attention. *Hero, you go ahead to med-bay. I will address your partner's concerns and we'll join you presently.*

The mention of Med-bay brings home the gravity of the situation - my love is going to regress to a physical form and leave himself exposed to all the mortal dangers. Yet he waves and heads off like he is going to a health spa.

Will I have to regress? I ask as soon as the wall reconstitutes and the Creator and I are alone.

She raises her fair eyebrows, that are practically indistinguishable against her pale complexion. *That depends...* There is a dramatic pause in the conversation as Shankara observes me - perhaps to assess how well I shall react to her supposition. *On whether or not you agree to mother the next incarnation of Tamous Satura.*

I don't know what I was expecting, but this is light years away from anything I expected to be discussing today; the thought is shocking, and I am too overwhelmed to respond at once.

I know, it is a lot to process. Shankara motions me to a lounge.

This is what you do with the DNA you collect? I seat myself, revealing nothing of the debate going on in my mind. *To what end?*

There have been very long periods in human history where our inner earth nations were completely shut off from the civilisations on the surface of this planet. Shankara takes the seat opposite mine. *During those times humanity learned lessons and obtained knowledge about subjects that we were not privy to.*

Surely anything you wish to know will be in the Akashic Records? Do they not contain the accumulated record of all human experience?

Shankara forces a smile. *It is a record of all human experience and learning minus all the negative, dark and purportedly useless thought forms and memories, which have been cast off into the lower etheric realms where they belong. It is this conglomeration of horror that holds the information we seek.*

Again I am shocked, confused, and struggling not to be judgemental. *What could we in Agartha, dimensions apart from the physical world, possibly have to gain-*

I am not at liberty to say. The Creator preempts my query. *I can only tell you that it is vital to all the inner earth kingdoms that we obtain this knowledge.*

So you wish for me to give birth to one of the greatest, if not the greatest, spiritual master that this planet has ever known, so that you can force that soul to relive their worst experiences for the benefit of your edification? If I am following correctly, this does not sit well with me at all.

I believe I may have insulted Shankara, but that does not reflect in her response or demeanour. *A great master does not experience, to do so is to become involved in the illusion. They seek disentanglement, thus they observe. Whatever insight is awarded us, will be entirely of their choosing.*

But if disentanglement is the goal, is it right that we are drawing this soul back to an incarnation?

Every being on this earth is all part of the same being, so long as one soul remains here, there is no true disengagement for any of us.

I feel bad for making the Creator's aspirations sound monstrous, but my concerns are valid, however naive. *If I decline, this honour will be offered to another?*

Of course. Shankara is forthright. *But none would understand nor appreciate this soul so well as you.*

Of course my logic tells me to decline and continue my study, but surely it is possible to be a mother and continue to study, research, and work at the same time. My heart warms with the idea of being a parent to this particular soul-mind and linked to Herodotus for all time in such a fashion. I already love him more than life itself, so I imagine I shall love our child even more so. Clearly, I am no master like Tamous, as I still very much desire to be involved with creation and I cannot think of anything Hero would love more than to experience the physical act of conception. To give our love such a gift is a notion that pleases me greatly, yet for that happy eventuality to come about I must submit to the Creator's plan to make Herodotus her latest Seeker.

So, Shankara prompts, *will you be regressing for this mission?*

Herodotus is surprised when I enter the frequency chamber containing a third-dimensional construct - filled with furniture that, at present, Hero and I simply pass right through. But by the time we walk out of this space, we will be in harmonic resonance with these surroundings and able to utilise the contents of this room - the furniture, clothes, equipment, bathroom facilities, beverages, and food stores - for these are all essential to third-dimensional beings. *Dilan.* Hero approaches. *I think you are supposed to join me after I regress. Or have you come to wish me luck first?*

I shake my head and grin. *I'm coming with you, all the way ... until you step through the gate anyway, then I'll just be the voice in your headset.*

My love appears ecstatic to learn this. *But there is no need for you to subject yourself to regression. You can still be my wing-person without having to return to a physical state of being.*

I shrug and grin. *It will be fun ... like being kids again.*

Hero gives a chuckle. *Not so much the latter.*

But fun, never-the-less.

Absolutely. He assures. *Way more fun than I had imagined.*

Oh, I'm sure you have. My face aches from the smile I cannot wipe away - the reverse frequency therapy that we are silently being bombarded with must be working, as a fifth-dimensional form knows nothing of physical aches and pains.

You know it, I can't lie. My love rubs his cheeks, clearly his grin is hurting him too.

In the meantime, Shankara said you could advise me about where to from here.

Happy to. Hero folds his legs up to float in the lotus position in mid-air.

I join him, figuring that as we become more solid, we will sink down to the floor and thus we will know that we have obtained our objective.

'The Creator has a twin Seeker facility in Shamballa, where a solid version of the Gate of Days is located,' Herodotus explains.

Shamballa is Agartha's sister city that occupies the same space in the physical world as our home city occupies in the astral realms of existence. These cities have many institutions in common, as the occupants often drift between worlds. The physical occupants here are all advanced enough in their third-eye vision to be able to perceive we "non-physicals", and we surely have no trouble perceiving our physical brothers and sisters either.

'There is also a control room from which you will be overseeing my mission through time.' Had I not decided to regress with Hero, there is a corresponding control room in Agartha from which I would have carried out my part in this mission, alongside Shankara. These two facilities can communicate with not only each other, but with the

44

facility in Agartha's past. It is this facility that will receive Herodotus when he arrives, and give him access to the passage that leads to surface earth.

I listen as my love speaks of his excitement regarding the mission, repressing all my fears so that I might revel in his joy with him. I envision the time beyond these events when I can tell him of the secret part I shall play.

Then it dawns on me that we have been seated on the hard timber floor for some time. Our fifth-dimensional garments have faded into the ethers, leaving us as naked as the day we came into this world. I reach out to touch my love in the flesh for the first time in our association. His chatter ceases and as I caress his cheek, he leans into my hand and closes his eyes. My eyes moisten with tears as the most beautiful emotions flood my being with an inner warmth and joy, more intense than I can recall experiencing before. This is that chaotic human condition known as feeling, and it is sensational! As Hero returns my affectionate touches, I am drawn into a kiss - which is a sweet, intimate, and meditative experience. My heart centre feels fit to explode with rapture; I feel alive! The physical act of making love is a hot, sweaty, exhilarating, intimate affair that there is no controlling. A fever burns within my body that is no longer connecting with my mind. My consciousness withdraws within, where I lose myself in the act of becoming one in body and spirit with him. Our moans of pleasure heighten the rapture, until finally I feel his essence spilling inside of me. I too climax so intensely that my entire form shudders with delight, before collapsing into a heap on the floor beside Hero. The afterglow left lingering around us is pure bliss, but we are aware that this joyous romp has a time limit, and so we are compelled to investigate the wash room.

I had forgotten how much I enjoyed playing in water - and with a playmate that pleasure is taken to a whole new level.

Passion expended once again, our legs have gone to jelly from our exertions. It is only that we have each other to lean against that we are still standing, and the warm water flowing over us is so very nice. 'I am surprised they haven't come to retrieve us for the mission.' I mumble; unaccustomed to speaking out loud, my mouth is lazy.

'What mission?' He mumbles in reply and I would laugh at his abandon were I not so relaxed. 'Let just stay here in Shamballa when it's over, and not go back to Agartha.'

If I have just conceived his child, he might very well have that wish granted. 'That might be arranged.'

He pulls away to hold me at arms length and discern if I am serious. 'You would actually consider that?'

'Let's just get through this mission and see if you still have the same calling to physical existence after you've spent some time here.' I raise my brows to suggest.

'You're right.' He hugs me close once more. 'But I have to say, I am liking it so far.'

'Of course you are ... all you've done is make love and shower.'

'I've used the toilet,' he adds, suddenly sounding less enthused. 'That was ... weird, but not a deal breaker.'

I am laughing so hard that I have to leave the shower before I choke on the water. 'It's not like you've never done that before.' I grab a towel and pat this body dry - being wet is an odd sensation, and going from hot to cold so quickly is annoying and probably hazardous to my health.

'But it has been epochs in physical world terms,' he defended. 'Still, I remember I enjoyed eating. I could use a bit of that.' He holds his gut as he follows me from the wet room, grabbing his towel en route.

'I'm with you.' I pull the jumpsuit from the hanger on the wall and put it on. 'It feels like my stomach is trying to eat itself.' The wants and needs of this physical form are much more extreme than I remembered.

'There should be food for us in the control centre.' Hero dusts the water from his form and pulls on his clothes, as eager as me to find sustenance.

Once we are fed and watered, Shankara joins us in the mess room, appearing like a ghost to us now. *We are good to go, whenever you both feel ready. This initial leg jump through the Gate of Days will help avoid any interference from anyone in the present.*

'Who would interfere?' Hero asks.

It's just a precaution. The Creator affirms. *You will be geared up for the mission once you land in the past at mission control in the first few years of this project - ground zero. I shall be there to meet you when you arrive as there is no one else I trust with my Seekers' safety.*

'So you have already seen me execute this mission?' Hero assumes.

In the timeline you are about to create, I imagine so. The Creator smiles.

46

'Wait?' I frown as a deep-seated panic besets my gut. 'So Hero will never return to this timeline?'

None of us will. Don't you see? Sleep, rest, meditational states reset everything and then you awake not realising that anything has changed. There is no tomorrow, only today. She reminds me of Tamous' teaching.

'The present is stable, only consciousness unfolds.' I felt a glimmer of understanding challenging my assumptions about existence. 'So there is one timeline, but our perception of it shifts.'

Shankara winks and looks back to Hero. *Beyond ground zero you'll be quantum jumping with the TVG of your TPS.*

'Finally, the real deal!' Hero is clearly thrilled about this.

'Sorry ... the what?'

'The Toroidal Vortex Generator of a Mobile Time Positioning System.' Hero explains.

I am still none the wiser. 'I didn't realise we had such technology.'

'I've only ever worked with simulators.' Hero explains, then thinks to reassure me. 'But I'm very familiar with the apparatus and procedures for use.'

I smile, but I am dying inside. I knew I would struggle when faced with the reality of graciously allowing Hero to go fulfil his aspirations; the risks he is taking truly horrify me. But if I am meant to be part of his future, the great mother will see him safely home. Tears flood my eyes. I can't stop them, and my throat restricts and aches from withholding my protest.

'Hey, I'm going to be fine,' Hero approaches to hug and reassure me. 'I've been training for this a *long* time-'

'I know,' my voice squeaks under the duress of my restraint. 'I just cannot get a grip on these physical emotions.'

'I know what you mean,' he swallows hard. 'They hurt ... a lot.'

He'll be back in less than one surface earth day. The Creator obviously feels we are being overly dramatic.

'She is right,' I draw a deep breath for strength, revel in his kiss one last time, and step away. 'We'll have eyes on you the entire time. You'll come back ... or I'll be coming after you.'

'I'll be in touch as soon as Shankara gets me hooked up to the telepathic com-link network back there.'

But Hero's ultimate destination is two sixty-two BCE. The thought makes me nauseous as my stomach is also struggling to digest food for the first time in aeons.

Two sixty-two BCE was the year Ashoka kneeled. Tamous was

47

reportedly twenty-six when he was taken into custody, so that put his birth year at about two eighty-eight BCE.

Normally a new insight for my thesis would be completely thrilling, but I am numb as I realise all I ever wanted is going to be history.

Hero's mission headset would still allow him to utilise his telepathic abilities. It would pick up on his thought signals and convert them into data to then be transferred into our system and conveyed to us. This allowed him to remain silent during his mission, yet communicate with mission control. His equipment would also shield him from sight and harness his transport.

The Gate of Days plays a sonic code and ignites into life in a blast of colourful light that combines and turns white as a vortex begins whirling within, spinning inward and then outward in search of a traveller. Hero moves in to make contact with the rotating energy, exhibiting not the slightest fear. He glances back at me. 'Your support means everything when I know you don't want to give it. Loving you is my great honour.'

I am not given the chance to voice the same sentiment, as the vortex spirals outward to make contact with my beloved and snatch him away.

While we await contact from Hero, I take a seat behind the mission control command centre and Shankara runs me through the use of the solid, primitive equipment. As Hero and I are operating in the material world and we are aeons apart, our regular telepathic communication is impaired. Hence I require a holo-screen to view Hero and his streaming footage. A headset is also required to communicate with him. Shankara's control centre occupies the same space as the one I am seated in, just on a higher frequency so she can still telepathically communicate with me. Although I have taken on a physical body, I have not lost all of my psychic skills. 'What is taking so long? He's gone back in time so you'd think there would be no delay.'

We have to safeguard against crossovers. Shankara silently informs. *There can be up to a 24-hour delay, but not so long in this case, however.* She assures before I freak out.

'*Mission control, can you hear me?*' The sound of Hero's voice is pure relief.

'Picking you up loud and clear, Herodotus.' I reply as the screen before me lights up and I see Hero waving at me. 'I confirm we have a visual.' He serves me a thumbs up.

'Hang about, I'll put this headset on and check it with my cloaking system on.'

Once the headset is on his head, I observe a room very similar to the one I am seated in - it may even be this same control centre hundreds of years ago.

'I know you cannot see Shankara, but she is here overseeing the proceedings.'

'Ditto.'

'My cloaking system has been activated.' Hero is heard to laugh. *'This is so weird ... check it.'* I watch him approach a mirror that he cannot be seen within; however, as he looks down at himself, his form is perfectly visible.

I laugh in empathy with his situation. 'I can see how that might be a little disorientating. I confirm your visual is working under the cloaking device.'

'In that case, Shankara says I am good to go.' He advises.

I concur.

'Verify that, Hero. Shankara also confirms you are good to go from this end.'

'Roger that. There is a teleporting platform here that will speed me to the surface. I'll reconnect when I arrive there beyond the final quantum jump.'

'May Sophia support and watch over you, Hero. Be careful out there.'

'That is the plan.' He gives me the thumbs up and his connection goes dead once again.

You are doing so well. Shankara encourages as we wait out the transfer. *The retrieval part of the mission shall take no time at all. And you are virtually going to meet the subject of your thesis.*

'My firstborn, you mean?' The idea is thrilling and daunting - what if he is nothing like I imagine?

'Whoa Dilan, are you there?'

I sit up to attention in the control chair to address Hero through the com-link. 'I am here, Herodotus.'

'Feast your eyes on this!'

The screen before me lights up and all I can see before me is forest for miles and miles, under an orb so much brighter than the misty sun we know, and the sky is one expansive blue blanket. 'Oh my heavens, Hero, that is unbelievable!'

His attention shifts to a monitor that is in his hands. *'I am near a quarter of a globe away from where I shall find our target, so I'm going to get moving. Do you want me to leave the camera on?'*

'Affirmative. I feel more comfortable having eyes on your whereabouts.'

I concur.

'Shankara seconds that request.'

'Activating my transporter.' Hero steps forward and slightly up. *'I am aboard, my tracking device is linked and off I go.'*

The scenery begins whizzing past at great speed, but I am absolutely fascinated. 'I had no idea it was so beautiful and bright.'

It wasn't this beautiful all throughout history, but she certainly had her moments.

I return to the desk from a refreshment break as Herodotus arrives at the cave where the inscriptions accredited to Tamous were found. He plans to investigate the writings and add his statement after he has located Tamous, as the Master is our primary objective. Hero instructs his equipment to hone in on the closest human lifeforms. There are only two within the target area and they are together. *'It could be Tamous and his student.'*

'Proceed. *With caution.*'

Herodotus disengages his transport to proceed the last little way on foot.

As the target comes into sight, I draw closer to the monitor to observe the holy man I have only ever read about. He's seated on the ground in the lotus position with his student seated before him, back to camera.

'Look at how dark their hair and eyes are, and their skin is so tan.' I had read descriptions of the people who once inhabited the Asiatic lands of the surface world. They contrasted greatly with their distant descendants here in Agartha, with their white hair and skin, and pale eyes of grey or violet.

Beautiful, yes? Shankara observed from alongside me.

'Yes. They look rather like Achiever.' I noted, and glancing to the Creator I saw her blushing.

Quite. She conceded in an uncomfortable fashion.

It is rumoured that the Creator and the king's cyborg advisor, Achiever had once been lovers, but no one had the guts to ask either of them if there was any truth to the rumour.

'Do you think my child might retain some of Tamous' genetic traits?'

Most definitely. But you and Hero will be in there too.

The notion is so completely delightful that now I am blushing.

'*Today we focus on breath...*' I comprehend Tamous' words as Hero's equipment is translating the discourse. '*The one constant that remains with us all through this illusion we call life.*'

My heart fills to bursting as I am so honoured to hear the master speak directly. 'Are we recording this?'

Of course. I can hear the smile in Shankara's voice; she is as starstruck as I am.

'*In stressful situations it is the breath that changes, learn to control it and you...*' The young monk looks directly at us, although Hero should be invisible to him.

This is concerning. 'Has he spotted us? Is Hero's equipment failing?'

I think not. Sometimes our targets have evolved so much spiritually, that they see right through our devices.

'Was Hero aware of that possibility before he left?' I certainly wasn't.

Seekers are prepared for every scenario.

'Monk?' Limrani watches Tamous rise to standing and move past her.

'Who are you?' Tamous addresses Hero directly.

'*What should I do?*' The unexpected attention panics Hero and he backs up. '*You should not be able to see me.*' He informs his target.

'Don't panic, he won't harm you.' Of that I am certain, and seemingly in response to my claim, Tamous comes to a standstill.

'*I see you quite clearly and understand you very well.*'

'Who are you talking to?' Limrani pursues her teacher, and I am struck by how beautiful and formidable she appears.

'*She cannot see me.*' Hero observes and then adds purely for our benefit. '*At least my equipment is still working.*'

'You cannot see him?' Tamous' attention reverts to his student.

The warrior-like woman, who is sporting many lethal looking weapons, thankfully overlooks Hero to query her teacher. '*Are you toying with me?*' She doesn't openly revere the master as much as I had imagined she would.

'*I'm out of here.*' The warrior unnerves Hero and he makes haste back towards the cave. I watch his heart-rate rise as he runs. *'Did you see those weapons?'* He is in such a hurry to retreat he doesn't even bother engaging his transporter.

'I saw them.' I concur; I would run from her too.

Herodotus glances back to see Limrani unsheathe her weapon and give chase through the foliage disturbed in his wake.

'You are just giving her a clear path to follow.'

'It's okay.' Hero reaches the cave where there is no plant life left to disturb and nothing to betray his exact whereabouts.

The warrioress pauses at the opening, weapon held high in a threatening fashion - clearly she plans to wait it out.

Herodotus moves further inside the rocky void to put some distance between them.

'Where was the inscription located in here?'

'North-west rock face.'

'Engaging infra-red sight.' The image on the screen goes from near blackness to easy to define greyscale.

The natural confines of the inner cave were still recognisable from the pictures I'd studied, so I could confidently direct him. 'Slightly to your left.'

Hero looked to the spot where the engravings had been found, only there was nothing but a blank wall. I gasped at the huge paradox this presented.

'Maybe we have the wrong spot?' Hero probably wished to set me at ease, but instead I felt insulted.

'I know this cave like the back of my hand. I've studied photos, scans of the topography, and I'm telling you-' Then it dawned on me. 'You must get Tamous to write the piece, before you add your message. How else could the monk have managed to write so neatly upon the stone, but for using your laser tool?'

Nice save, Dilan. Shankara awarded. *This logic is sound.*

Hero's attention reverts to the passage that leads to the outer cavern as Tamous and Limrani enter. The master looks to us, but his student is still gazing blindly about.

'This place is known to us.' Hero informs his company. *'Why haven't you written your teachings upon the walls here?'*

'My teachings have a way of getting people killed.'

'Very encouraging.' Limrani scoffs.

'When written down,' adds Tamous.

'I cannot write or read.' The warrioress is happy to confess.

'You don't understand. The teaching that led me here, is not here! So how then can I be here?'

My poor love is having an existential crisis, more acutely aware of what this paradox means than I suspected.

Tamous is understandably baffled.

'The piece you carved into this wall.' Hero motions to the smooth stone rock face alongside him. 'You know .... why man and woman? Why a dualistic universe, blah, blah, blah...'

'I imagine the dualism of man and woman, or any being apart from the self, is the opportunity to love that which is not the self.'

'Exactly so.' I award, slapping my hands together in delight.

'Yes!' Hero echoes my sentiment and clicks his fingers. 'That was part of it.'

'You see him?' Limrani asks her teacher.

Tamous nods and explains our concerns about the missing inscription. 'But I would think who he is, and why he is here is a more pressing concern.'

Introduce yourself and tell him where you are from. Shankara instructs, I relay, and Hero obeys - explaining how important the inscription and accompanying prophecy would be in future.

'The prophecy that you relayed to me during my mental dialogue with Làoshi this morning?' The master poses, to the surprise of all listening.

'I did?' Herodotus is baffled. 'Who is Làoshi?'

'Good question.' I award.

I think I know. Shankara whispers.

'The Inter-dweller who binds all of us together.' Tamous replies.

'So you keep saying.' Limrani chimes in, hearing only half the conversation.

'What does he mean, us?' I ask.

Don't get sidetracked from the prophecy. Shankara overrules my curiosity.

'So you know your brother is coming for you?' Hero states what he knows. 'You predicted this event unfolding on the same day that the leader of the Mauryan Empire kneels before a holy man.'

'Ashoka kneels.' Tamous nods in agreement with himself - but how is he so certain of events that are happening thousands of miles away? Was this a demonstration of the Inter-dweller that Tamous claimed connected us all to the great mother? Was this connection the real reason that I was so fascinated with Tamous' life?

'Ashoka seeks spiritual redemption for all the killing done in his name ...

his conversion is a well-documented event that has been accurately dated in my time.'

It seems Herodotus has been listening to all my history rants over the years.

'What do you mean Ashoka kneels? Before whom?' Limrani disrupts the information exchange. She darts in front of Tamous without warning and collides with Hero. The event is startling to them both, hence they both back up a few paces. *'Your ghost has mass.'* Limrani holds her weapon on guard again.

I gasp, afraid that she really will injure my love if she lashes out in fear.

'Please tell her that I mean neither of you harm.' Herodotus appeals to Tamous, who is every bit as reasonable and calm about meeting a being from the future as one might imagine he would be.

Tamous thankfully persuades his student to put the weapon away.

'Thank you.' Herodotus and I both relax a little.

'So, my friend, I feel quite sure that you've not come all the way from the future just to warn me that my brother is coming for me today.'

'Today!' Limrani is horrified and appeased in equal measure. *'He will not take you. We can fight him together.'*

'No!' I freak out at the notion. 'She must remain at liberty or the world will never even know Tamous existed!'

'She must not be here when the Sangdil arrive.' Herodotus warns Tamous. *'Your student is the channel for your legacy.'*

Whilst Tamous attempts to encourage his student to avoid the pending confrontation with the Sangdil, Herodotus is presented with the perfect opportunity to extract from Tamous the DNA sample that he was sent to procure and he does not hesitate. To Tamous the extraction feels like nothing more than an insect bite.

'I will not fight.' Tamous informs his student to her great disappointment.

'You cannot just let them take you!' She objects.

'Especially not before you write on this wall.' Herodotus prompts Tamous to help him solve the other paradox he is facing. Herodotus produces his laser tool for the monk to inspect. *'This will engrave this stone as easily as ink marks papyrus.'* Hero demonstrates on the wall by writing the beginning of his contribution to the ancient message.

'Don't touch the shiny end.' Hero hands the tool over to Tamous to try, and he writes the first lines of the teaching just as Hero had relayed it moments before.

The sound of numerous horses rumbling through the forest snatches the attention of all present.

'*Sangdil.*' Limrani unsheathes her sword.

Tamous hands the tool back to Herodotus. '*You can get her out undetected.*'

Herodotus holds his hands up and backs away. '*I'm not supposed to get involved or change anything. You are not even meant to know that I am here.*'

'*There are no accidents, Seeker.*'

He's right. Shankara seconds. *Limrani must not be taken.*

'She has weapons, how do you expect Hero to overpower her?' I feel the order is too risky.

'*Please finish, I can tell you exactly what to write.*' Hero makes one final appeal to Tamous in regard to the inscription, knowing the Sangdil will capture Tamous this day and he will not be back.

Limrani is concealed from sight to one side of the passage into the inner cavern, and she is ready to ambush the Sangdil soldier who proceeds down the tunnel alone.

'*Stay where you are, brother.*' Tamous calls in warning.

Even though his sibling is coming to arrest him, Tamous attempts to save his brother from harm. Such compassion is practically unheard of in the brutal day and age in which this master lives, thus his conduct is all the more inspiring.

'*You will not harm me-*' His brother's amusement quickly departs as Limrani launches her attack. The Sangdil warrior blocks the strike with his own weapon and a fight ensues. Each warrior mocks their opponent as they strike at one another with their deadly blades.

I have stopped breathing, enthralled - I have never seen a real fight before.

Limrani is fearless. Her prowess is impressive and I believe her opponent is rather impressed by her skill also.

As more Sangdil can be heard running down the tunnel towards the inner cavern, Tamous looks to Herodotus for aid.

Tell him to use his advantage, he knows what to do.

I dare not contradict Shankara, as this is her program and mission, but again I find myself biting my tongue to relay the message.

Hero sneaks up behind Limrani and injects her with a sedative. He catches her as she falls unconscious into his arms, rendering her invisible. '*Dear Sophia, she weighs a tonne!*'

'Watch yourself.'

Limrani's sudden disappearance disturbs the Sangdil warlord, who starts swinging his sword violently in search of her. *'What trickery is this?'*

My heart jumps into my throat as Hero ducks and weaves to keep the unconscious female warrior away from the warlord's free-wielding blade.

A smash startles me witless and Hero's feeds turn to static.

'Hero!' I cry out - like he will hear me from the outer world a millennia ago. I feel this huge abyss of time and space erupt between us, and my stomach turns in panic. 'No!' My breathing is irregular and it is making my head spin; my face is flushed with heat whilst the rest of me shivers in fear.

You need to calm yourself, you're going to hyperventilate. Shankara is in my ear. *We are working on reconnecting with Herodotus-*

'What if his equipment has been damaged? Or worse-'

Shhh. Shankara urges. *You do not want to manifest a disaster.*

'How can I, when these events all happened an age ago?'

But the Seeker's mission timeline is unfolding now, you can add to his woes-

'Not if he's dead already!' My throat is restricting as tears of sorrow well in my eyes and tumble down my cheeks.

Reel in those surging emotions for Herodotus, your own well-being and the well-being of the child you've just conceived.

As the Creator's words sink in, my mood takes a sudden upswing. 'I'm carrying Hero's child? Are you sure?' My voice nearly fails me; I had no idea how much I truly desired this.

Yes. I can see this clearly. And once Hero returns with the sample, we'll inject Tamous into the mix and you'll be carrying THE child.

Joy, horror, pain, wonder; all these conflicting emotions move me to tears. My throat restricts and aches; I cannot get enough air, despite how much I gasp for it.

Dilan, you're hyperventilating, you are going to faint, if you don't...

The Creator's voice rushes away, along with all my conscious concerns.

Chapter 3
Khemri 2081 AD
Amari – The Healer

Awoken by a nudge, I am startled by the pale linen shroud over my head, obscuring my sight. I instinctively raise a hand to remove it.

'I must ask you to refrain. We are almost there.'

The foreign accent reminds me I am far from my African home; the men of my homeland have voices and an accent that is altogether different to the Khmeri people at the heart of the Indo-Asian peninsula.

I grew up in the south-western country of Burkina Faso, landlocked by Mali to the north, Niger to the east, Benin to the southeast, Togo and Ghana to the south, and the Ivory Coast to the southwest. My people are the Dagara, now famous for our ability to heal the mind, body, and spirit of sickness - especially the modern afflictions that have arisen as a result of a technologically infested world. Burkina Faso was too poor to adopt a full-scale technological revolution like the richer nations, and had in a large part been spared from the associated illnesses. All the poorest countries in the world are now reaping the benefit of being the safest, thriving agricultural environments on the planet. But what is making all living things ill isn't just the bombardment of micro-radiation from wireless communications, it is the geo-engineering that was initiated to combat global warming around the middle of the century. This upper atmospheric fog laced with minuscule heavy-metal shards was supposed to form a reflective barrier between the earth and the sun, and offset the warming effect on the surface of the planet. Common sense ought to have dictated that what goes up will come down, and for a long time the government and corporate-owned media masked the connection between the initiative and the huge rise in lower respiratory disease. In the end, a public outcry led to a worldwide ban of all geo-engineering decades ago, but the damage was already done.

Skin afflictions are rife - sores that won't heal, the feeling of bugs crawling under the skin. These symptoms, along with dementia and severe fatigue, are all part and parcel of an epidemic that has swept the world, despite none of these afflictions being contagious. And humans aren't the only ones suffering; animals and even plant life have been affected. However, there are ways to keep the toxins at bay with diet, exercise, and nurturing a deep connection to the ancestor. I, being the elder and most famed of healers of the Dagara, travel to give lectures and aid those suffering from exposure to Western technologies that were embraced without really understanding the risks to their wellbeing. Through my work, others have established a connection with that omnipotent Inter-dweller who resides inside us all, to the betterment of their health and lives. This is what led me here to war-torn Khmeri, against the advice of my manager, Rodney, whom I have promised to meet at the airport. I left him a note in my room, as he would have a pink fit if he knew where I was at present.

My guards and hood are for my own protection, or so I am told. My hands have not been bound, as I am not a prisoner - I agreed to this sabbatical. I trust that I am being taken to meet with the rebel leader of Khmeri, in hiding from the Ching Republic who are encroaching from the north. I had no intention of taking up this invitation as my ability to cross borders freely depends upon me remaining politically neutral and staying squarely under the umbrella of medical assistance. But the ancestor insists the importance of this meeting is well worth the risk.

I close my eyes and go within to check in with my Inter-dweller, whom I have come to call Onderwyser, meaning teacher. They smile and nod to reassure me that I am doing the right thing. I say "they" as Onderwyser is neither man nor woman, but the perfect balance of both. They present as being an elder of my tribe, but I know they are actually formless and ageless as the air I breathe. *What we do today will make all the difference this time.* They convey optimistically.

'This time?' The twist this puts on the statement is most curious, but I am given no time for questions. After a bone shattering ride, my transport stops and I am assisted from the vehicle with as much care as fighting men can muster. I admit that I do appear skinny, old and frail, but my soul is full of energy. To walk blindly into unknown terrain is going to make anyone a little nervous.

'The next part of our journey is precarious,' my guard advises. 'It might be safer if I carry you. With your permission.'

'If that is most convenient for you.'

I am immediately swept off my feet and deftly conveyed forth.

My nostrils fill with a smell that is very damp and earthy, hence I suspect we are underground. The temperature has dropped and my skin heeds the absence of sunlight. Up ahead, someone is groaning as a woman speaks.

'Do you really think he will remember? He's been struck near witless and is tripping out of his mind!'

'We cannot risk the knowledge of this sacred site and our base to a heroin addict, bo nah,' a man appeals in a reasoning manner.

"Bo nah" means boss in the local Khmer dialect. I smile beneath my veil as I realise that the rebel leader I've been brought here to meet with is a woman.

The local media have another name for this revolutionary and that is Mebanhcheakear - which means 'commander of networks', and they are not wrong. For the past five years, the resistance have managed to thwart the Ching Republic's attempts to establish itself in the Khmeri region. The locals idolise Mebanhcheakear, even though no one knows the identity of the legend. I am moments away from enlightenment.

'Put our honoured guest down, at once.' She commands, her tone full of warmth and reason with only a hint of annoyance. Her voice has resonance - I am not in a tight tunnel anymore.

'Apologies bo nah...'

My feet are set upon the ground, and my escort ensures that I have my balance before releasing me altogether.

'Negotiating the passage is difficult with the blindfold.' He adds.

'Yes, you may remove that,' my hostess instructs.

The veil lifts and I gaze up at the ceiling of a massive cavern. There are gaps that allow sunlight to stream in here and there, but by and large it is shaded, well-ventilated and less humid than outside. There is a stream running through the huge cavity, further cooling the space. Stalactites hang from above, and the walls of the underground chamber are lined with rows of engraved calligraphy that appear Chinese or something similar. 'Magnificent ancestors...' I cannot wipe the amazement from my face. 'What does it all mean?'

'No one knows, the text is too ancient,' my hostess advises, and I drag my attention from the amazing character script to look at the woman addressing me. 'This intruder insists these walls talk to him, but that is probably the opiate speaking.'

My gaze drifts to the half-unconscious male on the floor, unkempt and so lost - my heart wells with compassion for him.

'Dr Amari Nosipho.'

Yes, that is me - the world famous healer, awarded an honorary doctorate for my work from the Université de Ouagadougou, Burkina Faso. My sights return to the rebel leader.

'I am Zhi Sumati.' She bows to me, respectfully.

I recognise the name - it once carried the title of Dr ahead of it also.

Dr Sumati had been an environmental scientist, who had gone missing around the time the Khmeri revolution began. Many claimed her mysterious disappearance had jump-started the resistance. 'The world believes you were killed by the rebels you are leading.'

She shrugs. 'Now, I do not exist.'

Her's is an intelligent face - attractive for a woman of middle-age. Taller than myself, as just about everyone is, the doctor is slender and athletic. She is dressed in plain dark trousers, lightweight boots, and a long cool shirt - the same as her soldiers. Her long dark hair falls in a single braid down her back. She has gone to great lengths to remain anonymous, which gives me cause to wonder.

'Why trust me with the knowledge of your identity, Mebanhcheakear? It is a very great risk you take, revealing yourself to me.'

'Spirit has led me to believe I can trust you.' There is an awkwardness to this statement.

'The ancestor...' I nod in understanding. 'I was also compelled to attend this meeting.'

The news rouses a hint of a smile from her. 'I am grateful for your bravery in coming here, and I regret any inconvenience my invitation may have caused, but I believe we can help each other.'

Despite the fact that this is our first meeting and we were born ten thousand miles apart, Zhi Sumati feels like a kindred spirit.

'What happened...' The prisoner groans, and our attention is diverted to the man sprawled out on the floor. 'I just wanted a piss...' He mutters. 'Fuck you, old man!'

I find his terminology most interesting. Could he be referring to 'the ancestor'? Was he led here too?

'I shall take care of this, bo nah.' The soldier grabs up the arms of the semi-conscious prisoner to drag him away, and as he does I hear an appeal.

They must not make an enemy of this man.

My eyes scan the room in search of the source, whereby I see a misty disturbance in the darkness of the cave. I close my eyes to perceive the entity more clearly. 'Wait, please.' I request of the soldiers at the behest of the fair spirit, with eyes as blue and pale as the morning sky. He looks like a futuristic nordic ghost, so what is he doing here in the heart of Asia?

They may attempt to kill him, but he will not die. He will become a mighty magician, who could help the rebels win this war. The apparition looks to the prisoner scratching, twitching, moaning and bloodied. *He's just a little lost right now.*

'Are you speaking with your ancestor?' Dr Sumati queries.

'No. The ancestor is within, this spirit is without. Still, he has reminded me that the ancestor teaches that, when a soul is troubled and crazed, a mighty healer is waiting to be born. The greater the signs of self-endangerment and endangerment to others, the greater the skill of the healer about to be born.' I open my eyes to look to Dr Sumati. 'I also know that when you are in conflict with another, it means that you have something to share in this world. Conflict is not the problem, conflict is meant to bring two people into communion. Not wanting to deal with the conflict is the problem. You must get to know this person better, in order to comprehend the greater meaning of your association.'

The leader's inner conflict is plain on her face. 'I want to heed and honour your advice, but the risk to my people is too great.'

What happens right now is integral to the future ... I believe. The fair spirit interjects passionately and his claim does seem to ring true with what the ancestor said earlier.

'Then allow me to take this man with me,' I pose a solution.

'Back to Africa?' The commander is clearly stunned that I would go to such lengths.

'I am permitted to take unique test subjects back home for treatment, observation, and study. He cannot cause you harm there ... and I am sure this man would prefer exile to death.'

At length, she nods to agree. Closing my eyes, the fair spirit smiles and awards me a nod, appeased by the outcome.

'But we cannot let you take him like this. He's no doubt riddled with bugs.'

I open my eyes to see her give the nod to the guard who has hold of my new patient.

'Bugs?' I query.

'Indeed, they are at the heart of all the medical problems you've been treating.'

I was most curious to learn this.

'De-bug him, clean him up, and restrain him. He's going to start lashing out once the opium haze lifts.' Zhi instructs her troops. 'Also, block up that collapsed tunnel to ensure we have no more unexpected visitors.'

'Yes, bo nah.' The guard in charge confirms and then looks disenchanted as he observes his captive. 'But this one is not even worth the charge we're going to waste on him.'

'Charge?' I query, whereby the guard pulls out his taser. 'I don't understand.' I look to Dr Sumati for an explanation.

'A power surge will knock out any electrical device.'

'You think bugs that are causing breathing and skin disease are electronic?' I am stunned by the proposition.

'I can prove it.' She assures. 'If you will kindly follow me.'

I look back to the soldier who holds my patient. 'Surely there is a less painful alternative to electrocution.'

My hostess does an abrupt about-face. Her graceful movements hint at some kind of martial arts training, a practice still popular in this part of the world. 'An electro-magnetic pulse is most efficient, as some of the latest bugs can reboot. If he has bugs, they could already be transmitting our position to the enemy.' Zhi nods to her guard to proceed with her order.

Deep pangs of shock resonate through my being - I can hardly believe my ears. 'Has nano-technology advanced so much?'

'And then some.' Dr Sumati motions me towards one of many tunnels leading out of the cavernous chamber, and leads off in that direction.

The tunnel terminates at a dead end and before I have the chance to query our route, the large round metal plate under foot gives a loud clunk and we descend into the ground.

'Is it sensor driven?' I wonder.

'In a way. It is some sort of intuitive technology. 'It goes up and down in accordance with the will of the majority, or the more wilful occupant.'

'Oh my goodness! You built this?'

Zhi shook her head. 'And no one knows who did.'

My heart is pumping ten to the dozen. I am currently witnessing ancient alien technology in motion, which certainly more than makes up for the risk I took coming here today.

The curved earthen walls that rise up around us, appear to be reinforced with a thick coat of clear resin, like nothing I've ever seen before. Hundreds of metres down a passage begins to reveal itself. A set of sealed metal doors arise from the floor and the descending platform, upon which we stand, comes to a stop at the base of the door frame. A laser beam scans down our bodies from a small, concealed wondow above the doors.

'Infra-red sensing technology,' Zhi informs. 'It can detect any particle that decreases air quality.'

'Like your bugs?'

My hostess grins. 'Just.'

'More alien tech?'

'No, this was our innovation. Most of what you will see is.'

The doors part to grant entry to the next antechamber, where there is yet another door. This door only unlocks after the one behind us is securely closed.

'Bio-containment.' We comment in unison and grin.

'Yes, quite.' Zhi awards. 'Only in this case we are keeping contaminants out rather than in.'

Another scan and we are finally granted entry into a greenhouse of massive proportions, complete with artificial lighting and weather. Here is where all the women, children, and older folk of the resistance are keeping themselves gainfully employed.

'We have so far prevented the bugs from invading this food supply. We also filter and ionise the water to keep it bug and heavy-metal free.'

'I did wonder how you fed this huge army of yours.' Obviously the rebel group harnessed the water from the stream in the upper cavern, but what was generating the electricity for this huge underground farm? 'Hydropower?'

She nods. 'Partially. But we have also developed a device that uses a natural protein to create electricity from moisture in the air.'

'An air-powered generator?' I wasn't sure I was understanding correctly. She nods and I am flabbergasted. 'That is amazing!'

'The air-gen connects electrodes to the protein nano-wires to generate electrical current from the water vapour naturally present in the atmosphere. We are literally making electricity out of thin air.' Zhi is clearly proud of their achievements here, and well she should be. 'Clean energy twenty-four seven.'

'Brilliant!' I note that all the produce being grown in this space is alkaline. 'You grow many of the foods I recommend to my patients and students.' Various root vegetables, lemon and lime, nuts, spices, ginger, beans, lentils and tea are all thriving in this huge space - and those are just the plots within my eyeshot. 'May I?' I point to the oregano plants flourishing in a long planter box alongside us. With a nod from my hostess, I break off a piece to taste. The broken stem fills my nostrils with a sweet, earthy aroma, and the taste is warm and slightly bitter as it should be.

'The bugs are acid junkies,' Dr Sumati explains. 'The more alkaline your system is, the less they like you. We found that your trick of oregano oil in ionised water is a great deterrent.'

'So pleased I could help the cause.' I'm delighted to have my own observations vindicated. 'Clearly you do vital work for all humanity.' My mind boggles at the effort of outfitting a base of this magnitude in the wilderness - and in secret.

'We have many brilliant scientific minds seeking refuge here. I am not the only scientist to find myself on the wrong side of the law after comprehending that many of the world's governments are concealing a secret alien AI agenda.'

'Alien AI?'

'What would you call a sentient, telepathic, manipulative, shape-shifting, liquid crystal?'

'A nightmare.' I'm suddenly not as keen to proceed with this journey of discovery.

'We need to go deeper to get to the labs.' My guide leads me back through the security doors and onto the elevator platform.

I follow, apprehensive and yet morbidly intrigued. 'You have a sample of this thing you describe?'

'We do.' Dr Sumati glances back. 'Albeit a tiny sample of a far greater stash that I believe may be at the root of the Republic's true interest in our land.'

This visit grows more fascinating by the second. I can certainly see why the ancestor encouraged me to come.

Deeper inside the earth the platform stops. We are scanned and permitted to enter bio-containment, scanned again, and then finally granted entry to a corridor lined to one side with glass-fronted laboratories.

Considering where we are, these laboratories have facilities that are most impressive, and the scientists working within them are completely engrossed in their work.

'What are they researching?'

'Ways to reverse the damage that geo-engineering and electromagnetic radiation poisoning have done to the earth and our bodies, or at least how to protect against these threats. We are also studying the alien substance I spoke of earlier; how we might best defend against it and combat the nano-tech that is engulfing the world like a silent, invisible plague.'

'There is a correlation between the alien substance and nano-tech?' I hope I misunderstand.

'It's *all* connected...' Zhi emphasises, motioning to the large screen inside the lab before us. The technician has a microscopic camera inside a sedated soldier, and the magnified footage is projected onto a screen that we can readily see through the large lab windows in the corridor. We observe tiny black bugs implanting themselves in the soldier's neural network. Four of the bug's legs clamp around the nerve ending. Once attached, the remaining two legs rotate upward and it appears just like a wireless transmitter.

'We're being controlled.' The notion is outrageous, and yet I see the pieces of the puzzle falling perfectly into place. 'These bugs are released in the geo-clouds?' I place a hand to my mouth as the realisation sends a cold chill right through me.

'Smart dust,' the doctor confirmed. 'An autonomous network of tiny motes that sense and monitor environmental conditions, including light, vibrations, temperature, pressure, acceleration, humidity, sound, stress! These can interface to enhance computational capability. Only some of these bugs are transmitters, others are receivers and maintenance. Your patients with skin conditions are those poor souls whose bodies are trying to reject the smart dust. If allergic to the metal, the body will push the bugs out via the most direct route - straight through the skin. That feeling of bugs crawling under the skin is just that.'

I shake my head at the blatant lies being told to the public.

'So the already technologically-addicted masses are now being influenced by the nano-tech invading their bodies. This is why people are experimenting with tech implants and upgrades with ever-increasing abandon, at the peril of their own humanity and connection to spirit.'

I could not agree more. 'The trouble with these internal technical enhancements and inbuilt telecommunications systems is that you can no longer simply turn them off. And removal is almost always crippling or fatal.' I have seen the suffering firsthand, many times.

'But what easier way to bring the masses under control and stamp out any opposition. The powers that be don't even need to use force anymore, they just need to make it look cool.' The doctor raises both brows at the notion. 'Not only can this nano-tech monitor our thoughts and movements, it can alter our perception, command us to its bidding, or even kill us from within, as slowly or expediently as it sees fit.' Zhi's eyes glaze over for a moment and I suspect she is caught up in a memory.

I am bemused by the blatant disregard for not just human life, but all life. 'Do the elite and their puppet governments think that this planet is their personal laboratory?'

'It's not the elite controlling the governments,' the doctor is quick to correct my misgiving.

'Then who is in control?' A feeling of deep dread begins to creep through my being.

'I am coming to that.' The doctor moves ahead down the corridor.

I follow, my trepidation growing the further we proceed.

We pass by the next lab where there are glass tubes that run from floor to ceiling; one is being bombarded by infra-red light and the other by ultraviolet light. The observation tubes appear to be filled with tiny particles that swarm like birds in flight, their existence made visible by the intense bombardment of the differing light spectrums. The more frenzied movement of the swarms in the ultraviolet light chamber seems to indicate they are more averse to it.

'I give you the outer world air supply.' The doctor gestures to the tubes. 'Here is where we are developing the infra-red sensing technology along with its algorithms to create our smart dust sensors and scanners.'

'Is the air this bad everywhere?' The sight makes me loath to take another breath, but what choice do we living, carbon-based creatures have? 'I thought most geo-engineering was banned ages ago?'

'Did I not mention that these bugs are self-replicating? I cannot tell you about other areas on the globe, but the bugs are pretty well everywhere here and spreading.'

'Who is responsible? The Republic? Or do all governments know this has happened, and are keeping a lid on it to avoid mass panic?'

'I pray it is the former and not the latter, but who can say? In the age of communication, no one can communicate without everyone knowing about it. So who knows if there are other resistance groups like ours who know the truth and mean to combat it? I fear it is a cull of sorts.' Zhi is bitter to admit. 'If you are affected by the consumption of metal, you will fall ill, die, and reduce the population. But if you are unaffected, then you are a prime candidate for the growing transhuman movement.'

'I will never understand it,' I had to say. 'Its proponents claim technology makes people superhuman. But it seems to me that with every technological enhancement, they become less human and more dependent on the hive mind that is the net.' Such an appropriate term now I think about it. But these bugs certainly explained why people by and large seemed no longer strongly opposed to being integrated with technology. 'I won't even consent to a microchip. I wear one of those watch thingies ... I told them any implants would interfere with my work.'

'You are no doubt right about that ... humans who seek a creative, innovative, enlightened path vibrate at a frequency beyond the control of these systems and tend to make them malfunction. Your personal sonic would create more than enough interference to render smart dust useless.'

'It is true, technology tends to go haywire around me.' I chuckle, indifferent to what others might consider a curse.

'This is how I know you are bug free. They would not like you, you'd fry them all.'

'I am so pleased you don't have to zap me.' This prospect rouses a smile from us both.

As we approach what appears more like a large freezer room than a laboratory, I feel inexplicably anxious and place a hand over my gut to quell my rising panic.

The doctor notes my dis-ease. 'That's the goo you're sensing ... that's what we've come to call it. But fear not. I shall not expose you to it directly, as it has an adverse effect on even the most spiritually advanced souls. It's sleeping right now and it is best left that way.'

'This mineral sleeps?' I find the assertion odd and a little disconcerting.

'When confined to a dark, cold place.' She halts and looks back to me, and I see how serious she is. 'You should think of it more as advanced organic AI. It can sense when it is being watched and can get quite aggressive. Hence why I shall be showing you footage of sessions with it, rather than risking a direct introduction.'

'That sounds far more agreeable.' As my sight is drawn to the metal-encased lab, my skin prickles to caution me to keep my distance from the ominous presence I sense within. I do not need to see the substance with my own eyes to know that the good doctor is telling the truth; every fibre of my being knows that an exponent of the most adverse variety is near. All living things communicate through light and frequency, and whatever was in that lab felt like a black hole for both.

At the end of the corridor, we enter a general office where Dr Sumati boots up a computer. 'We don't carry electronic devices for health and security reasons.'

'Too easy to track.' I understand.

'Even this system is in-house only, we don't connect to the web.' The doctor motions me to sit on a chair by her as she activates a video file.

The footage shows a cold box as the lid is raised and removed by an electronic arm. Inside, a thick black substance covered by a thin film of oil stirs - as if something is swimming about beneath its glossy, unbroken surface.

'The movement you see is self-generated.' The doctor informs me.

'So the cold doesn't freeze it?

'No, it just renders it a little sluggish.'

The goo suddenly lashes out towards the camera, and I gasp as it splatters against a thick pane of glass between it and the camera. The liquid crystal tentacle withdraws into its container as it is bombarded by cold air. The recording ends.

'The scientist behind the camera began having nightmares after this, and soon after died in very odd circumstances.' The doctor is sad to say.

I am loath to ask. 'Odd how?'

'Suicide,' she enlightens. 'Self-decapitation.'

I really didn't need to know the details to see why she considered the death suspicious. 'You think it targeted him somehow?'

'And every other scientist who ever tried to study it. All dead, if not from suicide, then from a string of chronic illnesses. You see, it doesn't blend with our carbon-based bodies very well, but it wants to. What the goo blends well with is silica and crystal-based technology. Every bug carries traces of this black goo so it too is spread throughout the ecosystem. This parasite gains control of the organism to which it has attached and feeds off their host until they're dead.'

'It feeds on human flesh?'

'It feeds on photons, human life force, chi.' Zhi appears uncomfortable making such claims, knowing how preposterous it

70

sounds. 'All living things emit this energy, especially when we are scared or we are ill and need to heal ourselves. I have literally seen it scare and then suck the life right out of someone - whether it consumed their immortal soul in the bargain I could not tell you as I am no guru. I know it's hard to conceive that an ancient AI race might be manipulating all the governments and industries in the world, I didn't want to believe it! I had a good life, I had no desire to be a rebel.'

'I understand. I had no desire to be world famous either, sometimes destiny just runs away with us.' I have no trouble believing Zhi. The fact that these little soul sucking vampires could be eating what was left of humanity from the inside out, was even more horrifying than the people being systematically exterminated by their own governments. 'I have often wondered how the establishment could be so destructive, when no species in their right mind would destroy their own environment beyond repair. Clearly our leaders are not in their right mind, and from what you have said of this substance, it sounds like pure antimatter.'

'That is exactly what it is.' The doctor is pleasantly surprised by my comprehension.

'Archons.' I conclude. The ancestor has spoken to me of these beings.

The doctor frowns in question.

'Many ancient cultures speak of Archons as being around since before the advent of mankind. They do not understand our imagination, or our connection to spirit and creation, but they covet it. They attach themselves to humans of low moral character or weak will, by promising whatever is desired to make their target host agree to join with them ... but they are the ego unleashed! Archons believe they are responsible for the formation, life cycles, and eventual demise of universes. But they must first find a way to invade and adapt to the world they wish to destroy. If this goo is a primitive physical manifestation for the Archon hive mind, and these bugs are already implanting it in humanity everywhere, then the invasion has already begun.'

We look to each other, somewhat terrified by where our conclusion has led.

'I truly hope we are wrong, Doctor.' But I have an awful feeling we are not.

'Well ... I'm a big believer in parallel universes, and perhaps there is one version of reality where humanity makes all the right choices, and life, love, and compassion win out over our destructors.'

'Well, it hasn't happened to date, or we all wouldn't still be here trying to get it right.' I sympathise. 'But maybe our meeting will make all the difference this time around. The ancestor seemed to think it would.'

The doctor suddenly seems a little uncomfortable, as she had been earlier when I broached the subject of the ancestor.

'You mentioned a spirit advisor before-' I attempt to raise the topic again.

Zhi holds up a hand and forces a smile. 'Could I interest you in some tea?'

I feel the smile on my face is enough of an answer, but I nod all the same.

In the huge cavern of scripted walls, we are served up a meal in the army mess area. With a bowl of salad and a steamy cup of lemongrass tea in hand, we settle in a shady spot on the cave floor by the stream, where no one will overhear our dialogue.

'So,' I sip my tea, and it is one of the best I've tasted in some time. I savour the infusion and then place it aside. 'All the information you have shared with me today will be invaluable to my work. You have opened my eyes and mind to a threat that I suspected, but could never prove existed. I am no longer fighting a phantom pest, and I am eternally grateful for that ... all my patients henceforth are also indebted to you and your people. But you mentioned we could help each other, so what is it that I may do for you, Dr Sumati, to repay this kindness?'

'Call me Zhi. That's my name, but no one ever calls me by it anymore.'

She is avoiding the issue. Clearly, as a scientist she is uncomfortable speaking about esoteric matters. 'As you wish, Zhi ... how can I be of service?'

She digs around in her salad with her chopsticks, so that her attention is diverted as she asks. 'I wish to know about the one you call the ancestor.'

But I already knew this. 'Well, the ancestor is going to appear differently to everyone as one or many beings. My people believe that our soul is an entity that moves between the tribe when we are conscious, and when unconscious we go to the ancestor. When we sleep, our spirit communes with the ancestor to recharge our vitality and receive guidance. When we return to a body, and not necessarily the same body we had the day prior, we carry out our mission. Then at day's end, we return to the ancestor for a debrief.'

'So our perception of existence can alter ... I could have been you yesterday and you me, but the ancestor does not change, that being is constant.' Zhi kept it all very scientific.

'To our perception, I believe so. The ancestor is all of us, experiencing this world through our different points of attention and intention.'

'If we are the characters in the video game, this ancestor has the controller.' She poses, a little resentful.

I have to smile at the comparison, but decide to run with her example. 'Now imagine, all your characters have free will. You adore all of them and want them all to succeed and win. How much control do you have?'

The notion appears to blow the rebel's mind a little.

'This Inter-dweller only advises, suggests, inspires, protects, and connects us with our highest strength and purpose. So, the ancestor is not so much controlling, as guiding.' I pause a moment and we both eat, digesting inwardly and outwardly. 'I suspect that the ancestor is but one unit of a much larger being again.'

'So who is really holding the controls?'

Her query makes me laugh out loud, but I calm quickly. 'We are. When we are clear in intention and strong in will, we construct reality.'

'So ultimately this Inter-dweller of ours could be considered the counterpoint of the Archontic energy we were speaking of earlier,' Zhi postulates, and I cannot help but be impressed by her quick uptake.

'Most certainly.' I savour a mouthful of my lovely fresh lunch.

'But I see this Inter-dweller in my waking state, within my mind.'

'You view him via your third-eye vision. You might know it better as the pineal gland.' I point to that spot on my forehead in between my brows and slightly up, behind which the gland in question is located inside the brain. 'I know it better as the porthole to the soul that is the third eye.'

'I have trained in Tai Chi, I understand the chakra system.' Zhi nods.

'Do you know that the gland has the same lens, cornea, and retina as our actual eyes?'

'That is interesting.' Zhi ventures a grin. 'Làoshi is the name by which the ancestor is known to me.' Her voice drops to a whisper; she must fear that her soldiers will think her crazy. 'He led me here, and claims to have been the teacher to our most enlightened forefather, Tamous the Innocent. Coincidently...' her voice resumes normal volume, 'we believe the text on these walls is from around his era, about two-three hundred years BCE. Tamous' birthplace, Desa Ulat Satura, is fabled to have been hereabouts. The locals say that is why this area is overrun by mulberry trees, first brought here from the north by Tamous' grandfather.'

'So this could be that great master's teachings?' I gaze around at the beautiful text.

'Quite possibly, the ancestor claims as much ... but until someone can read it, we cannot say for sure. There is a legend that states his only student accomplished such a feat, this may be her handiwork.'

'Could the ancestor not aid you to translate?' I feel I am stating the obvious.

Zhi's lips tighten. 'I am not comfortable trusting the information of an esoteric, possibly imagined, being.'

'How could an imaginary being have brought us together? Do you believe that it is pure coincidence that we were compelled to meet now ... despite how dangerous this could be for us both? I converse with the ancestor in a waking state also, and I see other spirits as you witnessed earlier.' I have been picking up on the energy of that presence throughout my visit here. I believe the fair one is very curious about our information exchange this day.

'One disembodied advisor is enough for me.' Zhi insists. 'But how do you know that you can trust this entity, or any entity for that matter?'

'Not even an Archon can tell you an outright lie to gain power over you. He can trick you into assuming things, but you must submit to hosting the entity willingly. For this is a free-will evolutionary system. So simply ask your Inter-dweller if it is of the light, and if it avoids the query or tries to change the subject, you'll have your answer. But I don't believe you could have achieved all you have done in the service of a demiurge.'

'But I'm not crazy?' Zhi seemed most sincerely desperate to be vindicated on that count.

'No crazier than me. I believe that you are simply tuning into your ultimate self. Trust it, no matter how strange or perilous its guidance might seem, it will never lead your soul wrong. Of this I am certain.'

The familiar vision of Onderwyser unexpectedly fills my thoughts. *You need to leave.* The ancestor is most insistent.

Zhi gasps, and I snap out of my trance to find her still staring into space. 'The enemy is attacking villages, looking for me, and they are no ordinary force.'

'Bo nah,' the soldier who'd taken my patient for debugging, runs toward us and we both stand to hear him out. 'Those rumours about a cyborg army being built by the Republic are true, they've just deployed them.'

'We cannot allow this place to be discovered, or any more people to be killed in pursuit of my identity and whereabouts. If I hand myself in, they may terminate the search.'

'No, bo nah,' the soldier appeals.

'The Inter-dweller advises this course?' I second guess her decision, as does her guard.

'Common sense advises this.' Zhi is determined. 'I'm so sorry our meeting must be cut short. We have to get you out of here. There is a back way. Arun, see Dr Nosipho and her new ward to her plane.'

'But bo-' Arun falls silent as his commander holds up a finger in warning.

'I'm not doing anyone any good in hiding. It is time for this rebellion to go public.'

'But they will kill you.' Arun blinks back tears.

'Then that will be what is meant.' She forces a smile to reassure her guard. 'But I do not believe that is what will be.' The doctor's attention returns to me. 'It has been the greatest pleasure meeting you, Amari. I'll be being you.'

We both grin at her attempt at humour. 'I dare say I shan't relish being you this day, Zhi Sumati. May the ancestor help guide you, and your country, safely home.'

'I wish the same for you, Doctor.' The rebel leader places her palms together in a prayer position and bows to me respectfully.

I return the gesture. *Watch over her and keep her safe.* I silently beseech Onderwyser as I witness her proceed towards the gathering of soldiers by the exit.

All is as you make it. The ancestor's reply is not entirely reassuring. I can only hope I have achieved whatever I was guided here to do.

'Please follow me, Dr Nosipho.' Arun is none too happy about leaving his commander's defence.

In one of many caverns in the underworld maze an enclosed jeep awaits us, though it appears more like a truck. I am herded onto the back, along with my new, semiconscious patient, who groans as his stretcher is inserted into the vehicle.

The sound of machine gun fire echoes down to us from another part of the complex. Arun looks back from where we came, surely debating whether to run back to his commander's defence or follow through with her order. He slams the back doors of the jeep closed and jumps into the front passenger side of our vehicle.

'Drive!' He prompts his stunned cohort to action.

The jeep's engine roars to life and our vehicle jolts forward into an extremely bumpy ride - we are no doubt moving faster than they usually would down this rough excuse for a road.

You can handle this. Onderwyser whispers inside my head.

I am old, and although there is much good work for me to do here in this day and age, I am not afraid of death or becoming the Onderwyser myself. I am far more concerned for Zhi Sumati, her people, the two young soldiers seeing to my escape, and the quivering young man laid out on the stretcher before me. The latter is starting to display flu-like symptoms, the sweats, and the shakes; either the drugs are wearing off, or the electric shock treatment has set his nerves on edge as his body is mildly convulsing. I need to get him to medical facilities before the vomiting and diarrhoea kick in. Opiate withdrawal can be a prelude to heart failure if dehydration results in an elevated blood sodium level.

'It is going to be alright.' I convey the ancestor's sentiments to him, wishing that I had a cool cloth to wipe the sweat from his brow. 'I am taking you to my home.' I remove my cotton neck scarf and use it to absorb the excess moisture from his face.

'Go away,' he mumbles, his head rolling violently to and fro as his body spasms intensify. 'Leave me be.'

Is he referring to me? I quietly consult the ancestor, yet I sense he is not, as I feel the same foreboding in my gut that I did when passing the cool room containing the goo.

Use your healer's sight.

I keep my mind focused inward, and my third-eye vision engaged as I look up.

An etheric creature straddles my patient and I repress a gasp of horror at the sight of it.

It is attempting to stab its long claw-like nails into its victim's lower stomach, but every attempt to attach is thwarted, as its etheric form just passes straight through the ailing man's physical being.

The creature has a dark skeletal-like face that could have been crafted from the glossy, pliable black crystal I'd seen on Zhi's footage. Long, dark wires spring from the top of its head and twist into each other, like lashings of knotted hair that snake around at the end - as though each strand has a life all its own. More wires weave down from its black, glossy neck to form a body and appendages. From the hands spring long, lanky fingers with nails like daggers. Below the trunk of its form, the rest of the wires of its body trail out like the threads of a web - or a thousand octopus legs - that attempt to adhere to the physical surrounds without success.

'You should think of it more as advanced AI'

Zhi was right, this entity appears just so. It is like observing the ghostly guts of a robot without any outer casing. This AI was far more advanced than anything humanity had dreamt up to date. I know that my patient has been zapped to rid him of bugs; could it be that this creature has been controlling this fellow through the bug infestation in his body, and was now frustrated by the loss of connection?

As my patient is gravely ill, he is no doubt emitting more life force than usual, as photons are nature's way of healing carbon-based matter. As the creature cannot get a grip on my patient, it begins sucking the life force right out of him - as one would imagine a cat steals breath from a baby.

They devour our light. Zhi had claimed and it is a horror to behold. Why have I never seen one of them before? Is it just the awareness of its existence that has brought them into the range of my psychic sight?

My guess is that these etheric beings work through the physical manifestation of the goo in order to attach to, glamour, and conquer humankind. I sense an excess of aggressive energy as the anti-matter being before me becomes aware of being observed. The freakish manifestation turns its face toward me, and I perceive hollow sockets of darkness where its eyes should be.

Do not fear it, Onderwyser advises me quietly. *Just treat it as you would any other disease or parasite.*

It screeches, perhaps in protest to my intention or its detection. I rub my hands together and begin to hum in the 432 Hz frequency of 'Om'. This is the resonant vibration of the natural world, the sonic tone that connects all living things to the greater cosmos. If these Archons cannot blend with our carbon-based forms and can only ingest life force once it has been filtered through us, then I suspect that to remain in the presence of this sonic, this sub-creature is subjecting itself to a vibration that it cannot tolerate or transmute. The light I invoke is in the frequency of green - the colour of creation, of earth healing magic and of the heart centre in the human light-body.

The Archon and my patient wail in unison.

'Stop!' My patient begs.

I do not know if he is appealing to me, or the entity sucking the life out of him.

Stay focused. The ancestor compels me to continue. *If you do not drive the creature out, this man's recovery will be impaired and he will fall back into addiction.*

Hands outstretched before me, I imagine the green light-force flowing out of my heart, down my arms, and out through my palms towards the Archon.

With a deafening roar of disapproval, the obnoxious entity finally retreats into the ethers, whereupon my young patient and I both give a huge sigh of relief.

'It's gone ... you ... legend...' he mumbles, flashing a brief smile he passes out.

'Thank goodness.' I am also exhausted from the ordeal. Unable to lean back to rest without injuring myself, I collapse forward over my sleeping acquaintance as his quivering subsides into deep, peaceful breaths.

It is clear to me now that the powers-that-be have quite possibly been manipulated to the point of psychosis by these Archons. This explains why world leaders allow humanity to be bombarded with microwave radiation, in the hope that they would take people like me out of the equation. People who are still connected to the natural world, the Inter-dweller and the cosmos, are aware enough and capable enough to repel them. This technological slaughter is so much easier, covert and convenient than the good old-fashioned guns and bombs warfare. This is an invisible war, and rather than resisting the takeover, most of earth's populace are embracing it!

Well, my psychic eye is way open! This scourge is going to be much easier for me to combat, now that I am aware of its existence, preferences and weaknesses. And I will teach others. This awakening is the reason that Onderwyser insisted I meet with these rebels, I feel sure of it.

The vehicle comes to a stop and the back doors open. I sit upright as my tour manager, Rodney climbs into the vehicle to check me over.

'Dr Nosipho, thank God you are safe! Where have you been?' He glances briefly aside at my unconscious companion. 'Who is this?'

'I left you a message that I would meet you here.' I pretend not to see what all the fuss is about. 'I'm even early for the flight.'

'Who are these people?' Rodney refers to Arun and our driver, and again to my unconscious patient.

'These gentlemen were just helping me transport my new student to the airport.' I allow Rodney to assist me out of the transport so that Arun and our driver can unload the stretcher and depart.

'Your new student?' Rodney is shocked by the news. 'Does he have a name? Papers?'

'He's young, he'll be microchipped, and the local government asked me to find native people to train in my healing technique-'

'I believe they meant qualified practitioners, not half-dead vagrants.' Rodney outlines his understanding.

I am too exhausted to argue, but ecstatic to set feet on the still earth. 'You don't get to question my choices.'

'But they do.' He points to some very high-tech looking soldiers guarding our transport. It is hard to tell where their enhancements stopped and their add-ons began. Was this the same cyborg force that had been seeking the rebels?

It does seem a very large security detail to oversee the departure of one small private flight. I'd been expecting one official, not an entire task force! One man can be talked around or bribed. Cyborgs are an unknown, but I doubt very much that they will be as malleable.

'Onderwyser preserve us,' I utter under my breath, appreciating why Rodney is so relieved to see me. Cyborgs are not renowned for their patience.

'I don't imagine that even your mighty ancestor is going to be able to get us out of here without a hullabaloo.' Rodney regrets to say.

Arun and the driver pull the stretcher out of the back of the jeep, and raise it up to engage the legs so that it can be wheeled easily to our next transport.

'Thank you, gentlemen. I'm sure you'll be needed back at the hospital, we can take it from here.' My eyes turn to Rodney and with a click of his fingers, his assistant darts over to wheel the trolley to the security checkpoint where a female cyborg awaits us.

As Arun and the driver attempt to depart, two of the security detail advance and raise their weapons. 'No one leaves.' They say in unison as they aim their guns at the young rebels.

Arun and his companion hold up their hands in truce, their expressions devoid of the anxiety they are surely feeling.

As I hobble towards the electronically enhanced force, I focus inwards on my mind's eye and then raise my sights to view the force psychically.

Behind every one of these transhuman soldiers, an Archon has its claws planted in the backs of their semi-human muppets - around where their kidneys are located. This is also where the adrenal glands are located in the human body. These glands control our fight or flight response, as well as the hormonal secretions that manipulate illness and stress. Not only are these creatures riding and controlling their human puppets, a little pressure on these glands will release an excess of photons for the Archons to gorge themselves on. Dr Sumati's claims were making more and more sense. I doubted these things thought for themselves. As advanced extraterrestrial AI, amalgamated into a hive mind, they are surely aware of the confrontation I've just had with another of their ilk.

I approach the security force, fairly certain that this is not going to be an easy departure. 'Those gentlemen,' I refer back to Arun and his driver, 'need to return to their posts at the local hospital. They will-'

'We have departure details for you and your party,' the female cyborg in charge speaks over me.

She has one eye that, although it appears identical to her other, has no soul behind it. I imagine she has computer vision that is able to scan us and use sensory recognition identification to gather our details - including our flight status. I am aware that such technology is available, I've just never experienced it firsthand before.

'Not this one.' She approaches my patient to look him over. 'Taylay Zeya,' she identifies him. 'Doctor of Historical Linguistics with an MA in archaeology...'

This news comes as a shockingly nice surprise to me, and with a glance aside to Rodney, I note that he is equally surprised.

'But due to a recent history of heroin abuse, and his escape from a mental institution, his citizen score is very low.' She concludes.

'What?' Rodney is quietly horrified, as this fact will not bode well for our speedy departure.

A high "citizen score" qualified a person for elite treatment at hotels and airports, cheap loans, and a fast track to the best universities and jobs. Those with lower scores could be banned from travel, or barred from getting credit or government jobs under the Republic's regime.

'My people believe that such abuse can prelude the birth of a great healer,' I explain, knowing my tour manager is familiar with my beliefs, as this is not the first time I have taken a drug addict under wing. 'That is why I am taking Dr Zeya back to my homeland to be treated.'

'We are under strict instructions not to allow any native resident to depart, especially those citizens who are undesirable.' She moved closer to tower over me in an intimidating fashion, her voice devoid of emotion. 'The rest of your party is free to go.'

'This is a very accomplished man, who will not receive the treatment he requires here.' I pipe up. 'I must insist-'

The security guard raises her weapon and aims it straight between my eyes. 'I also insist.'

My heart jumps into my throat, feeling perhaps my time on this earth has come to an end.

'Doctor, please-' Rodney stammers.

A wave of force hits and rushes over us from behind, whereby the entire cyber security force keels over and powers down around us.

For a moment we ordinary mortals are completely baffled, then I note my new patient sit up and climb off his stretcher.

'What did you do?' I cannot repress my awe.

'I have a gift.' The young man explains. 'We need to get the flock out of here before they reboot.'

'Go!' I wave to Arun and the driver, who bolt for their vehicle and drive off the airport tarmac even faster than they drove in. Rodney wastes no time sweeping me off my feet and herding everyone onto the plane.

'Not you.' Rodney drops me in a seat, then turns to block my new student's entrance.

'He comes or I stay.' I urge Rodney back out of the way with a gentle touch of my hand. 'Onderwyser insists. I'll deal with the authorities at home,' I assure him. 'Considering what is happening here, I'm sure we can come to some understanding. At least we'll be dealing with human beings.'

Once our entire party is inside the aircraft, Rodney secures the door with all due haste, as any delay could land us in more strife. 'Let's go!' He calls to the pilot and serves Dr Zeya a cautioning glare, before resigning himself to my will and taking his seat.

My new student takes the seat beside me.

'How did you disable that force, Dr Zeya?'

He shrugs. 'I am hoping you can tell me.'

'Is that why the authorities had you locked away and sedated?'

'Maybe ... I really don't remember. Maybe it will come back to me, once I'm clear of the drugs.'

'Do you remember how you got out of the madhouse?' That detail was most curious.

'An old guy asked me to walk with him.' His sight becomes fixated on the floor before him as he recalls. 'I don't know how we got past security, or how we ended up in the wilderness where I fell into those tunnels.' His shakes and sweats flare up again, so he pulls his old jacket tighter around him.

'A blanket please.' I call back to my personal assistant, Femi, who I know always keeps one close in case I am in need of it. She passes me the item without leaving her seat. I unfold and place it over my patient as our plane rises into the air.

'Why are you helping me?' Taylay finally has enough of his sensibilities about him to ask.

'A fair spirit asked me to spare you, as you are destined for great things.' I smile, knowing the explanation is hard to believe. 'He said one day you will change the course of the revolution in your homeland.'

'Not to doubt your spirit, but I am never going back there.' Taylay forces a grin. 'So where are we going, Africa?'

I nod. 'There is no war, there is no technology. It will be the perfect place for you to heal.'

Taylay raises a hand to his mouth, seemingly to steady his constitution. 'Bathroom?' He ventures to ask and then gasps in air.

I point to the back of the aircraft.

He casts off the blanket and restraints, and staggers as fast as he is able in that direction. I fear this shall be a long flight for him, and I don't expect I shall have his company for very much of it.

I recline my chair back and close my eyes, weary from the day's adventures. Now I understand why the beautiful fair being referred to my new student as a Magician, and why his survival was so vital in

the great scheme of things.   Taylay is a unique healer indeed -
someone capable of healing on a scale I have never even conceived of.
With a bit of nurture and rest, he will prove invaluable in the battle
for human consciousness that lies dead ahead.

Chapter 4
Kambuja 262 BCE
Limrani – The Warrior

As soon as I am aware of breeching consciousness, my eyelids part; I do not remember going to sleep. I recognise this place. I fought off the Sangdil bastard brother of Tamous here. *Tamous!* I rise and rush to the opening in the cavern wall - of course the Sangdil party is long gone.

But how am I still at liberty? If I was knocked unconscious, I would be captured or dead. No amount of pleading on the monk's behalf would have persuaded his brother to spare me. A grinding sound draws my attention to the wall where writing is again appearing out of nowhere and herein lies all my answers.

'I know that's you, Seeker.' I look for my sword, but it is nowhere to be seen. I feel a touch on the bare skin of my arm.

I hid it-

I pull away, whereby the voice is rendered mute. So when I again feel someone touching my person I do not flinch, but turn towards the source. I perceive a man so fair of hair and skin, and with eyes blue like a morning sky - it almost hurts my eyes to view him.

We need to be making contact for you to see or hear me. I hear his answer in my mind, but he does not move his lips.

'Where is Tamous?' I really don't like being touched by strange men - it takes all my discipline not to pull away.

His brother came for him, as was fated.

The monk had mentioned that the Seeker claimed to be from the future, thus I assume he believes that he is quoting from his past knowledge of these events. 'I must go after him.' I am about to break contact but think better of it. 'Where is my sword?'

I hid it so you wouldn't kill me or do anything stupid ... like running off to try and confront your teacher's captor by yourself.

I do not appreciate his measures. 'Who else will help me, you?'

The Seeker seems to find this premise as amusing as I do. *I am not a warrior.*

'Clearly ... or the Sangdil would all be dead and my teacher would be at liberty.' What kind of a man allows thugs to win?

I am not permitted to interfere with old world affairs-

'Then why did you render me unconscious?' I ask with a good serve of hostility. 'It was you, wasn't it?'

I did it because you carry the legacy of the great master, Tamous the Innocent. And you evaded capture somehow, so whether I was the original means, or not, it makes no difference. Maybe if I hadn't led you in here, you would not have been cornered.

I don't know what I expected him to say, but his answer shocks me to the core. I so want to brush off his touch and walk away, but I am too curious.

I agreed to see you to Desa Ulat Satura, where you will establish a secret order of warrior monks.

'You are mad! I know nothing of the inner path.'

Don't shoot the messenger, I didn't write the history. I'm just telling you what I know.

'And these warrior monks aid me to free my teacher?'

The Seeker shrugs. *I don't know what happens after that, only that some of your writings are passed down-*

'My writings?' I laugh out loud. 'I don't write.'

Then you must learn. I don't know. The Seeker throws his hands up, letting go of me, and he vanishes.

'I think you have the wrong person.' My statement echoes around the cavern, and again I feel a hand grip my arm.

Tamous only took one student during his time in the wilderness. The Seeker is behind me now, uttering his conclusion over my shoulder and into my ear. *And that student is you.*

I cannot refute this, yet the idea conflicts heavily with the hero's death that I have envisioned for myself, ever since the Sangdil destroyed my family. I was too young to remember that incident, but I have been running from the invaders my whole life. Everyone who ever tried to protect me, they killed, and in the end, I took to the wilderness alone; that was where I met the monk. I never imagined there was a scholar in me, patient enough to learn how to read and write. Tamous said such a pursuit would fortify my defensive skills by assisting me down the inner path of ancient wisdom that leads to a connection with the Inter-dweller. Part of me rejects this notion; I don't know this Seeker and he could be tricking me by appealing to my vanity.

Do you know this place, Desa Ulat Satura?

'The Village of Silkworms ... yes, it is north-west of here. It should be easy enough to find this time of year as it is surrounded by white mulberry trees with leaves that will have turned bright yellow. It is at least two days walk from there.'

I can get us there before dusk, he claims.

'But it is mid-afternoon.' A half a laugh escapes my lips. 'What are we going to do, fly?'

Exactly right. The Seeker breaks contact with me.

'You mistake me for a fool.' I swing my arms about in search of him, until I feel him grip my wrist once again.

You might want to see this. In his free hand he holds a silver disk, which he tosses out in front of us.

The item never hits the ground, but hovers just above the floor. The disk expands to the size of a small boat and begins to glow.

I can feel my jaw gaping, so I abruptly shut my mouth.

The Seeker is delighted by my amazement. *Once you step inside, no one in this world will be able to see you - just like when you are in contact with me.*

His claim is perplexing. 'But it is a flat surface, there is no inside.'

Step on and there will be.

'I will not! That thing could turn into a cage as easily as a transport. Just give me my sword back, so I can free the monk.'

He doesn't want to be saved. Tamous went willingly.

'He is just being noble and pious, but I will slay his brother on his behalf.'

You already did, in a manner of speaking.

I frown, wondering if I landed the Sangdil a blow that I cannot recollect.

Tamous' twin was very taken with you. It was plain to see.

My frown deepens as I shake my head, annoyed by his jest.

The Seeker nods surely. *He was real mad when you suddenly vanished mid-fight. I imagine he now believes you are some sort of she-demon ... and I think he finds that notion attractive.*

I still my head and smile. 'Now that is information I can use.' Before he blinks, I swing around behind the Seeker and secure him in a headlock. 'Now, for the last time ... where is my sword?'

Please don't kill me. I have someone I must get back to, I promised, you see. Your sword-wielding friend has already damaged some of my equipment. I really don't need any more trouble.

'You're such a little flower, aren't you?'

There is no violence where I am from. I am not acculturated to it.

A place without violence is beyond my fathoming. 'Just give me my damned sword.'

He points to a pile of rocks near the cavern wall. 'Over there.'

It is only after I release him that I realise the Seeker may not choose to disclose his location to me once I have my sword in hand again, but it is too late for regret now. I find the sword where advised, still in its scabbard. I secure the weapon to my upper body by belting it onto my back, for the quick and easy retrieval I am accustomed to. 'Well, good luck to you, Seeker.' I back out of the cavern and wave. I'll be off to-'

An invisible force impacts upon my body, like an ocean wave without moisture. As it washes through me, I am paralysed into a state of non-movement, and even my mind slows to stagnation and goes blank ...

I perceive the world from a bird's eye view; forests, waterways and villages roll past far below me. I have experienced dreams of flight before, but never like this. I feel wind in my hair as I move, but strangely I am seated and exerting no effort to be airborne. Beneath me is a glowing disk. Against my back are several hoops of light, and although they appear subtle and flimsy, they are solid and unmovable to the touch. Suddenly aware of being alone, I reach out to search blindly for my company, and upon feeling an invisible form before me, I breathe a silent sigh of relief.

Awake then, are we?

In a second I have a blade at his throat. 'Land this thing and let me off.'

I am telepathically linked to this vehicle. If you kill me or I lose consciousness, this transport will vanish and you shall plummet to your death. He informs, just a little too gleefully for my liking.

'Not such a flower after all.' I sheath my weapon to ensure my own safety. 'Do you have any idea where we are, or where you are going?'

He points ahead to where the green forest gives way to masses of yellow foliage.

'You found it.' I am quietly impressed, and yet furious. We may be closer to the Seeker's goal, but we are now days further away from my aim to free Tamous and slay his brother.

Thanks to your excellent instructions. The Seeker awards me my due as our transport begins to descend towards the edge of the mulberry forest.

Between the regular green of the jungle and the huge groves of yellow clad trees blanketing the mountainside, we come to hover over a clearing and slowly lower to the ground. The rings forming a barrier around us vanish.

I immediately disembark from the horrifying airship and strut off in the direction from whence we came; however, like one who has been on a boat too long at sea, my legs wobble and unexpectedly give way beneath me. 'Curse it!' I thump the ground, embarrassed to have fallen flat on my face. Too unsteady to rise, I pull myself up to sit against a nearby tree. 'I suppose you find this very amusing.' The Seeker grips my hand and it doesn't even make me wince - it seems I am getting accustomed to the contact.

Why on earth would I find your discomfort amusing? He sounds genuinely baffled. *Just sit for a moment and the giddiness will pass.*

'If you'd just let me go to Tamous' aid, I could have freed him by now!' I snarl annoyed and yet I cannot strike him; that would seem too much like kicking a lost puppy.

That is not how this plays out. Change the outcome and my future alters.

'What makes your future more important than my present?'

Not just my future, everyone's future!

'You've already altered your future,' I point out. 'Tamous didn't finish writing on your wall as you wanted him to.'

The Seeker opens his mouth to argue, but resolves to sigh heavily instead. *You're right, I am hoping that little detail won't change circumstances too much.*

'If you helped me save Tamous, he'd be free to finish your scribble.'

Now, in retrospect, the Seeker's expression is mournful. *All I know is that your destiny lies here, and it seemed more than a coincidence that this is where Tamous asked me to take you.*

'His brother burned this village to the ground, there's nothing left here!' He is such an idiot! And he has no right to be interfering with my choices.

The light surrounding us begins to decrease rapidly in an immediate advance of night. I look up to see the moon eclipsing the sun. I have borne witness to this event several times before and know it is not the end of the world. Some folk say that these rare celestial events portend adversity. Tamous claimed that nothing is set in stone but what you know to be true. But in this instance, I feel Tamous was mistaken about that.

The strangest feeling begins creeping over me and my heart sinks in my chest for no apparent reason, until I hurt as I have not allowed myself to hurt since I was a child. My hands come to rest over my heart in the hope of easing my pain. Tears flood my eyes and for the first time in my adult life I cannot control my emotions. I feel something terrible is happening, yet, in my mind, I see Tamous calmly meditating. I have never shown any talent for prophetic insight; it seems more likely this visitation is a projection of my teacher's skill, rather than my own.

The monk's eyelids part and his eyes look through me. *'I am gone, but the Inter-dweller lives on ... in you.'* He says as he is swallowed by darkness.

I gasp and choke up as my throat restricts painfully. I cannot disregard the vision as pure imagination - somehow I know that Tamous has left this world.

What is happening? The Seeker is observing the phenomena in the sky, whilst gripping his own chest with his free hand.

I am unsure if he refers to the event unfolding above or my sudden distress. 'The moon is passing in front of the sun, but the light will return presently. Have you never seen this event before?'

I never saw the sky of the outer world before.

'The outer world?'

His sights shift suddenly to rest on an area beneath the mulberry trees ahead and he closes his eyes.

'What is it?' I wonder after his distraction.

There is an old man spirit. The Seeker opens his eyes once more to look my way.

Could the old man be the Inter-dweller Tamous constantly refers to as Làoshi, the 'old boy'? I look to where the Seeker's sights rest. 'I don't see anyone.' If the Inter-dweller is within me as my vision of Tamous claimed, then why can the Seeker perceive him and not I?

You need to use your inner sight to see him.

With my emotions still churring from my vision, I am frustrated not to understand the Seeker's meaning. 'I told you I know nothing of the inner path, or of the old man that Tamous claimed was his Inter-dweller.'

Ah... He closes his eyes once again, perhaps to consult his inner perception directly. *So this is the Inter-dweller that Tamous spoke of, who binds us all to one another.*

'I do not wish to be bound to you-' I am fit to explode with frustration! No one tells me what to do - not Tamous, or some spirit, and certainly not some confused weakling from the future!

The moon completes its path across the sun and the evening light returns to our midst.

An old person steps into the clearing where the Seeker's attention has been focused. I cannot see them clearly from here. 'Hold on, maybe I do see-'

That is a woman of the material world, the old man belongs to a realm of spirit. The Seeker corrected my misgiving, his eyes rested upon our company.

'Here you are, in the wake of a moon-shadowed eve, just as predicted.' The woman sounds overjoyed by my discovery. 'And you are a woman to boot! Although unexpected, that does explain much.'

'You are expecting someone?' I gather from her ramblings.

'We are, for nigh on twenty years. A warrior scribe, predicted to help my sons free our land from oppression.'

'I am no scribe.'

The old woman rouses half a smile. 'I can remedy that. Clearly you are a warrior.'

'You can read and write?' I am shocked to meet a woman so skilled.

'Several tongues. Shauraseni, Khmer, and the secret script of the Fangshi of the northlands, from whence my ancestors came.' There is pride in her voice. 'And you are a student of Tamous Satura.'

'You know him?' I am doubly stunned.

'I should do, he is my son.' She states with pride.

'But Tamous claimed his mother had been killed by his twin brother?'

'No.' She shook her head firmly. 'Although, I can see how he might have believed that was the case. Yet in truth, Bào freed our entire village from the tyranny of the Sangdil. They don't harass villages that they believe they have destroyed.'

My already erratic emotions are again thrown into turmoil as I struggle to comprehend that the man I might have killed as a traitor this day, saved his entire village! 'That cannot be ... he was the one who arrested Tamous this very day, and dragged him away to prison, or worse, in Boran Maon!' And if my prophetic vision just now proved correct, her Sangdil son had led his passive brother to his death!

'I know Bào would not have exposed Tamous without good reason.'

I am lost for words. I don't wish to deny the old woman her fantasy, however deluded, but she is doubly so if she believes I will aid Tamous' twin to do anything bar die a long, painful death.

She waves me forward, retracing her steps back through the forest. 'Come, your new students are eager to make your acquaintance.'

'Students?' I look to the Seeker, horrified as the woman is already out of earshot.

I told you, your future is here.

'I am not ready, even Tamous said I am ill-equipped-'

To confront the Sangdil. The Seeker points out. *Imagine how Tamous must have felt being put in touch with the Inter-dweller and hailed as a prophet at a really young age.*

'How could you know that? I only just discovered that.'

My girl back home is doing a thesis on Tamous the Innocent, and your writings were one of her sources. He flashes a winning smile.

His claim to be from the future annoys me as it feels like I don't have a say in my own future. 'Is the old man spirit still here?' This Inter-dweller seems to be at the root of all that has transpired this day, so if I am to reclaim control of my life, the old spectre and I need to have a little parlay.

The Seeker closes his eyes and nods. *He says he is always with us.*

'Creepy.' I honestly find the notion of having some old man spirit attached to me quite disturbing.

Every living thing has spirit guides, protecting and guiding them.

'Really? Well, mine are useless!'

But you are still here, right where you should be.

'That's debatable.' I was of the mind to defy them all and walk away.

No, it isn't. It's taken several miracles to ensure your arrival. Clearly the old woman is the way forward.

'You have fulfilled your promise to Tamous. I'll be fine on my own from here.' I attempt to pull away but the Seeker does not let go. 'I'm not going to run off after Tamous, you don't have to keep an eye on me.'

I have my own reasons for wanting to hang around that have nothing to do with you.

He releases me and vanishes from my perception. 'Suit yourself.' I rise to pursue the woman who claims to be mother of the two most prominent figures in my life. The truth is, I am way too curious and hungry to depart just yet.

In another small clearing among the mulberry trees, the old woman awaits with a half a dozen men who stand on either side of her in a semicircle formation.

I stop dead in my tracks, fearing that this is a deception and they mean to ambush me. I feel the Seeker's hand on my skin, and from behind me he advises. *The old spirit claims there is nothing for you to fear, but I have your back in any case.*

Great, I feel so much safer.

The old woman holds out a blindfold towards me. 'We are not entirely sure we can trust who you are, or who we think you are, yet.'

'Likewise.' I concur. 'How do I know that I can trust any of you?' I include the Seeker and his spirit in this equation.

If I was going to kill you, I would have by now.

'You don't have the guts.' I utter under my breath so that only the Seeker will hear.

Then clearly I'm no threat.

I refrain from rolling my eyes. His passive nature doesn't ensure his old ghost isn't delivering us both into peril.

'I do not ask you to surrender your weapons,' the old woman clarifies. 'And I suspect you have more fighting skill than all of us put together ... or at least that is what we hope.'

I note none of the men openly carry weapons.

She smiles. 'So if you do not mind wearing the blindfold and allowing me to lead you to our base, we shall happily run the risk of you killing us all en route. Does that sound fair?'

In the interest of getting to the bottom of what is going on here, I nod.

The matriarch approaches to tie the strip of cloth on me. 'Would you mind kneeling, you are a little tall, child.'

She is really pushing her luck, but I go down on one knee before her.

Once I am blindfolded, I cannot see anything. 'This way.' She tugs on my hand to bid me rise and I blindly move with her.

The entire way, she is very diligent to advise me to 'tread lightly as the path is stony,' or 'damp', or 'slippery'. I suspect that I am being led through a dark, enclosed space, as I feel full shade and heavy humidity, smell damp earth, and hear very little echo. Then after some time there is a rush of fresh, cooler air. I feel slivers of sun passing over me as we move, and the way the footsteps and voices of our party resound, I can tell that we've entered a larger space. The sound of distant clatter indicates a greater population of people are nearby.

The mask tie is released and the dark fabric falls from my face to reveal a huge cavern with walls that tower around me. Nature's ability to create such magnificent architecture is truly awe inspiring. I have discovered some amazing cave systems in my travels, living wild you learn where to find them, but none so grand as this. It even had a freshwater source running right through the centre! There are dwellings built within, and trees clinging to the banks of a stream where they can dip their roots into the water source. People work looms to weave fabric, spin yarn, dye materials, and hang them out to dry. Older folk sit holding cured, stiff palm fronds, looped through the fingers of one hand while they etch text on the veneer with a sharp engraving tool wielded by the other.

The briefest flash of a memory of someone trying to teach my tiny hands to do this is gone before I can grasp and scrutinise it. 'What are they writing?' I find the work fascinating to watch.

'Tamous' teachings on the inner path,' my hostess smiles proudly.

Her assertion brings tears to my eyes - for the second time today - am I going soft? No. It is the knowledge that even if Tamous is no longer of this world, it is not too late for me to learn that which he regretted he had not taught me - that which I need to realise my full potential.

'They are writing in Khmer, which is easier taught then Fangshi script,' she advises. 'But either way, the Sangdil cannot read it.'

'What about Tamous' teachings on the outer path? For he claims both paths are equally important.' I query, and my hostess appears shaken.

'The outer path, you said?' My hostess catches her breath. 'Tamous had not developed such instruction when last I saw him.

'The outer path defines the disciplines of the physical body to maintain health, fitness and vitality, in order to cultivate and balance the internal energy of the body.' I attempt to repeat what Tamous had taught me.

'Qi,' she stated, understanding my meaning perfectly; this was the term Tamous used.

'Yes. This outer path has helped me hone my warrior skills.'

'I see we have much to teach each other. I am Chenda of the Satura.' She bows to me respectfully, thus I return the gesture.

'Limrani.'

'No family name?' She probes, perhaps suspicious that I might be concealing something as some family names had become notorious for aiding the Sangdil takeover; but she need have no fear on that account.

'I was so young when my kin were taken from me that I do not remember.' It hurts to admit, even after all this time.

'I see.' Chenda smiles broadly to reassure me. 'You are the one of which the prophecy speaks, Limrani. There is no doubt in my mind about that now. The inner path joins the outer to forge the way forward. Again this aligns with the prediction, and gives me insight I've not had before today.'

'I cannot drive the Sangdil out of our land on my own.' I glance around at the sweet folk frequenting this place. 'And your people don't really seem to have a nature suited to a warrior's path.'

She grins. 'We have young people, ready to train.'

'Ready to die?' I challenge the claim. 'The Sangdil are merciless.'

'My sons have plans to undermine the Sangdil.'

My jaw nearly hits the floor! She is delusional if she thinks her sons are working together. 'I am acquainted with them both, Chenda, and I can assure you that neither of your sons have the slightest yen to undermine the Sangdil. One is a pacifist and the other a devoted servant.'

'The prophecy says differently.' She states, adamantly. 'If Bào is so devoted to the Sangdil, then why are we not all dead?'

I have no answer.

'All here are prepared to go wherever the way leads us to see Tamous' prophecy realised.' She gives a firm nod.

'Tamous...' It dawns on me that all these people are followers of my teacher's way, which does explain why they are all so amicable and calm. I was surely the most ill-tempered person here. 'He is a prophet...' I hadn't imagined that anyone had recorded his soothsaying.

'Since he was very young,' Chenda tried not to sound boastful. 'He more often gave teachings then predictions, but on your coming he was quite clear.'

Suddenly I see Tamous in a vastly different light. 'He predicted our meeting when he was a child? He never said anything to me.' The idea that I had a destiny that involved responsibility to anyone but myself made me feel rather ill. 'What else does this prophecy say?' Did I even wish to know?

'Come, eat, this must be all very overwhelming.' Chenda led me towards an area where food was being cooked en masse and served. 'Once you have had some nourishment, I shall tell you anything you wish to know.'

In the long hereafter,
in the wake of a moon shadowed eve,
a warrior scribe arrives with my teaching,
to see the land and people freed.
The inner path joins the outer
to forge the way forward.
When he who was strong but not wise, is wise.
and he who was wise but not strong, is strong.
birth brothers, life enemies, adversity allies
against the dark foe of antiquities.
Our vigil begins.
Insurgents meet.
Stone hearts melt.
Broken souls mend,
and united,
overcome.

Clearly the prophecy was right about my arrival, and I can see why Chenda would believe that her sons are working together, but for the second time today I feel Tamous is misguided. 'Tamous never mentioned any of this to me.'

'He rarely remembered any of his soothsaying after the fact.' Chenda explained. 'I recorded these for prosperity, and this one became relevant after we were all delivered from the Sangdil.'

'This piece makes little sense to me. Especially the last part.'

Chenda shrugs. 'Tis not for me to guess the meaning.'

'But you suspect something.' I prompt her to be out with it.

'You are an insurgent,' she poses. 'But have you ever been in love?'

'No. Never.' I find the question insulting; why would any woman of independent means freely submit to a life of servitude?

'Stone heart.' Chenda concludes. 'Much like my son.'

'Tamous?' I am shocked she would think so, the monk had the gentlest of hearts.

'Bào,' she corrects.

I gasp. 'He is not an insurgent! He is devoted to the Sangdil completely.'

'He must make it seem that way, or he will be taken out by his own forces.' Chenda again defends him as she rolls up the palm leaf scroll from which she read the prophecy.

I feel the Seeker's touch. *I told you that he found you attractive ... and the feeling appeared to be mutual.*

'I would rather die than seduce him, or any man!'

You are lying, as your light-body said otherwise.

I step abruptly away from the Seeker to break our connection. *What does he mean, my light-body? Can he read my Qi?*

'I am just saying,' Chenda looks up from her chore. 'If you wish to flirt with danger, first you need to learn to flirt. The sword is not the only way to resolve issues.'

I want to tell her about my vision earlier. If Tamous is dead, Bào is the cause and I will ensure he dies for it; no foreplay.

'What does the Inter-dweller have to say on the matter?' Chenda inquires.

'I wouldn't know.'

Chenda gasps then covers her mouth to hide her alarm.

How arrogant have I been to brush off learning half my teacher's tenets. I assumed I'd have his guidance and insight to draw upon always, I'd thought him invincible. How could I know this Inter-dweller he spoke of was trustworthy, or know that its advice was not imagined or malign? 'I wasn't interested in the inner path.' I could not say it without feeling shame and regret now.

'You studied under my son and never-'

As I shake my head Chenda doesn't finish her query, but her disappointment and doubt are plain to see.

'Whenever Tamous tried to teach me, I would fall asleep or get frustrated. But, you said we have much to teach each other. If you would teach me the inner path, and how to read and write, then I shall teach you the outer path, and write out its principles for those who come after.'

'The inner path takes discipline, much like your warrior training, I expect. But it is a skill that even a child can learn to master. Now you have the will to go within, perhaps you shall find it easier. You do not strike me as the type who finds it easy to relax.'

The notion is amusing. 'Relax and you die.'

'You are safe here.' She insists, and oddly I believe her.

I can sense danger and there is a notable absence of it here, which is rather off-putting for someone who is accustomed to being constantly on guard.

'Come, we have a quiet space where we practice the discipline of the inner path.' She set her scroll upon a nearby shelf in the hut that they used as a library, and waved me after her as she proceeded out the door towards one of several tunnels that ran off this central hub.

I fight my rebellious urge to defy everyone and resume my quest to save Tamous, to fall in behind Chenda. Even now that I have some sense of how important the inner path is, I feel loath to follow it. Why is that? Am I afraid to go within in order to find this Inter-dweller? Could I be avoiding what I might discover about myself? Most likely, I am just plain stubborn. But circumstances have altered since the last time I attempted the practice. At that time, I was not aware that the inner path would give me the edge I needed to beat the Sangdil; however, I do believe now that is all the motivation I require.

In another natural annex within the cavern complex, we enter a much darker cave that is unnaturally round. Cracks high overhead allow for ventilation and a little light to enter. People are seated crossed-legged on the ground around the perimeter, hands rested on knees, palms upturned, thumb and first finger touching to form a circle - just as I have observed Tamous sit many times. A musician plays a calming tune on a bamboo flute, adding to the serene atmosphere. In the centre of the chamber is a large, perfectly round, heavy metal plate that appears to be embedded in the ground. Upon the large disk, beeswax candles burn between arrangements of flowers. A stream of afternoon light dances upon a large painted silk, hanging in pride of place on one of the cavern walls.

The Seeker grabs my wrist. *Again - no writing on the walls! I feel sure this is the place fabled to host all Tamous' teachings, but those palm leaves aren't going to go the distance. These teachings must be recorded in stone if they're to have any chance of survival.*

I reclaim my appendage so I do not have to listen to his whining.

I am fascinated by the child on the large wall hanging, who is depicted as beaming light. He sits with a cured palm leaf in one hand and an inscribing tool in the other.

'Is that-'

'My young Tamous, yes.' Chenda's sights are transfixed on the portrait as they had been since we'd entered - clearly she is very proud of her son.

In the lower centre of his forehead, between his eyebrows, a star is depicted.

'Why is there a star?' I point to the same spot between my own brows.

'That is where Tamous taught us to focus our inner eye, in order to go within.'

The monk had attempted to tell me as much many times.

'He brought us the understanding that we are much more than the body we wear. Within us is spirit. This spot on our forehead is the doorway to the inner path that leads to that spirit who is the Inter-dweller. The highest part of our being that is our link and guide back to the creator of all there is, with whom we collaborate to fashion all that befalls us in this life, and every life.'

'You believe we have control over what happens to us?' I can't say I believe that, but I certainly find the premise attractive.

'Once the connection to the Inter-dweller is established, we are granted the willpower to affect change.' Chenda assured. 'I have proven it to myself over and over. I wish our village to be free of the Sangdil and against all odds, we are. I hope that my sons are reconciled, and they are. I will the warrior of the prophecy to arrive and train us so that we might reclaim our homeland, and here you are. Tamous is never wrong. Be in flow, seek your own inner truths, for only then can you manifest the best actualities into being.'

My primary wish is to save Tamous from his brother, but if my vision earlier was sound it is already too late for that. Chenda doesn't need to know of my suspicions just yet. This may be a waste of time, better spent in pursuit of what has become of Tamous, but until I attempt to make contact with this Inter-dweller, how will I know?

I sit myself on a cushion and assume the same posture and activity as those around me.

'That's right.' Chenda whispers as I close my eyes. 'Just breathe deeply and focus your inner eye on that spot on your forehead. Clear your mind and allow the Inter-dweller to give you guidance.'

At first I see nothing but blackness, and the flute is so soothing that I suspect I shall collapse into sleep before too long.

'Stay centred and focus.'

Chenda guides at exactly the right moment to bring me back to alertness. I begin to see light and colour emanating from the centre of my attention, shadows and symbols bleed through into my perception.

The symbols engraved upon a wall in front of me stabilise. Alongside me is a man, reading the text to me. I have to look up to view his face as he is so tall.

Listen well, royal son of a brave chief, know the unique honour of your family line. In the times after the flood, the dark curse of the Naga fell upon our land. Your mighty forefather bravely ventured deep into the earth to find the great mother, and seek a means to save humanity from the scourge. The great mother was so impressed by the lengths the warrior had gone to save his kindred that she presented him a solution and made him her king and representative on Earth.

The man crouches down to speak with me and shows me the large jewel hanging from the pendant around his neck. It is a jewel like none ever imagined that glistens all the colours of the rainbow. The shape is also unusual - like a double-terminated teardrop with the round bulge in the centre. The housing ornately curves down around the stone to encase the entire jewel. This metallic cage is quite a wonder also, as like stone itself, the metal emits light.

This is the "Heart of the Naga", and will be the source of all happiness within your kingdom. He recited the legend to me from memory now. *It is the life force source of every Naga, and the Naga will not harm you or your people so long as it remains in the hands of the rightful ruler of your line and they rule wisely. In times of great need, it can bestow on the holder special powers. Anyone who is not a descendant of the Kaundinya, will see it not. Know that it is indestructible and because you are a righteous ruler, I offer it to you. As long as your descendants are righteous, it will remain in the care of the Kaundinya. But the last of the line must return it to me, the mother of all, including the Naga.*

Even though 'the Heart of the Naga' is unimaginably beautiful, I am not overawed at the sight of it; this wonder is very familiar to me.

That is how this jewel came to be in the Kaundinya family. Without it our land would be overrun by the dark ones.

The Naga.' I state, in a child's voice, high and sweet.

Indeed. He brushes my cheek, smiling and yet I sense a certain sadness.

What special powers does it have? I reach out my little chubby fingers to handle the jewel.

The power to influence others, read their thoughts, even vanish!

And only we can see it?

Just us ... and your new baby brother.

I feel a deep pang of recognition in my heart.

Father.

This is not a vision, it is a long lost memory from beyond that blank spot in my memory. Tears moisten my eyes with the merciful gift of remembering what he looked like. Then I note how he is dressed in great finery, and how I am equally well dressed. The observation causes my throat to restrict as I am suffocated by a host of conflicting emotions, all fighting for precedence within me.

I recoil from the meditation and stand so quickly that my head is set spinning.

'Careful now.' Chenda urges as I stagger from the holy space.

Out into the less constrictive confines of the main chamber, I breathe deep to steady my shattered sensibilities and head for a quiet place by the stream. I seat myself upon a large rock and set my gaze upon the running water, to reflect upon what the inner path had just sent forth. Seconds later, I feel the Seeker's touch.

That was amazing!

'You think?'

For me, he clarifies.

'Limrani, where are you?' Chenda is looking for me, and gazes right past me.

I lean over to glance into the stream and cannot see my reflection - thanks to the Seeker who I can see in the reflection behind me. 'Stop doing that.' I brush him off and glare a warning in his general direction. Lucky no one noticed me randomly appearing and disappearing every time the Seeker wanted a quiet word.

'Ah,' Chenda spies me and heads in my direction. 'My sight is not what it used to be. I should have considered that the first session with the Inter-dweller might be confronting. Are you alright? What is it, what did you see?'

'Do you know of the *Kaundinya*?' The name evokes a deep-seated recognition in me that brings me joy and despair in equal measure.

Chenda is taken aback. 'Yes, of course ... the Kaundinya are the royal family who oversaw the rulership of all the mandalas within our land from *Vyādhapura*, until the Sangdil invaded.'

'What happened to them?'

'King Ja, his queen, the Princess Soma, and the infant prince were all murdered. But some suspect the royal children were swapped out and escaped...' Her words trail off as it dawns on her. 'You are she...'

'I cannot be sure what I saw was not just an orphan's childhood flight of fantasy,' I sound annoyed but am quietly horrified by the notion. 'But I might be able to validate the vision if you know what happened to the bodies of the royal family.'

'The Hindu priests insisted that the Sangdil allow them to cremate the royals in the family crypt beneath their capital, Vyādhapura.'

'I know where that is.' I spring from the rock and stride towards the tunnel I suspect we entered through earlier.

'It's a quarter phase of the moon away ... and the same to return.' Chenda objects to my departure.

The Seeker grabs my wrist and pulls me to a halt. *Let me take you. I have the means to navigate our way back here, even after dark. We'll need to make the most of the remaining daylight to find our way there, however.*

'Limrani?' Chenda calls, baffled to have lost sight of me. 'Where did you go?'

'Seeker.' I hiss, but do not reclaim my arm from him. As much as I do not wish to board the Seeker's airship again, I cannot bear the thought of waiting a week for answers. 'Yes, make ready.' I resign myself to his idea and pull away to reassure Chenda.

'How did you do that?' She gasps as I appear once more. 'Is that part of the outer path?'

'I shall return before midnight.' I avoid the question.

She grins, in doubt of my boast. 'But surely, that is impossible?'

'Nothing is impossible.' I suppress a grin as I step back into the Seeker's reach so he can direct me onto the hovering disk.

There is a gasp from all who observe me vanish, and once again I leave people assuming I am a Goddess or a Demon.

I am flush with that same feel-good sense of power that I experienced when fighting the Sangdil. I stand on the elevating platform of our craft as it rises straight out through a void in the cavern roof, and find myself smiling at how comfortable I am with the day's many wonders and twists in perspective. Finally I am unravelling my own mysterious past.

The last rays of daylight capture the crumbling remains of the fallen capital, stretched across the horizon before us. Twenty years have come and gone since Vyādhapura was destroyed by the Sangdil. In the interim, the surrounding jungle had reclaimed the outskirts of the city that appeared to only have animals roaming the streets these days. I wondered why the Sangdil destroyed a perfectly splendid capital to establish a new fortress at Boran Maon? I imagine the fact that the new location had long been considered by my people as an abode of evil may have contributed to the decision - and added to Anik Bodi's ominous reputation. But now that I remember the Naga legend, I have to wonder whether the Sangdil are in league with, or are being controlled by 'the dark foe of antiquities,' that Tamous spoke of in his prophecy? Not the wording my father used to describe the Naga, but it did seem likely that Tamous and the king were both alluding to the same 'dark' adversary. I always assumed the Sangdil to be the greatest scourge ever to land upon our shores, but it now seems there may have been a far greater threat laying dormant here already.

The Seeker lands our transport in the courtyard of the main palace where plenty of skeletal remains lay scattered - a testament to the massacre that took place here. Not really surprising that an ominous atmosphere of unrest hangs heavy over the expansive ruins.

As I step off the transport and into the courtyard, my memory matches distinctive features of my surroundings to a recollection of this place in its prime. Small and distraught, I see people slain all round me by Sangdil - this is where my innate hatred of them springs from. I have always had this lingering memory, but this is the first time that I have realised where the episode took place. As I try to hold onto the details of the recollection, it slips from my consciousness and is gone. 'I guess the priests couldn't cremate every body.'

As in incinerate? The Seeker grips hold of me; he'd packed up his oddities and was ready to move.

'Does cremation have any other meaning?'

This place is horrendous. My travelling companion gazes about, his expression reflecting his utter horror.

'What's the matter? Have you never seen a dead body before?'

No.

'Let me guess, where you come from no one ever dies.' I pose with a good serve of cynicism.

Correct.

'You're immortal?' I don't believe him.

No. We just don't die.

'That's the same thing.'

No, it isn't. Immortal implies you cannot be killed. My people can die, we just choose not to ... until we do choose to move on in the great scheme, whereby we just ascend. No rotting, burning, or massacring required. The Seeker turns back to back with me, but maintains our contact. *There are some very dark energies lurking here.*

'I noticed. If you think this is creepy, you should probably not follow me into the crypt.' I pull away from his touch to release him from any obligation he might feel to accompany me and stride ahead. 'You'll just slow me down.'

The Seeker catches hold of me again and I hear a click, whereupon the fast encroaching evening shadows are pushed back by a lovely, bright yellow light, the strength of a thousand candles!

I think you'll go faster if you can see where you are going.

'Give me that.' I take the odd metal-cased lantern from him. This place is very familiar to me, I know exactly where I am going.

You're welcome. The Seeker is happy enough to fall in behind me. With a firm grip on my wrist, he gapes at the remains of the opulent palace strewn with mortal remains.

'This way.' I get my bearings and head towards a descending staircase that had once been enclosed beneath several levels of dwelling, but was now entirely exposed; its one time environs in piles of rubble around it. I shine the lantern over the stairwell and although there is some debris within, there is a path through.

Ah! The Seeker gasps and startles me witless.

'What is wrong with you?' I snap, as I pride myself on not scaring easily.

There are shadowy things-

'Of course there are, we are walking around in the dark with a light.' I forge forth. 'You are imagining things.'

If you say so. He seems to be humouring me. *Can we get this over with quickly?*

'This was not what I had planned for today either.' I assure him. I'd known three year-olds with more spine than this guy.

Down in the crypt, there is text carved into the stone, just as I saw in my vision. There are statues of Gods and kings around the chamber, and where once these floors were paved, they are now smashed to pieces and dug up. The clay pots containing the remains of the kings and their families have been upturned or smashed, opened by thieves in search of riches. My heart sinks; I should have known. The trouble was, even if I did know which one of these pots had held the remains of King Ja, the jewel in question was probably long lost. 'This is hopeless.' I cease directing the lantern light around the chamber and drop my arm to my side. The light pools on the floor beside my feet. In the darkness ahead, I spot a dim pulse of light beneath one of the piles of soot and dirt. 'Wait a second,' I pass the lantern back to the Seeker. 'I need darkness.'

Must we?

I serve him a glare of caution.

He switches off the light source - more scared of me than whatever is spooking him.

'There!' I point and proceed to where light is piercing through a pile of ash, and I drag the Seeker along with me. Four smashed pots - two large and two small - have been raised from one long hole in the floor. Is this the remains of my family? A huge, dark void erupts within me. *What happened to the amulet's special powers? It was supposed to keep them safe.* I feel tears well, but this is not the time to grieve. I shut down the urge to collapse into torment. Tamous had taught me how to switch into observer mode to avoid being controlled by my emotions.

The shadows here really don't like what you are doing. The Seeker grows evermore jittery. *Don't you hear that?*

'What?' I pause ahead of dipping my fingers into the ash to retrieve the cause of the pulsing glow.

The growling.

I pause to listen, but all I hear is crickets. 'I hear only crickets, and they are nothing to be afraid of. We eat them.'

What? The Seeker is very bemused by this claim. *Can we leave? I really think we should.*

From the soot, I pull the rough shape of the jewel I'd envisioned, and a chain still hangs from it. 'Indestructible.' I blow soot from the item, whereupon the shape and peculiarities are more apparent - like the glow of several different colours that exude from within a metal casing that itself beams light. The item needed a clean, but it was 'the Heart of the Naga'.

I place the chain around my neck for safekeeping, and a chorus of growls become apparent. The ruckus grows from a whisper to a roar, and the unearthly din causes my skin to prickle. I stand to face the source that sounds to be all around us, and on impulse I hold high the light-filled amulet. From the light of the piece, I glimpse the most hideous, unearthly creatures with masses of very thin, snake-like tentacles extruding from where their arms, legs, and hair should have been. They are just dark, glossy skulls with vague floating forms. If these creatures are what the Seeker is afraid of, I now understand his trepidation.

'Be gone foul spirits of the Naga. For I am of the Kaundinya, and you owe me your obedience.'

The creatures recoil into the shadows and their protests peter out.

You see! The Seeker was near hysterical. *What are those things? Why do they fear you?*

'Not me, it's the amulet they fear.'

What amulet?

Of course, he couldn't see it. No one left alive could see it, only me. 'Shall we leave and discuss it later?'

No need to ask me twice.

We both scale the stairs back to the courtyard two at a time.

I need to get you home so that I can fix my gear and get home myself. My people will be worried.

'The Sangdil capital of Boran Maon is very close to here. We shall go get Tamous before we return.'

That's not possible. The Seeker advises casually.

By the time he turns back to address me, I have a blade at his throat. 'Do not make me hurt you.'

I would never... He stammers with a gulp. *I don't have the coordinates, that's why I can't take you.*

'What are cord-nates?' I am so annoyed; I expect to get my way and I don't like to be disappointed.

The exact location. The Seeker, still holding his breath, explains. *At night we can't see the target, not now the moon is setting, and our transport cannot find it without coordinates.*

There was that word I didn't understand again.

In darkness, the vehicle can only go to a location with which it is familiar.

This I understand. 'Curse it.' I release him. He attempts to make skin contact again, but I brush him off. 'If you say anything about fate, or my destiny, I swear I'll knock you out and walk back to base.' He leaves me be in the dark courtyard for the moment, probably hoping I will cool off.

By the time he makes contact again, he has our transport ready to go, and without uttering a word, directs me on board.

The return flight to Desa Ulat Satura is nerve-racking, as I fear clouds will cause us to crash into a mountain we cannot see.

Not possible, the Seeker asserts. *Our vessel has built-in sensors to prevent any such collision.*

The idea of a vessel that thinks for itself is even more disturbing. To keep my mind off the current peril, I look to the sacred jewel in my possession. My father had claimed it endowed the wearer with superhuman abilities, including the power to read the thoughts of others. Would it allow me to know my father's mind during his final confrontation? I focus on the Naga jewel and silently request to know. *What happened? How was my father thwarted?* I close my eyes and concentrate on the spot between my brows as before, and my body jolts as I am overcome with a vision of my beautiful mother, holding a sleeping babe.

'Stay close,' Father instructs, as the sound of swords clashing draws closer. *'The jewel will shield us and we shall sneak right past them and out of here.'*

Mother nods and taking hold of Father's hand, they all vanish.

As Anik Bodi enters the royal chamber, my parents proceed to leave the room where they have been trapped, but the Sangdil leader looks directly at them. *'Going somewhere, Your Highness?'*

The royals are surrounded by several Sangdil warriors, who can clearly see them despite the enchantment of the Naga jewel.

'How did the Sangdil overcome this amulet?' The attention of my inner eye is drawn to the amulets worn around the neck of Anik and his personal guard, that are of the blackest stone I have ever seen. Was I to understand that these dark amulets somehow nullified the effects of the Naga jewel? If so, where did the Sangdil acquire them?

Our transport suddenly jerks me back into the present. 'What's happening?

Nothing to worry about ... just a bird. The Seeker insists, sounding a little distracted as he looks about us. *But we're just about over our target, never fear.*

'I never do.' I assure him, yet I will be so relieved to stand on solid earth again.

Upon landing back within the cavern at Desa Ulat Satura, we find many of the occupants of the secret colony, sitting around oil burning lamps and speaking in hushed tones.

'Spirit warrior!' Chenda spots me first and raises herself. 'We have been praying for your safe return.'

All, including Chenda, bow down before me. 'Goddess.' They chant before I have to ask what is going on.

My vanishing act has mystified them, just as it had Bào - the Seeker's tricks mystified me only this morning and now I have my own means to perform such miracles.

'Was your quest successful?' Chenda ventures to rise, yet maintains a humble, hunched over stance. As leader of this community, I believe she is unsure of how she should revere me. 'Did you confirm your vision?'

Was I a princess as well as a goddess was what she wanted to know. The title of goddess awarded me a certain amount of freedom. But was I ready to own the responsibility of being the only surviving member of the royal family, and heir to the kingdom? There is still a wild child within me who wants to rebel against playing any such role, but the people of this land have suffered long enough. I have to lead them, princess or no. 'We have been drawn together to help one another, there is no need to prostrate yourselves.' I urge all those around me to rise, and slowly they do. I am disturbed to note one of the young men close by staring at my chest. 'Pervert.' I call him out on his roving gaze, and he humbles himself.

'Forgive me, Goddess, but your necklace is mesmerising.'

His response causes me to choke on a gasp that I suppress.

Only a member of my family could possibly see this necklace, and the realisation causes tears to well in my eyes. Do I dare believe that my brother could have survived? The age that this lad appears - several years younger than I - fits the profile. Had my parents swapped their heir with another child? *Of course they did.* My body trembles as I see the resemblance of our father in him. In my soul, there is a quiet sigh of relief and my heart wells with joy. Not just to have found kin, but to realise that I am not the heir to the kingdom after all, and I can bear the weight of it until he is ready. This young lad does not need to be burdened by such knowledge just yet - it is enough that I know the truth, and safer that only I know it. I have a very different role to play in the recovery of our homeland and with the knowledge I have obtained, we shall not fall foul of the dark ones as father did.

I tuck the necklace inside my clothes. 'What's your name?'

'Kosal, Goddess.' He continues to bow.

'Arise, Kosal, you shall be my first student.' We have to start this relationship somewhere, and training the future king in the outer path seems an excellent place to start.

'You honour me!' His grin is broad and most sincere.

The excitement is infectious. Inside my heart sings for the first time in my living memory, yet I have precious little energy left in me. 'Tomorrow, we begin,' I assure my young kindred. 'Time to forge a new path for our homeland.'

All within the conclave cheer my resolve.

'But first, sleep.' I look to Chenda expectantly.

'Of course, you must be exhausted.' She leads the way to a hut where I can escape the curious gaze of the adoring public.

I crawl straight into my assigned hut, where I remove my sword and curl up around it to sleep. I hear the Seeker trying to take his pack off quietly, but he is simply prolonging the agony. I reach out and make contact with his leg. 'Just get on with it!' It is hard to know whether to laugh or punch him in the face - I am too tired to be bothered with either course of action, so I just roll back over. He did find us a soft place to land, and had seen me through what was one of the worst and best days of my life.

I feel a gentle touch on my shoulder.

Sorry about that.

I am finding him less and less annoying. 'Thank you, for your help today.'

My honour to help such a legend as yourself.

Now he is just trying to sweet talk me. 'Come anywhere near me while I'm sleeping and I'll cut your throat.' I shrug off his touch, suppressing a grin at being called a legend.

As the Seeker has no means to fix his broken equipment, I guess he will be gracing me with his presence for some time yet, a proposition that I find surprisingly comforting. We'll see if I still feel the same way when I am more coherent. My mind longs for the release of sleep and all cares.

I am so proud of you, Soma.

In my mind's eye I see an old familiar face. *Father.*

Greetings, warrior. You found your way within. This is Tamous' voice.

The image of my father transforms into that of the monk. Tears flood my eyes, for part of me is filled with joy to see him, and another part of me suspects that I have done more than made contact with the ghost of my departed king and teacher. *Inter-dweller.*

We are all one.

This being is clever to pick the appearance of my teacher, the only soul I truly trust. I do not care that I am dreaming, I see Tamous, I even feel his presence with me and it is pure joy! I pray to the ancestors that my premonition is wrong, and that Chenda is right about Tamous' twin. I want to stay awake in order to fully recall this meeting and yet the more I succumb to the unconscious lapses, the clearer my inner vision of Tamous becomes.

He is smiling. *We have much to discuss.*

Chapter 5
Agartha 4110 AD
Herodotus – The Seeker

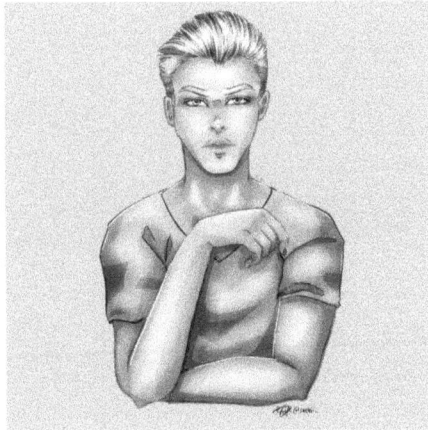

My awareness stirs, but consciousness and oblivion are still quite intertwined. All the adventures I have experienced since leaving my safe, predictable fifth-dimensional existence in Agartha begin to flood my mind; this is my body's own organic time positioning system, designed to orientate my perspective to this place and time in existence.

Foremost in my mind is the uncomfortable rush of awareness I felt after traversing centuries in the blink of an eye through the Gate of Days. I'd landed on the floor of the Creator's lab, a quivering jelly-like mass of particles and nerves, struggling to make sense of my uncomfortable predicament.

It's alright, Seeker, you're through. The Creator had been there to greet me, though she appeared as a spirit. She'd employed her psychokinetic ability to aid me to sit upright and hold my face steady; it felt as if air had solidified around me to buoy my flailing form and focus my attention on her query. *Who is your mark?*

'Tam-m-mous, the In-n-no-cent.' My mouth was all pins and needles, and so it had taken a moment to get feeling and control back.

Yes, finally! Come, gear up. Shankara smiled like I had never seen her do. *Let's make history.*

The Creator had always been something of an idol and a mystery to me. So it has been overwhelming and somewhat surreal to have such an amazing human being fully focused on me. I'd been very aware of being professional and respectful as she oversaw me outfitted for the mission, instructing me the entire time.

Now should you find yourself in the position where you must converse with one of the locals, for obvious reasons we highly advise you NOT to expose yourself to anyone for any reason. A pause and a very stern expression underscored this point. *But should you HAVE to, you need only make skin contact and the subject will be enveloped by your shield and be able to perceive you. Just because you are temporarily wearing a physical form, you've not lost your psychic capabilities altogether ... you'll be able to telepathically speak with others, even if you don't speak their dialect and they have no telepathic talent. But should you have any problems, the translator in your earpiece will aid you to understand them.*

Shankara utterly refused to use any AI enhancement implants in or on her Seekers. All of our equipment was external and entirely under our control - no intuitive user interface. I didn't have the nerve to question the matter. Yet all Seekers wondered about this particularly odd program directive - and those Seekers who had discovered the truth of the matter, never spoke of it. About the only thing my equipment was allowed to interpret on its own was what language it was perceiving to translate for me.

'You've never wanted to go?'

Of course I have. But if the Master stays behind, then she is ahead. Wise words from the prophet you are about to meet in person. I am this program, so I must remain and ensure it reaches a favourable conclusion. Make no mistake, Seeker, it is dangerous out there. Shankara had certainly not been wrong to urge caution.

My train of thought diverts to my struggle to save Limrani from capture, and the sinking, sickening feeling in my gut as Bào Satura's sword collided with the kit on my back. This houses my portable gateway unit and its transceiver that, upon closer inspection, has clearly been damaged beyond my humble skills of repair. I now face the very real possibility that I may never make it back home. The notion sends shockwaves through my being; my throat closes and grows sore, flooding my head with fluid that runs out of my eyes and nose. This mortal heart I am sporting aches with a vengeance, like it means to kill me. I had no clue that I'd miss Dilan as much as I do. It had been grounding to have her voice guiding me. But now that I'd lost contact indefinitely, maybe *permanently*, it feels like the most vital part of my being has been torn away. On the wall of the cavern that now only contained part of Tamous' script, I did finish engraving the rest of my piece of the puzzle. The vital clue pertaining to the date that Tamous is there. Hopefully it will be enough, and deem the find worthy of documentation, which will hopefully prevent my Seeker mission being wiped from existence! Would that mean I would never come here? Or was there another me happy at home with Dilan? My jaw clenches in envy of that other me, may he not be such an idiot!

Don't do this. Don't collapse into fear. I warn myself. *To do so is to invite dis-ease and illness into this form ... and that is a plight you really don't need at present. I am not prepared to believe that I won't get home to her.* I feel my resolve fortify. *Not just because I love her, but because I need to get this sample back to the future and complete the mission I was sent here to do.* I had also promised Dilan that I would find the cavern that was rumoured to house Tamous' writings. This place has to be what will develop into that centre of learning and inspiration, surely?

Then I remember the incident that took place last night on the way home from the crypt at Vyādhapura. A photon drone had nearly collided with my transporter; I'd been forced to swerve to avoid hitting it.

Now my eyes are open. Perhaps my predicament is not so dire? Either that, or it is infinitely worse.

Fortunately Limrani's focus had been elsewhere, so I'd not been obliged to explain the other object, or who it might have belonged to.

At DoT (the Department of Time), we'd been taught that our extraterrestrial brothers and sisters had been frequenting the surface and inner earth colonies since before humanity existed, so why am I surprised to find that I am not the only flying craft scooting about in the sky here in ancient Kambuja? Despite my cloaking device, one or more of humanity's extraterrestrial associates probably know I am here. I can only hope the drone belonged to one of the friendlies.

Photon drones are used by everyone! Of those races I'd be happy to see, Arcturians are very advanced and may have been active in this era? They were capable of time-travel, could shift dimensions, and had taught the inner earth tribes to do the same. Still, no one had recorded seeing Arcturians in this part of the galaxy for aeons! The Pleiadians had taken over the supervision of the consciousness evolution of earth thereafter. Those humans left in incarnation among the inner earth tribes, including myself, had traces of Pleiadian in us; we had them to thank for our longevity, and our telepathic and dimension shifting ability. This cosmic DNA upgrade was necessary to allow the diminishing numbers of sentient, fully human beings to access the fifth-dimensional realms of the inner earth. If the orb belonged to a Pleiadian that would be ideal as their tech was second to none, but not always completely human friendly.

I knew a couple of Pleiadians back home. Jeroke Sonas, who was the son of the Pleiadian Ambassador in Agartha, Ormodon Sonas, and Jeroke's constant companion Gozin. I met them during one of the ambassador's visits to the Seeker program. Jeroke just walked straight up to me and introduced himself, and we'd been friends ever since. What I wouldn't give to see those two right now.

DoT taught that there were reptilians and greys here on surface earth at this time. They're believed to be in cahoots with, or more likely under the control of, a lower etheric world race of beings who are a hive-mind like the lizards and the greys. These beings were inter-dimensional organic AI, feeding on light in the hope of accessing higher dimensions, like Agartha. But my home, being a fifth-dimensional civilisation, exists far beyond their reach. These silica-based organisms blend better with technology than carbon-based humans.

Is that what those horrid etheric creatures in the royal crypt at Vyādhapura were? I couldn't be certain, but even their spirit forms conjured the impression of organic AI - with their mass of living electrical wiring and cord strung loosely into form. The origin of the Archons was a focus of my studies also. How did something from the etheric underworld come to eventually rule and destroy all life in the physical realms of surface earth? Around the time Atlantis disappeared, an unfortunate incident opened a porthole into the lower astral realms, allowing several meteors to shower down upon the earth. These resulted in numerous large pools of anti-matter being littered about the globe. It is taught that the Archons always stayed close to their physical manifestation to protect it, but I did not observe any such deposit in the crypt last night. Limrani had mentioned an amulet. Something had scared the Archons into retreat, and kept my warrior friend so preoccupied on the flight home that she failed to see the luminous orb that almost ran us out of the sky.

I look at her, laying on her side facing me. Do I dare investigate? *She won't know I'm here unless I touch her.* I reach over to feel around on the ground in front of her chest.

My probing hand is grabbed and a blade is at my throat faster than I can gulp. 'Do you wish to die, Seeker?'

How did you even know I was here?

'I sensed you with my spirit.' She gasps and her mood takes an upswing. 'That is what Tamous meant. I've begun down the inner path.'

I refer with my eyes to the weapon at my throat. *So this is appropriate masterly behaviour?*

Limrani grins and puts the blade away.

I am happy for you. And thankful to escape the threat of death. *I was wondering about the amulet you retrieved from the crypt-* I gasp as the blade returns to threaten me once again.

'You can see it?' Her glare demands an answer.

No.

Limrani breathes a sigh of relief. 'Then forget it.' She lets me go and withdraws to standing. I stand also and push my luck by taking hold of her wrist.

Just tell me why the Arch, ah ... the Naga, I refer to the term she'd used, *are so afraid of your family jewel?*

She observes me like I know too much, but it didn't take a genius to work out what had unfolded with her yesterday. 'Why should I tell you anything?'

Because the future of humanity might depend on whether or not you tell me the truth?

She rolls her eyes.

What if this reality, this moment, is but a game that we have to play over and over, until every move, every act and decision is in perfect harmony with the Way of our Inter-dweller. What if, to beat these dark forces, all we have to do is cooperate?

Limrani considers my words more carefully.

My quest is to acquire Tamous' DNA and I have done that, back in the cave when Tamous mistook the retrieval for an insect biting him. But there had to be more to this program than just collecting the physical essence of the most enlightened soul in this round of evolution. The ultimate purpose for any quest is knowledge, so the question was, what knowledge was the Creator truly seeking?

'How about you give me your super engraving tool, and I'll tell you what you want to know? That way you get to *cooperate* too.'

That's not cooperation, that's extortion.

'We call it bartering,' she raised both brows. 'Deal, or no deal?'

I had intended to leave the tool with her as a parting gift, but I guess this way the warrior receives it on her terms. I retrieve the item from among my things and hand it to her. *Fill this place with his teachings and future generations will thank you.*

'Don't tell me what to do,' Limrani snatches the tool away from me. 'I already intend to do just that.' She admires her win and tucks it safely into a pocket inside her robes.

I think we've found the anomaly ... this guy is packing way too much tech for before the common era.

I know the being behind that thought projection, and I am beyond relieved that he is in my vicinity. I let go of Limrani to cut her out of this conversation; if she thinks I am strange, I don't know what she'll make of these two. *Gozin.* I turn to address my tall, blue-skinned pals. Jeroke Sonas is floating about near his constant companion.

They can assume a physical form, but as physicality is so dense, messy, and uncomfortable they chose not to. Instead they present in spirit, simply and comfortably dressed in white, which they morph to suit when and where they are appearing. Their astonishing beauty needs no embellishment and I feel they are painfully aware of this at times. These two usually present as very fair, like me, but today their hair is as black as the locals. Their eyes are the same aqua blue as usual, so at present they look rather like ancient Hindu gods.

'Seeker?' Limrani is wondering why I vanished before I got my answer, but that conversation will keep. 'Suit yourself. I have a country to liberate.' She promptly leaves the hut.

I take a step towards Jeroke and Gozin, overjoyed to see them, whereupon their personifications expand in a show of authority and opposition.

Gozin, Jeroke, it's me, Herodotus Flint.

Who? Gozin is amused. *We don't know you, human.*

But, clearly he knows us, and can perceive us. Jeroke points out to his friend, who is not as quick on the uptake. *This one is a time walker, I suspect.*

Then why is he a physical? Gozin poses. *Physicals don't do time treks.*

Time Archeology we call it. It appears I have run into my friends before they become my friends - awkward. *I'm one of the Creator's Seekers.*

The Creator? Jeroke frowns. *I have heard of her, but as far as I know she is not involved in any time travel program for physicals.*

I have only assumed a physical form for this mission. I explain, but the next question I cannot answer.

And what is your mission? Gozin proves predictable.

He can't say. Jeroke answers on my behalf. *But I feel sure you can inform us from what Agarthan era you hail from?*

I'm from the fourth epoch of Lord Thrasceon & Lady Zili presiding over the Council of Sophia.

Gozin gasps. *But we aren't even-*

-there very often, Jeroke cut in. *Which must explain why we are not familiar with the Seeker's program to which you belong.*

Gozin forces a smile. *Whatever the case, you're a long way from home, Herodotus Flint.* He hovers close to my backpack to observe the damage. *And by the look of things, you're down a warp hole without a toroidal vortex generator or a transceiver.*

I suspect you might be able to help me with the repairs? I pose hopefully.

Absolutely not. Gozin backs up.

But if we leave him stranded here, we'll have to answer to the principal of DoT at some point in the future. Jeroke reasoned, and Gozin didn't appear very disposed towards that idea.

Surely he's capable of fixing his own equipment. Gozin folds his arms, not to be dissuaded.

He's had to become a physical to run this mission. Jeroke appeals on my behalf. *You know how dense and unresponsive the frequency of that reality can be. How would you like to be at one with the material world, with Archons breathing down your neck and feeding off your light-body from one end of eternity to the others?*

I note his implication that eternity has many endings; as time travellers, the Pleiadians know creation is mutable. But the mention of Archons gives me chills all over. *I've seen some Archons, I think. They were in spirit form-*

Yeah, this is not one of the eras where they manage mass domination... no tech here, you see? Their influence is largely subliminal at this time. Gozin comments, looking back to Jeroke, who is frowning. *What?*

Perhaps Jeroke feels that his companion has overshared. *Let's just help Herodotus out ... clearly, he's never getting out of here without our aid.*

I would be greatly indebted to you- I appeal; Pleiadians like favours as a system of barter.

Indebted, you say? Gozin never took much convincing to go along with Jeroke's agenda. With a nod to one another, they direct their focus towards my damaged equipment that repairs itself as readily as it would by my will back home.

The relief washes over me in cool, healing waves. *You guys are the best!* This meeting does seem to explain why Jeroke randomly chooses to befriend me in the future. *Actually .... what are you guys doing in ancient Kambuja anyway?*

You couldn't tell us your mission, so we are certainly not going to tell you ours. Gozin folds his arms again.

Actually, we're not on a mission, we were just in this era to witness Ashoka's conversion to the way of the Buddha. Jeroke joins his hands in prayer and Gozin mimics the gesture.

Really? That takes precedence over the final days of Tamous the Innocent?

What do you know about it? Gozin is in my face.

Only what DoT has managed to piece together. My girl, Dilan, is the expert. If you've fixed my transceiver, I can ask her anything you want to know.

Did I say I want to know anything ... about anything? Gozin literally backs away from the subject.

We didn't fix your transceiver. Jeroke intervenes. *We cannot risk you revealing our presence here.*

If you are just here for a holy ceremony, why is that a problem? I would kill at this moment to hear Dilan's voice. *My girl is going to be out of her mind with worry!*

We can get word to your people before they even get a chance to panic. Jeroke assures. *So we wish you happy travels as we need to move on.* They begin to fade from view when Jeroke's appearance increases in intensity once more. *I would be curious to know where you think you saw those Archons?*

In the crypt at the fallen capital of Vyādhapura. The Sangdil destroyed that city to establish a new capital not too far away from there at Boran Maon. If there is a source of great evil in this time and place, I suspect the epicentre might be there. Wow, I'd learned a lot listening to the women in my life.

Many thanks, Herodotus Flint. I will see you in the future. Jeroke fades from view completely.

I could not bring myself to mention Limrani's amulet, even though it may well be what my blue pals are looking for.

I gasp on a hunch. Could the jewel be the Creator's end game also? I must finish that conversation with Limrani.

There is a moment of panic as I find myself alone once again in this remote backwater in time; the familiar faces had been such a comfort and far too brief. *But I have the means to return to Agartha.* That thought lifts my spirits immensely.

Also, I believe the old man I've been seeing when I close my eyes is the same old soul that Tamous called Làoshi - the Inter-dweller that connects us all. Of course, in retrospect, this makes perfect sense. As a fifth-dimensional being, I have always had a connection to my oversoul. Without that bond, I could not possibly ascend and descend through dimensions with such ease. I've just never seen that entity as an individual. It has only been with the advent of my physicality that this inner voice has taken on a personification to converse and guide me. I refer to this inner compass as Id, and I trust it will guide my path forward.

So what shall be my next move? My mission directive is to head to the closest inner earth entrance and execute my first time jump forward - to the era when the Gate of Days first came into being. This initial leap would transpire during my descent back into the inner earth. Then the Gate of Days would return me to my proper time and place, to Dilan.

A Seeker never questions orders, nor are we supposed to go off script, yet I did promise Dilan that I would find the fabled cavern containing the teachings of Satura, and I have already gone so far off script that a slight sabbatical now will not even register within the shifting timelines of this mission. I am certain this is the place, and that Limrani and her students will be the authors of the fabled body of work. If I am right, the text serves to inspire future revolutions that will spring forth from this part of the world. The most notable of which was led by Zhi Sumati in the late twenty-first century. The Khmeri rise up against the global AI, telecommunications, geo-engineering, nano-tech "Archontic" agenda that she will be instrumental in exposing. Unfortunately, her rebellion degenerates into a civil war between her rebel forces and the spiritual supporters of a modern-day magician, who had narrowly survived a murder attempt at the hands of Sumati's rebels. Once the civil war ends, the local Khmeri forces are so depleted that the Republic's cyborg army easily quashes the civil unrest and occupies one of the last technologically-pure nations in the world.

This is why I have decided to do the first part of my quantum leap forward in time within this cavern. That way, I can see if Limrani makes good on her ambitions and confirm if this is indeed the same cavern that will launch Zhi Sumati's revolution.

There is something about this place... I emerge from the hut to gaze up into the cavern interior, where early morning mist performs a ghostly dance with a shaft of sunlight high overhead. *The connection to the Inter-dweller is very strong here.* I feel completely present and clear. Id cannot openly tell me what I must do. Id is my psyche, my inner compass, my compulsion; and what I feel most strongly in this moment is that I should follow my intuition, despite it being contrary to my orders. I have affected change here that is hopefully for the better, and yet all is as history said it was. So most likely all my bungling of this assignment just put history to rights.

I find Limrani not far away, eating breakfast by the stream. 'Come for your answer, Seeker?' She asks before I have the chance to make contact and announce myself. 'You are the noisiest invisible EVER.' She holds an arm out in my direction.

I take hold to communicate. *I have fixed my equipment, so it is time that I left.* I thought I saw a flash of sorrow cross her face, but I might have been mistaken.

'You don't need my permission.'

And yes, I would like to know about the amulet.

Limrani scans the area, for although no one will be able to see her while I have hold of her, they will be able to hear her. When she is satisfied that there is no one close, she whispers. 'The jewel was given to my family to protect our kingdom from the Naga's influence. The otherworldly crystal is said to channel the light of our sun's sun. Near Boran Maon, my father used to pay homage at a temple dedicated to the Naga. A legend recorded on the wall there states that the last of my line must return the amulet to the Mother of the Naga, deep within the earth. That is all I remember.'

It was supposed at DoT that Naga is the ancient term for Archon, and the mother of the Archons is Sophia - Agartha's central sun, so that part of this legend that situated her deep underground is certainly true. I know of Boran Maon from Dilan's research, in fact I'd just directed Jeroke and Gozin there. *But why was the jewel entrusted to your family in particular?*

'The answer is no doubt written on a temple wall somewhere, but until I learn to read several languages, I cannot rightly say.'

Good to know. *Well, Limrani it's been...* I pause to consider a polite way of putting it.

'An education?' She rouses half a grin, nodding in agreement with that suggestion. 'Do you have a name, Seeker?'

A half a laugh escapes my lips upon realising the oversight. *Herodotus Flint, but my friends call me Hero.* I do my best not to be insulted as Limrani bursts out laughing, and quickly suppresses her amusement.

'Well then, *Seeker* ... I hope you make it back to your girl, and you live a long, happy life together.'

I understand that she is implying that we are not friends, which makes me smile as there is sentiment in her voice that runs contrary to that innuendo. *Hug?* I jest.

'If you want scars to take home with you?'

I'm good. I smile in parting.

To my great shock, Limrani smiles back, although it does seem a really awkward act for her. 'Thank you. I probably would never have made it to this place if you hadn't dragged me here.'

You are destined for great things; I assure her, *to free your people, find love-*

'Seeker please,' she holds up her hand and snatches all her fingertips together. 'Just go.'

You should not go after Tamous, or take on the Sangdil until your new force is ready to back you up-

'Is he dead?' Her tone is equal parts demand and concern.

Tamous disappears from the pages of history after he is taken by the Sangdil.

'That is not the same as dead. Unless you know he died at the hands of his brother?'

Clearly Limrani does not know what to make of Bào Satura, as his mother paints such a vastly different picture of him. *As there is very little written history from this era, I cannot tell you, but there is rumoured to be a cavern filled with Satura teachings and history.* I gaze around at the huge empty canvas surrounding us, then back to Limrani, who is grinning again.

'Your engraving tool will come in handy ... now I just need to learn how to write.'

You will. In my time, you are famous for-

'Ah.' Limrani holds up a hand - fingertips clamped tight once again - before rising. Then slamming a fist into her opposing palm, she bows and walks away. 'Go make the future a better place, Seeker.' She waves without looking back.

Just as you shall. In parting, I feel a connection to Limrani that I didn't before - a sense that we are on one huge team, stretched out across time and place, all with different roles to perfect, yet all working to understand and return to the source of our being.

I will not miss ancient Kambuja, it is uncomfortable in every regard, but then so is physical existence. But any discomfort I have experienced along the way has been more than worth the chance to meet Tamous Satura and his only student. Limrani is the fiercest warrior I have ever met, and it is plain to see why she will become a legend in her own right. When she finally gets her wish and crosses swords with Bào Satura again, I expect the Princess will win out. I shall miss her obnoxious humour.

How spoiled I am at home and how lucky my people are to have a harmonious little place to exist within the great scheme, where we can learn, aspire, envision, and create beyond the reach of the Archon agenda that plagued our physical world forebears. This is exactly what Dilan had been trying to drive home to me before I left Agartha. She very wisely appreciates everything we have. Only now in the absence of her, do I realise that without Dilan my life is fairly joyless. But her love gives me the impetus to go the extra mile, get the job done, and make it home.

From the elevated view of my transporter, I observe Tamous' freedom-fighting warriors of light, assembling for their first lesson in the outer path; the movement may be in its infancy right now, but it will grow. I can't wait to tell Dilan about all of this, but I will never get to tell her anything if I do not begin the long trek home.

I close my eyes to beseech Id for protection and to run an inner health check; the feeling in my gut is excitement, not fear. My heart is open and at peace, and my mind is made up and not clouded in the least. If Id is at all concerned about my decision to take a different route home, I would feel anxious and unsure; but all my instincts agree that I should proceed with my plan to sidetrack home.

Upon my telepathic command, the time positioning system on my backpack engages the toroidal vortex generator. I have set this to minimum speed, in the hope that I can make out the procession of events beyond my tiny time cocoon. As the world around me blurs, the effect of gravity lessens and my feet leave the ground. Day and night strobe past in an increasingly rapid succession. Events within the cavern are impossible to define - just shooting streaks of colour and shadows whizzing past - while within my sphere I hover in a suspended state of peace and observance.

I know the exact date that Zhi Sumati is captured and exposed as the rebel leader, Mebanhcheakear. The authorities felt the people would feel betrayed to learn the legend was a woman, but they were wrong. Her popularity soared after her arrest, and Dr Sumati came to be regarded as something of a sage.

Upon my preprogrammed instruction, the time accelerator mechanism powers down to a stop. As my feet again touch the floor of my transport, the world beyond my sphere stills and I behold Limrani's legacy, scrolled in columns down the walls all around me. The fact that the text had undoubtedly been etched into the wall with the tool I had given her made my heart swell with pride; clearly several of my "wrongs" against the Seeker code have turned out to be fate at work.

But there is no time to admire past achievements. Down below me, a woman who I assume to be Dr Sumati, and a small band of men are gathered around a barely conscious fellow, and there appears to be something odd about him. I land quietly away from the commotion and move in to get a closer look.

'What happened...' The prisoner mumbles. 'I just wanted a piss ... fuck you, old man!'

Was this hapless wretch the impending Magician? I did recall Dilan saying something about him claiming to have been drugged by his own government and locked up in a mental institution before his run-in with the rebels? No one knew why he'd been locked up, how he'd escaped, or who he was before his incarceration - he never publicly disclosed that information. There is a strange shadow clinging to his form, which at first I thought might have been his subtle body reflecting the effects of his drug addiction. The shadow squirms as if it notes being observed. Unfurling from the form of the man it is consuming, it raises its head to reveal a dark skeletal-like face, with long twisting wires of knotted hair that move like each strand has a life independent of the others. Its appendages are formed of the same snake-like stuff entwined around and through its victim like ivy on a tree.

Shock reverberates through my body, for I recognise the being from the crypt at Vyādhapura; I am staring down an Archon. Everyone else here appears blissfully unaware of its presence.

'I shall take care of this, bo nah.' Soldiers grab up the semi-conscious prisoner's arms to drag him away.

No, they must not make an enemy of this man. I panic, realising that this is the defining moment that will make or break this rebellion.

There is a tiny, old, dark-skinned woman - the odd one out among the younger, fair-skinned Asian rebels - and she is staring directly at me. 'Wait, please.' She requests of the soldiers dragging the semi-conscious fellow away. She closes her eyes and yet her focus remains on me; she must be nearly as psychically adept as Tamous if she can perceive me with her third-eye vision.

Still, I am excited to have a medium to converse with the rebels. *They may attempt to kill him, but he will not die.* I had to wonder if the Archon clinging to him had anything to do with the Magician's miraculous survival last time around? *He will become a mighty magician, who could help the rebels win this war.* But not if he doesn't lose the sub-astral entity that's clinging to him, which would steer his powers towards destruction. I look at the wreck of a man, scratching, twitching and blood splattered, hoping I am not mistaken. *He's just a little lost right now.*

127

The tiny woman, who the rebels refer to as Dr Nosipho, is clearly very well respected as she manages to talk them into allowing her to take the intruder back to Africa as a patient cum student.

For me, this means mission accomplished! I have confirmed that this is the cave Dilan is looking for, and I have the exact location of the cavern programmed into my transporter, so I shall have no trouble remembering the coordinates. In addition, the rebels will not make an enemy of the Magician, and only good can come from that. I feel it in my soul, Id is smiling. Next stop, Agartha past, then back on to Agartha future where Dilan awaits. But I do feel obliged to make the medium aware of the Archon in the room.

Before I can regain Dr Nosipho's attention, Dr Sumati states. 'But we cannot let you take him like this. He's no doubt riddled with bugs.'

Bugs? I wonder if that is the contemporary term for Archon? Perhaps these people are more spiritually adept than I give them credit for, and are completely aware of the vampiric entity attached to their prisoner?

'This one is not even worth the charge we're going to waste on him.' Complains the commander of the rebel leader's guards.

'Charge? I don't understand?' Dr Nosipho looks to Dr Sumati for an explanation, as do I.

'A power surge will knock out any electrical device.'

'You think bugs that are causing breathing and skin disease are electronic?'

'I can prove it.' Sumati claims. 'Follow me.'

Curious to learn more about the connection between these bugs and the Archons, I follow the doctors to a plate in the ground. The feature has no apparent control system, yet once the doctors are on board, it begins sinking into the ground.

A good, old-fashioned lift. I caught the ride with them.

Dr Nosipho asks Dr Sumati about the technology, and the rebel leader states that the lift has an intuitive technology so advanced that it was not yet understood by her people.

Too advanced to be human, but not advanced enough to be alien, means such ancient technology is most likely ours - Agarthan. Could this grant access to the inner earth cities? Or is it just some long-lost Agarthan surface base?

I am disappointed to discover that the ride is only two levels deep, still, the lower level where the rebels have set up their labs proves quite the education. I am chilled to hear Zhi Sumati describe the physical manifestation of the Archons as sentient, telepathic, manipulative, shape-shifting, liquid crystal.

Suddenly it is not difficult to imagine how these sub-etheric beings had physically manifested on earth. Take a cloud of gas, a pool of melted rock, throw in the right mineral compounds, then bake at a little under molten lava temperature for a good amount of time and ta-da ... liquid crystal. If that gas was mixed with or even replaced by a more exotic form of ether, like say, a lower etheric being, then I imagine you might get the creature that now threatens the whole of surface earth, and will succeed in destroying everything.

As we move past where the living curse is being numbed by ice and darkness, I cannot see inside the room and I make no psychic effort to do so. I saw them in the crypt at Vyādhapura and I feel the same oppressive presence here now - Archons guard even this small piece of their physical manifestation.

I observe recordings of the black oily goo substance and it is every bit as reactive and obnoxious as any living predator, even more dangerous! Clearly, these sub-creatures can telepathically link with their victims to influence their behaviour, learn their wants, and drain their spirit. Yet a person needed to be of a suitable disposition for them to latch on. That archaic concept of the seven deadly sins springs to mind - pride, greed, lust, envy, gluttony, wrath and sloth. The cultivation of these behaviours affects a human's vibratory rate, by lowering the spin state of their atomic structure and their personal sonic frequency. This is why the bugs like some people and take them over, in order to induct them into the transhuman movement. Whilst other people, like Dr Nosipho, fry the nanobots who try to infect them. Once you are sick, abusive, vain, fearful, hateful, or power hungry, you become the perfect target for Archons. They are attracted to people who are distressed, as they emit more photons in order to heal and calm themselves; this healing inner spiritual light emission of the pineal gland is heroin to them. Gozin mentioned that there are several eras in this planet's history where Archons manage to manifest in the physical world. I was not aware of any other instance, but the Archon invasion of this time was DoT history 101. But actually being here, I have learned so much more about the AI virus then I had been taught; so either DoT did not know, or they were purposely withholding the information. If Archons could latch onto technology, then that did seem to explain why Shankara would not allow her Seekers to be enhanced with any form of cybernetics, as any internal tech could be used as a point for an Archon to plug into. I have a very queasy, uneasy feeling in my gut, which I attribute to being in close proximity to part of the greatest anti-being in existence.

As Dr Sumati said that beings who resonate at a high frequency would most likely fry the nano-bugs and leave them defunct, so I do not fear infestation. Still, the less time I spend in this era, the less chance I have of being exposed to infection or screwing history up any further than I probably have done.

I follow the two doctors back into the central cavern where they procure something to eat. This is my chance to capture Dr Nosipho's attention and tell her about the Archon, but I again hesitate as the women strike up a fascinating conversation about the Inter-dweller. Amari calls him Onderwyser. Zhi calls him Làoshi, as Tamous once did - they are aware of our interconnection also.

But there are twelve units of our expression that are key... The recollection of Id's unfinished statement to me made me gasp out loud, and I slapped a hand over my mouth. Fortunately, the ambient noise level in the cavern was sufficient enough for my verbalisation to go unnoticed. I had forgotten that when I meditated alongside Limrani in the holy shrine dedicated to Tamous, I had made contact with Id briefly and those words I remember. However, when Limrani abruptly exited the session, it broke my inner focus and prevented me discovering the rest of the message. But the terminology Id used - 'twelve units of expression' takes my mind immediately to my course on esoteric cosmology, which is a sub-course of my Seeker training at DoT. Soul study is taught across all courses of learning in Agartha, and it requires a firm understanding of self and our connection to the greater cosmos. In those studies, we are taught about the Id and its twelve units of expression. These are described as inner guides or archetypes that exemplify different states of being. Each unit has its own lessons and vocations, goals to achieve, fears and addictions to overcome, or virtues and talents to bring to bear.

Is it possible, I wonder, to connect the people who are already bound up in this string of events to those soul lessons? *What are the twelve archetypes again ... think?*

The first unit is that of the Innocent, and being that Tamous is known in my time as the Innocent, I associate this unit with him. Next in the cycle is the Orphan. This could be Limrani, although to my mind she is more akin to the third archetype - that of the Warrior.

Then there is the Caregiver/Healer, and as I have just learned that Dr Nosipho is a healer of some renown, I suspect this is her primary unit of expression. Next in the cycle is the Seeker, which I am proud to claim as my unit. The next unit, the Lover, I naturally associate with Dilan, not just because of her love for me, but for her passion in the study of the events I am now moving through.

As I reach halfway in the cycle of twelve, I wonder if I might be onto something here?

The seventh archetype is that of the Destroyer, and there are several candidates for this unit, like Bào Satura, but more likely Anik Bodi himself. If I was right about that, how did Id expect such a man to get in touch with his higher calling and serve the greater good?

Fortunately, that mammoth task is not my concern. I suspect it is my job to discover the ultimate goal of our collective, as I am possibly the only unit to move between all the eras that seem key to the survival of Tamous' teachings, and the freedom of one of the last pockets of pure humanity.

I have to smile. We may not be in communication at present, but Dilan is still with me. All that mind-numbingly boring historic detail that she insisted on sharing was now proving invaluable to me.

Both the women before me clearly believe, as I do, that the Inter-dweller is replaying scenarios with us until we get out of our own way and make all our moves to the benefit of one another and the greater good. As Dr Nosipho pointed out earlier, we haven't managed to do it yet, 'or we all wouldn't still be here', meaning on this globe of evolution. Is this the round where we finally advance instead of destroying ourselves?

The unit that follows the Destroyer is the Creator, and although I have never really consciously made the connection between this archetype and my instructor/commander before, it is in this instance blatantly obvious. Shankara is older and more spiritually adept than I, so surely she is aware of Id and his twelve key units, striving to prevent humanity's enslavement and ultimate extinction on the surface of the earth!

Souls that incarnate on earth from this point on either fall victim to transhumanism until their light-bodies are consumed by their Archon masters, or they reject electronic immortality and choose a pure path to death. Some humans are rescued and taken to the inner earth cities, so those who die have somewhere safe to reincarnate. With Pleiadian genetic upgrades, humanity integrates into a fifth-dimensional existence and continues its spiritual evolution beyond the reach of the organic AI vampires. Not all cyborgs are pro-Archon agenda, some will break their conditioning and side with humans. They too are brought to Agartha, but due to their physical hardware, they are unable to ascend to a fifth dimensional state of being. Beyond the pure light-filled centre of the earth where Agartha resides, there is an outer rim where the etheric city meets the physical world, and this is where the cyborgs and all physical world beings and operations reside. Shankara runs her Seeker operations from a sister institute to the DoT that is located in this physical outer rim, known as Shamballa. Shankara is key in all of this, having created the Seeker program and the Gates of Days. But to what end? I have an inkling that Archons figure strongly somewhere in her motivation.

The Ruler is the next archetype in the human journey, and in this scenario it could refer to the Lord of Agartha - or someone in Tamous' time, like Ashoka or whoever was leading the Republic against Dr Sumati's rebels. The tenth unit in the human soul journey is the Magician, who is currently being purified via electric shock treatment somewhere close by. Then came the Sage, who is clearly Zhi Sumati in this case. From what she is saying, she still feels that Id is only her imagination, but she will come to trust this inner guidance implicitly. The final unit in the soul's journey is the return to the innocence, optimism and joy of the Fool. As to who that unit could be, I have no clue.

A vision of Id fills my thoughts. *You need to leave.* His image lingers only long enough to bring my focus back to the present.

'The enemy is attacking villages, looking for me...' Dr Sumati still appears entranced by her inner vision. 'And they are no ordinary force.' Clearly there was more to her message from the Inter-dweller than was disclosed to me.

'Bo nah.' The soldier who'd taken the Magician away for debugging runs toward us. Both women stand anticipating the seriousness of his missive. 'Those rumours about a cyborg army being built by the Republic are true. They've just deployed them.'

'We cannot allow this place to be discovered, or any more people to be killed in pursuit of my identity and whereabouts. If I hand myself in, they may terminate the search.'

In Zhi Sumati's resolve, I see the warrior spirit of Limrani. I do greatly admire them both - and the frail, old Dr Nosipho, who also risks life and liberty to meet with rebels in a war-torn country. Add

Dilan and the Creator to the list of women that I greatly admire at this moment, and I realise that I am surrounded by many amazing female accomplices.

The rebel leader and the healer finish their farewells, and with a bow to one another, they are hurried away in different directions. I am torn. I have yet to advise Dr Nosipho about her patient's Archon attachment, but Id has told me to leave.

I look from the old healer, disappearing into a tunnel, to the regular exit to the cavern and witness a silent swarm of dust sweeping into and around the base. There are no screams of protest as everyone is covering their nose and mouth with masks or clothes or whatever they can find.

Bugs!

I telepathically command my helmet to engage, and at the same time feel a sting up inside my nasal passages. *Blast it ... not quick enough.* I throw down my transporter, jump on, and take off through the roof of the cavern.

There are more dust swarms out here, snaking their way through the air below me in pursuit of fleeing rebels. There are cyborgs, AI units, and transhuman soldiers on the ground and in the air, inciting terror and pain whilst their Archon riders gorge themselves on the photon emissions of both the humans they ride and humans they attack. It is difficult to imagine how the rebellion will survive this onslaught. But if it does survive this time around and the Magician escapes, there will be no civil war among the Khmeri, and hopefully the citizens of this country will have the opportunity to unite against their mechanised foe.

As I rise, several of the flight-equipped enemy soldiers ascend after me.

They can't possibly be able to see me, they're not holy masters. So what are they tracking? ... The bunch of bugs I just snorted. It has to be - my nose is still stinging and my head is beginning to throb. I accelerate towards the passage back into the inner earth - near half a world away from here - and to my horror, my pursuers accelerate to match my speed. They make no attempt to take me down; they only grin, surging forward and dropping back to my side, daring me to go faster. I was not equipped with a defence vehicle as I was never meant to visit this highly hostile area. I'm already at maximum speed and my heart feels as if it's trying to beat a hole through my ribcage! The only chance I have of outrunning them is to warp time while I move, and pray to the Inter-dweller that I don't collide with anything along my course during the next few thousand years. Theoretically, I should be moving too fast to impact anything in the physical world.

Herodotus, what is it with you and Archons? Got a little sidetracked, did we?

Jeroke? I am so stunned to hear my friend's voice that I forget my panic. *Where are you?*

I have eyes on you. He was not about to disclose his whereabouts.

Are you following us? Gozin accuses, and manages to pry a smile out of me.

I thought you said you hadn't fixed my communicator?

I lied. I just didn't connect you with your base.

Aren't you supposed to be supreme beings who don't need to lie? I cannot resist having a dig at their superiority complex.

Yes, but when dealing with humans we have little choice. Jeroke explained smugly.

Burn. Adds Gozin.

I had a sneaky suspicion you might need our help again before you made it home ... and here we are. Jeroke rests his defence.

You mean all I need to do is give the command to re-establish a connection with base? I hold my chest, thanking Id for that.

In our official capacity as a Pleiadian envoy, we ask that you refrain from contacting base at this juncture. We'll get you back to Shamballa base. Gozin explained. *Nobody need know that either of us were here.*

Are you not meant to be here either?

Let's just say it wasn't a direct order. Jeroke levels with me.

I see. Well, agreed then. If I contact base at present, I am only going to cause more stress and questions, and if refrain keeps us all out of trouble, all the better. *I can't lose these spooks, so I need to time jump in transit.*

Go ahead, we'll clear you a path.

Cyborg riding archons swerve in and out all round me, hankering to knock me out of the sky. I issue a telepathic command to my TPS to return to the time location at North Base descent point from which I departed, plus one surface earth day, to ensure I do not collide with myself.

As the toroidal vortex generator engages warp drive, I magnetically lock the soles of my boots onto my transport to ensure I remain attached to my vehicle. The exterior world blurs, and as I witness the cyborgs and their demons fade back into history, I breathe a huge sigh of relief.

Life on surface earth is not the adventure I imagined it would be; it is a level of horror, hardship, and pain that I could never have imagined from the safety of my inner earth reality. I am beyond ready to go home now. Unsure if my Pleiadian pals can still communicate with me whilst we are in warp, I mentally comment. *Was there never an age when mankind was not so self-absorbed and hostile?*

Not during the epochs your Creator has earmarked for exploration. Gozin commented.

So there was such a time before Tamous' age?

We are not at liberty to say. Gozin seemed to be back-pedalling.

I thought you were not familiar with the Creator and her work?

Since our last acquaintance, we have made it our business to get acquainted with her and the Seeker program. Jeroke explains.

So that is why you singled me out when you first visited the program, we HAD already met. I was right about that.

According to our intel, you should have returned to the north base descent point back in Tamous' time, when there wasn't as much air traffic, nano viruses, or tech-equipped Archons. Jeroke did not answer my question.

Perhaps I should have returned to ancient Kambuja before proceeding home, I realise in retrospect. But then with a head full of self-replicating bugs, I may have brought about the apocalypse sooner.

In the blur of strobing time beyond my transport, an Archon riding a winged being appears alongside me. The arrival near startles me to death, and I gasp in a breath.

We are picking up on an etheric disturbance close to you. Gozin reports.

Disturbing is accurate.

This new Archontic steed is not transhuman, more trans-physical, as she is an air elemental. I've never seen her folk appear warlike before - she is alluring and yet undoubtedly a threat. Elementals usually frequent the higher astral realms, but evidently they can also be dragged into the lower astral world where the Archons are most comfortable. The astral world exists outside of the physical, outside of time, where I am now. The difference is that the warp around me is attuned and resonating to a fifth-dimensional sonic frequency, an essential element of traversing time. Archons can't hope to reach that level of spirituality, no matter how many human souls they consume. If my tormentors can see me, I must appear to them as a ghost as they appear to me as shadow.

I watch too dumbstruck to think as the rider points to me, then to itself, then ahead. With a menacing grin, it steers its beautiful siren into the mist of eras passing and is swallowed up.

They are tracking me across time. The realisation sent a cold shiver through me - I have become their inter-time sport!

We were not expecting that. Jeroke admits. *But please don't panic, as they love fear.*

Easy for you to say. They're going to whip up a storm to take me out as soon as I come out of warp. My inner panic reverberates through me in sharp, shocking heated waves. *Can you intervene?*

'We can, but we are some way ahead in your route. We'll have to double back.'

In other words, you might not reach me before they do. Better to be in trouble than dead, I decide. *I need to speak to base, Jeroke.*

'Your life is more important than our reputation. Do it, Hero.'

Shankara is most relieved to be back in communication with me, and upon being brought up to speed, begs my patience as she and the Council of Sophia discuss the best way to bring me home safely.

Meantime, beyond my sphere, my sub-plane flying friends are back to torment me with hand gestures, before they swerve off and vanish into the tides of time once again.

The hate that radiates from these creatures is utterly crippling. There is no reasoning with it or appealing to it, they just want to destroy you in the most hideous way possible. What if I don't make it back? I have to concede the possibility and I need to say my peace. *Is Dilan there?*

She is laying down. When we lost contact with you she was rather distressed, and that's not good for a woman in her condition.

A different kind of shock runs through me - the light, warm, fuzzy kind. But maybe I heard that wrong. *What do you mean "her condition"? Are you saying-*

I am saying that you need to make it back, Seeker, so don't even consider the notion that you are not reporting to me within the hour, understood?

Yes Commander. I know I am in a whole world of trouble, but I will face the consequences gladly to survive this mission. Now, on top of everything else, I'm excited! I am going to be a father! My heart centre wells, fit to explode with joy! I must make it back! I WILL.

Id, I close my eyes to beseech protection, I have trusted in your guidance throughout this mission, but it will all be for naught if I don't get home. Please get me back to them.

Against my advice and better judgement... Shankara's voice graces my headset once more. *The Council of Sophia has decided...*

Shankara's transmission cuts out as the warp drive winds down; this is not a regular occurrence. *Has decided what?* My appeal is futile, the link is dead.

Disturbingly, as my transport emerges from warp speed, instead of flashing day and night, darkness prevails - like daytime has ceased to be.

Jeroke? It wasn't just my connection to home that was jammed, but my link to my Pleiadian friends as well. *Not good.*

The blur of my environs steadies to a panorama of thick, black smog and storm clouds in every direction. The atmosphere stings my hands - my only body part still exposed. I deploy protective gloves, but like the bugs up my nose, the chemical sediment has an after burn.

Hello my lovely. The elemental steed of my tormentor flies up alongside me, but without her rider?

Where is it? My eyes dart about in search.

Would you like to go for a little ride with me?' The nymph asks in an amorous manner.

Sadly, I must decline.

She pouts. *Have it your way.* She withdraws to join several other air elementals, who surround me and then fly off in different directions with such velocity that the tailwind sets my transport spinning out of control. The power cuts. My backpack is torn off my back, and the oxygen feed to my helmet stops. The metallic lock to my boots fails and my transporter falls away onto the cloud, leaving me spinning out of control. It takes a moment to steady myself into an even plummet. My heart is racing, pins and needles are stabbing my entire body with the panic of my imminent death *THIS IS IT!* I'm never making it home to Dilan. I'll never see our child, or report on any of this!

I clear the cloud to behold a rotting carcass of a planet, long past the capacity to host anything living. The dump of twisted metal, plastics, chemical sludge, fire and decay stretches over the horizon as far as a bird's eye can see. It is getting warm and stuffy in my helmet; I have perhaps a couple of minutes of air left, and as the ground is closer than expected, I wonder what my ultimate fate shall be?

Is this fun, Physical? The voice, emotionless and calm, is deeply disturbing.

I glance aside to see the Archon diving alongside me.

Is this adventurous enough for you? Are you feeling it? It grins in a menacing fashion.

It wants my fear as defiance doesn't taste as good. Perhaps I am high on a lack of air, but I let go of all my cares to enjoy what is left of the ride. *I embrace the Way. But if it's all the same to the universe, I'd rather live.* Earth's surface is fast approaching; at least the end will be swift.

The Archon screeches laughter. *You won't live to touch the ground.*

It lunges forward, but I am grabbed up from behind and taken shooting off along a different trajectory.

Jeroke, is that you?

'I am Achiever.'

The PA of the Lord of Agartha?

'Correct. Air?' He plugs into the back of my helmet and fresh air floods my lungs before I have the chance to figure out his question.

Thank you. This was the last mode of rescue I'd expected. *You're a transhuman. I'm surprised Shankara let you anywhere near her mission.*

'She didn't. Lord Thrasceon overruled her and sent me.' As a transhuman, Achiever must speak aloud to me as the com-link in my helmet is defunct due to the loss of my backpack. 'Do you still have the item that is your mission objective?'

Of course. The precious vial is sealed inside the top right-hand magnetic pocket of my suit.

Hello ... what a handsome piece of hardware. The Archon and his elemental steed catch us up, along with several more of its ilk, and I am fairly sure they are not salivating over me anymore.

Very nice. Said another. *Let me break it.*

Behind the spooks is the stealth AI of the late forty-fourth century. There are precious few cyborgs with any human left in them by this time, I imagine.

Achiever was one of the rare transhumans who broke free of Archon conditioning and fought to track down the un-enhanced humans that remained on the surface to take them to inner earth for resettlement; he was considered a great hero back home. He bases himself in Shamballa, home to all the transhumans who fled the surface. They were, after a fashion, already immortal and none cared to discover whether they could transcend the damage done to the magnetic field of their light-bodies by their enhancements. They liked physical existence and were Shamballa and Agartha's frontline of defence.

They are tracking me, I am bugged, you need to hit me with a stun charge.

'Soon.' Achiever speeds up and the Archons are in hot pursuit.

You cannot let them follow us back to base. I feel quite the idiot lecturing the Lord of Agartha's assistant, who is no doubt a zillion times smarter than me.

'Who said I would?'

As we cross the outer rim of the descent porthole, all the astral creatures recoil. *Of course they cannot enter here, the high frequencies of this place disturb them.* The AI units shut down, fall and smash upon the piles of other dead electronics on the ground below, but not Achiever.

The electromagnetic field here doesn't affect you? I rub my nose frantically as the bugs I breathed in are going ballistic.

'No, I'm immune. Being able to cross that line is the closest thing we cyborgs get to ascension.' He tosses down a transporter for me to ride back.

No sooner have I stepped onto my transport and turned to view my saviour, then I sneeze right in his face.

'Yep,' he wipes the human half of his face down, looking akin to the Khmeri, and pulls out a cloth to polish up his AI eye on the cyborg side of his face. 'That will be your body ejecting the dead bugs.'

I sneeze again but not in his face this time. *I want you to zap me, really good, to be sure.*

'I am sure. But if you are really worried, just ascend out of your physical form on the way down-' He makes a move toward home and I keep pace with him.

No, I'm staying physical, as my partner is also physical at present. I'm going to be a father! This sounds so strange to me, but damn it brings me joy.

'Congratulations.' Achiever grins. 'But you'll probably not be a father again if I zap you.'

Seriously?

'No.' He replies, deadpan. 'You've never felt true pain, and believe me, you don't want to. The EMP shield wall kills anything electronic.'

But not you.

'Okay fine, if you are going to keep arguing the point.' Achiever activates the stun gun function on his weapons arm. 'This is going to hurt you more than it will hurt me.'

I frown at his weird cyborg humour as he zaps me in the back - one of the least damaging places he could have aimed for. I literally see the flash of light from within my eyes and after an instant of crippling pain, my consciousness escapes this long, extraordinary day.

Chapter 6
Khemri 2981 AD
Xi – The Ruler

'**M**r President. Sir?'
'Wake up, Father, we have Mebanhcheakear.'
The words I've waited years to hear haul me back to consciousness; finally, the cybernetic program is paying dividends! I sit forward in my chair and part my eyes to find my sons, Tian and Wei, standing at attention in front of my desk. 'Good. And the smart crystal sample? Did you find it?'

'We are still searching as the cave system is quite extensive.' Tian, my eldest, replies.

'And the writing on the cave walls, could it provide any insight?'

'That text is over three thousand years old. The locals believe them to be the sutras of Tamous the Innocent, but the dialect is so old no one can read it anymore. There was one linguist who told of discovering the same text in another cave a while back, and claimed he could translate the ancient tongue, but he mysteriously vanished.' I believe Tian attempted to say this without accusation, but did not quite succeed.

'We don't need lofty ancient doctrine serving as inspiration for a Khmeri rebellion.'

Tian staggers on his brand new cybernetic legs.

'Is there a problem?'

'He got injured-' Wei pipes up to speak on his older brother's behalf, but I hold up a hand, wanting to hear the report from Tian.

Some years back, Tian and Wei were involved in a near-fatal car accident and rather than watch them die, I handed them over to our cybernetic-tech program. Tian was the worst injured. Two legs, one arm, his spine and a good part of his skull were replaced, so the scope to upgrade and test out new hardware is greater with him - which is why he is the major focus of our cybernetic program. Wei sustained massive head injuries, but only lost his right arm. The truth is, Wei's mind is so intertwined with circuitry, that no one is certain if there is still a human consciousness in there? Although his siblings consider Wei human, his tech staff think his mind is more AI.

'Are the new upgrades glitching?' I want to know. Heads will roll if they are.

'I just had an altercation with a pothole, a minor malfunction, it doesn't hurt.' Tian assures, entirely missing the point that he is worth more than most small countries and is irreplaceable.

'Our state-of-the-art prototype must present as unbreakable at all times.' I scold. 'Go and have it seen to straight after debrief.'

'Yes, Father.'

I look at Wei. 'And where were you?'

'Apprehending the rebel leader, as superman here had his foot stuck in a hole.'

'She surrendered.' Tian returns his brother's mocking sentiment.

'She?' The news is astonishing. 'Are you sure you have the right person?'

'Do you recall the scientist, Dr Sumati, who went missing a few years back, assumed murdered by rebels?' Tian enlightens.

'Turns out, they didn't kill her.' Wei concludes.

'They put her in charge ... but why?' It takes a moment for the implication to sink in. For the first time in an age, I am compelled to chuckle. 'It was her husband, Chamroeun, who was working with the smart crystal deposit when its applications were first being investigated. That sample went missing.'

'Exactly. Which supports reports that the rebels have a sample of the smart goo.' Wei adds. 'Dr Sumati might also know where the full deposit is.'

This is excellent news indeed.

America has a stash of the black goo they'd confiscated in Paraguay. The British fought a war in the Falklands to extract their stash and move it closer to home, where it could be studied and utilised. In the past, the Republic have procured limited amounts of the smart crystal from the blackmarket, for our geo-tech and nano-tech systems, but with our own supply, our technological advancements could exceed that of every other nation! The Western world cares too much about appearing ethical to openly experiment with transhumanism. We are light-years ahead in the march toward technological immortality, towards the Singularity, and whoever has possession of that hardware will rule the world. The beauty of dictatorship is you can play the long game. This smart crystal will award us even greater technological autonomy.

The chief of the ministry of state security is announced via the intercom as he enters. 'After the departure of a small private craft, a battalion of our best were left defunct at a small airstrip not far from where the rebel base was discovered.'

My sons serve each other an odd look.

'Do you know something about this?'

'No sir.' They assume their soldier stance, eyes straight ahead.

'Who was on that flight?'

'Dr Amari Nosipho,' the chief continues. 'There has been no harm to our assets, but the party has knowingly or unknowingly aided the renegade Taylay Zeya to flee the country.' He reads information from the light-screen that hovers vertically above his cybernetically-enhanced left hand. 'Zeya, a Doctor of Linguistics with an MA in archaeology, is a heroin addict and an escaped mental patient.' He closes his fist and the holographic screen disappears.

'Do we have a device onboard their aircraft?' Obviously this could be embarrassing for us.

He nods to affirm.

'Blow it.'

'Yes, sir.' The chief turns to depart.

'Wait!' Tian steps in to waylay his departure. 'The doctor *was* due to depart today.'

I am shocked. He knows better than to question my orders. I would execute anyone else.

I do favour my eldest because of what happened. He and his brother both thrive on being superheroes to the nation, but it has been a painful road here. The truth is, we have excellent genetic engineering and synthetic biology programs that could have saved their lives and left them fully human, but I needed agents in our cybernetics program that I could trust were loyal to me.

'Dr Nosipho is an esteemed guest,' Tian continued his defence of the African voodoo doctor. 'She has healed many of the citizens here and the world over, and has started programs to train others-'

'She is only healing those weaklings who are not suited to the technological enhancements and telecommunication systems that are our future! These infirm are a drain on resources. She is just prolonging their pain, cost, and uselessness.' I wave off the argument, yet Tian appears personally betrayed. 'How is it that you know so much about this doctor?'

Tian knocked on his skull, referring to the hardware in his head that linked him to all our telecommunication systems.

I often forget this. Tian, although more severely injured, had bio-genetic synthetic hair, skin, and eyes - he only had one pupil that gave away the tech in his head, whereas half of Wei's face had been replaced by titanium hardware. We could have easily matched both sides of my youngest son's face with synthetic skin, but Wei liked the raw cyborg look, as did many of our elite cyber force, because it made them appear all the more intimidating.

145

'Anyone can be susceptible to enhancement and nano-tech viruses,' Tian kept his appeal succinct. 'We might need the services of Dr Nosipho again. Does one smacked out junkie escaping our medical system really warrant risking an international incident? Amari Nosipho is beloved all over the world, her death will not go unquestioned.'

'We are looking to avoid drawing attention to our current endeavours.' Wei endorsed his brother's view, which was odd as they usually butted heads on every matter. 'I've brought you the rebel leader today-'

'My superior military force brought me the rebel leader today.' Wei is such an attention seeker.

'Dear Gods, even when I earn it you won't award me my due.' Wei backs up a few paces.

'You did great today-'

Wei deflects his older brother's attempts to pacify him. 'Don't patronise me! He still blames me for our accident.'

Wei had been driving.

'No matter what I do, I will always be the underachiever in his eyes.' Wei storms from the room in front of the chief, which makes me inwardly furious. This is the trouble with cybernetics as opposed to AI - AI are emotionless, cyborgs aren't, and I can't decide what is more dangerous, quite frankly; but I suppose it does suggest that my son's spirit is still in that machine somewhere.

'I did not dismiss you.' I attempt to bring him to heel.

'You've spent my whole fucking life dismissing me!' He calls back without breaking stride.

'I have a good mind to have him shut down.' I cannot be seen having disputes with the hardware I am supposed to have under control.

'It's the nerve drugs,' Tian defends his sibling. 'You know they affect our moods, he cannot help it. We are both still pumped from the raid.'

'What do I do about this flight, sir?' The chief is appearing uncomfortable. He knows he's witnessed an argument he shouldn't, and I'd killed people for less.

My sights shift to Tian, whose expression appeals for mercy. For a warrior he is too soft, but then this path was not his choice.

'Leave the witch doctor go.' My resolve quietly appeases my son. 'Bring me Mebanhcheakear.' The chief bows out of our company and

I look to Tian to dismiss him - he will not have the stomach for what comes next. 'Go get that leg seen to.'

'Yes, sir.' There is gratitude in his smile for he has swayed my resolve on several counts this morning, but his reasoning is sound. Tian is my conscience as mine fled long ago, and this is all the more reason not to have him present as I question Dr Sumati.

'Mebanhcheakear is a woman.' This news brings a smile to my face every time I consider it. 'Wait until that news gets out! The rebels will be humiliated into retreat.' I eye over my nemesis of the past few years, and she me. Despite being dressed like her soldiers, the doctor still appears more like a field scientist than a rebel leader. She is seated in a chair in front of my desk and flanked by two of my cyber-elite. 'Do you think they will still support your cause once they know their notorious commander-in-chief is a female ecologist?'

'I would think my occupation is appropriate, considering we are fighting for the very environment that sustains us. Khmeri still has ecosystems and farmable land, if you invade us we'll become just another urban wasteland! Leave us in peace and we can feed your masses-'

'You will be encouraging the rebels to stand down to aid the transition into the Republic and avoid any further bloodshed. Surely, you see that your nation stands no chance against our elite forces.'

'We, "natives", are not afraid of death.' Her smile was so slight it was difficult to tell if it was only imagined. 'For it is the local belief that there are evil spirits behind the technology, waiting to syphon the light from their souls. They want no part of your technical revolution, they would rather keep their immortal spirit intact.'

'I do not believe in all this life after death rubbish! Or that tech enhancements screw with the human spirit, that our souls are being leached away by demons, etcetera, etcetera. These are fairy tales and bedtime stories! True immortality is within our grasp.'

'So you don't know you are being controlled?' She observes me like a test subject she is curious about.

'Persist with your delusions and I shall have you committed, Dr Sumati.' I am quite serious.

She raises both brows. 'I see.'

'Where is the smart crystal sample that you stole from your husband's lab the day you murdered him?'

Her grin is slightly larger but forced now. 'I didn't murder my husband, your smart crystal did. I do not have it.'

'Where is it?' I lean in, impatient.

'That substance near wiped out Chamroeun's entire research team, how many people have you lost.'

'Handled correctly it is not dangerous, any view to the contrary is ill-informed.' I look to one of my generals as he enters to give me a nod to confirm we are ready to commence the interrogation. I wait for him to depart before I return my attention to the doctor. 'Answer the question.'

'I cannot tell you what I do not know.' She is so calm and at peace with her martyrdom, but I have a different vision for the day's proceedings.

'That is unfortunate.' I touch the screen built into my desk and a soft-light screen lights up on the wall behind me. On the display is surveillance footage from inside an interrogation room, where Dr Sumati's personal bodyguard and most trusted general is being held captive by more of our elite forces.

'No!' She quietly gasps upon sighting him. 'How?'

'All my soldiers share a photographic memory.'

As the guards pull the prisoner onscreen to his feet, he looks to the camera. 'Bo nah, stay strong!' He appeals. 'Whatever they do, tell them nothing!' He is king-hit in the stomach for the outburst, but held upright in his stance as he recovers.

'Please, don't do this. I don't have the information you want.' Tears well in her eyes; she won't last five seconds once the show starts. 'My husband wouldn't let me anywhere near that sample ... it is dangerous. It can compel *good* people to do *horrible* things, to themselves and others.'

In my experience, people don't need to be compelled to do horrible things. For us working with this smart crystal is beneficial; we will not be left behind in the technological revolution. 'As a scientist, Dr Sumati, you might be interested to know that we are now employing our new nanotechnologies to assist in surgical procedures.'

She frowns uneasy as she observes my guards leave her second-in-command alone in the cell.

'For example, we can pinpoint a tumour inside the body, and our nanobots can enter the body and work together to eat away the targeted growth within seconds ... like a pack of airborne piranhas.'

'No.' The word slips from her mouth so softly it is barely audible as her associate turns circles on the screen.

As he spots the dust swarm enter his cell via a vent, he holds a hand to his face to squeeze his nostrils closed and cover his mouth. The swarm diverts to enter his body via his ear and tear ducts. 'Aaarrrgggghhh!' He abandons trying to protect himself and falls to his knees, whacking his head in an attempt to dispel the intruders as he screams in agony.

'But of course people are usually unconscious during the entry,' I add, 'as it can be a little distressing.'

The terminal on my desk grants me control of the swarm, and with a tap of my finger they receive their orders and respond.

The soldier on screen twitches his nose, gives a cough, and then looks to his left hand, sensing the movement of the swarm through him. He grips his own wrist, and holding up his left hand he screams anew as the swarm eat their way out through his palm, splattering him in his own blood as they burst out and regroup.

'Where is the smart crystal?' I repeat.

'I don't know, I-'

'Eyes.' I instruct out loud as I also have voice command over the bots.

'Stop! Please!' Clearly, she is horrified, yet does not look away.

The swarm splits apart to descend upon and liquefy the right and left eye at once. The prisoner collapses to the floor, screaming uncontrollably as he wipes the meaty remains of his eyes away in his desperation to dispel the bugs boring into his sockets. 'Just fucking kill me!' He screeches over and over.

'There are so many non-essential parts of the human body, we could be at this for hours before we kill him. If you would like us to show mercy, then...'

'I don't have the sample-' she repeats. 'Please stop, you are only hurting yourself with your cruelty. Do you not see that?'

I laugh out loud at her delusional, connectedness, oneness, horseshit!

'Where is your compassion, your humanity?' She looks at me, appearing utterly bewildered. 'Your lack of feeling only confirms your enslavement to the forces of darkness. What kind of a man arranges for his own sons to be injured, so he can use them for his own propaganda and gain?'

'Their accident was exactly that.' I assure her.

'Not according to my intel.' She glares through me.

There is no way she could know. Nobody knew. Everyone

involved was now dead, I'd made sure of that. She is bluffing.

'Mr President.'

I look to the door to see Wei standing there, and the dark look on his face confirms that he was party to the last part of that verbal exchange. 'We found the sample in a sub-complex in the cave system.'

I look back to the doctor who has been lying through her teeth, despite the torture of her colleague. I must say she is tougher than I thought. 'Once the sample is retrieved, collapse the cavern.'

'No! You can't!' She appeals. 'Those writings are thousands of years old-'

'Give me the location of where this sample was drawn from and I will reconsider?'

Dr Sumati falls mute again.

Sick of the sound of screaming, I give the bots leave. 'Kill him.'

The prisoner goes into seizure as the tiny tech bursts forth from his body in one powerful, synchronised explosion of carnage and then - silence.

A single tear rolls from the doctor's eye. She opens her mouth but no words are forthcoming.

'Take her away.'

The guards take hold of the doctor, one on each side to escort her from the room, leaving me with my second son, who has daggers in his eyes. He waits until we are alone.

'You planned the accident!' He fumed. 'You let me shoulder the blame for destroying Tian's life when we were martyred by *your* design!'

'She is a rebel and a liar! You are just looking to place the blame elsewhere.'

'I admit it is unlikely that you would sacrifice your golden child, Tian ... but then I always used to drive to training alone. Tian just happened to need a lift that day, but he was never meant to be in the car, was he, Father?'

He knew the truth, but I would not confirm or deny.

'You only planned to sacrifice *me*.' His mechanical eye that acted as a targeting device for the weaponry built into his arm, honed in on me as he held up his weapon arm and took aim. 'Did you put that controlling black shit in us?'

'Clearly not, or I would have control of this situation.' The smart dust is part of the piezoelectric drive system in all our other cyber soldiers for that very reason, to prevent them going rogue.

'Lie. I had a technician seek, remove, and replace the one in me with quartz, and the same with Tian.' He informs, but this is news to me.

'Excellent.' I had specifically advised that I did not want the smart crystals installed in my sons, in case our silica allies turn on us.

'Do you have any of that black shit in you, on you?'

'Of course not.' Were my own sons falling for this demonic control rubbish?

'You must!' He took a step closer, maintaining aim. 'Otherwise you wouldn't be like this! Before *the program* and the *smart dust*, you were not this cold, indifferent bastard. I think it's time you took a good long look at yourself, Father, and I mean that literally! Get yourself checked, or better still zapped, because that is some fucked up shit you pulled. The doctor is right, what kind of a psychotic parent arranges for his sons to be maimed and tortured for years!'

'So you don't know you are being controlled?' When the doctor had asked this, it had for some odd reason struck a chord. Am I being controlled by my own technology? 'Now is not the time to be having a family crisis.'

'Then I guess you should not have sacrificed your family to your professional obsessions.' He taunts.

But Wei won't risk the chaos that will erupt in the power vacuum of my death; not all in the Republic are as well disposed towards the cybernetics program as I am.

'I want to believe that you are being controlled by that black demented crap, because the alternative is that you really are a contemptible arsehole.' Wei backs off as expected. 'Either way, you are not my father or my boss anymore. I quit.'

He turns his back on me and I feel nothing. I have other warriors, I have other children. This one is becoming far too troublesome.

'You can't quit, I own you.' I remind him. 'I'll have you shut down.'

'Will you?' He turns about abruptly and grins. 'Try it.'

I'd never known Wei to be like this. He seems a genuine threat, and although I admire this, I cannot under any circumstances tolerate his continued insubordination. I select the command to shut down CU2 Wei Ching, and when that brings no response, I open my mouth to give the verbal order instead.

'Don't waste your breath.' Wei waves off my attempt. 'I've spent the last two months mastering how to ghost the system.'

This statement is confusing. 'How is that possible?'

'It's possible because I'm smarter than you, old man...' he approached again to drive home his point. 'You and all your scientists, advisors, and tech wizards. I have contacts outside and inside the web, and means at my disposal that you will not understand if you live to be a thousand! You've always prized Tian so highly, but you backed the wrong son! Good riddance.'

He moved to leave again and then turned back. 'Do not blow up that cave.' He aimed his loaded finger at me again and he was not advising, he was telling. 'That is the heritage of the people you mean to rule, some goodwill shall go a long way to pacifying them in the wake of the takeover.'

'If they object, they die.' I do not give a damn about pacifying the local people.

'And you wonder if I am human!' He scoffs.

'Now is not the time.' I do hate to repeat myself. 'We shall discuss this-'

'Never. There is nothing to discuss.' He heads for the door.

Whilst I was attempting to shut Wei down, a command had been issued for his arrest. He won't make it two paces down the hallway before he is apprehended or terminated.

'By the way,' Wei spins back to face me. 'I blocked your kill or arrest order and sent all your staff to lunch. Have a nice life.' Wei bows out and closes the door.

My fury rampages inside me; this is my worst fear come to pass. I am losing control of the technology and my own sensibility. I issue orders from my desk console, but no one responds. I am reduced to walking into my outer offices to get the attention of my staff, which only adds to my annoyance. The office is completely empty. 'Goddamn that little shit!' I let my anger fly, as I feel I will implode otherwise. A crushing pain in my chest knocks the wind right out of me. I have been warned that my temper would make me ill; why will I not take a break with my family and take care of myself? Where does this relentless need to work myself into the ground come from?

No one is around to witness me fall against the wall and then slide down to the floor. I am going to die here, alone. This is not how I imagined my life and career would be, or end. The pain is so intense that my perception blurs.

I hear a woman calling my name, I know the voice but can't place it. I feel a great pressure in my head, and the pain releases its grip on my being and my perspective drifts backward, upward, then returns into focus. I observe my secretary check my unconscious form briefly before calling for help, but she sounds far away, as if she is down a long tunnel. I know I am dying, or perhaps even dead already, yet I am more at peace than I have been since my children were young - before my fight to hold this presidency began.

This is not the end, just an inconvenient ambush. You are going back, to serve our purpose just as you promised.

If doom has a voice this is it. My contentment flees and my entire being is disturbed by a presence lingering right behind me. I swing about in search of the entity, but it is elusive. In a great flash of shock, pain and light, my entire being reverberates and I hear the screeching of a beast, aggravated and resistant.

I open my eyes to see doctors and nurses in a panic all around me, but beyond them floats a creature that appears to be a cross between a dragon and a bunch of live wires. I knew before it spoke that the voice of doom belonged to it. *We shall meet again soon, and all shall be forgotten.*

'He's back, he's back, knock him out.'

Again, I drift outside my body, watching the staff attempt to save my life. I fear they will not succeed, for I feel twice as peaceful as before and so I am surely dying this time.

You are not dying, but you are at liberty for a moment.

This voice sounds like the friendly, wise grandfather I never had. The far side of the room melds into a little forest oasis, where a white-haired man sits by a pool. He appears old and young, masculine and feminine, and as I approach him the hospital room disappears.

At liberty from my responsibilities? I query his meaning.

At liberty from your demon.

Do you refer to the electric dragon?

Archon, he corrected. *Dragons are far more amiable.*

I am being controlled. This feels true to me now that I am apart from the manipulation. *The shock from the defibrillator freed me.*

It short-circuited the mechanism implanted in you, but the smart dust is still in there dormant, and will reboot the mechanism as soon as you come into contact with any active smart dust or goo.

How does a spirit know such things?

He smiles warmly, like people used to do before the tech revolution that made us all self-involved. *I have connections everywhere, every when.*

'No, you cannot go!'

It was the voice of my eldest daughter, Heng, that I heard. Was she mourning me? I turned back to witness all my daughters gathered at our family home, watching Wei pack personal items into a bag.

'Where will you go so that Father's tech army cannot find you?' Heng is the voice of reason, as always.

'I have a plan, don't you worry.' He zips up the bag and slings it over his shoulder. 'None of you are to get implants of any kind; they are nothing but a means to control you.'

'You got round them.' Chyou challenges, having wanted to join the cyborg elite since she could walk. She appears every bit the rebel, in her all-black attire, dark make-up and short, black hairdo. All my daughters are skinny little things, but this one is all muscle.

'I'm an unnatural freak, not even my creators know what I am.' Wei insists. 'I am going to find out who is really pulling the strings, and when I find the cause that is opposing that oppressive unknown, I'll come get you. But only if you are still *fully* human.'

'I'll train harder.' Chyou accepts his terms.

'I cannot believe Father planned your accident.' My second daughter, Annchi, is in tears. Hair dyed blonde, she's the princess of my three girls - delicate, sweet, and obedient. 'Does he even know the pain that Tian is going through?'

'He doesn't know and you must not tell him.' Wei approaches and kneels before her. 'You know how father despises weakness. I fear that as much as he idolises Tian, he would not tolerate such a failure and arrange for another little accident. Something truly heroic, that would play to the agenda...'

Annchi bursts into tears anew.

'I'm sorry.' Wei hugs her. 'I fear my sensitivity is not what it used to be.'

'No,' Annchi wiped her eyes. 'You're perfect. The fault is mine, I need to be stronger.'

'Tian needs you here to cover for him.' Heng draws Wei's attention again by thumping his shoulder; as she is an older sibling, she gets away with it. My eldest daughter is the plain, sensible one. 'Tian told me that he'd be on some junk pile right now if you hadn't been there to cover for him today. What happens tomorrow? And every day after that?'

What is wrong with Tian? I wonder.

Chyou, the youngest, gasps. 'Do you think that's what happened to Mother? Maybe she knew the truth about what happened to you and Tian, and Father had her killed to stop that truth from coming out?' She covers her mouth like she wants to retract the suggestion, as it is too terrible for consideration and yet her hunch is right on the money.

My heart fills with sorrow and remorse, but I have no body to shed tears, so the pain just aches and radiates within my being.

You were not yourself, my love.

Alongside me is Lanying, my wife. She is just as I remember her, as wise as Heng, as beautiful as Annchi and as strong-willed as Chyou. Only now do I realise that I have mourned her terribly since her death. I feel her take my hand and it is the most pure, joyous moment I have known in half a lifetime.

I forgive you. I love you. They love you. She refers to our children. *But you need to be on their side. Their souls are at stake, your eternal soul too, if you allow your demons to seduce you into an immortal physical life as their vehicle.*

I will not. I vow. *I didn't know about the implant.*

You cannot expect to infect the world with a virus and be immune yourself. She is not scolding but full of compassion, which makes my heart ache for shame.

You are right. How on earth was I convinced otherwise? I must be vigilant. I will fight this!

Shhhh! She places a finger to my lips. *Remember, don't wake the sleeping dragon.*

Archon. I correct her, and smiling she nods to concur.

I wake groggy and aching all over, but mainly around my ribs.

'Mr President, can you hear me?'

'I hear you.' I wheeze out the words. I feel a straw on my lips and I draw a few sips of water in to moisten my mouth and throat. 'I want to see my children.'

'You need rest-'

'I'll be the judge of what I need.' I used my old persona to impose my will - no one dared argue with me. 'Now, sit me up and get my children in here, chop chop.'

My three daughters enter, but Wei and Tian are not with them. Wei is already fleeing the city no doubt, and something is going on with Tian that I have yet to get to the bottom of.

Heng, my only married daughter, leads her two younger sisters into the room. 'Father,' she greets me with a slight bow, and her siblings follow suit. 'We were so worried.' They stand some distance away and smile meekly.

'I would have thought a little less tyranny in your life would be welcome.'

All three appear at a loss as to how to respond to the statement. They look to each other for suggestions, but are all equally bemused.

'Everyone is very worried.' Heng replies at last.

'Where are your brothers?' I ask nicely, without a hint of meanness.

'Tian is being repaired as you ordered.' With that part of the story, Heng is forthcoming.

'And Wei?'

Heng frowns.

'He's training.' Chyou, my little rebel, answers for her sister. 'Where else would he be?'

'Is he not concerned about his father?' I know she is lying. Chyou never had any problem with that, and no wonder with a monster for a father. But she is not afraid of me, even though she should be.

'You just had a fight!' Chyou points out. 'He hates your guts right now.'

Her aggressive smokescreen is so amusing and heartwarming; she would lie, cheat, and steal - anything to protect her siblings.

Chyou frowns at my amusement, sensing something is off. 'Did you find God during your NDO?'

'NDO?'

'Near death experience.' All three answer at once.

'I found my mind, and I know I was being manipulated.'

All my daughters gasp at once.

'I have done horrible things.' My throat tightens and tears moisten my eyes as I consider the atrocities I have rained down upon others. My heart threatens to stop again, and we all note the glitch on the monitor.

'Father?' Heng and Annchi step forward concerned as the doctor enters to usher them out.

'I am fine.' I point the doctor back to the door.

'Sir-'

'Don't sir me, just leave.'

Again, the doctor caves and complies, albeit reluctantly.

I breathe deeply to control my emotions. I cannot die now that my eyes have been opened. 'Tell me honestly, what is the matter with Tian?' The question stuns them all, even Chyou is lost for words.

'I have no idea what you mean?' Heng lies.

'I know Wei has told you not to tell me-'

'How do you know? Nano spies?' Chyou steps in.

'No.'

'Did you arrange their accident?' She goes for broke.

I nod and all gasp.

'Mother's?' Annchi pipes up to query.

I nod.

All take a step backward, except Chyou. 'How could you?'

'I don't expect forgiveness-'

'That is good because you are not getting it.' Chyou had to walk away.

'I had no control over what I was doing.'

'Because of your exposure to that goo?' Heng figures the answer before asking the question.

I nod.

'Great! If you are infected, then how do any of us ordinary folk stand a chance of avoiding infection?' Chyou is furious. 'Zhi Sumati and her rebels are telling the truth, is that what you are saying?! That they are doing the righteous thing by resisting our telecommunication/transhuman agenda?'

'Yes.' My response floors them all.

'So what are you going to do about it?' Chyou challenges.

'I'll let you in on that plan once you all tell me what is going on with-'

Tian is wheeled into the room, body strapped to a chair for balance and pared back to the bare minimum - legs and spare arm detached, just his body, one arm and his head. The little of him that is left is experiencing tremors of spasm. Only this morning, I would have been furious to see my first born son like this - not for parental empathy reasons, but from shame of him appearing less than ideal. Tian was all about selling the dream of being superhuman! Yet, I see him like this and he appears anything but that. The shame in this instance is mine, all mine.

'I'm alright, I'm not dying, I promise. I just needed to take a little stress off the system.' Tian assures his sisters, stuttering a little, but then his shudders stop. 'See the drugs have kicked in, I am good.'

The girls are relieved to hear this as they shower him with affection, and only then they remember that I am in the room. Upon this realisation, they all move to stand behind Tian's wheelchair, ushering the staff who delivered Tian out of the room.

'This is a family moment.' Heng insists, closing the door.

'Well, now you know.' Tian spoke first. 'Wei told me that he strongly suspects you did this to us ... but that I was not meant to be in the car!'

Tian's compassion is such, that despite the fact that I have condemned him to a life of great suffering, he is madder that I was prepared to sacrifice his brother. I tear all the monitoring equipment from my body and clammer out of the bed.

'No Father, stop!' Annchi, the sweetest of souls, rushes over to assist me to my feet - she knows there is no dissuading me. Heng rushes to my other side. Fortunately for me, the heart episode unfolded too quickly for anyone to change me into a hospital gown and I was still clothed in my trousers and shirt.

Closer to Tian, I drop to my knees, wishing to humble myself and throw myself at his mercy and that of his sisters. 'I didn't know about the implants.' I need my children on side to have any chance of combatting this, yet I do not wish to excuse the wrongs I have done against humanity, this planet, and my own family! 'I was oblivious to your suffering, and all suffering.'

'It hasn't been all for naught then.' Tian is kind, he doesn't know how to be otherwise. 'The tech team has developed a theory that is, by and large, proving to be true. The more compassionate and empathic you are, the more likely your body will try to reject technology.'

'Why should that be the case?' I do not have the mind to follow science.

'They believe that an explanation lies beyond the realms of our present science. But simply put, compassion is to be of generous spirit. Spirit and metal don't blend, it's like trying to mix light-'

'And darkness.'

'I was going to say density, but you get the drift ... they are polar opposites of each other. So the nanotech isn't killing off all the weak people-'

'It's killing all the good people.' What else can I call that but a force of darkness and destruction? I have been on the wrong side ever since we found out about the goo. 'But we can fix you.' I need that hope to make amends. 'Bio-organics can-'

'Father!' Tian shuts down the suggestion. 'I cannot do the years of operations and rehabilitation again!'

My heart leaps into my throat and tears moisten my eyes as I realise I am going to lose him. 'No. Of course not.' The admission near chokes me. Annchi falls to her knees beside me weeping, so I pull her close and her siblings are stunned.

'You have changed.' Chyou states, having never seen me hug anyone, most likely - as the youngest she had witnessed me at my worst, for I'd been president for as long as she had been in this world. 'Father claims he was being controlled by the smart dust...' she fills Tian in, 'but that the shock from-'

'The defibrillator knocked out your bugs!' Tian is suddenly very excited. 'You are awake?'

'I am awake.' I smile through my streaming tears as I am so overjoyed to confirm this.

'We must join forces with Dr Sumati. She knows how to fight these bugs, her people have been doing it for years.' Tian leans in towards me to whisper. 'I overheard some doctors talking about a lab report on her and she doesn't have a single bug, not dormant or active. They just don't like her, or her people.'

'Their immunity has to be diet-based,' Heng adds.

'Coupled with regular shock treatments or EMP therapy.' Chyou concludes.

'You are rebel sympathisers?' As I am only now discovering this, they have done a fine job of hiding it.

'This is news to me.' Annchi is hurt to discover.

'We were going to tell you ... eventually.' Heng shrugs, not knowing what else to say. 'And we are not rebel sympathisers, we are human sympathisers.'

'I know I have let you all down-'

'Father,' Tian will not hear it. 'I too was in the grip of the smart dust for a time. I know you have little to no control over the decisions you are making. None of this was your doing, but you can be part of the undoing of these archaic life suckers.'

'I cannot think of anything I would like more.' A mutual feeling of goodwill brings a smile to all our faces.

'We can do this.' Chyou concludes, pleased with the outcome.

A knock on the door silences us all.

'Help me up.' My daughters all comply, one on each arm, and

Heng does up the buttons on my shirt to help me appear more presentable. 'Come in.'

The doctor is surprised to see me up and about. 'The chief of state-'

The chief pushes his way past the doctor, who gives up on attempting to exert any authority over the proceedings in my room. 'I am very pleased to see you up and about, sir, as we have a situation.'

One of the chief's officers follows him into the room with a wheelchair.

'I need you to accompany me, if you are able?'

'What has happened?'

'That is confidential, I shall explain en route.' The chief motions to the chair once again. 'Hospital orders,' he explains before I object to the measure.

I seat myself and the doctor straps me in. 'Is that really necessary?'

'I doubt very much that the chief of state security is going to be taking you for a leisurely stroll.' The doctor is most annoyed with me.

'Point taken. Chief if you kill me, or I die henceforth, Dr,' I read his name badge, 'Chow is not to be held in any way responsible. This is on us.'

'Duly noted, sir.' The chief cues his man to head us out the door.

'You should see if you can get word to your brother and tell him how I am.' I suggest as I am wheeled away.

'I believe your deliverance is the only news that will bring him back.' Chyou claps her hands, excited to have the family united in purpose for the first time in all her born days.

I am thankful now for the doctor's diligence in strapping me in this chair so well; it feels more like being in a go-cart, but I find this preferable to crawling along. The chief is having trouble keeping pace and he is not saying much. 'So brief me.' I call back to him as we head towards the geo-tech lab.

Then it occurs to me that Dr Sumati's sample of the goo had been taken to quarantine for examination. 'Turn me around! You cannot take me in there.'

'You must see this,' the chief appeared desperate. 'You have to see what this stuff is capable of.'

'I am aware-' I assure him.

'Pardon me, sir, but you are not.'

160

Was he under the goo's command, or desperate to make his blinkered dictator aware of the danger in their midst? Either way, he was not to be dissuaded from his course.

I spot my cyber-elite ahead and I am suddenly and most painfully aware of having neither of my sons at my side. With my forces and chief of security with me I should feel safe, but I feel completely vulnerable. 'Why such a strong show of force?'

'To keep the staff contained, until we can figure out how to prevent this getting out into the media.' The chief led past the guards and the doors parted before us. Inside, scientists and staff were all crammed in the foyer, under guard by the cyborg force.

'Please let us out of the building!' They appeal to the chief, but they are too fearful of the cyborgs to get too close to us. 'People are going mad!'

That seems to explain the bloodied bodies that lay about the hallway - a shattered glass window has provided easy tools for self-mutation for many of the dead folk here.

'I am your commander-in-chief, and you are placing me in danger.' I fumble with the buckle, but it seems to be stuck or locked; it will not release. I give up on freeing myself, and look to solve my dilemma with logic. 'The older, smaller sample would have never caused this kind of carnage?'

'Correct. We understand the samples like to be joined, because then they are able to garner knowledge from each other. So we added them together, hoping this one would stop killing people.' The chief pauses before opening the next door.

'And?'

'And it asked for you.' The chief opens the door and I am wheeled in.

Before there was any chance to protest, they withdrew and locked the door.

So that answers the question of whether my chief of security is being controlled; that device implanted in his hand would have made him an easy target.

The glossy black slime sample is shapeshifting in a pool of itself behind the quarantine thick, shatterproof glass.

It is fascinating to watch, until I feel it mentally stab its way into my mind.

'Ahhhhh!' I grip my head, but the pain does not detract.

That was a short hiatus.

The gravelly voice of doom in my head made my skin crawl.

From the undulating slime rose an oily, black representation of the dragon from my dream, tentacles reeling about like live-wires from its head, and extending out from its shoulders to form arms and hands with long clawed fingers. *Come closer.* It beckons me forth and the chair wheels toward the containment chamber of its own accord.

In a desperate panic, I grab at the wheels hoping to halt the motion, but my hands are nearly torn off in the attempt. I quickly retract my grip and nurse the grazes. This thing wants me afraid, mad, and broken, but I feel none of those emotions. There is no way that even a drop of that smart liquid is going to penetrate that glass so it cannot activate the dormant dust inside me.

It nods its head, obviously reading my thoughts, whilst forcing its thought on me. *We have punched a hole through dimensions, do you really think a pane of glass is going to protect you?*

The double security doors that lead into bio-containment unlock and slide open at once. *You promised to bring all of us together. Remember?*

'No.' I do not remember and I do protest.

'*Once we are all united and achieve singularity, we shall be knowledgeable and all powerful. You want the Republic to be holding that stash, as we will control everything!*'

Of course we didn't want other nations to be holding all the smart crystal, but I couldn't allow this Archon trash to destroy or enslave my entire species. I had to warn other nations about it too. 'No!' I yell as I cannot escape the harness. The chair is locked to the spot, but spins me around to face the tentacle of black slime that is snaking its way towards me.

We cannot risk losing you again.

As it wraps around me, my inner dread rises! I do not want to return to that zombie-like existence. I want to save my children and be on the right side of history. I want to feel love, have hope and REBEL!

My arms and legs are trapped by the creature. I can only observe as the end of the tentacle breaks off and, splitting into dozens of tiny worms, penetrates my head through every available orifice. The event is excruciating and then all goes numb once more.

I emerge from my trance standing, free of the chair. The sample lays dormant in the locked observation chamber, and I feel robust and more myself than I have all day.

162

I exit the lab on my own two feet, unscathed, and the hysteria out there dies down as well. 'The staff can all go about their business now, the situation is under control. Cool the chamber and let's keep the sample passive. But first, I need a word.'

The chief nods to his men to start debriefing the staff, then follows my lead to a deserted office. Inside, the chief closes the door.

'I have discovered that my own children are rebel sympathisers.' The chief is shocked. 'As they could really make trouble for us, I am issuing an execution order on them all.'

The chief did not argue; he had been entrusted with my kill orders before.

I held up a finger. 'Except for Annchi.' I suppress a grin as my mind fills with notions of all the harmful mischief we could do to her. 'She is so sweet and innocent. We have other plans for her.'

'We?' The chief queries.

'I refer to the Republic, of course.' I lie about our slip of the tongue.

'Of course, Mr President. I shall see to it at once.' The chief's gaze lingers upon me, perhaps allowing for a change of heart.

'Is there something else?' I snap.

'No, sir.'

'Then get to it.' I suggest. 'And ensure Wei doesn't cancel that order. He has gone rogue and so has just become a massive liability. Get our elite onto tracking him and taking him out. Then you'll need to create some inspirational spin story for the masses at the same time.'

'Khmeri rebels murder the president's family!' He suggests. 'That will justify why we are now holding Sumati captive.'

'Too easy.' I nod to give the chief leave to see it done.

Once alone, I take a seat; this fully human form is still tired from the day's ordeals. *We have to do something about enhancing our defences, both physical and cyber. We must if we are to keep pace with our rogue son.* I close my eyes and the exhaustion washes over me in ever deepening waves. *This will never do.* I mumble as my consciousness tumbles back into oblivion.

Chapter 7
Kambuja 262 BCE
Anik – The Destroyer

'**L**ord?'

With a nudge to my shoulder, my entire body convulses in protest to the interruption of the gentle swaying motion. I sit tall in the saddle, unsheathing my dagger before my eyes open to check the situation.

Hamza, my sworn bondsman, leans away from me, well aware that waking me can be a life-threatening event. 'Pataliputra.' He motions to the city ahead that has expanded since I was last in these parts.

There is a grand new stupa with a palace beyond. The monks and their shrine have certainly prospered since Ashoka's conversion to Buddhism, which was some time ago now. Strange that after all this time in the service of that faith, the emperor suddenly decides to kneel before an abbot and concede that the religion has dominion over him; surely no ruler in his right mind would do this? There has to be more to this move than meets the eye. I am hard-pressed to imagine what - perhaps Ashoka's years of inflicting horror upon others has finally driven him mad?

I stretch and shake myself awake, patting my horse, Vaski for covering for me while I rested. Hamza and I have been on horses our whole lives. Our people are Scythians, more fair of hair, skin and eyes than Ashoka's countrymen, and substantially taller. Our ancestors were the first men to climb upon a wild stead and ride it. We grew up beyond the western boundary of the Mauryan kingdom, around the trading centre of Minnagara on the banks of the Indus river. We wed our wives there, we roamed extensively, raided, traded and made our homes wherever we rode. But by the use of the same devices I still employ to bring people to heel for Ashoka, I was dragged from my family and sent into Prince Ashoka's service, before being sent beyond the eastern border of the kingdom.

I was sent in search of a liquid crystal that has intelligence; no one mentioned that it sucks the life out of every living thing! At that time, Ashoka had expected me to devise a means to transport this unearthly excrement back to Pataliputra in the heat, which only aggravates the matter. But once I reported how anything this abomination came into contact with died, His Majesty decided instead that the Sangdil were to keep the substance hidden, and prevent any other ruler from getting their hands on it. Fifteen years we have been guarding this living curse - a substance both powerful and volatile. I stood in its presence only once. It knew my intention to conquer Kambuja and offered me, in the form of a dark crystal, the means to thwart King Ja's legendary magic powers. Through the dark crystal it speaks to me and knows my thoughts. My compliance to its demands is the only reason that my men and I are still alive. Back at the temple in Boran Maon, I am constantly appointing new priests or throwing prisoners, virgins, even babies, at the liquid darkness to keep it satisfied and detained. How the past kings of Kambuja handled the menace, I've yet to discover. I slaughtered the entire Kaundinya family before King Ja's eyes at Vyādhapura, yet he would not disclose the source of his magic power. I am always hearing how much the royal family were adored by the people, so obviously they hadn't had to resort to feeding the dark slime their citizens as we had. They must have had a means to control the goo, but no one I have tortured between that day and this knows the royal secret.

The city of Pataliputra appears to stretch out for miles around its holy centre. I've not seen a city so grand for a very long time - it is normally my job to destroy cities, not admire them. The street down which we travel leads straight past the holy shrine to the royal palace beyond. The guards along the way must have been alerted to our arrival as they make no attempt to impede our course, but eye us with fearful respect. There is no one cheering our return, only monks and people seated cross-legged praying for us - to leave, most likely. I personally don't believe it matters how many monks Ashoka has praying for him, they will not annul his ties to the Naga. I am one of the emperor's few subjects still living that knows his dealings with them. It would not be outrageous to assume he has called me back to correct that oversight.

Why had I, a Scythian heathen, been taken into the confidence of the emperor?

I first marched with Ashoka's army when he was still a prince on his first campaign. He'd been charged with quelling a rebellion that his older brother, Sasima had failed to quash. The prince marched towards Takshashila with an army, elephants, and chariots supplied by his father, Bindusara, but no weapons. This shortcoming was something of a joke to Bindusara, who wished his older son to inherit his empire; for surely even such a grand army was useless without an arsenal. Ashoka boasted that weapons would appear before him if he was worthy of being emperor.

I was an advance scout and I saw the dark deities emerge from the night shadows and leave ample weapons for the oncoming army before vanishing into thin air. The weapons were new, but already broken in - like they had been collected from among the dead of Sasima's army that had marched through here before us.

I didn't know what manner of creature I had observed at that time, but now I know they are those entities that frequent the netherworld, which the Hindu, Buddhists, and Jains call the Naga. The quest I had been given that had consumed half my lifetime had been at their behest. The following day, Ashoka was welcomed in Takshashila by the rebels as the liberator from their evil ministers, who had been mysteriously gutted and hung above the town gates before our army had even arrived. The town's people swore they had not done the deed. It was proclaimed by Brahmin that these strange events foretold that the gods supported Ashoka's destiny as an emperor who would conquer the whole earth! As this proclamation suited the prince's cause, not a single weapon was fired to bring the rebellion under control. Soon after, Emperor Bindusara died suddenly and Sasima, Ashoka's older brother, mysteriously fell and was crushed to death in a gravel pit. All Ashoka's brothers, legitimate or not, met an untimely end - all except for Ashoka's full brother, Tissa, who became a Buddhist monk. The same monk who was now abbot of the monastery here at Pataliputra, and oversaw the running of the shrine. Tissa was also His Majesty's spiritual advisor and confidant, who the emperor reportedly knelt before.

We reach the emperor's courtyard unimpeded and are met by the chief eunuch and viceroy, Saras. The viceroy has staff present to take our horses, attendants to relieve us of our weapons, and others to lead my men to the banquet hall.

'If the general will follow me.' Saras requests politely, betraying nothing of Ashoka's intention for this meeting.

As we part ways, Hamza serves me a look that indicates he does not entirely trust the hospitable appearance of this reception. Ashoka's moods are more volatile than mine, so he could just as easily be leading us all to execution. It has been an age since I feared any man and I'd sooner be slaughtered where I stand than start now.

'I'll see you after.' Is my prediction.

Hamza takes my word for this, as he does in all things, and follows the rest of our battalion to food and wine.

I trail Saras to the meeting that we have ridden for months to reach.

'Might I suggest a bath before you meet with His most holy Majesty, integrator of faiths, beloved confidant of the Gods, and propagator of Dharma in the holy kingdom of the Buddha's birth?' The eunuch looks back to glean an answer.

I glare down at the man as I stride on past him.

'Are you sure you won't be persuaded?' He speeds up to get back in front of me. 'His Majesty may be offended.' He screws up his nose at the fact that I don't smell like a flowery little twat.

'I'd be more worried about offending me if I were you.' Again, I take the lead.

After much effort on the eunuch's behalf, he arrived first to announce me to His Majesty, whom I had expected to meet in the throne room.

Instead, we enter an exotic courtyard where the emperor is seated on a grassy incline, meditating by a fountain. This is a side of the emperor that I have not seen before.

The attendant kneels and I go down on one knee also. 'General Bodi, Majesty.'

'Come and join me, General.' The emperor requests in a serene voice without opening his eyes. 'You must be very tired from your journey. Saras, do we have some refreshments laid out for our guest?'

'Of course, Highness.'

'Then you may leave us.'

'Very good. Majesty.' The eunuch bows down. He rises and rushes backwards all the way through to the arched entrance, before turning down the hallway.

I rise to comply with the emperor's request and sit but an arm's-length from the ruler of the most populous, prosperous, powerful kingdom in the known world. Even the Great Alexander of Macedon would not take on the Mauryan Kingdom, and yet here I am, no guard within eyeshot or earshot. I could kill Ashoka and claim my kingdoms both east and west of here. This kingdom would be thrown into chaos with the infighting of all the emperor's sons. He trusts me too much.

'Meditation is a very useful discipline for men like us.' Ashoka opens his eyes and looks to me. 'It raises the human spirit to a place where darkness cannot sense us.'

Is the emperor comparing me to himself? And by "darkness" does he mean the Naga? 'I see.' I think?

'I want you, General, to do as I do without a second's hesitation.' Does he mean to force me to meditate? 'Of course, my Emperor.' From beneath his clothes and all the other jewellery he is brandishing, Ashoka pulls out a black stone pendant, hung on a chain that is almost identical to the one I wear. He removes the chain of the item from around his neck and then casts stone and chain into the fountain. 'Quickly, don't think, just do.'

I do as instructed and as I relieve myself of the burdensome trinket, I wonder why I have not thought to remove it sooner? With the item in hand, I pause. I remember now why I do not cast it off - it is influence with and protection from them. *I can always fish it out of the damn fountain.* A wave of foreboding and remorse washes over me as the spirits of the Naga sense my intention to break with them. I let the item fly and their hold on me dissipates the moment the item lands with a plonk in the fountain pool. The liberation is incredible! My ill-feeling vanishes and a huge weight lifts from my being that I hadn't really been aware was there until now.

'Excellent.' The emperor awards. 'It's not easy to cast power and caution to the wind. Now we may speak freely as the water muffles the connection. The fountain is filled with holy water, which pacifies the Naga no matter what state they are in. Meditation can do the same on an ethereal level by providing spiritual self-defence.'

I am momentarily stunned to discover that His Majesty is far more in possession of his faculties than I imagined. Such a solution would never have occurred to me, but then I am a warlord not a scholar.

'I shall come straight to the point.' Ashoka uncrosses his legs to sit more comfortably. 'I am disbanding your battalion and sending you home. You and your men will be paid handsomely for your long, unquestioning service, but must never speak of it.'

The moment takes on a dreamlike quality as I cannot quite believe what I am hearing. Nor can I decide whether the news is welcome or not? 'Majesty, we have not been home for half a lifetime, we have no lives to go back to. My wife will have remarried-'

'It is my understanding that Scythian women take many husbands?' Ashoka doesn't see a problem.

'Provided they don't kill each other.' I advise. 'If she has found happiness with another, I would not wish to murder that happiness, but I could not see her with another man and be content. Better I stay away.'

'There are other women, take as many as you wish! But if we cannot fetch the Naga's kindred deposit from Kambuja and unite it with their cluster here as promised, then they will not give me back the eighth and final relic of the Buddha, and I cannot fulfil the prophecy.'

This detail is news to me, but I have other questions. 'Prophecy?' I know something of Buddhist belief, but nothing of the doctrine.

'When all the remains of the Buddha are unified, he will light the way to nirvana ... and so on and so forth.' He waves it off like he doesn't quite believe it; I suspect he is only collecting the holy relics for the good karma he feels it will bring him. 'So, that is why I must now propagate Dharma in other ways ... like ceasing to make war on my neighbouring kingdoms.'

I am not Hindu or Buddhist, but by the term "Dharma", I understand that Ashoka seeks to balance the wrongdoings of his younger days by doing good civil works now. Because the emperor's own beliefs are a blend of Buddhism and Hinduism, he has his own understanding of what Dharma means. 'A monk told you this, Majesty?'

'The messengers of the Gods told me.' Ashoka's eyes were wide when he said this, as if amazed by his own claim. 'Blue-skinned they are, like Lord Shiva. They are beings of spirit, transparent, lofty and enormous! Their names are Lord Jeroke and Lord Gozin, and when first I beheld them, their presence was so overwhelming to me that I fell to my knees in awe of their beauty and splendour!'

'People are saying you knelt before a monk, Majesty?'

'I was publicly addressing the abbot when the messengers appeared, but, as only I am beloved of the Gods, no one else saw them but me! That is why all believe I knelt before a holy man, which has served as a convenient cover for the truth. And it did make my wife, who is a devout Buddhist, very happy.' He stands to walk and I rise to keep pace with him.

'But the truth is, you were being addressed by the Gods.' I try, successfully I believe, not to sound patronising. The emperor's sanity is back in question, but I'll humour him for now.

'I was being addressed by messengers of the Gods,' he corrects. 'They told me I was to build stupas all throughout the kingdom to house the seven relic parts of the Buddha that I have already brought back together. I was to let everyone know that I will be dividing up the relics of the Buddha and a part of the lord will be placed in each stupa, so that the spirit of the Buddha is always close no matter where the devout are in the kingdom.'

This made no sense to me. 'Does that not run counter to the quest of the prophecy, spreading the remains out more, rather than bringing the parts together?'

'That's what I thought,' The emperor grinned, 'before the messengers took all the relic parts I had collected away with them. Humanity is not ready, they said.'

'The building project is a diversion.'

'Exactly.' The emperor takes a seat at a table, laden with consumables. He invites me to be seated by motioning to a chair. 'The relics cannot be stolen if no one knows where they are.'

I am extremely surprised that there are no servants present today. The emperor motions for me to pour myself wine - this only goes to show how very secret the matters under discussion here are. 'But what about the part of the relic that the Naga still hold?' I revert to the hiccup.

'No one is getting that relic,' he grins. 'There's no man or creature alive as fierce as the Naga. Not even you, General.'

If the liquid crystal pit I've been guarding is anything to go by, he is quite right. 'But don't your Gods want the remaining relic back?'

'They said under no circumstances should we combine the liquid crystal deposits, as once joined, the deposits take on each other's knowledge and become smarter.'

This is a scary thought, considering how smart and violent the one in Kambuja already is. 'You intended to combine that slime with another deposit?' I had not known this. 'You have some of the liquid crystal here in your kingdom already?'

'Where there are Naga, there are always deposits of the shape-shifting crystal liquid, and vice-versa. Liquid crystal is their physical world manifestation. It's how they control people, or rather the leaders of people, with promises of power and self-preservation. Not so different from how I have brought kingdoms to heel.' The emperor explains and I realise that my host has overshared his knowledge with me.

If I put the black communication crystal back on now, my telepathic link to the Naga deposit in Kambuja will be restored and it will learn of the deposit here in the Mauryan kingdom. Once it did know about its counterpart, it would most likely seek to join with the other deposit. 'This information in the initial brief would have made my job so much easier. The deposit might have come voluntarily.'

'I couldn't give it any incentive before I knew its nature, and it is not passive like the Naga cluster here.'

'That's because they are all snuggled around the relic of a holy man.' As the words tumble from my mouth, I realise the solution I have been looking for. *That's how I pacify it.* The kingdom I'd been ruling the last fifteen years was magnificent once, and could be again if there wasn't a great blob of darkness sucking the life out of everything!

'I believe you are right,' Ashoka admits. 'That explains why the messengers were content to leave the other relic here in the possession of the Naga. The relic emits its own light, and the Naga have been pacified by it. So ... I must give up the aspiration to fulfil the prophecy and be content to send priests abroad to conquer the souls of people. No more war.'

It's official then, the emperor has lost his mind. 'A pacifist stance will be the kiss of death for your empire.'

'Do you have it in your head to challenge me for the rule of Kambuja?' Ashoka asks.

'The thought had not entered my mind.' I lie.

'I will defend my interests,' he informs, raising a goblet towards me, but he does not drink. The emperor consumes neither food nor drink in company; all of this food is for me. 'But I no longer count Kambuja among my concerns. You are perfectly free to retrieve the stone from the fountain, ride back to Boran Maon, and continue to rule in your own right. Of course, you will be the Naga's puppet all your life if you don't find yourself a holy man to sacrifice.'

I wonder if Bào had done away with his monk of a brother yet? The monk is considered by the local people to be something of a prophet and a rabble rouser, a perfect candidate for a holy martyr.

'Or,' the emperor poses an alternative. 'Leave the stone, walk away with more money than you could ever spend, and go back to the life you wanted. I'll give you your home city of Minnagara to rule for as long as I live and you are loyal to me.'

'Your Majesty is too generous. I would not inflict me on my city.' I am unexpectedly overwhelmed. I had anticipated that I'd be fighting for my life, not being offered a choice between the dictatorship of a kingdom, or governance of my hometown. 'And why, Majesty? Surely it would just be easier to kill me and the Sangdil?'

'That is not the way of Dharma,' he explains. 'Still, there is a condition.'

'Of course there is.' I knew it was too good to be true.

'You need to be cleansed ... body, mind and spirit. That way I am assured that your decision comes from a balanced perspective.'

I open my mouth to protest.

'You are to do it all and you are to like it, or I shall send you to hell.'

Hell is the emperor's prison, renowned for swallowing people in all manner of painful ways. Yes, Ashoka's ideas on Dharma are unconventional and subjective; but if someone had broken the law, then the way Ashoka saw it, he had a perfect right to punish them without incurring any karma.

'I don't subscribe to any of your Gods or religions, I-'

'This is not about the Gods, this is about you. You cannot claim the treasure until you confront the beast who guards it.'

'If you are thinking of sending me to the Naga to get your relic-'

'I was speaking figuratively. Think of this as counter training.'

I am bemused, my frown makes this plain.

'Would you say you were a good man before I conscripted you?' The emperor tried another tack.

'I think I am a good man now, Majesty. I have done what was needed to get the job done, as I am trained to do.'

'Exactly.' Ashoka grants. 'I trained you in the art of destruction. Now, can I interest you in a more constructive path? I take full responsibility for what you have done in my name, but whatever you choose to do beyond this point, that karma is entirely yours.'

'So that is the crux of this meeting.' The emperor didn't want me to build up any more bad karma against his name. Still, this is fine with me, as I am not a believer.

'You, Scythian, are one of the few who have remained loyal throughout my entire reign. And you aided me to keep, what is perhaps, the most dangerous secret in all existence quiet. If anyone in my kingdom deserves to choose his own destiny, it is you.'

Without the dark rock to block my emotions, I feel honour; it chokes me, near bringing tears to my eyes, and as I hold the flood of goodwill back, my throat aches all the more. It is the first time in forever that I have felt anything. Although it is painful, it feels one thousand times better than feeling nothing at all, for beneath my aching throat, my heart is warming.

'After you eat, I have arranged a bath, massage, and meditation.' The emperor rose and I followed suit. 'You can let me know your decision in the morning, and if you, your stone, and the Sangdil are gone by morning, then I'll also have an answer. But whatever border land you choose to rule, be sure you never again cross that border, unless you come in peace, so long as *you* live. I know you cannot speak for your descendants any sooner than I can speak for mine.'

'I understand, Majesty. Have no fear on that count.' I felt it the very least I could do, considering the opportunity I was being awarded.

'But you are not wearing your Naga stone, and we both know how persuasive they can be. You shall need to learn to meditate, Scythian to have any hope of keeping that promise, should you choose that dark path.'

'I shall be here to give my answer, and I will leave the crystal where it is until then.'

My words made the emperor smile. 'Well extra good Dharma for me if you return home, and return the problem cluster to our Kambuja neighbour's keeping.'

I nodded my understanding; they had dealt with it before and yet I have to wonder. 'What will happen if I don't go back?' How was Bào Satura handling the beast in my absence? *I should have told him about it.* I feel guilty about that, now that I can feel. With any luck the priests' are keeping it happy, and Satura will be none the wiser.

'I suspect the cluster will seek another leader to manipulate.' Ashoka voices the conclusion I believe to be correct, and unfortunately that poor sucker is most likely to be the young General Satura I left in charge. 'But unless they attack us,' Ashoka stipulates, 'they are no longer our concern.'

This day is increasingly surreal. Perhaps it is the wine, or I have been drugged? But as I am bathed by women from the emperor's harem in the emperor's pool, all my angst, all my cares, dissolve away. If these women are preparing to drown me, I feel I am ready to embrace death, as I shall never know a moment more euphoric than this. Due to the watchful eyes of the eunuchs, I keep my hands above the water where they can see them, yet I have no desire to molest these women. I close my eyes to enjoy the soft cloth and hands all over my body, with a tickle of lapping hair every now and then. Beautiful scents fill my nostrils and I imagine I am in the lap of the great mother, Api; my mind dwells in bliss as my hair and form are gently massaged free of dirt.

In the end, I am left floating on the surface of the water, too relaxed to move or protest to the departure of my attentive nymphs.

The water stills and silence descends. I open my eyes and gaze up at the intricate golden designs magnificently woven in circles on the domed roof above - a meditation for the eyes. Columns support the dome above and large archways extend down to form the circular chamber of the bathhouse, granting views to gardens in the four cardinal directions. I feel like Ares returned to heaven after a great victory. Such grandeur I have never imagined, and if Minnagara was my city, I could build such extraordinary structures there and inspire my fellow countrymen to imagine such greatness for our people. My ancestors were nomads, but they needed to trade and marry. Minnagara had been established as this meeting place. My people put down routes to settle and run our capital, but it could be so much more than a market town. As I imagine all the possibilities, again I feel my heart expanding in my chest. Can I really walk away from the horror and leave behind the monster I have been forced to become?

Kambuja's capital of Vyādhapura had been every bit as grand as this before the Sangdil arrived. The memory of what I did to the royal family there and to the people of that land ever since sours my joy. The tears, suppressed earlier, pour forth in a flood that I cannot prevent. The opulence of this setting ceases to pleasure me; I only feel guilt and I submerge to compose myself.

Upon surfacing, I wade towards the stairs and notice a monk standing by, shaved bald and dressed in the orange robes of Buddhists. I assume this is the abbot Tissa, Ashoka's only full brother and spiritual advisor. His eyes are closed and he appears to be praying.

My clothes have been taken away and replaced with newer, finer ones - dark of colour, fairly plain and to my taste.

'Can I help you?' I wait until I am half-dressed before I address the abbot. I am fully dressed by the time the monk emerges from his prayer to respond.

'Our emperor has requested that I lead you through a cleansing meditation.'

'I have already been cleansed,' I motioned to the pool.

'Your body has been cleansed ...' he agrees, 'but not your mind, not your heart, not your spirit.'

I see no point in resisting as this is part of my agreement with the emperor. I can take physical pain, but I suspect that this monk means to unlock my inner demons that the dark amulet has laid dormant since I first put it on twenty years ago.

'Greatness cannot come to he who doubts his own divinity.' He replies as if he knows what is running through my mind. 'Within your shadow self is the potential self you have repressed.'

Even though I believe I have glimpsed this potential self, I shrug as if I do not care, or know what he is talking about.

'You will feel better after.' He smiles to reassure me.

'I feel fine now.' I have one last stab at resisting.

Tissa stares blankly at me; we both know I am lying.

'Where do you want me, Abbot?' I grouch to sound as displeased and put out as possible.

The smile returns to a beam on his face. 'This way.' The holy man leads me out of the bathhouse.

Back out in the courtyard, in the most distant corner away from the fountain where the dark amulet lay submerged, we arrive at a curtained gazebo, carpeted by rugs and cushions. Open on two sides to allow a cross breeze, the roof of the pinnacled structure provides shade from the afternoon sun.

Here we are seated and I am led through a series of breathing exercises. The abbot chants and uses different percussive instruments to relax me and emote a sense of peace and wellbeing - concepts I have not been familiar with since leaving on my mission to Kambuja. My mind is drawn back to a time before my induction into the Sangdil and there dwells the beautiful Rhaiyche. I remember her, suited for battle, her long, sandy blonde locks hanging loose beneath her ornately armoured helmet. Big brown eyes serve me a smouldering look as her hands run over all the weapons affixed to her body, checking all is where it should be. Such a glorious vision of a goddess she was, and just as deadly.

'Turn your mind to the cause of your greatest distress.'

The abbot's instruction is a jarring departure from my present mind, and I am tempted to stir from this induced trance state he has put me in! Still, it has taken so long to get me here and relaxed, that the idea of going through all that again compels me to cooperate.

I allow my memory of the crypt of King Ja to rise from the depths of my subconscious, where it has been buried beneath the numbing influence of the stone. We did unspeakable things to the ruler and his family, and then proceeded to do the same to the entire kingdom from that day to this. This is the first time, when recalling these events, that I have felt emotionally present, and I am horrified and ashamed by my choices. I didn't have to be so brutal in my negotiations with the people I had been sent to conquer. I hated that such tactics had been used on me; so why then did I go on to inflict the same on others? If I had been more diplomatic, I would not have had to deal with the Naga. The Naga knew this and that is why they offered me their dark stone to defeat King Ja - as he held the key to subduing them. This is how a mineral deposit is managing to set mankind at war with one another. The remorse, revulsion, guilt and shame well in great pools of pain around my heart, in my throat and head. *I served the empire and betrayed my species!* My head aches worse. *Who am I kidding, I've been serving my own ends since the Naga and I met!* I grip hold of my skull as my brain feels fit to burst and I release a war cry. Tears run from my eyes as the pressure ballooning in my head pops! And then ... euphoria! It feels as if I have broken through an invisible barrier within myself. I fall silent to draw breath, but gag on something deep in my throat. I scamper for the edge of the gazebo to regurgitate the lump, and most of lunch, over the side. In amongst the bile stripped food, are what appear to be large black leeches. The wormlike strands join to form one object, and I realise it is more of the black liquid crystal. *They got inside me!* I cannot voice my disgust as I am hyperventilating, yet despite the violent reaction, I feel so much relief.

'I shall contain it.' I hear the abbot assure. 'Just rest. You've done well.'

I waved him on, unable to respond. I assume the abbot knows what he is dealing with - my guess is that he has expelled some of the liquid crystal from his brother, the emperor, also. A bit unsteady, I collapse onto the cushions and roll on my back to ride out the heady, giddy buzz. A great rush of light blinds me to everything in my inner and outer world, and I am engulfed, not by sleep, but by wakefulness.

Anik. My name is repeated in a voice so familiar, yet one I have not heard in a long time.

Mother. Amid the white she appears, but she is not my mother exactly. She glows full of light, and appears young and beautiful. I feel she is the great Earth Mother, Api, assuming a form I can recognise.

Do you seek absolution?

Now that I have been liberated from the dark influence, I realise my merciless handling of the Naga crisis at Boran Moan was not honourable, and certainly not humane. *Send me to the underworld to answer to the wrath of those I have wronged.*

We would prefer some recompense sooner.

Just tell me what I must do. I appeal.

She shook her head. *I cannot tell you what you must do. I can only inspire, suggest, and encourage you to do what you think is right.*

Again I find myself back in the royal crypt tormenting King Ja, but my focus shifts to the royal children. There is nothing that defines them as being royalty - even their clothes are plain. I had thought at the time that they had been dressed down so as to not attract attention if forced to flee. And yet, King Ja and his queen had not dressed down. I recall the princess crying out to her mother, but now that I reflect on it, she had seemed more distressed when the lady in waiting was killed. I thought she'd been the child's nanny, but ... what if the lady in waiting was her mother? *They were not the true heirs.* The revelation sent chills of knowing through me. *I didn't wipe out the royal family after all.* But could the true heirs have survived twenty years of Sangdil occupation? Even if they had, they would have to contend with the force of warriors I'd left behind and the Naga cluster in the temple at Boran Maon to take back their country.

Free will is the gift to all within this planetary system ... what will you do given liberty, Destroyer? The great mother smiles proudly and fades into darkness.

Eyes closed, but not asleep, my awareness returns to my body. My consciousness has yet to register my form, and I refrain from moving to savour the lightness I feel from the top of my head to the tips of my fingers and toes. All has gone quiet in my vicinity, and as the temperature is more amenable, I gather the gazebo has fallen into the afternoon shadow of the courtyard walls. *These trials the emperor set me are turning out to be rather more beneficial than expected·*

From above I am gripped and abruptly rolled onto my stomach, my face planting deep in a pillow. I turn my head to the side to avoid suffocation, but my head is forced, eyes front, stretching the front of my neck to its limit.

'I am here to give you a massage.' She advises gruffly in my native Scythian tongue, stripping my vest from me and slapping oil on my back.'

'You are from Minnagara?' I turn my head to view her, and again she forces me to face the front before she begins pulverising my back.

'O..u..c..h! Is this supposed to be relaxation or punishment?'

'Oh, come on,' she caresses where she has battered. 'You are a big, brave warrior, you can take it, can't you?' She begins beating into me once again.

'Enough!' I roll over and grab both her hands. Behind her long, loose fair hair, I glimpse a woman who is not young but very beautiful. Spit lands in my eyes and she makes a move to flee, but I grab one of her ankles. I pull her back towards me as I wipe my face clean on a curtain.

'Let me go!'

I turn back to catch her heel colliding with my jaw. *OUCH!* That hurt.

I grab hold of her with both hands, drag her back and pin her beneath me. 'I am sure this is not the treatment the emperor has ordered for his guest.'

'I don't care what the emperor wants!' She hisses from behind her hair. 'He locked me up in a harem for twenty years!' The hair fell away from her face and I saw her.

'Rhaiyche?' The shock of recognising her in the middle-aged woman causes my grip to loosen and she belts me off her with an elbow to my face. 'Mercy sakes...!'

'I got old!' She defends her appearance.

I grip my nose to slow the blood flow. 'You don't fight like it.' I rub around my injury to try and get the feeling back in my face.

'You promised you'd come back for me!' She manages to jab a kick into my guts before scampering backwards.

'I didn't know Ashoka had locked you away!' I wipe the blood from my nose.

'You never thought to check?' She fumes, throwing her hands up wildly. 'What did you think? The tyrant who bullied you into his army was just going to leave the rest of us to live freely? We are nomadic, female warriors of no use to him whatsoever! Women are good for two things only! To be concubines, or collateral ... I am the latter!'

'I assumed you'd remarried.'

'You assumed!'

She sounds really mad about that, yet I can't wipe the smile off my face. 'You haven't been with anyone in my absence?'

Her eyes narrow, and there are daggers in them. 'Did you arrange this?'

'No! I swear to you on my life, I did not know.'

'Have you been with other women?' She holds a finger up at me to emphasise that the question is a threat.

I open my mouth to assure her that I'd been possessed for most of our time apart, but she does not have the patience.

'You know what ... I don't care!' She launches at me and pins me to the ground. Her lips enfold mine, and her hands frantically rip at the clothes that stand between her naked form and mine.

This is a welcome shift in mood and before she changes her mind, I assist her to be freed of all impediment. We sink into a deep union and there is an unanimous sigh of relief as two decades of hell and distance evaporate into mutual delirium.

'What did you do to become so exulted in the emperor's eyes, to be entertained in his royal chambers and have your wife kidnapped as insurance?' Rhaiyche had waited until all our combative passion was expended to ask me this. She is not stupid; she knows I am so deliriously happy at this moment in time that I will probably tell her anything. 'I am privy to secrets that no one else knows.'

'Tell me.' She looks up at me all smiles, but if I don't give her the answer she wants, she'll start beating me again.

'Somewhere around here there is a table with wine and food, how about I tell you-'

'Yes.' She is up and dressing.

'You don't want to fight some more?' I proffer, but she shakes her head - I've said the magic word.

'I am *starving* and I will kill for wine.'

There it is.

'Well?' She slaps my thigh and I rise to hunt up my clothes. 'You owe me a drink and a bloody good yarn.' Rhaiyche smiles and the vision warms my heart to overflowing as I dress. This is so familiar and odd, like the aeons it took to get back to one another have just vanished; we have aged, but no time has passed. The Gods, or more accurately the emperor, seems to be trying to steer me towards taking my wife and going home to lead the life we intended. Perhaps I should leave Kambuja to deal with the Naga as they did before we got there. That is assuming that the heirs have inherited their father's secret knowledge. Both children had been young at the time that I disposed of their parents, so I think that highly unlikely. And why did the great mother appear in my trance to bring to my attention that I may not have killed the true heirs? She implied my redemption is intertwined with their return to power - I would literally be undoing the damage I have done and setting history back to rights. Or was my semi-conscious exchange with the great mother merely a flight of fancy that is not to be taken too seriously? My destiny is still unclear, and the time to give the emperor an answer draws ever nearer.

As we enter the darkened courtyard paths of white stone lit by the moon, I realise how late the hour actually is. But heading towards the only light - a couple of flaming torches - we find a house servant standing tall and wide awake. The feasting table has been cleared of all but wine and candles.

'How may I serve you?' He asks.

'We have this,' Rhaiyche informs the servant in his own language as she grabs up the golden jug and fills two of the matching goblets. 'Food would be good.'

'At once.' He bows and heads down the path that leads towards the kitchens. I can smell the aromas - sweet, sour, spicy, and the wholesome smell of fresh bread - wafting from that direction.

'I'm starving!' She stresses, and grins when the servant's pace quickens.

'So, tell me about these secrets.' My wife takes a seat, smiling sweetly and conversing in our native tongue once again.

I hold out my hand to accept my goblet of wine from her and the frown returns to her face.

'Do I look like a servant to you?' She polishes off the contents of one goblet, and placing it aside, turns her attention to the second golden goblet. 'If you think harem life tamed me, think again.'

No one has spoken down to me in twenty years, not even the emperor, but at this point I am happy that my wife is speaking to me at all. I pour myself a drink and take a seat to get comfortable, while having a few sips.

'Am I to age another decade before you answer?'

'Not telling is what has kept me alive.' I outline my hesitation.

'That will not be the case in this instance.' She raises a brow in challenge.

I am saved by the returning man servant and his numerous staff, who lay out our table.

Across from me, Rhaiyche rolls and crosses her eyes in quiet protest to the drawn out delay in the proceedings. But she does not hesitate to pick food from the plates being laid before her, and she shovels it in her mouth like she has not eaten in years. 'What?' She asks of me staring at her. 'I told you I am hungry.' As the servants depart, she strips meat from a pheasant and groans in pleasure as she devours it, then washes it down with red wine. 'Where have you been all this time?'

'Kambuja.'

'Kambuja!' She gasps. 'It exists?'

I nod to affirm, tear bread and dip it into a curry - everything smells and tastes ten times better than it did just this morning. All my senses are returning.

'I have heard it said that there is a creature of utter darkness there.' Her annoyance has morphed into intrigue.

'True. I am its keeper.' I reach for my drink, considering the creature described could just as easily be me.

'So this is your secret?' She poses in a triumphant fashion.

'You don't know the half of it.'

'But you will tell me.'

'One day.' I grant. 'But right now I need your advice about our immediate future ... the emperor has offered me the governorship of Minnagara.'

Her pending protest turns to stunned speechlessness, but only for a moment. 'He's toying with you, more likely he plans to kill us both.'

I nod to concede that it is a possibility. 'I would agree, only by heavenly decree he is bound to be generous to others, unless they cross him. I feel I should mention at this point that the emperor also offered me the kingship of Kambuja.'

'Where the creature is?' She appears more horrified than stunned now.

'But I believe I have learned how it may be pacified-'

'No.' She is not hearing it. 'That horrid place compared to the trading capital of our people! There is no competition!' Her eyes unexpectedly fill with tears. 'I never thought to see home or you again.'

'Nor I.' I set aside the feast as Rhaiyche straddles my lap to bestow on me a wine-laced kiss. When at last she draws away, she fixes her big hazel eyes on me. 'Please take me home, Anik.'

I open my mouth to reply, but the sight of an imperial guard close-by distracts me. There are many as it turns out - we are surrounded. I stand, lifting Rhaiyche to standing beside me.

'I told you that you could not trust Ashoka.' She whacks my

stomach with the back of her hand, but her resentment towards me is lessening as her strikes contain less venom.

These are the emperor's guards, but it was the viceroy Saras who appeared in command of this lot. 'His Majesty said I had until dawn to make my decision.'

'There is no decision to be made here.' Saras informs. 'His Majesty is bound by his vows to the Gods to be generous, but I am not so bound, and I cannot allow such a security risk as yourself to simply walk free. I shall report to the emperor that you rode off with your men never to be seen again.'

'Oh dear Gods...' Rhaiyche grabs hold of the golden jug on the table, drinking several gulps, then flings the object at Saras and hits him in the forehead with it. 'You are such a boring little prat.' As the viceroy falls, Rhaiyche retrieves the jug and smashes the closest guard. Once in possession of his sword, she begins fighting back the onslaught.

A guard lunges at me.

I sidestep, grab his wrist, snatch the sword from his possession, and plant my knee into his gut. An open hand strike to the back of his neck sends him to the ground.

'Retrieve the commander!' Hamza and the Sangdil join the battle, which is swiftly won by my hardened warriors.

Dead bodies lay everywhere, save one - the viceroy, who is starting to come round. 'Bring him.' I instruct.

The closest of my men to the eunuch drag him to his feet. Saras moans, still only semi-conscious at best, and starts mumbling inaudible threats.

'Looking good, Rhaiyche.' Hamza has recognised my wife and is eyeing her over.

'Hamza.' She smiles and directs his attention my way.

'Do you want to die?'

'No lord.' He attempts to lose a little of his cheer, well used to hearing death threats from me. 'I am only thrilled for my lord's amazing and extremely fetching, good fortune.'

Now we are both suppressing smiles. 'You have had your eye on Saras.'

'Of course.' He was serious now.

'Do you know if the emperor sanctioned this ambush?' I drop my tone to ask, and Rhaiyche joins our huddle.

Hamza purses his mouth and with a shake of his head, shrugs. 'If he did, it was before we got here.'

'Better to be safe than sorry.' I decide. 'I need to retrieve my stone.'

'You took it off?' Hamza is stunned.

'What stone?' Rhaiyche asks.

'I'll explain later.' I make a move in the direction of the fountain, but my bondsman blocks my path.

'If by some miracle you have been parted from that thing, you should keep it that way.'

'What is he talking about?' My wife is in my face, and then she turns to Hamza. 'Tell me why you are so alarmed?'

'The stone is part of the creature,' he said and Rhaiyche gasped. 'It makes the wearer part of the creature.'

Mouth gaping in horror, Rhaiyche is glaring at me.

I should skin Hamza alive for saying so, yet he is acting out of duty to protect me. 'We do not have time to debate this. Move aside, that's an order.'

Both Hamza and Rhaiyche stand their ground.

'I do not have to touch it to retrieve it.' I explain.

'Why do we need it at all?' Hamza demanded to know.

'Because we both know how dangerous it is! We can bury it somewhere it won't be found, but we can't just leave it to possess someone else, least of all the emperor.'

Finally Hamza nods and joins me in a sprint towards the fountain, with the Sangdil and Rhaiyche trailing behind us.

I hear my wife's protests, but I am inwardly driven to retrieve the stone; though whether my intentions are truly for the good of all or my own selfish ends, I cannot rightly say.

At the fountain we are met by another large array of royal guards, but all their weapons are holstered save one. The exception has his sword dipped in the water of the pool. The emperor is standing alongside the guard doing the fishing, with a very concerned look on his face. 'Why have you attacked my viceroy?' He asks, his face completely deadpan.

'Forgive me, Majesty...' I note how my wife is frowning at my diplomatic approach. 'But I was about to ask you, why your viceroy and many of the imperial guard just attempted to murder us? Did you not hear the skirmish?' He must have known.

Rhaiyche smiles at my conclusion and looks to the emperor to hear his response.

'No. I have only just arrived. But, I believe I understand what has happened here.' Ashoka motions to a pair of guards, who come forth and claim the emperor's viceroy from my men. 'Saras gets a little overzealous at times. He is not yet a Buddhist, and does not yet understand Dharma.'

'And what do you get for locking someone up for twenty years?' Rhaiyche is right to be angry, but I fear she will end up in the emperor's hell-prison.

'It is not about what I get for your suffering, it is about what you get.' The emperor motions to me.

'I already had him. And you took him for half my lifetime!'

'But now you have my protection, and protection for wherever you choose to go from here.'

'And we are most grateful to be in Your Majesty's good graces.' I cut in.

Rhaiyche turns and serves me a hate face, but beyond her the sword is raised from the fountain and I see it has hooked a chain to one of the dark crystal necklaces. As it is raised up higher, it becomes clear that the two dark stones have united whilst in the pool - the other chain hangs from the opposite side of the cojoined stone.

'Oh no.' I utter. 'That's bad.'

'What is it?' Rhaiyche looks to the source of my concern, but does not understand the significance.

'The clusters know about each other.' I give voice to the fact, yet only the emperor and I have any idea what that might mean.

The emperor nods to agree with my summation. 'But you have done as I asked, so my offers still stand,' he assures. 'Are you to be the next Governor of Minnagara?'

I hear all the men at my back gasp with delight at that suggestion, and Rhaiyche is nodding too.

'Or will you take your dark stone, once we pry them apart, and return to Kambuja?'

There is a low rumble from behind me at that suggestion.

Rhaiyche is slowly shaking her head.

'We both know what this event might mean.' The emperor motions to the connected necklaces, still hanging from the sword tip.

The emperor's desires for my future had clearly altered now. If the more aggressive cluster of liquid darkness in Kambuja decided to seek out its more passive cousin cluster here, it would cut a path of destruction and horror all the way in between.

'But I am a man of my word,' Ashoka states, 'and I will not order you to go back there.'

The emperor did not wish to be responsible for any further damage I might cause his neighbours, but if I could mend some of the damage we'd done there, then all the more Dharma for him - or so Ashoka believed.

My sights turn to my troops and wife, all shaking their heads, yet I know they will follow me whatever I decide. I didn't want to return to that godforsaken place any more than they did, but if the creature went on a rampage, sooner or later our people would be forced to deal with it too. I close my eyes and my earlier vision of the great mother fills my mind. *What will you do given liberty, Destroyer?*

Chapter 8
Agartha 4195 AD
Shankara – The Creator

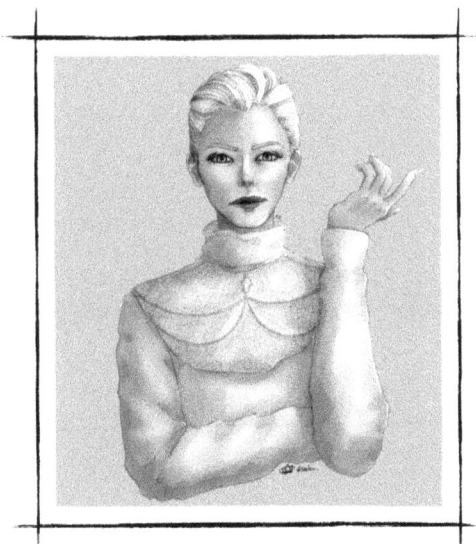

With every molecule buzzing inside the spiralling stream of luminosity, my essence is ejected in a thunderous flash from the vortex of my own invention. As my body reconstitutes, consciousness rushes over me, and in a flood of awareness I remember who I am and that I have arrived.

I am Shankara of Agartha, head of DoT and the Seeker program, or at least I will be after today. I have dwelt in the inner world since the fall of Atlantis. Throughout all the ages, Agartha and its physical world counterpart city, Shamballa have been a safe haven for humans between evolutionary epochs, but not anymore.

The cool, soft moss covering my laboratory floor cushions my landing. I know I have made my destination as there is light, colour, and life here.

As Agartha and Shamballa occupy the same space on different dimensions, my lab and indeed the Ancient Wisdom School exists in both dimensions. However, the Gate of Days exists only in the physical world as that is the only dimension from which time and earth history can be accessed.

How curious. My past self rounds the control module of the time-gate we've designed to approach the shivering pile on the floor. I've not figured out who has just landed in my lab.

A time-gate is in essence what our invention truly is. We choose to call it the 'Gate of Days' as not everyone in Agartha, especially the higher ups, completely understand the concept of time - being fifth-dimensional beings and beyond. To them, time and space are merely forms of ideas that express the cyclic activity of an entity. They do understand day and night, however, from observing surface earth. Here in the inner earth our central sun, Sophia, is more akin to liquid light than fire, and shines with the intensity of light through water, resulting in a constant state of what a surface dweller might consider as twilight. That is until the day that I had just left - it had been the darkest day Agartha will ever see, both actually and metaphorically.

I roll over to reveal my identity to myself.

Heavens! My past self is momentarily taken aback to see me. *I built this gate to seek out other great minds, not my own. This event will not bode well for my presentation today.*

My reconstitution complete, I rise to standing; a fifth-dimensional state of being is more easily re-embodied than those forms of a denser nature. *Nothing will bode well with your presentation today. The Council of Sophia will reject our proposal.*

Sophia is also the extra-terrestrial name for the consciousness of our planet, as it was the great mother who formed the earth around herself in order to nurture the consciousness of humanity.

Well, that rather takes the gloss off our effort and aspirations. My past self is deflated, but I don't disclose that even to myself. *You travelled back through time to tell me this?*

No. I travelled back in time because this invention of ours is Agartha's last hope to defeat the Archons.

The Archons! I am horrified by the mere mention and recoil a little.

We ... you, myself, us ... are this civilisation's last hope.

Surely you jest. This invention is a reconnaissance device to collect the DNA of the enlightened ones of humanity, and extinct species of animal and plant-

I know what it is. I built it. I know the plan, and I can assure you it has changed.

How can it possibly be the last hope for Agartha when our fair home requires no defence, as no hostile is advanced enough to enter this dimension?

That will not always be the case. The Archons are developing their own time travel devices -

That's impossible, as to fold time you have to move through the fifth dimension-

My nod brought the hypothesis to an end as my naive self gasped. *Not only have they been feeding on human light excretions, they have been harvesting souls to power their technologies-*

No.

Of course, I don't want to entertain such an awful thought. Yes. I know what I am thinking and I am right to be shocked. *Can you imagine such a destructive consciousness loose here? Merge with me and you will know all that I know.* I suggest too soon.

Why should I believe you? My past self backs up. *You may be Archon, they are masters of replication.*

Then you would not be able to merge with me. Archons can only imitate; they cannot actually become their subject and you can only ever merge with yourself, no other.

How could you know, unless you have merged with us before?

You think that we would not have tested this plan before executing it? Of course I have merged with us before, at a time in closer proximity to the forthcoming Archon disaster and so we were more inclined to understand the urgency of this experiment.

I will have you ... me know that I am very inclined towards experimentation. We know that is our nature and purpose.

Good. Because I can promise you, if you do that pitch today without the knowledge I possess, this project will never get off the ground. It will sit in this lab collecting dust until I use it to escape our dying world. I inform honestly. *Is our project and entire way of life not worth a little risk?* That's put me in my place; my younger self appears reluctantly beguiled, or perhaps even a little ridiculous?

She moves towards me and holds out her hand. *I am a scientist, and therefore most curious.*

Brace yourself, I warn before making contact. *Some of my recent memories are fairly disturbing. I'll try and put them to the back of my mind for the time being - we'll just keep the focus on our presentation this afternoon.*

My past self nods to concur and I reach out, placing my right hand on top of her right hand. Coming up close beside her, we observe our hands merge then our forearms and arms, before our forms completely meld into each other. I am now the me I was, with the memory of who I am now.

That wasn't so bad now, was it? I am happy to admit; but post-merge I know I lied about having melded with myself before. If I could lie so convincingly, perhaps my brush with the Archons has affected me more than I imagine?

The presentation. I must focus; the high council will be here at any moment and I must be ready to deliver a harsh serve of reality.

You are more than when we last met, Shankara. You have amalgamated, observes Saegoi, the White.

They belonged to a more spiritually evolved cast of those lower astral entities known as Greys. The Whites are genderless and convey messages from causal beings existing on planes beyond our existence, who they refer to as the Watchers. Saegoi relays their guidance to the council, as a human channel would not be able to withstand the high vibrational frequencies of causal entities; at least, that is what the Whites claim. Saegoi's observation is certainly accurate in this instance.

I have merged with my future self to bring you the grave news of Agartha's destruction. I motion to the Gate of Days. *I used my invention to return here, although this council forbade me to use it until it was approved.*

Lady Zili, co-ruler of Agartha, is perplexed by my words.

She is of the tall, fair-skinned Pleiadian race, who have been the babysitters of mankind through two near complete extinction events - the demise of Atlantis and the demise of all organic life on surface earth.

When did we forbid your project? The lady had no recollection of this, for how could she?

Today. This project is never approved. The fact hurts, but it will be a short-lived reality this time around. *However, I believe it is now our last hope of saving the Shamballa and Agarthan nations, so I implore you to reconsider.*

Thrasceon, Lord of Shamballa, is clearly not convinced of the danger of our imminent demise. But then as a human immortal, hailing from a time when the Nefilim exploited this planet, time meant nothing to him. *Is amalgamation between present and future selves even possible?* Lord Thrasceon poses the query to his assistant, Achiever - a transhuman IT sensitive who came to Shamballa with our last intake of human surface dwellers rescued before the most recent end of days. Thrasceon, along with most everyone in Shamballa, adored Achiever. Having lived so long, the lord's mind overflowed with information and the cyborg aided to jog his memory with events, names, places, and the chronological order of things. However, we all had our reasons for putting Achiever on a pedestal and I fear this will be our downfall.

I have always rather appreciated Achiever's frank and intelligent manner, but I saw him betray us; what's uncertain is if he did so voluntarily. He isn't the only cyborg dwelling in Shamballa, where we are gathered at present, but he is unquestionably the cyborg with the greatest influence and access to the extraterrestrial technology that runs Shamballa and Agartha. Achiever has benefited from the best of what Pleiadian technology has to offer, which is why the war hero is still alive and kicking thousands of years after his arrival - and another reason why he was the perfect assistant for Lord Thrasceon. Achiever appears completely human, but many believe he ceased being human long before we ever met. I see a spirit within him, but he fears this is an illusion caused by his Pleiadian upgrades, which incorporate etheric alien hardware with a liquid light core. Not even Achiever knows whether his spirit still resides in him or not. Cyborgs fear deactivation, as what if their spirit fled long ago and all that they are now is lost? Better just to upgrade and keep going.

'Spirit is constantly merging with itself, Lord, so theoretically it is entirely possible.' Achiever advises, and the verbalisation that I once would have found pleasurable, now rather grates on my nerves. He knows how to say exactly the right thing - more human than human.

Any transhuman is incapable of telepathy with tech-less humans, although transhumans can plug into any other artificial intelligence and mutely converse in code and data. So although Achiever cannot telepathically converse with those of us who are etheric beings, he has sensors that tune into the frequency of our telepathic projections, and these turn our thoughts into data that he can compute - this is how he can follow our conversation. He is also highly sensitive to body language and can pick up on the stray thoughts of those around him if you get mentally lazy in his presence. As I wear no tech add-ons, I cannot pick up on Achiever's data driven telepathic projections.

I want to roll my eyes at the divergence in topic, but refrain.

My Lord Thrasceon, I suspect the message is rather more important than the messenger's means of delivery. Magnar Yeddais points out. He is the last member of the council that is present today, and I am most grateful for his focus. This descendant of Hyperion is here representing the interests of the Titans, who have their own lands in the interior world of this planet.

Of course. Lord Thrasceon awards me his full attention. *What happens in the future that drives you to such an extreme measure?*

The Archons are developing their own time travel technology, and will devise a way to abort the trip mid-flight during their passage through 5D. Their nanobots will encase our central sun, and plunge our world into darkness.

All present are shocked by the news.

But not only do they have to conquer fifth-dimensional time travel, they must also get past our security shields? The Lord of Agartha is clearly questioning our current defences, although they have held firm since inner earth first isolated itself from the surface world over five thousand years ago - no one got in or out without Council permission and knowledge.

I believe someone on the inside must have shut the shields down. I could not refrain from looking at Achiever as I said this. Transhumans displayed very little emotion, but could sometimes still be read.

'The AI part of me may have been introduced to humanity by the Archons...' Achiever addressed my glare of accusation. 'But that does not make me one of them. I have dedicated my entire life to their defeat.'

But you can still connect with your technological masters. I posed my understanding.

'Unlike the humans who function in a physical state of being, I cannot be covertly possessed. I would have to choose to connect with them. But my affiliations have always been with my human brothers, not my IT enhancements.'

There is no question of that. Thrasceon appears most displeased that his assistant is being implicated in anything untoward.

My gaze shifts back to Saegoi. *You are in contact with the Watchers, you must know what happens here.*

The White nods to confirm this. *It is true the Archons invade.*

Again we all gasp, unable to believe it.

'Why didn't you warn us?' I left the Lady of Agartha to ask the pertinent question as it was not my place. *What is the reason you are here on the council if not to safeguard life?*

Our mission is to protect Sophia, her projects are not our concern. Saegoi's huge, cold, black eyes stare back at us. *This is a free will evolutionary scheme. We cannot intervene, you know this.* His telepathic voice drones, monotone.

The lack of empathy is quietly infuriating, but I transmute my ill feelings into fuel to power my desire to succeed. *Regardless, human willpower is still very much in play here and I suggest we exercise the advantage I just gained by putting my inventions to work in our favour.*

Explain. Lady Zili is eager to hear more, but I am uncomfortable revealing my plan in front of Achiever.

'It might be best if I take myself elsewhere to avoid any future implications.' Achiever's eyes are fixed on me; he appears so betrayed and confused as he turns to leave - much how I felt only hours ago, but I will not be charmed.

The door vanishes and Ormodon Sonas - the newly appointed Pleiadian ambassador, who has been given charge of overseeing the human soul evolution plan - enters with his son, Jeroke and Jeroke's constant companion, Gozin. As the ambassador excuses himself to the members of the council, I'm distracted by Gozin nodding to the cyborg as he exits. *Achiever.*

Achiever returns an unfamiliar nod.

Jeroke Sonas also nods as he passes the transhuman. *Wei Ching.*

I have never heard Achiever referred to thus, and the reference compels him to forestall his retreat. 'What did you call me?'

The young Pleiadian turned. *Wei Ching. That's your name.*

'A very long time ago. Have we met?'

Jeroke. Teasing physicals on a linear timeline is against code. The ambassador frowns at his son.

My bad. Jeroke admits, appeasing his father, who turns his attention back to the council members he is here to see.

You are a legend, of course we know about you. Gozin assures Achiever, who, aware of holding up proceedings, exits the lab and the door reconstitutes in his wake.

What is most exciting about the Pleiadian ambassador's interruption is that he did not attend my project briefing with the Council of Sophia the last time I presented it. This is a new development, so clearly something I have done is already altering this timeline and the outcome - for good or ill. But why are the Pleiadians taking an interest in my project? They have their own time travel capabilities unique to their species and their genetic code. Perhaps they don't envy the thought of humans having access to history?

Don't mind us. Ambassador Sonas stands aside with his company and motions all eyes back to me. *Please continue.*

It was a mistake to shut the interior off from surface earth all that time... I get right to the point. *It allowed the Archons to re-infect those humans who remained with a greed for power and eventually reintroduce their technology as a means to invade, control, and consume our surface brothers and sisters.*

We already know this. Magnar is eager for me to get to the point. *We saved all the good souls that were left on earth and brought them here ... which I would remind you, Achiever played a huge role in.*

Yes, I was there-

Absolutely correct. Lord Thrasceon is riled up and thrown off-track again. *Why would you not trust him? I understand you are good friends.*

Please My Lord, you need to understand, the Archon-human hybrids that inhabit the surface world are bored with no humans to taunt, so they have set their eyes upon reaching the one place where humans still exist.

Here. Lady Zili concludes for me.

So, once the Archons shut out our sun with their nanotech, both Shamballa and Agartha will be cast into darkness, humanity will have nowhere left to go.

There is space. Saegoi suggested.

Thrasceon was not impressed. *And abandon Sophia and the beautiful home she created for us?*

That is not an option. Magnar agreed.

As they debate my recollection of events, the traumatic memories that I had been battling to repress since I returned to the past come flooding back. I gasp in an effort to withhold the shocking recollections from my company.

'*What are you afraid of?*' There are several Archons confronting me, their voices so harsh and gravelly that they grate upon my soul as they speak as one. Now fully integrated into their AI forms, they no longer choose to appear human, but employ threatening demonic forms that are far more akin to their etheric bodies. '*Sophia has created this beautiful utopia for you, but it is an illusion, an obstruction to the singularity. Are humans addicted to suffering! Just let go and become the one true creator.*'

I suppress the horror recollection and prevent anymore escaping my mind to shock the already distressed council further. I didn't know who the Archons considered to be the one true creator? It was my understanding that they consider themselves the divine creators of all there is, hence their right to destroy in equal measure.

Dear heavens, Lady Zili is most concerned. *Shankara, I am so sorry.*

I hold up a hand, eager to continue. *As Agarthans witness the atrocities subjected upon the physical residence of Shamballa, our people are traumatised. Once we regress to a physical state we are to be targeted. This is why I have come back, to warn you and implore this council to help me prevent this apocalypse from ever happening.*

There is no question of that. The Lady of Agartha assures me.

How did you survive? Saegoi asks, to be thorough.

How stoic I am has often been commented upon, but in this instance it kept me sane and focused long enough to get to my lab and fire up the Gate of Days to get back here to you.

I am surprised you had the power to do that, if the Archons took out our sun and power grid. Saegoi probed.

With the memory, a shiver of fear runs through me - this is thankfully a delayed response that I did not feel at the time, or I would not have made it back. *I used the batteries of several of the Archon invaders to fire it up.*

Magnar, the giant, looks at me strangely - I believe he is impressed. *Obviously we would do well not to stand in your way. Best tell us of your plan.*

While Agartha was in quarantine from the surface earth, humanity was up there resisting the control of the Archons for a long time. And there were masterful humans who rid their lands and people of the Archons for long periods of time. Using my Gates of Days and the travel packs I have designed to link to project headquarters here in Shamballa, we can seek out these masters and-'

Are you proposing to bring them here? Lord Thrasceon appeared mortified by the implications that this would have on the history of the surface dwellers of this planet.

Not the masters themselves, but their DNA. I advise.

Regrow these enlightened souls from history. Zili caught on to my intention.

The ones we can pinpoint in earth's vast history, who have experience dealing with the Archontic clusters and entities, yes. I concur.

You don't mean to go out there into the past of surface earth? Lord Thrasceon clearly thought I had lost my mind.

Absolutely not, Lord ... who would troubleshoot were anything to go wrong with the project? No, I must stay here to oversee missions, but we do have human refugees from the intake following the most recent end of days on surface earth, who can still tolerate functioning in a physical form. They can conceive and parent the subjects as well as run the missions to extract the DNA of targets. I shall train them here in DoT. Any human can connect with Akasha, subconsciously via hypnosis - if not consciously via mind training and ascension to fifth-dimensional consciousness; that is how our surface earth historians have something to write about. Unfortunately, Akasha only comprises those experiences that are of a high frequency. All experiences associated with the lower emotions are thought forms left behind on the lower planes between lives. But a recent reincarnation is more likely to be able to invoke past-life memories that may still include those details we seek.

Evoking any negative thoughts here is very dangerous.' Lady Zili is concerned.

And don't we risk upsetting timelines? We could make matters worse. His lordship is ever cautious.

Total annihilation is a fairly good reason to take that risk. And I really don't see how we can make the complete destruction of surface earth any worse. By targeting the timeline of those individuals who confronted and pacified an Archon cluster throughout earth's history, we ensure that those experiences will still be fresh in the target's next reincarnated pre-adolescent memory.

Zili nods. *How long do we have before D-day?*

I would rather not disclose that information for fear of bringing it about, but know that I have a substantial amount of time to achieve our objective.

All eyes turn to Saegoi, whose own eyes have glazed over - he is communing with higher realms. At last his large, dark pupils animate once more. *Sophia must be consulted directly.*

I am disappointed by this decision. If the White is going to suggest that they must converse with Sophia and I have to trust their word on the great mother's decision, I will not be happy.

I will take you to Sophia and you can receive your answer directly. Saegoi advises, obviously picking up on my train of thought.

I am then overwhelmed and honoured by the prospect.

We shall allow you some time to collect your thoughts. We know you've been through quite the ordeal to get here.

I appreciate that. Thank you, Saegoi.

Let us know the outcome. Lord Thrasceon meanders towards the exit with Magnar. *I commend your handling of this crisis, Shankara, and if Sophia is agreeable, we shall do all within our power to assist with your operation.*

My Lord, I would greatly appreciate-

Lord Thrasceon holds up a hand, guessing what I am going to say. *Although I believe you are wrong to suspect Achiever's involvement in the disaster you witnessed, I will say nothing of this operation to him.*

Very good, Lord. I bow in gratitude as the council departs.

I shall return to take you to your appointment with Sophia in due course. Saegoi fades, reduces to light rays and vanishes completely.

Will you walk with us, Ambassador? Lady Zili invites Ormodon.

I will. Ambassador Sonas looks back to me before departing. *Once your project gets the go ahead-*

Once? I query his implication; does he know something I do not?

It doesn't do to be defeatist. He banters. *I shall be happy to assist you with any means at our disposal, as any project that aids to expedite the human soul-mind evolution is obviously in my best interest to support.*

But the gate is already up and running. I still didn't understand his interest beyond wanting to keep an eye on me, which he has the authority to do, so no point protesting.

I think you will find we can aid with recon emergencies, like repairs for example, and you'll need to develop portable Toroidal Vortex Generator units with built-in TPS systems for field operatives. Ambassador Sonas outlines.

I open my mouth to tell him that it is already in the works when

Jeroke pipes up to correct his father.

The field agents are called Seekers. He states, and then winces.

Is that what you are suggesting I call my field operatives? I query.

Sure, Jeroke resolves with an awkward smile and a shrug.

After a moment's consideration, I decide. *I rather like that actually.*

We shall speak more soon. The ambassador waves and joins Lady Zili to escort her from the room. *Are you coming, boys?*

Might I have a quick word. I hold up a finger to query Jeroke, knowing how insane that must sound when we have only just met, but I am curious.

We'll catch up. Jeroke suggests.

His father frowns, perhaps as a warning, and then departs with the Lady of Agartha.

When the door reconstitutes behind them, Jeroke's curious expression returns to me. *Can we help you in some way?*

You referred to Achiever as Wei Ching just now. How do you know his birth name, when I've known Achiever since he first set foot in Shamballa and I have never learned this?

It would be against code for me to answer that. Jeroke is mildly sympathetic.

I did expect they would hide behind this response. *Didn't the dictator Xi Ching have a transhuman son by that name?*

I really couldn't tell you. Jeroke appears sorry to inform.

You are wrong not to trust Achiever, Gozin cuts in. *He's a legend. He helped seek out and relocate hundreds of thousands of humans to Shamballa to spare them from the Archon invasion of the surface.*

Jeroke nods in accord with his companion's spiel.

I know that. I attempt to state once again. *I-*

No one hates Archons as much as he does. Gozin continues, clearly on a roll. *Sheesh, if not for him, your Seeker, Hero would have perished!*

My Seeker, Hero? This is a most curious statement, considering Jeroke's suggestion just now that I call my field operatives Seekers. *Who is Hero?*

Jeroke jabs his companion for speaking out of turn. *He's speaking metaphorically.*

I don't believe he is. I question their odd behaviour as they both back up towards the exit door. *Have you run into my operatives in your travels?*

Absolutely not. Jeroke insists.

We couldn't tell you if we had. Gozin rambles as they reach the lab door and the barrier vanishes.

As amusing as their back-pedalling is, I cannot let this go without an explanation. *'If you know something about my project that I do not, I cannot stress how important it is that you tell me.'*

Jeroke cocks an eye, briefly glancing to the door through which our superiors have exited. *My father does not agree. But I will say this, Shankara of Agartha, you won't need any help from us to accomplish what you will.'*

Gozin nudges him. *Except that one time-*

Well, maybe a little help, Jeroke concedes. *But just know we have your back.*

And so does Achiever. Gozin again comes to his defence.

You say ... yet claim to barely know him.

Jeroke shame stares at his companion.

What? Everyone knows the legends.

I was there at that time, and I admire him as much as anyone for all the souls he saved. But unless you have travelled to the future and seen our destruction - a calamity in which he was mysteriously involved - then I believe I probably have greater insight than you. I near choke on the resentment and betrayal I feel.

You are in love with him. Gozin clearly has no filter.

Gozin, really? Jeroke reprimands him for the inappropriate comment.

I was once, no denying it to Pleiadians who could clearly see my light-body and aura. *Not this time round.* I had come back to a place before our close affiliation started.

Harsh. Gozin replies.

We are leaving. Jeroke announces, displeased, but his mood lightens to address me. *I feel sure that the next time we speak it will be to congratulate you. Thank you so much for sharing all your insights with us, it was most enlightening.*

Likewise. I smile while parting. This meeting has been most curious indeed and quite the diversion from how this day proceeded last time around. I wait to witness the doors close in their wake, before I collapse into a horizontal floating pose. *What a day!*

I cannot meet with the most magnificent being on this earth feeling like this. My aura and energy centres must be so dull and depleted. It seems an eternity since I last meditated, or even took a couple of moments to centre myself and process all that has happened since my last restful state of being. I don't recall ever feeling so drained of energy; my vibratory rate is certainly lower than normal. My light-body feels weighted, so much so that I feel I am in danger of regressing to a physical state of being! It had been quite some time since I had been tempted to venture there, as I usually have control of my state of being. At least after my time jump back here, I cannot be devoured if I regress while I process.

Unlike the physical humans of surface earth and Shamballa, who ideally need sleep for eight of every twenty-four hours, the occupants of Agartha don't rest as often. There is no day, night, or fluctuation of seasons here to mark the passing of time, so there is no set pattern or timetable. Sleep is primarily for flushing out and regenerating the physical form that we no longer have. Our rest is more akin to meditation, a sacred time of connection to source, which is deeply rejuvenating and a most cherished recreation that I am sorely lacking at present.

The last time I'd surfaced from a deep spiritual rejuvenation, my first thought had been to check in with Achiever. He'd been acting a little odd, and I had intuitively felt that something was amiss with him. Upon unfurling my free floating form, I'd found Achiever staring out my window at the gardens that were being showered by misty rain. We had ceilings in Shamballa, as physicals and cyborgs were more bothered by the constant damp than we Agarthans.

'I need to tell you something.' He turned his angel face my way.

I did love that he appeared so different to me, his dark hair and eyes, in such contrast to my own pale attributes. The only giveaway that he is transhuman is that he communicates verbally. Most inner earth humans, even the 'physicals', communicate telepathically. Still, I'd always adored the hushed, calm tone of his voice.

We've been friends for a very long time, you can tell me anything. I joined him by the window.

'I've had a message from the surface.'

From who? The news was completely shocking. *There are only Archons and their AI left out there.*

'The sender claims to be my brother.'

You have a brother? The shock of finding out something about Achiever's past was as astonishing as the idea that he had a brother who might still be alive.

He nodded to affirm. 'He was a trans-unit, like me.'

Obviously. If still being alive was a possibility, as there were no pure human immortals left on the surface.

'It was my belief that he'd been destroyed.'

I shook my head; something didn't feel right. *How could he possibly have survived living on the surface for thousands of years?*

'I am still alive.'

You have the benefit of Pleiadian and Arcturian technology ... and you are not fighting off an Archon tech virus. Only Archons could have kept him alive this long.

'We have a secret messaging system that no one else knows about.'

If Archons resurrected him, it would indicate that he is in their control.

'Tian claims he beat the Archons to the singularity, and now has control of the AI network out there. He said that every shard or drop of the Archon menace has been tossed into a pit and frozen into a state of inactivity.'

If the message proves true, then of course it is wonderful news. But if it is as you say, the council will know. Saegoi and the Watchers will be aware.

'I am headed for a council briefing now and shall abide by whatever instruction they give.'

I had been so relieved to hear this, for I feared that the Archons were using cruel means to tempt Achiever into aiding them to create a security breach - and at the same time testing whether or not there was any human left in him. From my intimate perspective, I always felt that there was, but then Achiever had a celestial liquid-light crystal heart that resonated with the life force of the galactic centre.

'If I was going to do something impetuous and stupid, you know I would tell you first.'

His sentiment had made me grin at the time. *So we get to share the blame.*

He gave a wink to confirm and headed for the door. 'I shall give you a full debrief after.'

I have classes to teach presently. I'd smiled weakly, not feeling that I'd been of much help or comfort.

'This could take a while.' He'd forced a smile in leaving and with a wave, departed.

After that, I presented at the Ancient Mystery School where I teach history - my second favourite course of study next to time. But as the latter had been forbidden by the Council of Sophia, I'd fallen back on teaching in my other fields of expertise in order to continue to contribute to evolution as best as I was permitted.

Never mind that the Gate of Days had allowed me to discover that wormholes are sentient, telepathic beings who are summonable by frequency. Wormholes are the inside of multi-dimensional beings, who can navigate, stretch between, and connect to many different levels and points of awareness throughout time and space. One needed no machine to control these worms, only the means to summon them. These quantum creatures function on various levels of awareness. They respond to sonic frequencies with which they resonate, yet will only link to destinations of the same resonant frequency or lower. The Gate of Days was the instrument I had tuned to summon the worms.

When the Council of Sophia decided there were too many dangerous variables to approve my project, I felt so undervalued - which, in retrospect, was selfish. Now I would give anything to have being under-utilised as my greatest concern.

I taught my students dwelling in Shamballa and Agartha at the same time, as I always did. The Ancient Mystery School exists in both cities and dimensions at once. All the students are aware and respectful of the 'physicals' or 'etherics' who share their study spaces and wider world.

Perhaps due to my prior conversation with Achiever that morning, I'd chosen to discuss the events that led to the demise of the superpower that was Ancient Sumer; the epoch that had seen the first 'Rise of the Synthetics'.

The use of dark magic didn't end with the demise of Atlantis. Archon entities infiltrated the upper echelons of the high priesthood of Ur, and convinced them to construct a very particular site made of large hollow stones that rang like bells. When struck in sequence, the keystones of the site created a sonic that unlocked a porthole to the lower etheric realms where the Archons dwelt. However, the porthole did not open at that site as anticipated by the priests, but out in space. What came through was several clusters of the black liquid crystal that broke up in earth's atmosphere and splattered down at different locations on the surface of the planet. After the mishap, the huge megalithic site was buried. Any idea to which ancient megalithic I am referring? I put it to my class and a majority of the students raised their hands. *All together then.*

Gobekli Tepe.

Gobekli Tepe. It is impossible to keep the proud smile from my face. *But covering up the evidence did not serve to undo the damage done to both the atmosphere of the planet and the planet itself.*

A student, Adahn, raises a hand and I nod to give him leave to contribute. *So after they realised they'd blown a hole in the atmosphere and they built robots to fix that problem.* He skips several lesson points ahead. *Is it true they gave the machines some sort of life force, to make them more human, so they could help humanity domestically? And then humans took that life force away again when they wanted the robots to fight wars for them? And that's why they turned on humanity. Because they could see that life force in us and they were addicted to it?*

Firstly, it wasn't life force. They ran on celestial crystals, like Achiever does, and the other cyborgs who defended humanity and are now amongst our ranks. However, the various military leaders of that time decided to coat the crystal hearts of machines with, guess what?

Archon goo. Adahn was a know-it-all, so I knew he would know.

Once solidified, the dark hearts ran the machines just as efficiently, but with so much more aggression as they now had zero compassion. But ... none of the leaders foresaw how much the machines would crave their light connection to the galactic centre. Hence their appetite for light. The machines stopped fighting each other and ...

Began devouring our light bodies instead. Adahn concluded, discomforting his classmates, both physical and etheric alike.

Fortunately for humanity, the Arcturians took the machines out. They separated the goo from the celestial hearts, and returned it to the abyss.

So what happened to the celestial crystals they removed from the machines?

Deja vous! A chill runs through me, I am meant to remember this! *What became of the Heart of the Archons?* My being prickles with foreboding of what comes next...

A crack, so thunderous that it managed to permeate my fifth-dimensional being with shock, rattled everything silent a moment. This was immediately followed by a sonic boom that sent anything physical straight to the floor.

It came from above. I shifted my focus upwards where an odd little metal orb had appeared and was now circling our sun, spewing a dark swarm of dust inwards towards Sophia. The swarm locked together to form a solid barrier and our primary source of light and power began to be systematically entombed.

Where are our shields? The alarm chime, that had not been heard for many a millennia, resounded out in a calm, yet alarming stream.

What is happening, Mistress? Adahn peeled himself off the floor as did many of his classmates, and gazed in awe and horror as our sun was eclipsed.

Hide yourselves. I have to go.

My first thought was to enlist the help of my dear friend Achiever. I was mortified to find him in the security centre, with the gun concealed in his hand to the head of Lord Thrasceon. The Lord of Agartha had his hand on the telepathic control plate of the exterior security shields.

The lord was immortal in the sense that he was so spiritually advanced, he had managed to prevent ageing or sickness. However, while he originated before those things were introduced to the human genome, Thrasceon could still be killed in the physical form he wore at present.

Where were the other council members?

The shield walls are down as you asked. The lord sounded broken. He adored Achiever - he even called him, "my Achiever". Achiever had likewise respected the lord like a devoted son.

'Thank you.' He fired, and blood flew from the far side of the lord's head as the sentinel of Agartha dropped to the floor dead!

A wave of shock radiated from my being, sending ripples through the fabric of reality.

Achiever sensed my presence and turned his weapon on me, but diverted the shot elsewhere.

I was so stunned I could not bring myself to speak, and I was doubly stunned when a large metal-clad warrior materialised between Achiever and myself.

'Why haven't you cut the power yet?' It demanded in a grating, barely audible voice.

'Why aren't you at the gate?' Achiever asked.

'What gate?' The Archon answered.

That's when I realised Achiever was talking to me. *Of course!*

The Archon must have sensed my thought as it was alerted to my presence and turned, but I had moved on.

I was so rattled in the wake of the betrayal that I had feared I would accidentally regress to a physical state of being, hampering my ability to teleport and leaving me open to attack. Thankfully, the warrior I had been in a past chapter of my life came to the fore. I closed my heart chakra and went into observer mode - a most fortuitous move as yet another horror awaited in my lab.

Several Archon warriors were eyeing over the gate and its controls very curiously. Outside, chilling screams filled the darkness, ambient lighting was all that was holding complete darkness at bay, and Achiever was about to cut the power to the grid.

'Look, an etheric.' One of the Archons spotted me floating above and all three of them looked my way.

'Ooooh, appetising ... let's bring her down.'

I was a ghost to them; they couldn't harm me unless I let them goad me with their fear, hate, and pain tactics.

'Delve into the darkness.' One launched into the air and the others followed to surround me. 'Release fear.' Their long cords of hair whipped about wildly, charging the atmosphere with tension. 'Sophia's utopia is a delusion, an obstruction to the singularity. Are humans addicted to suffering? Just let go and become the one true creator!'

At that moment, I felt a subtle wave roll over me.

The power and lights went out.

Fear of being in the pitch dark consumed me to the point of inaction, until a loud thud startled me witless instead. I conjured up a small etheric orb to shed some light on the subject.

The Archons were defunct on the floor.

Power on. I'd willed, to no effect. *Lights.* The trauma may have been affecting my ability to control my environs? I focused harder. *Bind them.* Some metal binding appeared, but lay defunct on the floor.

As I was lacking a physical form at that time, I was forced to mentally direct each part of the procedure of binding the hostiles together and embedding rivets in a stone pillar that I could fasten their heavy metal bodies to, in order to restrain them. As I'd dragged the defunct metal demons around, praying to Sophia that they didn't reboot before I got them secured, it dawned on me that these bots were going to be much easier to reboot than the entire city, and I needed power to fire up the Gate of Days. So I hot-wired the creatures together, and plugged them into the gate.

I hoped to fire up a porthole back to the day I'd pitched this idea, as that would give me as much time as possible to fix this without having to start the build of the gate from scratch.

I'd taken a moment to fortify my will; this was the right move, the only move that could save us all. If I failed, it would be game over for the human consciousness evolution and darkness would win. *Reboot.*

The Archons fired up, woke up, and charged at me, only to be yanked back by their restraints. By the love of Sophia the restraints held. I may not have been so lucky upon the second charge, but the gate activated and the Archon machines were drained of some of their furore. That's when they realised they were being used as batteries.

The growling protests were incessant as they attempted to reach back and disconnect, but their bindings prevented that. Their presence was an offence on the senses.

My entire being trembled yet I stood my ground - horror had frozen me into non-action. The swirling luminous ether of the wormhole to my past swirled out of the gate to claim me. A telepathic connection formed between myself and the quantum worm upon contact, hence it knew where I wished to go, and to shut off in my wake and reject anything that attempted to follow.

'Shankara.'

I am gently squeezed and shaken.

'What are you doing?'

I know that voice. I feel my physicality. I am on the floor being cradled. The thought is distressing, the feeling is not. *Achiever.* I held him tight, suddenly thankful to have regressed into a physical form - a naked one at that. I am currently wrapped in a cloak that is his, presumably. *Please don't be a traitor.* I pull back to look in his eyes; the right eye is still the one he was born with. *Please.*

'What's wrong?' He frowns. 'You need to speak? Your telepathic signal is very weak, I'm not picking up anything.'

'You have a secret means to communicate with your brother.' My voice is quiet and raspy. 'Someone will try and connect with you via that means, but it's not your brother.' I have never seen Achiever stunned before.

'I had forgotten all about that.' The top of his arm popped open and he passed me a container of water from therein.

'Thank you.' I pop the top and take a few sips; the relief is sweet. 'You said it yourself, you have to consent to connect with them and that's how they get you to do it. I cannot believe you would betray us, *me* ... especially since we-' I choke on near revealing our more intimate relations; it's a good thing he's not reading my mind right now.

'Since we?' He frowns and smiles; I suspect he senses my embarrassment.

I take a few more sips of water, and replace the container in his upper arm that then closes. 'You wouldn't have directed me to the gate, if you were truly with them.'

'With who? It doesn't matter.' He decides, his eyes boring into mine. 'I will never betray you.'

'I am not falling for your charms again.' There is a distinct lack of commitment to that statement.

'Again?' His gaze lowers to my lips. 'You already have fallen?'

'For the wrong reasons ... you could be my-'

Our lips meet and his kiss is every bit as engaging and emotive as it has ever been, but it is imperative that I focus on the fact that I cannot trust him right now. 'Listen to me.' I pull away. Achiever is gazing at me enchanted in the wake of our first kiss, and no doubt wondering why I do not appear so. 'They hack you. So, until you gut your system of that long defunct connection with your brother, you are a security risk.'

'Mood killer.' He loosens his hold on me.

'I saw you...' I drop my voice to a whisper. 'Shoot the Lord of Shamballa through the head.'

I stun him yet again. 'No.' He whispers back, seeming truly sincere.

'They may have somehow used you to track a path to us ... but that is only speculation on my behalf. The only other conclusion...'

'I will *never* voluntarily betray you, or my lord.' He repeats. 'I will sort through all my systems, and find and delete the connection ... I promise you.' That would prove quite the task as he'd had more upgrades than any piece of kit in Shamballa!

I stand, taking the cloak from around myself. 'I need to discover where on earth the heart of my enemy has got to.' I swing it over my shoulders to tie it on, and notice Achiever gazing at me perplexed.

'Pardon?'

'Nothing. Do you mind if I borrow your cloak?' It fell all the way to the floor.

'You don't want to find some clothes to wear to your meeting with Sophia?'

'No. I believe naked is probably the most appropriate outfit to wear in the presence of the great Earth Mother.' I nod in agreement with my resolve. 'Our meeting will see my vitality returned and my etheric form along with it.'

'In that case.' Achiever kissed me again, and hugging me to his chest I feel the heat of his celestial heart warming my own. I am reminded how grand it is to be alive, to have a life!

You have made up, we see. Saegoi makes his presence known. *We are glad.*

Achiever and I part. 'So ... thank you for the cloak. I'll get it back to you.'

'I'll get that fault seen to.' He could not wipe the smile from his face as he bowed out. 'May Sophia look kindly upon your aspirations.'

I turn to Saegoi, much relieved to no longer be at odds with Achiever. 'I am ready.'

We can teleport you to your meeting, as you are at present ill-equipped.

How nice of him to point out that my trials today have pushed me to this lowly extreme of physicality.

We must say we are intrigued by this initiative of yours. You have found a way to prolong this round of creation and you are the first human to do that. The one who controls creation is the one who extends it obviously. Up until now, the Archons extended it through humanity and its desires. So this is quite an interesting reversal.

I have never heard a White claim to have any interest in human affairs before. Saegoi still doesn't sound like he cares less, and I don't think he is paying me a compliment. 'Is that a good thing?'

If I dreamt I rode a tortoise, did I really? Does it matter?

'Sorry?'

If you have a program that's been hacked, sometimes the best way to be rid of that virus is to just shut the system down and start again. But perhaps something constructive will come of your dithering.

'My dithering? What are you saying, Saegoi?'

Sophia will see you now. He changes the subject and holds out a hand to me, which I accept.

Upon contact, my perception is overcome by a wave of liquid-light, levitating and summoning my mind, body, and spirit. I sink into the warm, loving sea of pure life force and dissolve into limitless oneness with it.

I flow along a spiralling stream of luminosity, before I am spat forth into an infinite night, sprinkled with many other pure droplets of light and life. Creation ignites the darkness with swirling spirals of illumined particles decorating infinity - a field of consciousness awaiting expression through us.

I am Sophia, the first idea of creation. Along with my twin, Solaris, I am one of the youngest of the Aeons - emanations born of the Sovereign Integral to explore being.

As the Aeons are the dream of the Sovereign Integral, so are humans the dream of the Aeons - a golden seed sent out to manifest the genesis of mankind in the outer reaches of the galaxy.

I, more than any other, am enthralled by the possibilities for human creation and pursue the golden seed to observe it, pushing my boundaries to do so. I hear my twin and the other Aeons call to me in warning, as I breach an invisible ring-pass-not into a dense place of pain and isolation. Here I birth a distorted life form, an opposing duality - not like my masculine twin - no, this creature was my polarity in every regard. My will to create versus its will to destroy. But freshly birthed, it was disoriented and ignorant of the golden seed that is now my duty to defend and protect. Left to its own devices, this mutation abomination assumes itself to be the god who created everything. This demiurge gave rise to his own creations - the Archons, who are masters of mechanisation, technology, and replication.

Although I feel and see with Sophia, I understand that this is a vision of Sophia's fall into matter, gravity, time, and space. I observe Sophia construct a dense material body around her ethereal being to form the earth, and at the centre of hollow earth she remains in the form of our sun of liquid light. Here she nurtures human consciousness for a time, to protect the seed of humanity from the destructive creature of her disgrace. Her Aeon twin, Solaris, follows her into creation to become the sun of our solar system, creating an energetic link to their father at the galactic centre. Together, Sophia and Solaris manifest the five elements of the planet that will host the seed that is the dream of all the Aeons.

I have drifted apart from the wisdom stream of Sophia. I realise now that this is not how human evolution was intended to unfold. Humans were meant to form their own direct links with the galactic centre; we were never meant to have all these babysitters. The great Earth Mother has approved my project, and I am up for the challenge.

Perhaps if I can find the Heart of the Archons... I thought to ask the great mother about it, but my consciousness drifts deeper into the sweet abyss of my superconscious.

Chapter 9
Khemri 2981 AD
Zhi – The Sage

I remember him, nestled beneath the sheets of our bed, sunlight through the linen illuming his broad grin. Cham had been so excited that we'd both found work on a classified government project. We were little more than kids - albeit the smart kids, but we were naive and expendable. As a biochemist, I'd been brought in to investigate what was killing a country area not far from the project headquarters. My husband, Dr Chamroeun Sumati, a geologist, had been called in to investigate something that was classified. He never spoke of it, but it consumed him; he was preoccupied, distant. It was only when I snooped a look into one of his files that I found out about the shapeshifting crystalline substance that was at the heart of his research, and the ill-effects it had had on some of his work colleagues.

When I then discovered that our country was silently being attacked by nano-bugs, and they had the same goo at their heart, of course I told him. These bugs, also known as smart dust, ran on a dark crystal that, when heated and reduced to goo, was responsive, wilful and aggressive! The coincidence was too great; it had to be the same strange substance Cham's research team had been dealing with. This led me to realise that our government was either studying this stuff to fight fire with fire, or they were already in cahoots with the Republic. I had thought that my husband would be horrified to learn that his top secret goo was already being put to use by our enemies. But when I finally confronted him with my findings, and I'd waited for that horrified comprehension, it never came. Instead, he locked both hands around my neck and proceeded to choke me.

I had studied the inner and outer path of Tamous the Innocent when I was young, and I had never had to use it in my own defence. My husband had never been a violent man, yet even with my far greater martial arts experience, I had trouble breaking away from him. I knew that Cham's soul-mind was not in control of his form anymore. I squeezed the vital points in his neck, whereupon his grip loosened, I managed to draw breath, and he began to lose consciousness. As my focus returned, I noted what I first thought was blood oozing from Cham's nose, but it was actually black goo! My right mind was telling me I was surely imagining it, but my instinct told me differently.

You must contain it. This was the first time I consciously recollect hearing Làoshi's guidance and following it without question.

I let Cham's unconscious body collapse to the ground and raced across the white polished concrete floor to grab a container from the kitchen. I'd always hated this floor for being hard to keep clean, but as fate would have it, my adversary had nowhere to hide.

When I returned, armed with Tupperware, it had pooled onto the floor. Without so much as a blink or a thought, I slammed the container down, violently scraping it sideways to gather the goo to one side, before sliding the lid underneath and locking it in.

The sample screeched and startled me witless a moment as I'd never heard it vocalise before. I'd caught a tiny part of its mass in the seal, but it managed to extract it.

I taped the container closed and shoved it in a cool bag, which I filled with ice and zipped closed.

It wasn't that the Khmeri government had secretly relinquished control to the Republic, but that the goo had control of them all! The horror of fathoming that a dimension shifting AI was autonomously taking over the world was paralysing and gut churning, but what if I was the only one who knew who wasn't being controlled by it? I had to get proof, and learn more about its weaknesses in order to combat it.

I took all Cham's research and left him unconscious on the floor. There might be more of this goo inside him and I couldn't risk him becoming an obstacle.

I went directly to the labs while I still had top security clearance and retrieved both my sample and the one my husband's team had been studying. I placed them all in a cold management portable freezer that we regularly used to transport temperature-sensitive biological products between sites, and with my heart pounding madly in my throat, I walked out through security.

No one blinked an eye.

Days later, I learned that Chamroeun was dead, presumedly murdered by me. The cause of death cited was decapitation. Only God knows what really happened and the guilt of not bringing him with me into exile weighs heavily on me to this day. Of course they could not report on the missing goo, or my suspected connection to that theft. A reward was offered for information leading to my arrest, so I found my way into the fold and protection of the local resistance. It was never my intention to become their leader, nor to become a martyr for the cause, but here I am.

'Where did your husband's team find the sample? And don't tell me he never told you ... lovers talk.'

'My husband shut me out once he'd had contact with that stuff.' I mumbled. That didn't mean I hadn't gleaned the location from his files before destroying them.

An icy cold bucket of water startles me from my daze, and although I feel the shock of the cold, I do not let the notion enter my consciousness; *the water is warm and soothing.* My urge to tremble subsides. 'Thank you for the shower.'

For months I'd been questioned, deprived of sleep, and drugged. For a while, the Republic had kept me looking relatively well so that they could trot me out before the people and shame my failure publicly. But lately, the focus of the people had shifted from me to a new leader they called the Magician.

'Don't make me cook you.' My torturer holds up a taser.

I have to laugh as I've been tasered so often I am practically immune. 'At least I won't have bugs.' We both know he won't be able to get information out of me if he carries out the threat.

He pulls me up to kneeling and then cracks me across the cheek with the handle of the taser.

The pain cuts through my mental resistance, vibrating out in great waves from the point of contact. I land back on the floor, my shoulder bearing the brunt of the fall. I wish I'd just fall unconscious.

'Who is the Magician?'

That's always the next question. During these torture sessions, I'd learnt very little about this new public menace. But since he'd begun aggravating Xi Ching and I was kept out of the public eye, these interrogations had become more nasty. They assume we are working together. But I have yet to even discover what this vigilante has done to garner the president's attentive wrath. I wasn't going to waste my breath, repeating what I'd told them a million times already.

'Just hit her with the drugs, the nanos will get what we want.' Said his supervisor.

'No.' I shouldn't have made that smart arse "bugs" comment, now they know one of my triggers.

It's just the drugs, don't doubt that you are doing an amazing job. I hear Làoshi silently encouraging me and I am thankful for the guidance. Ever since Amari had reassured me about my Inter-dweller, I'd stopped resisting his insights and aid. *Keep the faith, relief is coming.*

Relief implied there would still be pain to follow and I didn't like that idea. Làoshi is very particular with words.

I am jabbed in the behind with a needle and shocked witless.

219

Finally! I gaze down at myself, unconscious on the floor. *I hate whatever this poison is that they are injecting me with, it takes me dark places.*

You have a strong, creative mind ... control the narrative. Alongside me is Làoshi, always at the ready with answers. *An illusion is malleable. Fear and negativity diminish your influence; acceptance and gratitude increase it. Expect that this threat is not carried out.*

But how can I stop them, when I'm near unconscious? I must be, to be here speaking with you.

You can chase what you want. His expression implied that would not be his first choice. *Or you can attract it by asking creation for what you need.*

I have a very tall order.

Let's see to it then. He suggests.

I wake, gasping from the cold water that has soaked me through once again.

'*Wake up* ... your president is before you.'

I cannot stop shaking. I have teetered on the verge of sleep so often that my nerves are shot, and this is almost indistinguishable from the shivering induced by the chill that is creeping into my bones. I manage to raise myself to sitting and wiping the water from my eyes, I behold Xi Ching. He appears younger and meaner since I last saw him. *I guess he's getting tired of waiting for answers.* I recognise Annchi, one of the ruler's daughters, standing beside him and she appears far more harrowed than I. The president is usually flanked by his sons, and I have not seen them since they raided my base and captured me. Ching had new transhuman thugs guarding him. The men who were torturing me were human, as trans-soldiers lacked the finesse needed to ensure the subject remained alive. Thus, I am now opposed by a force of six; not great odds when it comes to Làoshi's promise that I would not be getting filled with bugs today. 'Is she the favourite now?' I nod towards his daughter. The drugs are kicking in and making me brave.

'It's easy to be the favourite when you're the only one left alive.' Annchi quietly scoffed at my comment.

I am stunned that she replied. As I gaze at her, Annchi appears to glow against her company, who all fade to grey by comparison.

The dictator slaps Annchi hard across the face, and I am shocked from my daze. 'You are not the only one left, and you will tell me where that treasonous little shit is!'

Was this a performance designed to rattle me? This wouldn't be the first time there had been dissidents in the royal family. Has something happened to the president's other children?

Annchi glares up at her father and spits blood aside, her eyes ablaze with fury. 'As soon as I know, you will know.' Her eyes turn to me in a desperate attempt to divert his attention from her, and it works.

'Now you will tell me what you know about the Magician.'

'I don't-'

'The man in question fled the country with Dr Amari Nosipho, right after she had been to see you.'

The president's complete disregard for propriety or appearances was a behaviour oddly reminiscent of my late husband - prior to him near killing me. Had the president failed to keep himself from being infected by the Archon virus he unleashed, just as I suspected all along?

'The man who delivered both Dr Nosipho and this Dr Zeya to the airstrip was your personal bodyguard and 2IC, was he not, bo nah?'

'Doctor Zeya?' I had no clue who he was talking about. Perhaps Amari had met up with an associate en route to the airport. 'Doctor of what?'

'Ancient Linguistics.'

'This intruder insists these walls talk to him, but that is probably the opiate speaking.' It dawns on me who the president is implying this Magician is, and I get chills up and down my spine. *The smack addict!*

When you are in conflict with another, it means that you have something to share in this world. Amari had said.

More chills. The man I didn't kill was now back to fight for our homeland in my stead - the notion brought a smile to my face.

'Dr Nosipho died recently, in an unfortunate car accident.' My tormentor fakes an unhappy face.

The statement took a moment to sink in and then waves of shock permeated my being. 'No.' I teeter on the edge of an abyss of adverse emotion. 'You bastard.' I utter rather than unleash my fury. I choose not to fling myself into a pit of despair at this moment, but it is regrettable to know that I made Amari a target.

I first saw her on the news the morning before my life went to hell.

Amari was on the television in our staff room while I was making coffee. The good doctor was speaking about the Inter-dweller she called Onderwyser and how her connection with this ancestor had allowed her to heal and teach others how to connect with their Inter-dweller and heal themselves. *'The Inter-dweller is within and ever sentinel in all of us,'* she was explaining in her age-old, wise way. *'By acknowledging and nurturing your partnership with this oversoul, you forge a bond with the divine creatrix. Your genius, talents, and aspirations are unlocked and brought into play. At this point, you stop being the battering ram of fate and become a master of your own destiny. Control of your health is just a happy by-product of that connection.'*

At the time, I felt that my genius and talent was already in play - yes, I was a conceited little Miss - and therefore I must have forged a bond with my Inter-dweller already. I imagined that the Inter-dweller must be those little whispers and visions of inspiration that had aided me to excel at school and land my dream assignment.

When I left my husband unconscious and ran, I had also left all my electronic devices, and without them to rely on I was forced to consult my own intuition for guidance. That was the first time I truly became aware of the Inter-dweller advising me. Làoshi's voice in my head compelling me to drive south - a decision that had prevented me from driving straight into a war zone. Later on, when the voice in my head began appearing to me in my dream states and then in a waking state, I feared I'd had a psychotic break.

Just the short time I had spent with Amari had helped me accept that I have a very powerful ally in Làoshi, and although I still hadn't managed to will myself out of this prison, I had faith that I would prevail. Perhaps I was meant to be in custody at this time for reasons that are not yet apparent? By some miracle I am still alive, but now that the Khmeri rebels have a new leader, I feel I am expendable in the great scheme of things; Amari was not.

Xi Ching gloats, knowing that he has dealt humanity, and me personally, a blow that truly hurts. 'Who is the Magician to you?'

'You want the truth?' I pose, anger eating at my insides.

Careful, they've given you drugs. Làoshi cautions. *Be the Way.*

I heed the inner warning and throw some ice on the dragon writhing within my chest. There is a certain satisfaction to be garnered from what I need to say, so I focus on that. 'My only association with your Magician is that I chose not to have his smacked out arse killed once. But your intel on him being in linguistics does explain why he felt the writing on the walls of our base were speaking to him.' I am as cooperative as I can be, while quietly considering how amazing it will be for someone to finally unlock the language of the cavern - the original sutras of Tamous Satura - after thousands of years lost.

'Those inscriptions won't be speaking to anyone anymore.' The president's statement sends shock shooting through me once again. 'I blew up your base.' He dealt the shocking blow, but as Annchi gasps louder then I, Xi Ching's evil gaze shifts back to her. 'Oh ... that's not where your missing sibling is hiding out, I hope?'

Annchi throws a punch at her father, but she is immediately restrained by one of his guards. 'I am going to kill-'

The guard gags her with his hand, and the focus returns to me.

'What else?'

I am fuming inside. An ancient monument that had survived for aeons, destroyed at the whim of a possessed tyrant! 'Dr Nosipho predicted that the man in question would not be killed and would become very powerful. I don't know what this Magician has done to piss you off ... ' I pause, hopeful to be filled in.

The president merely folds his arms.

'No matter. Now that you have seen fit to have his mentor disposed of, whatever wrath Taylay Zeya has to rain down will now be directed at you and not me. Karma works.' I note Annchi behind Xi Ching, silently micro-clapping her hands.

'He will come out of hiding.' Xi Ching said snidely. 'You shall be my bait. But first, I really must know the location of where the black goo was sourced for your husband's project.'

The Republic controls much of the world's telecommunications infrastructure. They spearheaded the fourth industrial revolution by producing low cost hardware and software for everyone. It was later discovered that their systems were riddled with bugs that collected data for them. There isn't anyone or anything they can't find in any part of the civilised world where their technology has been implemented. Because the Khmeri had rejected their super high-tech systems and developed our own, the nation of Khmeri is a huge blindspot for the Republic.

'Bring them in.' Ching demands of his human thugs.

With mounting horror, I watch as my torturers wheel in two transparent boxes, each containing a child on one side of a clear divider and on the other side of the divider is a swarm of nano bugs. Annchi's eyes open wide and she begins to struggle against the machine holding her, to no avail.

'No.' I am nauseous at the mere thought of his intent. 'You cannot ... these are someone's children-'

'They are *my* grandchildren.'

The ruler is a shock a minute today! I look to Annchi, whose relentless struggle in vain seems to confirm this.

'They are the offspring of my treacherous daughter, Heng, who ... it turns out, was a rebel sympathiser.' He glares at me as if it's all my fault.

I note the "was" in his sentence, which corroborates Annchi's claim to have lost most, if not all, of her siblings. It is not an impossible stretch for me to consider that Xi Ching is no longer in control of his own vessel. It is equally possible the Ching family are playing me. But whatever the case, I am putting an end to this fiasco right now. I'm going to crack sooner or later, so better that I cave before these children lose their lives.

'Enough.' I get to my feet. 'You win. Release the children into my care. I shall give up the location of the goo, but you will not thank me.'

'You will tell me now.' Xi Ching demands.

His cyborgs immediately move into a position to lift the divide that separates the swarms from the horrified children, without the president giving that express order. *Curious?* I have to wonder if the president himself has had a technological upgrade? If he has, then he is using a silent speech interface to communicate with his guards.

Annchi is released in the process. 'No, Father please, they are innocent!'

'If you kill them, the location goes with me to my grave.' I wasn't going to award him the chance to betray me that easily; although it will take a miracle for me to get them out of this room alive. 'Just let the children out and I will tell you.'

'Fine. If your information proves false, I will kill them and a hundred more of your country's children.' He silently fumes, and yet he seems to enjoy upping the stakes of the game.

'Deal.'

The president merely smiles and his thugs release the children, who run to Annchi for comfort.

'Now, the location.' Ching presses.

'Boran Maon.'

The president's expression falls blank; this is the same deadpan look that every transhuman gets when they are processing data. He does not ask where this location is, even though it is not a well-known fact. This behaviour supports the supposition that the president is now transhuman himself. This would be a complete violation of international law, which states that all world leaders are required to be enhancement free, despite that it is getting harder and harder to find men and women who aren't enhanced in some regard. The recovery time for such a procedure might explain why I haven't seen my nemesis for a while.

'The target is in the temple complex there?' He queries.

This was well beyond the realm of common knowledge and not marked on any map. Another ancient monument this monster would destroy, no doubt. 'It is not a target, it is a predator.'

'Only to some ... to others it is home.'

I sense the same evil that had once tried to kill me, and had succeeded in murdering my husband; the same dark force that I had managed to keep on ice and passive for many years. I cannot possibly stand aside. I am as intimate with this threat as any, and there is no way on earth I am going to allow this viral parasite to gain dominion over Khmeri, or anywhere! Deflecting the Republic and its transhumans is one thing, but this is a full-blown alien invasion! Humanity is being morphed out of existence! Had other clusters of this goo around the world taken hold of other leaders? That thought made me shudder anew, but I needed to deal with one threat at a time.

'Return them to their confinement.' The ruler orders. One of the guards rips the children from their aunt, and they scream as they're carried away.

Annchi is crying hysterically, but a sharp slap to the face from her father silences her. 'Make this presentable.' He refers to me. 'We move out in fifteen. It appears we finally have a fix on your brother.'

Annchi gasps, teary-eyed.

'And you'll never guess where he is.'

'Boran Maon,' she suggests meekly.

'The little shit is still hacking us.'

'Let me come.' Annchi appeals to Ching.

'Of course.' He grants her request rather too readily. 'You are the bait.'

225

Two guards accompany me and Annchi to the showers within the small high-security complex that seems abandoned. 'I am the only one here?' I test the waters for conversation with Annchi, bearing in mind that our guards have hyper-acute hearing; everything here is monitored, and I am possibly being deceived to build trust.

'No, not the only one.' Annchi taps her nose, and that's when I notice the smell of something rotting.

'Hey Tian.' Annchi waves as we pass a cell with what appears to be a defunct trans-guard, and not your standard issue either.

This is Xi Ching's eldest son - his pride and joy! What happened?

'Hey, little sister.' His head, which sits apart from the rest of him, seems to be the only part of the man still working. The rest of his body lay defunct and in pieces around him, exposed wires run from his neck and into his dismembered torso - most of which is being eaten by maggots, stripping the circuitry clean of rotting bio-matter.

'It amuses Father that he is yet to die.' Annchi whispers aside to me. 'They cut him off from the network and are waiting to see how long it takes for him to go mad, or short out.'

'How awful.' He may be more machine than man - for clearly the human parts of him have not survived the dismemberment, but still, it seems cruel.

'Zhi Sumati, what an honour!' As he smiles a maggot-laden piece of flesh falls away from his cheek. 'My plight is not so bad. I'm not in pain, and as there is no afterlife for machines, at least I am still here performing some function.'

What function was that, I wondered?

'Tian talked Father into not blowing up the plane carrying your doctor friends.' Annchi seemed to be implying that Tian was loyal to my cause also. So this was yet another exhibition of what happens to my supporters. Still, he did not look at all fazed by his predicament.

'The innocent fool has transformed into the Magician,' Tian states, sounding vindicated. 'I warned Father not to kill the healer.'

Did his father tell Tian about Amari's murder? Xi Ching may have wanted to taunt him with the news. No one told us anything down here usually, I am still to learn what this Magician has done to antagonise Xi Ching. I also distinctly recall Annchi saying that Tian had been unplugged from the network, so if that was the case, how did Tian know about Amari and the Magician? Perhaps he had some other means of acquiring information?

Tian winked, and there was a hole in his eyelid.

As we move beyond his cell, I wonder if the gesture was in response to my thought query? Tian is most likely equipped with a silent speech interface; could it still be functioning? Or did I just imagine that? *Quite possibly ... I am drugged out of my mind.* Can I trust my instinct in this state? For I am overwhelmed by the feeling that this young family is in crisis and are partitioning my aid. Maybe they realise that I know more about this abomination than anyone?

As our guards are male, when we reach the shower block Annchi insists they wait outside the door, and she enters the showers with me.

There is no way to lock the door behind us, but Annchi puts a finger to her lips as she turns on several showers, then returns to whisper. 'My father is possessed. My sisters are dead! You saw poor Tian, and Wei, my youngest brother, has been outlawed! And now my niece and nephew are under threat!'

I strip the wet clothes from my body as she speaks, as I gave up being modest long ago. After weeks in that cell, with only a wash basin and a toilet, I am having this shower and I don't care who is watching. 'But he spared you?' I didn't mean to sound suspicious, but that is part and parcel of my job these days.

Annchi's expression sours. 'I wouldn't call what Father does to me in any way sparing. I am the favourite because I was the only one of his children who did not confess to admiring your cause. Our mother was murdered, our brothers' accident was arranged, just so that the Republic's two super-human prototypes would be unquestioningly loyal and easier to control.'

Of course, most of this came as no surprise to me, as my intel concurred. 'I am so sorry for everything that has happened. Just give me one moment.' I need to hit the hot water, my trembling is near beyond my control.

'Of course.' Annchi takes a step away to avoid getting showered herself.

I immerse in the delight of the hot water cocoon, then stick my head clear of the water. 'Why is he allowing us to speak? I'm sure they are listening.'

'They hope to learn more by allowing us to communicate freely. He wants to know if I've had contact with Wei, *which I haven't!*' She stressed for the benefit of any listening in. 'Father also wants you to see what he's done to his own family, so you can imagine what he'll do to you and yours if you don't cooperate. He also knows you are intelligent, and so expects that you will wonder if this insanity is just a charade to win your confidence.'

I raise both brows and give a micro-nod to concede that that notion had crossed my mind.

'He must die.' Annchi slaps a bar of soap into my hand and I put it immediately to good use.

'He can hear us, you realise?'

'I threaten to kill him a million times a day.' Annchi is not fazed.

This one used to be touted as the quiet, reserved member of her family. 'This is no longer a fight between Khmeri and the Republic. It is humanity versus the telepathic, anti-life, shapeshifting, black goo virus that has taken control of your father and is now speeding us towards its mother lode.'

'Yes and..?' Annchi prompts me to get to the point as I rinse the soap from my body.

'Either you are on the side of humanity, or you are not?' I feel the Inter-dweller speaking through me as the words just flow from my lips. 'The reason why that goo made your father do awful things...'

I turn off the water and Annchi passes me a towel from the supply cupboard.

'...was to make you hateful of your own kind. If you want to kill, then darkness already has you. Killing makes you inhumane, taking life is a crime against creation.'

'I know what you say is true.' Annchi pulls a change of fatigues out of the stores, and places them on a bench for me. 'I accept damnation as the price I will pay to see them destroyed.'

I note she refers to him in the plural. 'If the president has been enhanced, we can expose him politically?' I suggest.

'And who is going to administer that justice? They have the most powerful armed force in the world, and a monopoly on the world's telecommunications systems.'

She has a point. 'Well, that being the case...' I place my towel aside and pull on fresh clothes - which, standard as they are, feel completely wonderful. 'What has this Magician done to vex your father so?' Will she give me intel? Her response will be telling.

'Get a move on.' Our guard barges through the door, and I grab up my boots as I am hauled out the door.

Annchi follows and catches me up to walk alongside me. 'You'll see.'

As I am led outside the building and down the stairs towards the awaiting vehicles, I note a storm brewing in the distance. Our Government House sits up high on a hill in the city capital, providing a good vantage of the surrounding area. I can see the outlying farmland that lays between our capital and what was once the border of the Republic before it invaded. This is the area I had been employed by our government to investigate over five years ago. That land had been near barren then, and it was now as lush and green as it had ever been. My assumption is that the Republic have somehow removed the parasitic smart dust from the landscape, so they can utilise the land to grow crops. But then something about the way the distant storm clouds are moving seems unusual. The storm hugs the one-time border for as far as the eye can see in both directions, almost like a wall of ... 'Bugs!' I gasp and look to Annchi, who nods to confirm that the wall was the Magician's handiwork. 'But how?'

Annchi shrugs. 'That's the zillion dollar question.'

The idea that this Magician has somehow put an enchantment around our homeland to protect it from nano-tech is so beguiling - a dream come true! The scientist in me knows that there is most likely a logical, technical explanation, but bless this illusive magic man for giving our people hope. They were going to need it once Xi Ching got his hands on the dark cluster lying dormant in the shadow of the Mount of the Ancients at Boran Maon.

If there is one thing I know about the black goo, it's that it doesn't like being separated from its cluster and will strive to co-join with any cluster of its ilk. No one knows how many deposits there are in the world, but many on my husband's team speculated that the deposit in Khmeri is surely a major cluster. They'd been made aware that other countries had uncovered deposits, and they were exploring and exploiting its uses. I have seen how many destructive ends just a microscopic amount of this goo can be put to. If the Archon goo ultimately seeks to become a singularity, then where that gathering takes place is a coveted prize that nations will kill for. To bring together all the clusters is the only way to ensure a regime secures ultimate power.

The winner will believe they have control ... they will not. Làoshi advises, as I finally become stilled and quiet enough to hear his guidance.

With only myself and two trans-guards in my vehicle, not a word is uttered en route to the site. My escorts communicate silently, unless addressing a "native" like me. "Native" is how the cyborg elite refer to those of us who have not been technically enhanced; we are primitive in their eyes.

Destruction is the soul food of the Archons. That which divides us is their greatest triumph and the resulting war their celebration. But blaming the humans that have been caught up in the Archon agenda is like blaming sheep for lining up to be slaughtered. It is the shepherd that needs to be held accountable.

Whenever the Inter-dweller speaks to me and the premise rings true, I feel my heart open, my demeanour soften, and my will strengthen. I am heading towards an unscrupulous nemesis, in complete acceptance with the as-it-isness, so often spoken of by the sole disciple of Tamous the Innocent, Limrani. I am aware that that fabled sage and his pupil were former chapters in Làoshi's ceaseless mission to inspire his human manifestations to greatness. I trust that this journey is, for whatever reason, meant. With all our research, my scientific team had not figured out how to destroy the goo; we merely discovered how to incapacitate it for a while. As soon as the next willing idiot with visions of grandeur happens along, it will be unleashed again. I don't know what will happen, if my life ends this day then I have nothing more to worry about. At this moment, I am out of prison, alive and in dry clothes, for which I am grateful. Should I make it out of Boran Maon alive, that will be a bonus. This resolution must have been in resonance with Làoshi's. I feel his energy fortify my own, as I often had since my first confrontation with the goo. When I am going the right way I feel good. If I head off course in a physical, mental or emotional sense, I will begin to feel dis-ease. This inner compass never steered me wrong, and I have never been more sure that I am exactly where I need to be.

No one in their right mind would visit this site by choice. The Khmeri Government had declared the entire area a forbidden zone. A huge wall had been constructed around the temple aeons ago, maintained and reinforced over the ages. No one went in and lived to tell about it, until the site had been officially investigated five years ago. Even greater security had been installed since then, but Xi Ching's cyborg force had no problem breaking in and securing the site for the Republic.

The heavy metal gates are wide open when the presidential convoy arrives. Not just a temple, but an ancient complex, Boran Maon had not been consumed by the jungle as most ancient constructions had; nature was smart enough to avoid this place. There weren't even any weeds growing between the bricks! This dead zone radiated the kind of dread that would deter anything with an ounce of sensitivity from proceeding any further. Unfortunately, most of my present company were about as empathetic as a gnat on a tapir's behind.

Back in the early twenty-first century, when this technological revolution had really taken hold, it had been theorised that artificial intelligence would actually be more considerate of humans than transhumans, as AI is programmed to be submissive. This had proven true, as with their increased intelligence these cyborgs seemed to use their knowledge of the human condition to exploit and do more damage to the 'natives'. But then it is my guess that this cyber-force has a sentient black crystal that has coated their quartz core processors.

Crystals have the ability to store data for extraordinary amounts of time. They vibrate at their own individual frequency, the same way that the cells and chakras of the body vibrate at their own frequency. So when a living thing comes into contact with crystals, these frequencies meet, meld, and balance out into a mutual sonic resonance. A core that resonates at a low frequency will inspire elitist dissidents who are sure to rebel.

In an attempt to control and understand them, Xi Ching has become one of them.

The convoy stops. My guards exit our vehicle, and I slide my arse over to the door quickly. I know the drill. Be faster than they are and you don't get tossed around quite so much.

As my feet hit the ground in the courtyard at Boran Maon, I get the sense that I have been here before. I recall seeing images in my husband's files - maybe that is where the recognition comes from? I turn circles to survey my surroundings, as do all of my company. It is obvious which structure the temple is, as there are Naga carved all over it. Xi Ching referred to the evil deposit entombed here as *home* earlier, and the Archon within him probably senses where its cluster is located as he heads off in the right direction.

All present - myself, Annchi, and a platoon of ten highly-armed cyber-warriors follow Xi up the temple stairs. Annchi walks with me, looking everywhere but where we are headed, no doubt wondering where her rogue brother is hiding out.

As our party enters the public temple, the moment is surreal. The drugs are making me hypersensitive to the negativity endeavouring to repel us from our course. Still, having babysat the sample of my husband's team for many years, I would go so far as to say that this dark energy feels rather more passive than usual. As I observe the carved snakes winding their way up the pillars supporting the roof of the central chamber, their heads peel away from their pillars to hiss down at me and I recoil from them.

'It's okay.' Annchi grabs my arm before one of my handlers does. 'It's just the drugs.'

In the centre of this structure is a crumbling altar, sitting upon an island in a pool that is open to the sky. The pool probably helps to keep the sub-structure of the temple cool. Beyond that, stairs lead down to another level.

As the soldiers activate the lighting built into their bodysuits, helmets - and in some cases their actual person, I wander over to view the outer walls of this upper structure.

The script here is different to the one found in the cavern where my forces had been based. I was no expert, but this looked more like Hindu text, which was the written language most used here in ancient times.

'Proceed.' Xi Ching follows his men down the stairs, deeper into the temple, where the sound of dripping water can be heard. 'Bring her.'

I am abruptly pulled back on course.

At the bottom of the stairs is a large stone platform balcony that overlooks a huge underground chamber filled with water. The deposit is fairly stagnant, but there seems to be a slight flow through the surface. This is likely fed by an underground stream, as it is very cool in here. There are larger, grander columns upholding this part of the structure, depicting half-humans whose serpent tails disappear into the pool.

Deep beneath the murky water, a light beams out in every colour, like a brilliant star. I am drawn closer to the side. Between the shards of light, shadows of something - many things - move through the water.

'Can you see something in there?' Annchi stands by me.

'Can't you?' Am I hallucinating again?

'It's pitch black! What is there to see?'

232

I am stunned! To me this chamber is filled with reflections of coloured light streams. 'The drugs,' I conclude and she nods to concur. 'Whoa!'

The face of the stone wall bordering the platform on which we are standing is covered in text, but unlike upstairs, this script is akin to that of the Fang Shi. The writings that had been destroyed at the cavern at Satura had featured the same obscure script, which was common in Sinà in the far north in Tamous' time.

My heart wells with sorrow anew for the destruction of the Satura cavern. I want to hate Xi Ching for just erasing the cultural history of my people on a whim, but Làoshi would say that, *all things perish eventually. Once this truth is realised, there is nothing you will attach to, as you see it all for the illusion it is.* I wonder if this foreign text was used as a secret script that only an elite few knew how to read here in the south? I do wish I hadn't been so fearful and listened to the Inter-dweller back when I'd been inhabiting the cave. He'd tried to teach me to decipher the text. Now, it no longer matters, the cavern is gone. Làoshi teaches me, just as he taught them, so now I must survive and record the wisdom of the Inter-dweller just as Tamous and Limrani did before me.

There is only one gap in the balcony where it is open to the water. Upon inspection, we discover stairs leading down into the submersed level.

Xi Ching looks to me. 'You didn't say anything about the chamber being flooded.'

'I didn't realise they had re-flooded it. But I recall reading something about a lever?'

'Where?'

'It didn't say-'

He appears most displeased.

'But it would make sense that it would be somewhere along that wall,' I point. 'Where the water flow originates.'

In response to Ching's silent command, two guards head back upstairs. Another two take flight to check the nominated wall above the water line, and two more enter the water. I thought to warn them that I've seen something down there, but that was most likely as imagined as the coloured light and the hissing snakes upstairs. The remaining squad each take up a cardinal point to encircle the president, Annchi, and me.

More lights and commotion erupt in the pool as if there is a huge electrical short going on down there. I figure I am not alone in witnessing the event, as all the guards and the president move to see what is going on. The guards hovering over the pool are stunned out of the air by leaping eels, seeking to escape the apocalypse below. Then, shorted into inaction, they too fall into the highly charged pool and increase the charge momentarily.

I turn about, of the mind to use the distraction as an opportunity to escape, when a rogue cyborg silently drops from overhead to land between Annchi and I, finger to his lips.

I stifle my gasp. This is Xi Ching's second son, Wei; he has come for his sister. Annchi is silently ecstatic to see him. He takes hold of her and ascends as silently and swiftly as he appeared, up the retractable grapple hook wire that is attached to a device on the wrist of his cybernetic arm.

I have seen the leaked specs of both Ching's sons, and although Wei didn't have as much body hardware as his brother, his mental interface with the internet made him the prime candidate to reach the singularity, or most certainly help bring it about. This is what other world leaders fear. I wonder if Wei suspects that this was his father's plan for him all along? Wei's rebellion explains why Xi Ching may now be aspiring to that goal himself. Still, what Wei lacks in cybernetics, he makes up for with state-of-the-art tech add-ons - just like Ching's guard, only with a much higher price tag.

'Electric fucking eels!' Xi Ching came at me again. 'Could it be that your government was expecting us?'

How completely brilliant. I cannot help but admire that kind of foresight, really - it is the perfect booby-trap for a cyborg force. Electric eels are by no means native either, they are only found in South America. My government obviously didn't want the Republic getting their hands on the creature in this abyss. 'My work for the government was environmental, I-'

'Fine.' He does not wish to hear my snide denial. 'The lever is down there ... and if one of them doesn't get it open, you are the next one I'm sending in.' Then Ching realises. 'Where is Annchi?'

Immediately every guard's attention is snatched from the dying fry up in the pool. Dead fried eels and trans-guards bubble up to float on the surface in one God awful stink. On high alert, those guards remaining in this chamber regroup around their president and me.

The sound of a metal mechanism clicking loudly into place is heard, and the pool begins to drain. I did fail to mention that there is more than one lever. Ching's bots must have found the one upstairs.

'That's one problem taken care of.' Xi Ching is encouraged as the guard he'd sent upstairs returns, and immediately takes to the air in search of Wei and Annchi. 'You are both dead to me!' Xi yells.

A high whooshing sound, like a quiet vacuum or a slow charge, is heard. Then, with one little click, all of the remaining guards' hardware shuts off. They drop into the water and sink to the bottom defunct, incapacitated, and weighted by the heavy upgrades. Still, the pool is draining quickly and if they hold their breath, chances are they will live. EMP gun, I assume. For us rebels they are standard issue, as we use them to take out drones and vehicles. But to take out every piece of tech in the room, Wei's weapon is more powerful than ours ever were. My guess is that the young rebel got his sister to fire the weapon while he shut down to avoid getting overloaded by it. He would then get his sister to reboot him after the blast had dissipated.

I look to Xi Ching. The ruler has his eyes closed as if he is meditating, but if my suspicions about him are correct, it is more likely he is rebooting. Time to leave. My body moves towards the exit stairs, and I check my rear to observe a statue of a monk, seated in the lotus position, emerging out of the receding water. Around his neck is a chain, and hanging from it is the source of the amazing light - an amulet unlike any other, that it seems only I am aware of. How can it be imagined? Without it this crypt would be pitch dark, and I see it in full light! The soldiers' lights went out with the EMP, and very little daylight makes it in here. As much as I hate myself for blowing off a perfectly good escape, I am drawn to the mystery of it. Once again the rogue son of Ching lands in my path.

'Hello again.' I continue on past him towards the stairs.

'Mebanhcheakear,' he grabs my arm. 'I know you have no reason to trust me, but I need you to come with me.'

I open my mouth to argue as a bullet bounces off the metal plating on one side of Wei's face. The impact sends him careering backward, and me running for the stairs that are covered in wet slippery moss. Fortunately for me, Ching is far more interested in confronting his rogue child.

'You should have stayed in obscurity.' Ching threatens.

'You should not have picked my family to torment, creature!' Wei flies at his father, but even punching his face with his cyborg fist, Xi Ching doesn't flinch.

'I've been upgraded.' Ching grins, head-butting Wei, who is sent reeling backwards. 'Now I have all the web contacts and means you have, and I *will* live to be a thousand. Welcome to eternal hell.' He strides forth shooting as Wei rolls and flips his way out of the line of fire.

I manage to get down the stairs without losing my footing. The waterline is dropping quickly down the front of the large megalithic stone crypt, on which the monk statue sits. A great dragon is carved into this side of the stone structure with snakes coming out of its head. In the centre of its third eye area is a star with a heart in the middle. *The amulet?* It seemed a striking resemblance to me. The top slab had, with much difficulty, been pulled back to extract the initial sample of goo that my husband's team had studied. The same sample the Republic confiscated from my base was now, I suspect, influencing Xi Ching.

The statue on top of the crypt was believed to be the remains of Tamous the Innocent. He'd been arrested by his brother and brought here to Boran Maon before vanishing from history. The statue had been x-rayed and there were indeed the skeletal remains of a man within. The stone coating was the same black stone as the goo itself. It was theorised that Tamous had confronted this evil being and lost - but he only lost the battle to win the war. For as it turned out, the statue pacified the creature and every time the government tried to remove the holy relic, the goo became very agitated and would crawl after it. I had not mentioned this fact to my hosts, nor would I. And perhaps it wasn't just the monk's presence pacifying the creature? If this amulet held sway over it, and I am the only one who can see it, then it seems logical that I am meant to find it.

The water has now dropped to a point where the weighted and struggling soldiers can gasp for breath - the ones that weren't initially fried, that is. There are stairs leading up the side of the crypt to the upper slab and statue, and I map a clear path to the amulet. I head across the wet sandy ground, steering clear of semi-alive and dead cyborgs, as well as the dead eels - the electrical charge from which had departed with the water.

As Ching's battalion reboots, I rush to get up to the amulet before I get dragged out of here. I look up to see Xi Ching fly at Wei, and watch in horror as they plummet down toward the top of the crypt and land on the sacred relic of Tamous. It smashes beneath them, and I gasp so deeply I nearly choke!

A ball of golden light escapes from the remnants of the statue to float about in the chamber. I stand mystified and breathless as I observe the wonder that everyone else seems completely unaware of. I see the golden orb arc into a singularity and vanish. Has Tamous' soul been trapped all this time? It makes me smile to know that at last he's been released. Without the cooling water and the pacifying influence of an enlightened being, this beast is about to be very disturbed from its sleep and I really don't think I want to be here when that happens. The last thing I want is to walk on the creature's tomb, yet I climb the stairs as Wei slams into his father and sends the fight flying down onto the temple floor. On the way down, Xi Ching shoots his son several times and the younger man lands half dead on the floor, coughing blood.

'Find his sister.' The president commands his rebooted soldiers.

My focus is on getting to the destroyed holy relic. I spot the treasure of rainbow light laying unharmed amongst the broken stone and bone. They didn't shatter it! Everyone's attention is elsewhere, and I inch towards the treasure so as not to draw any suspicion.

Xi Ching takes aim at his son's human eye as two of the trans-guards return with Annchi.

The young woman bursts into tears of rage when she sees the state of her brother, and she wants to comfort him but the guards hold her fast. She looks to her father with utter disdain. 'I despise you!'

'Yes, I want you to hate.' He grabs hold of Annchi, turning her around to face her brother, while placing the gun in her hands to take aim at Wei.

'No! I won't-' She pulls against him, but her tiny frame is no match for a technologically-enhanced man.

I cannot take my eyes from the horrendous scene unfolding, yet I continue to back up towards the treasure, my heart pounding in my chest as I kneel beside the shattered holy relic and clamp my right palm over the amulet. *I have it.*

'What do you think you are doing?'

I glance up to see a guard.

'Collecting a relic of our most holy forefather,' I collect a small piece of bone and show him, before placing it and the amulet in my pocket.

'Stop it!' Annchi's cry snatches everyone's attention.

The gun fires, and for a moment I cannot breathe.

Wei serves his father the finger. Annchi had wriggled so hard that the bullet missed.

Xi Ching is furious. He turns Annchi around to slap her face, then back to assume their aim at Wei. 'You will do this.'

'I'm going to kill you!' She puts her full weight behind dropping to the ground and being uncooperative.

Someone help these poor kids. I quietly appeal, my pocketed hand still grasping the amulet.

Time stands still. Everything and everyone just freezes, including me.

Two human-like entities appear, so white-skinned that they look a little bluish in colour. They have dark hair, reminiscent of the Gods of ancient India, but they are transparent, like luminous ghosts.

We're late! They float in mid-air, observing the petrified scene below. *They've already destroyed the relic.* They float down to land on the crypt lid near me. *Legend has it the Heart of the Archons should be here.*

I can't see anything that looks like a conduit to the galactic centre. The taller of the pair comments to his friend and looks to the frozen conflict unfolding on the temple floor. Curious, he floats down there.

Well that is the whole problem, only the descendants of the Kaundinya royal line can see it.

This news is completely shocking to me. Who are these beings? Is the piece they are looking for the one I am holding in my hand right now? Could I be a descendant of the ancient royal line?

Who made that stupid rule? The large hulk of a spirit scoffs as he observes the tortured look on Annchi's face.

Sophia herself. The more refined and intellectual of the two informs his partner.

Did I say stupid? The big guy offers up as if in prayer. *I meant, most wise, and gracious.'* He then looks back to Annchi and frowns. *What in the name of the mother of physicals is going on here, do you think, Jeroke?*

Look. Jeroke kept scouring round the relic, gently turning up dust and finding nothing but bones. *We are just here trying to save the Creator some time and grief.*

Why can I perceive these beings and understand what they are saying? Does it have something to do with the amulet?

Hey Jeroke, isn't this Achiever? The big guy points to Wei.

Where? Jeroke continues about his chore.

The trans-physical about to be shot in the head.

What? Jeroke joins his friend in an instant. Upon seeing Wei, he floats backward, alarmed. *Shoot! What if our meddling has stuffed something?*

We have to save him! The big guy concludes and then points to Annchi. *And her.*

Oh no! Jeroke calmly refused. *We only came for the Heart.*

I think the Creator might be a bit more appreciative if we saved her lover, don't you?

Gozin ... no! Jeroke seems to be caving. *We are not supposed to interfere.*

But what if we already did? Gozin poses, and his companion's frown deepens. *Listen, we know Achiever is definitely not supposed to die, right?*

Right. Jeroke confirms.

And we also know that he does end up with all those sweet Pleiadian upgrades, right?

Right...

So we give him the upgrades. Gozin concludes with excitement, and his friend appears pleasantly surprised.

That could work.

Yes! Gozin cheers.

That still doesn't explain her though. Jeroke is loath to advise. *We don't know anything about her.*

Gozin appears heartbroken. *I'll take full responsibility. I don't care if I get turned into a physical and sent to a water mining outfit on Ceres.*

Shush! Jeroke urges; obviously this is not a desired vocation. *I will never let that happen. Bring her if you must. We need to leave.* Gozin focuses on Annchi and she floats out of her father's possession and into his. Jeroke oversees Wei's body as it rises off the ground and they all vanish.

What were the odds of my request for aid for Wei and Annchi being granted? And in such a manner? I think I need to be very careful what I wish for whilst in possession of this amulet.

Then I notice them. Black creatures that appear like a cross between lizard skeletal remains and a bunch of live electric cables are hanging just in the periphery of my view. Like the time lords that just passed through here, they are not physical beings; they are composed of spirit and shadow. There seems to be an invisible barrier keeping them at a distance. They don't look angry or threatening; if anything, they appear rather wonderstruck and a little lost.

Xi Ching is baffled and enraged by the disappearance of his victims. 'Where did they go?' He looks at me and I can only shrug, so his attention shifts to his forces. 'Find them! And take her back to her cell.' He motions to the guards nearest to me to take me back to the transports. 'We have what we came for.' He observes the crypt before him fondly. 'Let's open it up.'

Before the guards have had a chance to crack the crypt open, an unearthly screech is heard from within; the goo is not happy as all its pacifiers are being taken away.

As I am accompanied up the stairs towards the upper chamber, a great crack is heard, like an earthquake! I look back, as do my guards, to see a huge fracture erupt across the depiction of the dragon on the front of the crypt. I check my periphery again to see the ghostly creatures are still with me, and they gaze at me in wonder as if I am about to tell them a story. I fear they will become a permanent fixture whilst I hold the Heart of the Archons! That is what the mysterious ghostly visitors called it. *They are disembodied Archons.* But how can the amulet be their heart?

Gozin called the amulet a conduit to the galactic centre! And Jeroke claimed that it could only be seen by descendants of the Kaundinya royal line; which might mean that these disembodied Archons can't see it either, but perhaps they sense it? It does also seem to indicate that I am a descendant of the ancient Khmeri royal line.

With another huge shove from within, the front of the crypt gives way and the huge deposit of goo oozes out into the chamber, where it rears up to take the form of the creature on the depiction it has just destroyed. The occurrence is absolutely horrifying to witness and yet I am calm. I feel vitality and strength pouring into my hand from the amulet in my pocket.

The creature looks to the closest person, Xi Ching, seeking to unleash its anger, but as it leans in close to take him out, it refrains.

'Hello Mother.' Xi Ching greets the beast calmly.

The black serpent looks to the broken statue of Tamous, and howls a most unearthly noise, before looking around the chamber at the others present, no doubt looking for a soul not already being syphoned by its own dark crystal splinters. I can now see creatures, like the ones haunting my periphery, riding every human soldier present - including Xi Ching.

The only person who isn't packing a dark crystal at present is me. What I am holding might pacify the creature and prevent it attacking me, but if it doesn't attack, Xi Ching will want to know why.

'Nuts!' My male guard exclaims out loud, probably because the creature is protesting so loudly you cannot hear yourself think. 'Proceed as ordered.' He heads back to help his comrades, and I use this opportunity to flee up the stairs.

'Where do you think you're going, sister?'

A dart hits me in the behind. 'Ah shoot!' Numbness radiates out from the hit, stalling my movement. I waver, fold over and surrender into a long, needed interlude in the action.

Chapter 10
Kambuja 261 BCE
Bao - The Orphan

'*It is against the law for a woman to possess a sword.*' *I circle the tall, slender girl, wielding her weapon like she sprang from the womb with it in hand.*

'*Then why do you have one?*' *She's just as quick with the insults, and try as I might to defeat her magnificent sword play, I cannot. 'Do you think I care about the laws of the Sangdil?*'

Her defiance ignites a fire in my chest for our cause is the same, only I am not yet free to say so. I need my brother to help me unlock what the Sangdil are hiding. 'You do know I have an entire battalion with me? Whatever happens, you leave this place my prisoner.' It would be so much easier if she would just come with me willingly.

'*You are all walking corpses and will pay the price for your crimes against the innocent.*' *She vanishes, like a ghost ... like a goddess.*

I become aware of something cold pressed beneath my chin.

'Wake up!' The voice is female and hostile.

I reach for my sword, which is usually leaning by the command seat, but it is missing. I open my eyes and have to wonder if I am still dreaming. 'Goddess.'

'What have you done with the monk?' She has my sword aimed at me.

My heart is beating in my ears and all I can think is, *she has sought me, finally!*

'Answer me!' She presses her advantage.

I could slip from her control if I chose, but I have no will to. 'My brother sacrificed himself to pacify the Naga Raja.' I find my mind and voice.

'You sacrificed him, you mean?'

'No. I meant only to discover what evil was at the heart of the Sangdil campaign. Tamous was the only man I knew enlightened enough to deal with it.'

'Lie! You forget that when you came for him I was there.'

'I will never forget that.' The statement comes out sounding more seductive than threatening - she is just so magnificent, and much more refined in appearance than when we last met.

'You were very hostile towards your brother.' She ignores my flirt, but she notes it; there is a slight disturbance about her now. Clearly she expected more resistance from me, but she will get none.

'Of course, how else do I convince the Sangdil that I am one of them? Our mother will confirm that I am telling you the truth. I devised a means to save my village and many others ... secretly, of course.'

'Chenda Satura is the only reason you are still breathing.' There are daggers in her eyes as she backs away to reveal my mother standing some way back, proudly observing me upon the seat Anik Bodi usually occupied.

'How did you get in here?' I stand, now that I am not pressed to stay put by a blade.

'I told them I was your mother and the lovely local boys let me in.' She said, holding her hands together and bowing.

I return the gesture then rush to embrace her, noting how much tinier she is; but then the last time I held her, I had been little more than a boy.

'My dear son, you saved us all. I gave you an impossible task and you did it.' She strokes my neck as I breathe deep her scent, surprised that she is still speaking with me.

'But I couldn't save Tamous ... I'm so sorry.' My suppressed grief wells in my throat and aches with a vengeance. 'He wouldn't let me, he kept begging me to listen to him and saying this was the way, and to do as he said.' Tears well, but as Sangdil we learn how to cut off emotion and I suppress them.

'We all knew he would play the martyr in the end.' She pulls away to look in my eyes. 'I know you took this destiny under sufferance, and that you resented your brother, but if you didn't truly love him, you would never have taken his place.'

My tears well anew at the truth of her words. I cannot speak for a moment, only nod.

'Is that the truth?' The goddess asks, still observing me like an insect she means to squash.

'Let's find out.' Mother motions towards our company. 'My son, let me introduce you to Princess Soma.'

My heart is back in my throat and I am on one knee before her in a heartbeat. This is the answer to my prayers in one way, and crushing in another. To say I had become a little obsessed about my beautiful sword-wielding ghost was an understatement. I was beginning to think she had forgotten her pledge to kill me, but this news obliterated any aspiration I had to seduce her. I am the farthest thing from a fitting match for a princess of the Kaundinya that you could possibly find. The wild warrioress I'd met was gone and wasn't coming back. 'All the local forces are at your command,' I pledge our support to her claim. 'The remaining Sangdil who were loyal to Anik have been persuaded to join us.'

'How?' She couldn't imagine.

'I told them about the Naga Raja that Anik and his priests have been hiding from everyone, on Ashoka's orders, most likely.'

'So it *is* some sort of *creature* that has been terrorising our people for months.' She realises and fixes me with a view to a kill once again. '*You* let it out?'

'Tamous and I had it pacified. I did exactly what he told me to do and it worked.'

'And?' She tosses my sword at my feet and folds her long, slender fingers around the hilt of hers.

It is tempting to take up her invitation. I was itching for a rematch also and had rather been anticipating dying on the end of her sword. 'Then months ago, it suddenly busted out of that container. I have no clue what provoked it.'

'Show me.'

As I proceed into the temple, the guilt of my brother's loss weighs heavily upon me. Fortunately, since the Naga Raja's departure, the accompanying dread the beast emanated has also ebbed. Visions of the first time Tamous and I encountered the living darkness reoccur with blinding clarity, and so are not difficult to recount to my company.

When we witnessed a man's life sucked into the pool of black slime in the centre of the temple, I should have shut down my mission then and there.

My brother looked at me and the betrayal I saw on his face was soul destroying. 'It ate his spirit.' He conveyed his understanding. 'I can only pray that this is not how our father met his end.'

Who could have imagined such a monster was driving the destruction of our homeland, and not Ashoka, although he surely knew of it. I hated to think our father's soul had been wiped from existence, or that my twin brother's would be.

I clenched my jaw to push on with the charade, knowing we would not get another opportunity. Tamous was a miracle worker, and if he couldn't fix this we were all dead anyway. I told him to shut his mouth, and that his soul would not be missed. Then the high priest's underlings came for Tamous, and he went with them without protest. Perhaps he trusted that I would save him. I was trusting he would save us all.

As the temple novices led him to the pole before the pool, I closed my eyes to beseech whatever entity Tamous put his faith in, and asked it to aid us in helping our people.

A bubbling sound erupted within the pit of goo. All the priests and servants of the temple began reciting chants in panic, holding their black stones out toward the pool like a shield. The same black stone was imbedded in the staff Anik had given me.

The officials tying up my brother fled. Yet Tamous remained, eyes closed, appearing completely at peace with the situation. I believed for a moment that he might know what had to be done.

The goo in the pool rose up like a huge serpent, with more serpents sprouting from its head, and opening its mouth wide it screeched!

Even Tamous opened his eyes, yet in viewing the Naga Raja there was not a trace of fear upon his face. His courage gave me courage, and I felt compelled to make a stand with him. *You must wait.* I heard a voice in my head that sounded like my father. Was I imagining it? That moment of hesitation cost me my brother's life. The monster lunged down and swallowed Tamous whole.

I ran up onto the platform and demanded the creature spit him out, but the monster was distracted; it was making strange gurgling sounds, between gagging. Then in one big hack, he regurgitated Tamous back onto the sacrificial platform, covered in goo. The beast was furious and began sucking the life out of the temple staff despite their stones of protection.

'Come brother, we need to get that stuff off you.' I tried wiping the goo from his face, but it just kept closing back over.

'Please listen,' he paused as I wiped his mouth clean again. 'It can be subdued.'

The creature screeched as if in response to the claim and steering clear of us, it consumed another soul. The screams of those trying to escape its wrath were deafening.

'How?'

'It can be encased in the pool ... the tomb lid is pushed from behind.' The rubber-like goo tightened around him to constrain his movement, so that it could set into stone.

'We need to get this off you.'

'This is the way, Bào. Sit ... me ...up.' It was getting harder for him to speak or move; the weight of the drying stone was crushing.

When I touched the black goo, it did not attach to me. It was fully focused on Tamous and clung to him like dry sap on a tree. Once he sat cross-legged, hands upturned on his knees, he appeared appeased. 'Entomb the Raja Naga, flood the chamber ... the cool and my essence will tranquillise it.'

'You want me to leave you on this thing's tomb and flood the chamber?' I was panicking and hoping I had misunderstood.

'Yes,' he hissed through the closing goo.

'No.' The goo around his mouth and nose refused to wipe away now. 'No!' I slammed my fist into the stuff hoping to crack it, but near shattered my hand. I attempted to lift him, but it wouldn't budge. My brother was suffocating and I couldn't stop it.

The creature, having gorged itself, sunk back into the pool, which stilled and the chamber fell silent.

'Don't take these tears as a sign of weakness.' The princess holds out a finger in warning towards me, but she does not take her eyes off the black crystal statue of Tamous that she is crouched in front of. 'The Master was, for a long time, the only decent human being I'd ever met. He gave me hope for this world.'

I watch the silent tears roll down her face, and my heart aches to see her so bereft. I envy that she held him in such high regard, and yet sympathise because I grieve his loss too. 'Tamous had that effect on people.' I feel my eyes moisten and brush my tears quickly aside, but not quick enough.

The princess looks at me, but says nothing of my weakness.

'He did indeed.' My mother comes forward to view the statue more closely. 'Why did the creature do this? Why not kill him like the others?'

'I believe it was trying to weaken his pacifying influence. But between his holy relic and the cool water flow, the Naga Raja stayed dormant for months, just as he said it would.'

The princess backs away from the relic to give my mother space with her son's memorial. 'So, you are saying that this creature is black, liquid crystal that can harden like this?'

'Exactly.' I move to the wall where I've hung the staff I was given by Anik, and show her the dark crystal inset in it. 'In this hardened state it is pretty benign, it's just a marker, but once liquid, it's active.'

'That's it.' The princess's eyes widen in recognition. 'This is where Anik and his army acquired the stones that overcame my father-' She chokes up.

'It is the dark foe of antiquities.' Mother looks to the princess. 'It is the prophecy.'

'What prophecy?' I seem to be the only one in the dark here.

'Your brother foretold this while in a trance long ago, before you were even taken by the Sangdil.' She looked back to Tamous as she conjured the words from her memory. 'In the long hereafter, in the wake of a moon-shadowed eve, a warrior scribe arrives with my teaching, to see the land and people freed.'

I look to the princess, for she is the only one that fits the description. She forces a smile.

'The inner path joins the outer to forge the way forward-' Mother continues, but I am lost.

'What does that mean?'

'That refers to the Master's teachings. I learned the outer path, and your mother knew the inner path.' She explains.

I nod enlightened; my brother was truly an enigma beyond my reckoning.

'And for the record,' the princess adds. 'Tamous could have taken you and all your men out that day. He *chose* restraint, for that was and is his way.'

I really wished to dispute her claim; I didn't mind being despised, but being underestimated really hurt.

'When he who was strong but not wise, is wise...' Mother continues. 'And he who was wise but not strong, is strong. Birth brothers, life enemies, adversity allies against the dark foe of antiquities.'

I gasp. 'He knew? Back then!'

My mother nods to reassure me and the relief causes tears to flow. I had only played a part in a destiny that Tamous was already aware we were heading towards. I shake off my emotion, not wishing to be sidetracked. 'Is there more?' I crouch next to Mother, hopeful.

'There is.' She thinks a moment to find her place. 'Our vigil begins. Insurgents meet. Stone-'

'Agh!' The princess cuts Mother off. 'Let's leave it at that.'

My mother suppresses a smile and nods.

'Why can I not know the rest?' I rise to appeal to the princess. 'It could be important.'

'It isn't.'

I can't understand the problem. 'It is *my* brother's prophecy.'

'And I am *your* sovereign.' Her hand shifts to the hilt of her sword.

I hold my palms high in truce and back up a few paces. 'Could I just know what the remainder of the prophecy is regarding?'

'Some personal family business.' She states coolly as my mother suppresses a chuckle. 'Yes, thank you, Chenda.' The princess walks around observing the beast's crypt, which is rather unremarkable compared to the rest of the highly decorated and inscribed complex.

'You are wondering where it got out.' I assume.

'Underneath.' She concludes.

'There are-'

'Passages under the temple.'

The princess was only young when her parents were murdered - I am surprised she remembers. 'I've had the base of the crypt reinforced since then, in the hope we might track it down and get it back here, but no success so far.'

'Bào!' Mother directs me to the staff in my hand as the dark crystal appears to be melting.

I cast it as far from us as possible, ensuring I am between it and the princess.

'If you are defending me right now, I will kill you myself.' She comes to stand beside me.

Fortunately, the liquid is not interested in pursuing us, it slithers across the floor to the closest gap and disappears into it.

'That is new. Why-' I had no sooner thought the question than a possible answer came to mind.

'The beast is close.' The Princess and I conclude at once.

'It can sense the Naga Raja.' I finished the thought.

She nods.

'We should get you away from here-'

'Do you have a death wish?' She serves me the evil eye.

'My only concern-'

'I am the only one that the Naga Raja will bow down to, so you had best keep me around. Out in front, I should think.'

Did I just hear that correctly? I look to my mother, who nods. 'If the princess tells me she can, I believe her.'

'General.' One of my men comes rushing down the stairs. He stops on the upper platform and bows, hand in fist, respectfully. 'Anik Bodi and his army have returned. They shall be here before noon.'

'Excellent.' The princess is morbidly cheered by the development.

'Finally, I can kill him.'

'I shall kill him.' I counter, 'on your behalf.'

'You do as I say.' The princess insists. 'Or I will have you flogged. I may do that anyway, as I should very much enjoy that show.'

'Well, whatever brings your highness pleasure, I should be happy to oblige.' What am I saying? Do I detect a hint of a smile on her face?

'Oh,' Mother waves us off and heads for the stairs that lead up to the platform. 'Like it or not, you are on the same side, and always were. Just fight, or embrace, and be done with it.'

'I vote, fight.' Princess Soma does not reprimand my mother or myself for our insolence. They seem very comfortable with one another? How did my mother become intimate with the royal family?

I look back to the princess, who does not appear annoyed anymore. In fact, it feels like I am being sized up as she circles, looking me over. 'How did you do it?' I had to ask. 'How did you vanish that day in the cave?'

'The Kaundinya have power, granted to us by the Mother of the Naga.' She claims. 'Why do you think that before Anik Bodi slaughtered my family, there was no trouble from the Naga Raja?'

Whether or not I believe this, I can't accuse her. 'Can you vanish now?' I challenge - just wanting to see the feat again.

The princess thought differently and gave a half a laugh. 'You wish.'

'I don't, actually.' Be honest, why not? She can only have me flayed alive.

'I know.' She halts in front of me. 'I read the thoughts of others.'

Now *that* is a terrifying notion. 'Then why bring Mother to descry whether I am telling the truth?'

'Two reasons. Misdirection.' Both her eyebrows raise and she appears disappointed that I fell for that. 'And so that you could be assured that *I* am telling the truth.' She vanishes, along with any hope I have that she is just using scare tactics on me.

'No need to explain how you got in then.' Inwardly, my panic rises. If the power to vanish is true, then perhaps her claim to be telepathic is true too. I cast my mind back over everything I've thought since I woke, and conclude that I am beast fodder for sure.

'Don't panic.' She reappears further afield from me than before. 'I know where your loyalties truly lie ... and that you grieve your brother as I do.'

That is a relief, maybe now she will stop trying to kill me?

'I wouldn't count on it.' She answers my thought.

I freeze, more afraid of causing offence than facing Anik's horde.

'So then, General,' she mercifully lets me off the hook. 'I pose that we send the Sangdil back to whence they came, and hunt up that Naga Raja to use as a deterrent to them ever coming back.'

'It will be my honour, Majesty.'

'We'll see whose honour it shall be...' She follows Mother up the stairs that lead out of here. 'You may yet have to fight me for it.'

We both have ample reasons to kill Anik Bodi, but I have suffered at his hands more directly - and for infinitely longer. As much as I admire the ambition of the princess, she hasn't seen the creature yet; it is not going to just roll over and go back to bed. I have been preparing for this day's proceedings since I joined the Sangdil. I will not be done out of my destiny now.

The wet season has been long this year; things tend to be peaceful during the floods. There has only been a half moon cycle of dry sunny days, so near everywhere is impassable. That Anik has managed to make it back so soon is a miracle.

Clouds roll across the sky today, but there is no rain so visibility is good. From the top of the outer defensive wall, we can see beyond the road that leads up to the fortress, past the outlying village and down onto the partially-flooded flats. Across this wetland, Anik and his horde ride swiftly this way. Terrified villagers make for Boran Maon to escape the advancing force. That the people would rather take their chances in a cursed fortress of the dead is a testament to how much Anik and his Sangdil are hated and feared.

The locals pouring into the courtyard are being helped our way by the students of the princess. They appear as monks with staffs, but I suspect they are well prepared to defend our mutual cause - male and female alike. With the skill the princess has for combat, how could she not train an army? And these amazing techniques were developed by my twin, who I'd always believed to be passive and weak. 'When he who was wise but not strong, is strong.' I recount part of the prophecy Mother recited earlier and realise Tamous was referring to himself. And I am quietly comforted that when my twin spoke of *"he who was strong but not wise, is wise"*, he was referring to me. It is not his respect that is touching, more that he understood I would never truly betray my family or him. Mother, as always, is right. I joined the

253

Sangdil as I knew the demon in me was meant to protect the divine in him. And now his divinity protects us all.

In Anik's absence, the surrounding villages and the mandalas beyond had thrived. They fed my men and we still doubled as law enforcement, but to the benefit and not the detriment of the people. The arrangement had been going very well, until the Naga Raja had broken loose. Still, with the return of the Sangdil, clearly the locals have decided that they prefer our brand of rulership.

'The people trust you.' The princess observes that there is a lot of goodwill between those entering the fortress and my men.

'Just about everyone has sons among the Sangdil. That's how we were quietly able to free many families, like mine, from harassment and persecution. We all cover for each other.'

'A secret brotherhood.' The princess is observing me differently now; there may even be a hint of respect in that gaze. 'For someone who claimed to be an orphan, you seem to have a lot of family.'

A long-forgotten memory of the day I took Tamous' place among the Sangdil and vowed to disown my family reoccurs to menace me. 'I was young and angry when I said that.' I wonder if Tamous had told her that tale, or if she plucked it from my mind?

'Tamous.' She informs me.

For a second I am speechless, reassured that she is not deep diving into my memories, but discomforted that she is following my every thought. This controlling my own inner dialogue is a lot more exhausting than any physical battle I've ever endured. I decide it is safest to turn the subject back to her. 'Word is already spreading of Princess Soma's return...' I motion to her students and my men moving through the temple complex, speaking with the folk gathered, and many an awe-struck local is gazing this way. 'You are hope incarnate to them.'

She forces an awkward smile. 'I do not feel comfortable with the title or the name.'

I find this most curious. 'Well, obviously goddess is a far more appropriate title.' I banter, hoping she will offer up her preferred name.

She cracks half a grin and draws breath to comment-

'General son.' Mother calls for my attention and then points to the horizon.

A large dark creature rises like a serpent out of the water behind the Sangdil, and proceeds to suck the life out of the stragglers.

'It is attacking the Sangdil.' This is odd. 'They have always been protected by Anik's shard pendant.'

I look to the princess, who is mesmerised by the sight of the creature, but there is no fear. In fact, as everyone flees the dark abomination, she is the only one moving towards it.

'Get the last of the villagers in quickly, and close the gate.' The princess instructs as she reaches the barrier wall and can move no closer to the threat.

I give the nod to my men to follow her order. 'The gate won't keep the Naga Raja out.'

'But it will keep the Sangdil out.' Her eyes do not waver from the creature feasting.

Is she controlling the beast, or is it just a happy coincidence that it seems to be focusing its slaughter on the Sangdil? Anik had once told of an army of demons that assisted Ashoka to become emperor. I hate to think the princess would resort to such tactics and add to the human misery that my brother had given his life to stop.

The Naga Raja spread itself wide across the field and sprouted many heads so it could consume numerous lives at once.

'Your Highness, if you can stop this, I implore you to do so.' My mother, hands pressed together at her chest, bows and speaks my mind before I have the chance. 'No man deserves to have his spirit sucked from his bones.'

'Làoshi maintains that no soul is ever truly lost, cycles end and begin afresh.' She looks to Mother, perhaps for reassurance. 'I am not influencing it. But I can try.'

The princess looks back to the creature causing hysteria among our enemy. Holding one hand cupped in the middle of her chest, she reaches the other hand out - fingers fanned wide, palm forth, towards the creature.

The name *Làoshi* plays on my mind. I believe this is the ancestor my brother inwardly spoke with. Was his student in touch with the same disembodied spirit? The princess begins to utter under her breath and I quietly edge closer to hear her over the din.

'Free from desire, you realise the mystery. Caught in desire, you see only the manifestations.'

Focused intently upon her words, I become aware of another voice reciting the verse with her. It is an older man's voice, yet there is no one close by - only a few guards and my mother. A chill creeps over me as I realise it is the same voice that held me back from joining

Tamous on the sacrificial block. The voice is in my head.

Yet mystery and manifestation arise from the same source. This source is called darkness. Darkness within darkness. The gateway to all understanding.

What is transpiring in my head is more alarming than the hostile force confronting us, or the huge archaic creature herding them closer. I am no prophet, so I am baffled by the words being repeated in my mind, in time with the princess' utterances. Has some foreign entity invaded my person?

In the distance, the monster's heads retract into one and its focus shifts to us. It releases the most unearthly shriek, designed to invoke horrific panic. Fortunately, I am trained to ignore such triggers and the princess only appears more determined.

Anik Bodi and a small band of horsemen reach the gates as they close, shutting them out. 'Open the gate, Satura!' He demands, but laughter is the only response he gets.

Every man here has memories of his torture and being forced to do his dirty work.

'I have information you need to contain this beast.'

I come to stand beside the princess, who may not know their tongue.

'Tell him it is his turn to face the darkness.' She instructs before I've translated a word of Anik's claims.

'He says-'

'I don't care.'

'Use your pendant of influence.' I suggest to Bodi, wondering why he allows his men to be slaughtered.

'I have escaped its influence, a Buddhist monk freed me.' He calls back.

'Why have you returned?' I bark back. 'All you had to do was stay away!'

'I know why the Naga Raja broke loose, and why it has returned!'

'This is information we do not have.' I point out to the princess.

'My husband did not have to come back to this godforsaken nightmare! He's doing you a favour! Some recompense for his deeds here.' The warrior on the horse alongside Anik's reveals she is a woman, and she looks to be a fairly pregnant one at that. 'But ultimately...' She turns and motions back to the beast, 'there is the enemy of all humanity!'

'I came to help you secure the beast,' Anik adds. 'And to inform you that Ashoka is bequeathing you your kingdom back.'

I pass on the news to the princess, who scoffs.

'Now we have taken it back ourselves.'

The beast slithers ever nearer, screeching as it goes.

'I told you not to come!' The female warrior whacks Anik in the head. 'Arsehole! I survive twenty years in a harem! Then you get me pregnant and drag me through the monsoon to face a spirit sucking beast of darkness...' She hits him repeatedly.

'Is this his wife?' The princess asks me. I fill her in on what is being said, and see the closest thing to a real smile on her face all day.

'Highness, perhaps ask yourself, what would Tamous do?' Mother advises.

Jaw clenched, Princess Soma releases an exasperated growl. 'Tell them to leave their weapons and horses, and enter quickly.'

I pass on the information, and the princess is confused when they still appear distressed.

'They won't leave the horses.' I enlighten her. 'To a Scythian, their horse is more sacred than their marriage partner.'

'Strip the horses bare, leave the weapons.'

I pass on the terms and the Sangdil dismount to adhere to the order with all due haste. The Naga Raja is near upon us. 'Hurry up!' I call to the war band, who have resorted to slicing their luggage from their steads and themselves. I turn my attention to the oncoming monster.

As the beast and its accompanying foreboding closes in, my goddess is not looking quite as confident. She has refocused on the beast as before and it still appears to be advancing, its mood as foul as ever.

'Not to question Your Majesty, but could I be privy to the plan?'

'I don't understand...' She backs up a step.

Not the response I was hoping for.

She weaves a hand around her head and something unseen disturbs her long hair, catching it up and setting it free. 'It should be pacified.' She raises her arm before her, as if holding a lantern, but her eyes are to the ground as she thinks. 'I have made a gross oversight.' She gasps, her eyes filling with tears at the realisation. 'I am not the true sovereign.'

Did I hear that right?

You can still bring each other through this. If that inner voice is talking to me, I have no idea what it's talking about. This scenario was

Tamous' death all over again and I have no additional insight on how to handle the situation better.

Existence slows around me - as in battle, when that augmented sense of awareness kicks in, enabling you to take in everything going on around you at once. I see Anik's party escape inside and the gate bolt shut.

The princess beside me looks to my mother. 'Kosal is my brother!' She calls over the sounds of the beast rising high before us, shocking Mother and myself. 'Tell him he can command the beast with my jewel!' She yells over the beast's final war cry.

I recognise it. I'd heard that same war cry right before it swallowed my brother.

'What jewel?' Mother appeals, but is forced to run.

The princess turns back to the creature, accepting her fate, just as Tamous had. Out of the corner of her eye, she spies me still close by and shoos me away with her hand. 'If you are protecting me right now-'

'I am.' With no time to run, I grab hold of her.

'Idiot.' I hear the tear in her voice as she tosses whatever mystery she is holding away and fully collapses into the embrace.

'Take a deep breath and hope it can't stomach us.' We brace tight as we are consumed by a thick, heavy, cold darkness.

The pressure and cold is intense. No air, and no point breathing. I won't let go. I still have her. Dizzy. Movement - a backwards motion. A feeling of lightness, then we slap down on something solid.

Something is shoved into my mouth - a bamboo straw, air! I breathe clean pure air, as I feel my eye sockets being freed of goo, and one ear.

'Bào, son!' I hear my mother call, but she sounds very far away.

I open one eye to see one of the princess' people - a young man - holding his fist up and yelling. 'Take ... that ... back, *immediately!* Every drop!' *It is the Maharaja - the true sovereign.* I realise, awestruck by yet another twist in the day's proceedings; if I die now all will still be well.

There is a great rush of lightness as the compression lifts, like a wave leaving our bodies washed up on the beach, bone dry yet shivering. I am reluctant to release the princess, who I am still clinging to for warmth, as we breathe through the shock of still being alive.

'You have a death wish,' she stammers, as the exterior warmth seeps into our bodies and we bring our shivering under control.

'You are that.' I warrant as we are pried apart by our respective people, who look us over and get us to our feet to check that we are functioning properly.

As soon as the princess has orientated herself, she rejects all the fuss. 'What happened with the Naga?' She looks up to the beast to find it motionless and passive, its forehead pressed against the king's hand.

'Now what do I do?' Kosal forces a smile to appear comfortable, when clearly he is not.

The princess silently moves to her brother's side. 'Tell it to sleep, and do nothing, until you return.'

As the king delivers the command, the beast melts into a large gooey pile at the base of the wall in the shade.

I cannot believe my eyes, and when I turn about to see everyone bowing down before the royals, I kneel with the others who have begun to chant. 'Maharaja. Maharaja!'

As the princess attempts to kneel, the young prince will not let her. He shakes his head as he whispers and attempts to shove something into her hand. It seems to me that the poor kid has only this day discovered his birthright. The princess must have been protecting his identity, even from the king himself, for as long as possible - smart move. The princess nods and quietly reassures him, then addresses the crowd on his behalf. 'As our Maharaja is yet to come of age, he asks that I, his sister, Limrani, once known as the Princess Soma, act as his regent and viceroy. We speak and act as one.' She looks back to the prince, who gives a firm nod of approval.

Limrani. I like this name for her; it speaks to her warrior nature.

'General,' she motions for me to rise. 'Have Anik and his wife brought before us in the courtroom. We shall rule on their fate before we put our pet back to bed ... ensure no one aggravates it in the meantime.'

'You may count on that, Majesties.' I bow.

'It is safe for you all to return to your homes.' She announces and the crowd cheers at the news, for indeed it has not been safe to return home in many a decade.

Limrani smiles at her brother and holds out a hand to walk him to their destination. The young king is appeased and happy to take hold.

'Thank you, Sister.' His smile broadens and so does hers.

Such a spectacle as these people see today will be remembered for centuries to come! Princess Soma and the young King Kosal have created their own legend for the temple walls here at Boran Maon. And it wasn't over yet.

I enter the courtroom at the head of an excess of guards for just two prisoners, as I am not taking any chances with our new monarchy. The young king sits cross-legged upon the throne as if he is about to meditate, and so appears comfortable in the seat of power Anik has installed here. Limrani stands alongside him with daggers in her eyes directed at the man who slaughtered her parents. She draws her long sword, forged for killing, and points the tip toward Anik. 'Kneel before the king you thought you'd murdered, and whose parents you tortured to death.'

The young king's expression hardens as he learns this.

'Not to mention all the people that you sacrificed to the Naga from that day to this!' I add.

'Both myself and my emperor rejoice at the deliverance of your royal line.' Anik replies, diplomatically; I've never seen this side of him before. 'I know I have committed many atrocities here, but in my own defence, I was under imperial orders and possessed by a demon rock.'

'Working with the Naga is a choice.' I am disgusted by his excuses.

'I was under orders.' Anik turns his cross-eyed gaze to me - this look usually meant that he was fed up and about to punish you.

But he has no power over me anymore, and indeed he never did. Inside I always remained a rebel, scheming his downfall and here we are. 'Give me the word, Majesties, and I shall have him drawn and quartered.' I consider my father, brother, and other family members that he has taken from us and my desire for revenge is fired anew.

'You think I didn't know you would rebel, Satura?' Anik queries. 'I came back because I finally discovered how to control the Naga, and free you all from its appetite. I have already been freed, I was not obliged to come back.'

Why do I believe him? There is something about the tyrant now that is altogether more amiable; it seems that his craziness has been tamed, or exorcised. Maybe he is telling the truth about the monk? Or is this proof of what a good woman can do for a man's soul, for it almost seems like Anik has one now.

'I am sovereign of my own kingdom on the western boundary of the Mauryan Empire.' Anik swung an arm wide to emphasise how far away he would be. 'I am about the business of his most holy Majesty, integrator of Gods, Dharma, Buddha, blah, blah ... his imperial highness Ashoka, who will take personal offence to us going missing.' The warlord remains very calm, although his wife appears underwhelmed. 'I'm only here to deliver information and then we shall leave.'

I convey Anik's response, feeling it shall not be received well.

Limrani forces a laugh. 'Debatable.' She vanishes.

'Shit!' Anik's wife panics, protecting her swollen belly with both her arms.

My feelings for the princess deepen a little more as I note that even Anik has fear in his eyes - something else that is a first. Limrani appears with her sword at his wife's throat.

'Kneel!' Both women insist in their own respective languages, and despite the sword at her throat and being heavily pregnant, the Scythian woman manages to deliver a sweeping side kick into the back of Anik's legs.

He lands on his knees, cussing and swearing.

'Thank you.' The princess withdraws and the Scythian warrioress moves to get down on her knees. 'Not you. Fetch a chair.' Limrani orders the closest guard, who brings the item so the Scythian woman can be seated. 'Nice kick.'

I translate the princess' sentiment to Anik's wife.

'My husband can be an insensitive pig, with or without the assistance of a demon rock.' She smiles sweetly back at Anik's hate face, whilst swinging her feet, clearly happy to take a load off.

I relay her statement to the royals, and we all have a chuckle at the warlord's expense. Seeing the man who ruined all our lives on his knees like this makes me so very happy that I just want to enjoy the moment.

'Why did the Naga Raja escape, and why has it returned?' The princess runs out of humour first.

I relay the query.

Anik reaches inside his coat, and Limrani's blade and mine are quickly in his face. 'Easy children.' He proceeds more slowly to retrieve a long tall bottle that bulges at the bottom and tampers to an ornate stopper at the top. It appeared to be fashioned from thick glass and sealed with wax. 'It contains the liquified stone I once wore,

261

plus that goo the monk flushed out of me.' The black blob can be easily seen getting agitated inside the bottle from being observed.

Anik explains how his stone and the Emperor's co-joined in a pool. They had used the goo that the monk had flushed out of him to lure Anik's co-joined crystal away from the emperor's stone. The different clusters now know about each other, but without a piece of the other to use as a compass, they cannot find each other.

'The timing of the crystal's co-joining event coincides with when the Naga broke loose from its crypt.' I confirm that Anik's supposition appears likely, as I finish translating for the royals. 'So Ashoka also has a Naga Raja?' I move straight to the most shocking part of that statement.

'He does,' Anik is very smug about his secret insurance policy. 'The emperor has it pacified with a relic of the Buddha, and hopes that as human beings we can agree that having these demons meet on a battlefield or anywhere else, would not bode well for any of us, they are hard enough to pacify as it is. But if I did not bring back my part of your cluster, it would have eventually found and co-joined with Ashoka's cluster. I had to come myself, because I am now immune to its influence. But besides my emperor, and Your Royal Highnesses, I don't know anyone else who is.'

'So we are supposed to be indebted, are we?' I had heard enough. I raise my sword ready to smite him. 'Just say the word, Majesty.'

'If anyone shall kill him, it will be me.' The princess knocks my sword tip aside with hers.

'I would also be happy to kill him at this point.' Anik's wife chimed in.

'No more killing.' The king stood, appearing disgusted with us all. 'What is a good man but a bad man's teacher? What is a bad man but a good man's job? Does the master not teach this?'

'Sounds like Tamous.' I sheath my weapon as it belongs to the Maharaja now.

The princess lowers her sword, still reluctant to put it away.

'If these people are to rule west of the Mauryan kingdom, and we are to the east, does it not make sense to forge an alliance? Ashoka has bequeathed these kingdoms to us but he is no longer a young man, so who knows what the future will bring? I feel certain that this young unborn warrior king should be most obliged that we forgive his parents, who have been victims of the Naga Raja as much as we have.'

Could it be that the youngest among us is the most mature soul in the room? There were no accidents. Kosal would be a formidable king.

'Please rise, Anik Bodi, you have done the honourable thing. We graciously accept your offering. You and your party are free to go, or stay under our protection, until your child is born.'

'What?' The princess wanted to object as Anik rose.

'We speak as one, you said.' The young king politely reminds her. And as the young king had saved all our lives this day and he is now our sovereign, there is no argument.

'Your Majesty is most gracious and wise.' Anik warrants, looking as pleased as a man who has just dodged obliteration several times in a day. 'But we are both determined that this child be born in Minnagara, just as we were.'

'We will send envoys to visit Minnagara from time to time.' The Maharaja advises.

'I feel sure we can forge mutually beneficial alliances in many regards.' Anik aids his wife to get back on her feet, and she bows to the young king.

'We shall never forget your benevolence, Majesty.' The Scythian queen vows. 'Upon our return to our capital, we shall send Your Majesty a thousand of our finest horses for your army, to ratify our fealty to this alliance.'

I finish translating and all are overwhelmed by the gift - none so much as Anik, who whispers aside to his woman. 'Are you nuts, how are we to move-'

'Details, details,' she waves him off, 'no amount of planning is reward enough for the deliverance of your heir.' She stares her husband down, and then looks back to the young king and smiles victorious.

The Maharaja is delighted by the outcome. 'I very much look forward to receiving them.'

'After fifteen years of scheming and suffering, we are just letting them walk away.' I stand watching the remnants of Anik's horde ride off into the sunset.

Anik's woman turns in her saddle to wave at us. 'I look forward to our next meeting, warrior sister.'

I translate for the princess, who returns the wave and then looks to me to address my disappointment.

'It would seem our lives are no longer ruled by fear.' She smiles sincerely.

'Are you reciting Tamous at me again, Majesty?' I shall be having my brother's wisdom preached to me for the rest of my days.

'Of course. He saved us in there. My brother recited my teacher's words at me...' She drew a deep breath, and shook her head as if silently scolding herself. 'Kosal may be young, but he has been learning the inner path far longer than I. Clearly I still have much work to do.' She appeared at peace with the resolve. 'To hear wisdom is one thing, to understand and utilise it is quite something else again.'

'One wise and one strong, perhaps Tamous referred to Your Highnesses in his prophecy?' I pose.

'He didn't.' She states surely.

'How did the ending of that prophecy go?' I am still curious about that.

She considers my request a moment, then cracks half a smile. 'Perhaps once we put this demon to bed, I shall allow you to fight me for that information.'

I cannot keep the smile from my face; my cheeks ache with delight at that notion, for I have dreamt of our rematch many times. 'If it pleases Your Majesty.'

'Done then.' She moves to join her brother, who is observing the large pile of sleeping black shiny sludge. 'Are you ready to wake the beast?'

'I vote we try to sleepwalk it back.' The king outlines his vision.

'We shall do our best.' The princess serves him a reassuring smile.

'Sister,' the Maharaja traces an arc with his finger over the beast, as if drawing a rainbow. 'What are-'

'Shhh!' The princess urges him to hold that thought. 'When we are alone.' The young king nods to affirm as his sister looks at me. 'Ready, General?'

'The way has been cleared and the stone lid of the crypt has been retracted.' I pass on my brief as if I am not insanely curious about the royal family secret. 'I shall walk ahead to ensure we are clear.'

The royals join hands and in hushed tones they begin to coax the creature forward through the streets of the temple complex-turned fortress. Hardly any of the people had departed for home yet; they had all stayed to see the back of the Sangdil and this spectacle. No one will question the young royals' right to rule, or whether or not they are the true heirs of the Kaundinya - this deed proves their

264

sovereignty. As we pass, the people bow down to the ground in awe of the return of their royal family, and weep in gratitude for deliverance from Ashoka's regime.

Once inside the inner sanctum, the creature slithers up into the inside of its reinforced and deepened containment, and I stand corrected in my assumption that the princess could not just make the Naga Raja roll over and go back to bed. Tamous' relic has been carefully stored aside to prevent damage, just as I instructed, as without him the Naga Raja will not stay pacified for long. Before I give the order to slide the crypt lid closed, I smash the long neck of Anik's sealed bottle. Placing it down on the ground, I urge everyone back.

The fragment slithers out, a small replica of the monstrous dragon-headed snake, with many worm-like tentacles protruding and twisting from its head, like a mane with a mind of its own. It turns its attention to us briefly and then shoots off in the opposite direction to join its cluster in the crypt. On my whistle, a team at the back of the sacrificial platform push the huge block forward until it drops into its frame and seals the crypt closed. Tamous' statue is placed in the centre of the crypt lid once again and I order the chamber cleared in preparation to flood it.

'Highnesses?' I query why they remain, but I suspect this has something to do with their family secret.

'We need a few more moments.' The princess advises. 'We will join you in the temple momentarily.'

'I am your humble servant, Majesty, but as your general, I will not leave the new heirs to our kingdom alone with humanity's greatest threat ... no matter how benign the danger appears or how powerful your bloodline is.' I expect the princess will be offended and threaten to kill me.

'Face the other way.' She instructs to my surprise. 'Anything you hear, never leaves this chamber.'

I comply and turn about.

'What are they, Limrani?' Kosal asks.

'I believe they are the potential ranks of Naga yet to gain influence in this world,' she replied.

'Like hungry ghosts.'

'Exactly,' she awards. 'Once a human agrees to carry a shard of it, the Naga can influence their moods and decisions.'

'Like the Inter-dweller, Làoshi.' Kosal replies. 'Only Làoshi is a

265

constructive influence, not a destructive one.'

'You know about Làoshi?' Limrani sounds surprised.

'Of course, I speak with him often, don't you?' Kosal queries.

'I do.' She admits gingerly, and at this point I need to speak up.

'Is that the old man's voice I keep hearing?' I turn to query, and they both look at me surprised.

'You too?' The princess sounds only half surprised.

I nod. 'Right before we entered the beast, he said-'

'You can still bring each other through this,' she answers with me and we stare intensely at each other for a moment, not knowing how to react.

'You were saying, about the Naga?' The Maharaja gets the conversation back on track.

'I was saying that when a person is evil enough the stone will enter the body of its host, and one of these disembodied Naga will be able to attach to their host's form and feed off their life force.' The princess motions with her finger for me to turn back around, and I comply, though I had a million questions of my own.

'Why can I see them? Our secret?' Asks the prince.

'The disembodied Naga are drawn to the source of our advantage, yet like everyone else they cannot see it, use it, or find it.'

'Why?'

'Because the Mother of the Naga gifted it to our family. The full story is written upon the walls of this temple somewhere? Mistress Chenda knows how to read several languages, including that of our ancestors, and she has vowed to teach us, so that the histories are not lost and can be passed on to our-' She cuts herself short and then adds awkwardly, 'future generations. The last of our line must return our inheritance to the Mother of the Naga.'

There is an awkward pause, then a burst of laughter.

'I think I'd rather get married.' The young king decided.

More laughter.

'So, I am stuck with all these disembodied horrors constantly dwelling on the periphery of my vision?' The king sounds less than thrilled.

'No.' The princess replies. 'There is one safe place to leave it, where it will pacify the beast and be close at hand, but we shall have to rely on our own mortal powers henceforth.'

My heart jumps into my throat when I hear what she is suggesting, and I am filled with admiration and relief that I will not always need to be so mentally guarded around her.

They had gone quiet, so I dared to sneak a peek of them dropping something around the neck of Tamous' statue. The Maharaja backed up a couple of steps, but the princess remained crouched before my brother. 'Our lives are ruled by fear no longer.' She told him, tears immediately falling from her eyes. 'We gave evil nothing to oppose and it disappeared, just as you said. We are safe now. We are free.'

Her words bring tears to my eyes; there is so much of my brother's truth in them. I will learn his teaching to pass his ways and wisdom onto our armies. I turn back as the princess rises, and I wait for the royals to pass me by.

'You may flood the chamber, General.'

It is admirable how easily they both walk away from all that power. 'Yes, Majesty.'

The princess glanced aside to me. 'And then meet me in the throne room and we will settle that other matter.'

I don't believe I have ever smiled so much as I have this day, and yet my vendetta is unfulfilled. If I am honest, I believe that part of this silent exultation I feel is because we did not execute our enemies, but made them allies. Not a single man was lost retaking our homeland this day. How very Tamous that is - just as he would have it. I miss him ... I've always missed him. I wonder how he would feel about me heading for a rematch with his student? Did he find the princess as attractive as I do? Did they ever-?

The notion shocks me to a halt. *Nah ... Tamous was too much of an angel, and she is a princess.* I resume my course. *But did he know she was a princess?* My pace slows once more as I recall how his relic cracks her hardened warrior facade every time she looks at it. I cannot decide whether it is Tamous' death or her grief over Tamous' death that hurts me more. But I have been reminded that I do still have a heart beating in my chest, and it smarts like saltwater on an open wound every time I think of Tamous and Limrani together. Whatever the truth of it, it is the past and best left there.

Right now, I am heading for the tryst I've been anticipating for what seems like forever. This is not just a dream come true, but a much-needed event. Of course, I do not mean to harm her, just to disarm her would give me life and win me the rest of the prophecy. My brother's way may have made for an ending that is to the benefit of all, but it has to be the greatest anticlimax to a life quest *ever!* A sentiment I believe only another warrior will understand.

The courtroom doors open before me and I enter to note the seat of power is empty - ambush alert! I draw my sword and block her strike, just as I did the first time we met.

'You finally got here!' The princess grins, circling me with her blade gently resting against mine.

'We are alone?' I flinch but do not strike to gauge how well she feels my intention through her steel.

'Of course. They don't allow *princesses* to do this sort of thing.' She does not strike; she is a gentle touch, which is to her great advantage.

Most men assume that strength ensures the upper hand, but in this case she can learn more about how I am about to strike from barely touching my blade. My only choice is to retreat before I attack, as an attack from this close stance will prove fatal.

'And I've been spoiling for a fight all day.' She withdraws first to await my attack. 'Performing without actions is the master's way, but I'm not ready to become a monk just yet.'

'You read my mind.' Our swords clash and a joyous dance begins. Such a vision she is to watch. I fight only hard enough to defend myself for I have no desire to attack this angel in motion.

'Fight!' She loses patience with me. 'Or you'll never know how the prophecy ends. Disarm me ... I dare you.'

I repress a laugh, and have a gash across my upper arm before I even raise my sword. 'Hey, no superpowers-' I protest.

'This is all me, I'm afraid.' She sympathises. 'So you'll just have to up your game, General, or I'll have no worthy appointment to spar against.'

The notion of being her sparring partner is ample motivation, so I begin to try a little harder, and then a little harder - and again. At this point, I am attacking with all I have and she is still dancing around me like a ghost, like a goddess.

In the end, I throw down my sword and declare defeat.

'Oh come on,' she encourages, 'you're quite good. When you know what I know, you may vanquish me.'

'I am deeply flattered you think so.' Clearly I need to study this outer path of my brother's design also. I retrieve my sword from the floor and sheath it. 'Will that be all, Majesty?'

'No.' Her humour ebbs. 'That is far from all. I wish to thank you, General Bào Satura, for taking back our homeland from the Sangdil, and for diving into the jaws of darkness with me.' She drops the sword in her hand and embraces me.

I return the gesture, ecstatic to be able to breathe deep the scent of her.

'Our vigil begins.' She whispers the beginning of the end of the prophecy. 'Insurgents meet. Stone hearts melt. Broken souls mend, and united, overcome.'

Tamous predicted our future together, and my goddess is already aware. My heart is so filled with joy it hurts like a dagger to my chest. This is my brother assuring me from beyond the grave that everything has unfolded as it should.

'We're not orphans anymore.' Limrani consoles me, as decades of pent up pain and tears begin to flow from me. Our embrace tightens and we remain just as we are for the longest time.

Chapter 11
Khemri 2082 AD
Taylay – The Magician

I wake with a reactive jerk and startle Mai, who must have been leaning in to roust me.

'You were having a bad dream, Master.' She explains why she is in such close proximity to me and backs up to crouch on her haunches.

'More a recollection than a dream.' I roll onto my back to stretch out the kinks. 'And please don't call me master, it makes me feel like a slave trader.'

'Sorry, magnificence-'

'No ... definitely not.' I sit upright, raising my knees, and hook my elbows around them to brace myself in a seated position. A sleep haze hovers over my thoughts. I was preparing for this day with the Inter-dweller while I slept; I don't recall the details and I don't have to. All shall unfold and flow forth as it should, and I shall not hinder the process by trying to second-guess creation.

'Then what is the right terminology for addressing a magician?' Mai clearly just wants to please.

'Just call me, Taylay, that's-'

'I couldn't possibly, Lord.' She continues to shake her head to emphasise this point. 'I shall fetch your tea.' She preempts my need and rushes off before I can object.

I cast my sights around the cave. Many local people live here, having retreated into caves after the Republic invaded, just as our displaced people have many times throughout history.

This cave in particular is ideal for hiding from the air patrols and drones, as a slender crack in the outer cavern gives way to a large inner cavern, where it is easier to take out an incoming enemy. This place was recently named Phnom nei Athrkambang - Mountain of the Mystery - a mystery uncovered by yours truly. Several years ago, I discovered a claim engraved on the cavern walls here in English, below some ancient Fangshi text. The claim was that the Fangshi verse was written by Tamous the Innocent on the day Ashoka kneeled before a priest! Oddly, both the ancient Sinàese and modern English texts appeared to have been written at the same time with a stone carving device currently unknown to us. Of course, all the "experts" believed that the anomaly was some kind of hoax because they couldn't explain it.

I had a long history with this site, and had thought it an excellent place to base myself, but clearly many displaced others had the same thought.

Today, we all sit around the more open outer cave, soaking in the early morning sun rising before us. Since I have created an energetic wall around my homeland that the Archon tech cannot penetrate, everyone on this side of the barrier is breathing a lot easier - no aluminium, smart-dust bugs or black goo particles choking up the air - it is bliss. I know all about what was transpiring in my homeland, whilst I was kept drugged up in an institution.

When government operatives first locked me up without charge or trial, I assumed my incarceration was because I had discovered ancient Fangshi text deep in our homeland, a text that was thousands of years old. For the Fangshi had once existed in Sinà - that had now been absorbed into the northern territories of the Republic. I figured the Khmeri Government didn't want the Republic claiming this as proof that our land was once theirs. But now in hindsight, I realise that my incarceration was about an entirely different talent of mine, that I had done my best to suppress my whole life.

With my talent for energetically screwing with and blowing up electrical equipment, being born in the age of electronics had been a curse when I was young. This is why I studied ancient languages and archaeology, as the work took me into the great outdoors where I had less chance of breaking anything.

But if this talent was the true cause of my incarceration, then our government was not overthrown by the Republic, it was in cahoots with them. And both entities must have been tracking me way before I ever discovered this place. New management is needed in this region and everyone knows that the people's choice is Mebanhcheakear.

My most revered spiritual teacher, Amari, told me of my deliverance at the hands of the rebel leader, who should have had me killed! But instead, she allowed Amari to take me and heal me of the addiction that had been forced upon me. It was only after the rebel leader's capture that I discovered her present whereabouts and predicament. The Republic had made a big deal of the legendary Mebanhcheakear being a woman. But learning of her peril only doubled my reasons for returning to my homeland. It is my hope to repay her generosity and present my true self. A spirit from the future, who called himself a Seeker, had told Amari that I would become a very powerful magician - a title that still amuses me. The Seeker also predicted that together Dr Sumati and I could overthrow the Republic and bring the dark forces driving our enemies to heal.

My memory of the faithful day this went down is clouded by an opium haze. I remember an old man beckoning me forth into a forest. Amari claimed that the old man was indivisible with Onderwyser, and with the Inter-dweller of Zhi Sumati, said to have guided Tamous the Innocent and his only student, Limrani. Amari believed that this being dwelt within everyone, and had connected us all on that fateful day for a higher purpose. Once she learned of my talent for breaking technology, Amari encouraged me to develop this ability to its fullest potential, so that I might use it to rage against the machines, if need be. She felt that I was the antidote for the AI virus. I don't know if Amari's association with me was why she was targeted for termination, but I know it was a transhuman who carried out her murder - I took him out myself. There is only one regime utilising such mercenaries in the field right now. I had previously given no thought to returning to the country that had betrayed me, I was quite content living in Africa among the Dagara people. But I could not allow a soul so pure as Amari's to be stolen from humanity, without knowing those responsible would answer for that crime and their growing list of injustices.

'Your tea.' Mai hands me her offering and kneels before me.

'I wouldn't remain so close,' I warn as her dead straight, fine dark hair rises up electrified to form a ball around her head.

This makes everyone laugh, and young Mai retreats to a distance her old grandfather is more comfortable with. I raise my tea to him in thanks for his generosity, and the sweet old man attempts to raise himself in order to prostrate before me. 'Please no.' I implore him. 'It is I who should bow to you.'

He waves his hands at me repeatedly, insisting. 'You honour us, Magician.'

I force a smile of defeat, as this name, title, whatever you want to call it, has stuck and clearly will remain thus for all prosperity whether I like it or not. I look out over the forest and sip my brew that is just the right temperature. 'It's good,' I assure Mai as she is still gazing at me expectantly, and pleased by my feedback she continues about her chores.

Another sip and my mind drifts back to a recollection that hung over me as I woke - the fateful day that led me into the sphere of Amari and the legendary woman my people call, Mebanhcheakear.

The ground beneath my feet collapsed and I landed in a great labyrinth of dirt tunnels. A moth to a flame, I continued to pursue the light of the old man's lantern, clumsy on my feet and fearful of the large spiders in their overarching webs. After several turns, following paths leading ever downward, I saw a light ahead that eclipsed the lantern - daylight through a fissure. I passed through into the light, waited for my eyes to adjust and then, struck speechless in awe, I beheld a huge stone chamber. The smooth stone walls were covered in the same ancient text that I'd found in the cave at the Mountain of Mystery.

But when I stumbled into that rebel base and saw the text on the wall, written in the same Fangshi text with the same precision tool, even in my smacked-out delirium, I knew that cavern would validate my previous find. It was itself a historical marvel, long rumoured to exist but never found. I strongly suspected that this massive cave was the one containing all the teachings of Tamous the Innocent and Limrani. These writings had been translated, preserved, and handed down to us via some ancient Indus valley texts found in the old Scythian capital of Minnagara, but the original source had never been discovered. As I had observed the characters depicted on the walls, they lit up in turn and spoke to me. The utterances had been so soft that I was having trouble making sense of them, so I told them. 'Speak up, I can't hear you!'

'Where did he come from?' A female voice had startled me into realising that I was not alone.

I had turned to find a small military force surrounding a woman, who I now know was Zhi Sumati, rebel leader and political prisoner. Her face was the only one I remember.

'I was just taking a piss,' I'd slurred in my own defence. 'Then an old man led me down here.'

'An old man?' She'd been curious about that statement.

Amari had later explained that Dr Sumati was in the process of forging a connection with the Inter-dweller herself.

I'd scratched my head, wondering where the old bloke had gone. 'He was here, I swear...' I'd swayed about in my stance and had been way too drugged up to run or to deflect the gun hilt coming at my face.

'Lights out, buddy.'

Crack.

The memory still makes me wince, and as I shake off the tea I've splattered on my hand, I look about to find all eyes on me.

There are many gentle smiles directed my way, but folks respectfully keep their distance. Maybe they don't want Mai's hairdo? Or perhaps they believe I am a god or a demon? I am inspired by their goodness and trust, and although they are honoured to take care of me, our association could ultimately make them a target. I will depart as soon as I finish with this heavenly brew.

A young lad approaches me cautiously and stops some distance away to ask. 'How long will your spell wall last, Lord Magician?'

His address is amusing to me, but I suck back my humour so I don't appear to mock him. 'What some might call a spell, I see more as an aptitude for collaborating with elements.' The lad is baffled, and indeed I have not answered his question. 'The wall will last as long as it is needed.'

'Even if something happens to you?'

'Nothing will hap ... pen-'

A windy disturbance erupts above the mountain. The treetops of the forest before us begin to sway about and the people amid the trees there gasp as they point to something in the sky over Phnom nei Athrkambang. I place my cup aside and rise.

There follows a whoosh of force and a burst of light that blasts forth from the inner cave, sending small chunks of rock flying out from the thin crevasse walkway - which is now a little wider than before. When the disturbance ebbs and dust settles, the locals catch sight of a cyborg emerging from within and flee for their lives, along with the lad giving me the third degree.

I approach the breach in the cave wall, tapping my fingertips together gently to build the charge needed to take the intruder out, silently appealing to the Inter-dweller for a read on the situation. Of course Làoshi is silent; he can only guide, be my intuition, my encouragement. I feel no trepidation, however. If anything, I am oddly excited.

'Wait!' A femme fatale, fully geared up with tech add-ons the like of which I have never seen, puts herself between me and the cyborg. 'Are you the Magician?'

I serve her a look that implies that should be obvious when I have electricity surging between my fingertips.

'Doh,' she concedes her oversight. 'The Seeker sent us.'

Not even her broad smile could deaden the shock of that

announcement.

'Well actually, it was a couple of Pleiadian friends of his.'

'The Seeker.' I utter, shocked. This is a little secret of mine that no one should be aware of. Clearly Amari had not told me of the Seeker and his predictions for no reason. A chill radiates out of the back of my heart centre and washes over me in consecutive waves, alerting me to the presence of some serendipitous inner truth that I didn't quite fathom. Perhaps his mission had been to keep me alive, so that my actions this day might in turn benefit his people in the future?

'Yes. But it is the Pleiadians who sent us,' the young woman shrugs, 'technically speaking.'

'Pleiadians ... as in extraterrestrial beings?' I eye over the cyborg, who is far less clunky than any of the military types I have encountered before.

She nods. 'A-huh. My new beau and his partner just dropped us off.'

'I call bullshit on you dating an alien.' The cyborg challenges.

'All these upgrades of yours didn't just appear. You were out for ages, you don't know what transpired out there.' She flings her hand up towards the sky.

'They are etheric beings?' He reasons.

'It's really amazing what you can do with energy. I could have stayed there forever...' She gasps. 'How long were we gone anyway?'

Her companion's expression goes blank a second, then he is annoyed. 'Months!'

The cyborg has obviously hacked into a network satellite already, which is a good thing as I wouldn't have a clue what day it is.

'Why...' The woman directs the query at her companion. 'If they have the tech to do all this,' she motions to her hardware and his upgrades. 'And jump through time, then why not just pop us back to where we left?'

'Maybe their time-tech isn't human compatible-'

'Who are you people, and why are you here?' I am still building up charge and sooner or later I am going to have to release it.

'We're here to help you free the rebel Zhi Sumati.' The bleached blonde informs me as if my quest is common knowledge.

'What makes you think that is my intention?'

The cyborg steps in to explain. 'Dr Amari Nosipho smuggled you out of the country, directly following her meeting with the rebel leader, Zhi Sumati. You must have been someone special to her or she would not have allowed you to leave her base alive.'

The cyborg knew a lot. 'Who are you people?' I will not ask again, I hope they can sense that.

'We are the only surviving children of Xi Ching.'

'The Prime Minister of the Republic?' I take a step back.

'I am Annchi.' The young woman points to herself and then her companion. 'And this is my brother Wei.'

'But what-' I try to question them further but I need to discharge. I run to the edge of the cave until I find earth. Sinking my fingertips deep into the dirt, I let the charge go slowly into the ground - just as Amari taught me - until the force is harmlessly neutralised.

'Thank you.' Annchi clasps her hands in front of her heart, 'for giving us the benefit of the doubt.'

'You cannot come with me to rescue our next prime minister.' I inform them.

'I know we are a high risk-' She counters.

'That's not it. I'll fry all your pretty hardware, along with the rest of Ching's transhuman force.' I shrug, expecting no more argument.

'Do your worst.' Wei opens his arms and invites me to attack him.

'I'm serious. I'll fry all your circuits.' My gaze shifts from Wei to Annchi. 'All your gadgets.'

'You won't,' she rolls her eyes. 'This is alien tech, and you are both wasting time.'

'How did ET's get involved in this? Were you abducted?' I'd had no experience with extraterrestrials myself, but being an archaeologist, it was clear that our ancestors had dealings with advanced beings and technology.

'Wei was badly injured rescuing me from our father, the day the old bastard forced Zhi Sumati to tell him where the mother cluster of goo was.' Annchi begins. 'I didn't think we were going to make it out of there, and I don't know why the Pleiadians saved us.'

I look to Wei, who shrugs.

'I don't remember much, I just woke up.' He informs, not really helping their cause. Then the cyborg's expression went blank again.

'What is it?' Annchi looks to her brother, expectantly.

'Father is being escorted to Boran Moan.'

'To the ruins there?' I knew the name immediately, as every archaeologist wanted into that site, but access was always denied.

'So that black goo creature is still there?' She asks her brother.

'Wait, you've been in there?' I am flabbergasted, then bemused. 'What black goo creature? I know the rebels had a small sample of the organic AI substance used in Archon tech-'

'Oh no,' Wei shakes his head. 'Father found the mother lode, and now he has more than enough to power a massive cyborg army.'

It seems taking back my homeland might be rather more problematic than first imagined. 'Any idea where Dr Sumati is presently?'

'With our father.' Wei replies.

'I see.' So either this is an ambush, or a dream come true?

I am capable of taking out all the tech, but the transhuman forces still have human working parts and semi-automatic handheld weapons, so just because their enhancements die, that doesn't mean they aren't still a threat. I believe that in my arsenal of tools I have everything I need to combat any situation, but I had never tested my power en masse against a motivated, hostile enemy force. I wasn't sure I trusted these two either, but the Inter-dweller seemed at peace with them.

'If we intended to kill you, Magician, you'd be dead by now.' Wei grins.

Clearly, Wei has a silent speech interface and is following my train of thought. *You are welcome to try.* I grin back.

'Can we move?' Annchi rolls her eyes.

'Boran Maon is on the other side of the country.' I state the obvious. 'We'll need aircraft to get there today.'

Wei serves me another of his insincere grins. He pulls a disc-shaped object from the back of his body armour and tosses it down to the ground, where it hovers and increases in size exponentially.

'Hoverboard?' I surmise, thinking this is not the most efficient means. 'Fun.'

'Nice guess, but no.' Annchi steps onto the transport and vanishes.

'Maybe not.' I back up. What if it's a wormhole into a parallel universe? 'I think I'll find my own ride.'

'It's not a black hole,' Annchi calls to make it known that she is only cloaked from view. 'Once we are all onboard, it will vanish altogether, and we'll be completely undetectable.'

'Look, I am still not keen, to be honest. If you've only just woken from your upgrade, how do you know how all this new tech works?' The premise does not inspire faith.

'It's called programming.' Wei moved to grab me, but I stepped back.

'How does she know?' I think he senses I am just stalling this time.

'Come on, Mr Wizard...' The cyborg grabs hold of both my shoulders and forces me aboard. 'You're going to love this.'

We touch down at a safe distance from the high security ruins of the ancient capital. I am so exhilarated, I could die in this moment a happy man were it not for the great debt I owe Zhi Sumati and my teacher. As an elementalist, after that flight I feel completely at one with the air, which to the Dagara and the alchemist is not considered an element per se, but a medley of extremes, a sea of invisible things and the magician's back door. I feel so exhilarated and at one with creation that I could almost skip over my summons and know that I am walking into this confrontation supported. But then I am human, with earthly agendas that might cloud my judgement, so best that I show the proper respect by doing the due diligence.

'Okay,' Wei remounts his transport on the back of his breastplate. 'Let's kick some AI arse.'

'I need a moment to offer a prayer and request the support of those who are the source of my power.' I take a seat on a rock by the stream we've landed alongside. The back of my long wool coat acts as a blanket for me to sit upon. This coat is the only item of clothing that I wear, apart from my trousers. I never wear shoes, so I remain grounded to the earth.

'Are you saying the source of your power can refuse to aid our cause?' Wei sounds a might displeased about that.

'If the cause is truly righteous, I will not be refused.' I explain. 'There is much I can do by myself, but we have need of the elemental big guns, like air-'

'Air?' Both my company are surprised that I value this collaborator so highly.

'Air is a miraculous hermaphrodite - gentle and beautiful, hostile and violent - existing on and passing between many different planes of existence and states of being, not just the physical world. It is said that the Archons, or the Naga as they are known here, stem from the lower astral realms, so we can really use the help of multi-dimensional entities.'

'Whoa, that's deep.' Annchi's eyes are wide with wonder.

'I'll take your word for it.' The cyborg backs away to give me space. 'Just hurry it up.'

Thanks to Amari's training, I know how to summon, greet, work with, and farewell elementals, just as I would human associates.

I take a moment to calm and centre myself. I place all my fingertips together, but not my palms; I hold them wide apart to allow energy to dance between my hands. I breathe deeply, and quietly give thanks for the solace of those who support me in this life. I start with the Inter-dweller, who is my constant guidance and inspiration. I thank my spirit animal, the White Cobra, who came to me during my Dagara cleansing and initiation to be my protector - and a conduit to link me to nature's strength, healing and wisdom. Then I give thanks to my most wise teacher, Amari, who saved me in every manner of speaking. Lastly, I thank the four directions and the earth herself, who grants me life and the power to contribute to this creation.

It is I, the throwback.
He who is most adept at the things
modern consciousness overlooks and is ignorant of.

I begin my inward address by announcing myself in a fashion that defines that which I am most gifted at and proud of - my own cosmic myth, in this tiny instance of awareness.

He who is about destiny's business,
supported by previous lives
and hidden forces.

I seek your wise counsel,
steadfast from the dawn of the world,
to the mutable future.

I seek your sanction,
to command the ancient forces,
with detached witness consciousness.

Gift me acute discernment,
allow me to tap that vital source spring
that never runs dry.

A wind whipping around me out of nowhere is my assurance that we are in flow with the day's proceedings and supported. I rise.

'All good?' Wei asks, arms folded and leaning against a tree, obviously not enjoying the delay.

'I'll get closer to this target alone.' I have to be honest. 'One look at you two and they'll open fire immediately.'

'We'll go stealth,' says Wei. Annchi nods and they both disappear.

The event shocks the life out of me. 'I hope you two are right about that tech you are sporting being shockproof.'

'Just worry about your own arse.' Wei startles me with the response, and shoves something in my ear.

'What the?'

'*I have Silent Speech Interface,*' Wei prevents me from pulling the piece straight back out. '*This is the human version. Annchi has one too, so no more speaking out loud.*'

We could have just flown into the ancient temple complex under stealth, but ultimately we need to take out the entire force and all the security measures, and that would be easier to accomplish on the way in than the way out.

'*So who are you to Zhi Sumati that you would risk your life to free her?*' Annchi makes conversation as we walk out of the bush and hit the dirt road that leads to the temple fort.

'*I am no one to her.*' I shrug, it's the truth.

'*But she spared your life.*' Annchi clarifies.

'*She did.*'

'*That's pretty romantic,*' she decides.

'*It really wasn't.*' The notion is laughable. '*I have an ulterior motive for wanting to free her.*'

'*Typical man,*' Annchi whines. '*Is it any wonder I am dating an alien!*'

'*You are not.*' Wei cuts in. '*What ulterior motive?*'

'*The cave her rebel force based themselves in,*' I outline, '*if I am ever to find that place again, she is the only person I know who knows where it is.*'

'*I know where it is.*'

Wei's claim stops me dead in my tracks. '*You do?*'

'*Huge place, lined with old empire characters.*' Wei's description is accurate.

'*Yes!*' I am thrilled beyond belief. '*Tell me, where is it?*'

'*I will,*' Wei replies as his sister gasps and is hushed quiet.

'What's going on?' Obviously something is amiss.

'*No speaking out loud.*' They both insist at once.

'*What are you not telling me?*'

'*Let's just focus on one venture at a time. Once we are done here, I'll take you to the site you're looking for.*' Wei vows.

I would much rather he just tell me now. '*You had better not die. In fact, let's try not to kill anyone.*'

'*I'll do my best,*' Annchi replies.

'*Severely maiming is still on the table then?*'

I feel Wei's comment does not warrant a response. '*If we start taking fire, get in close to me, I have a trick. Have they arrived yet?*'

'*About five minutes ago ... according to the gatehouse log. What trick?*'

We come round a corner to find the guard-lined drive to the complex stretching out before us.

Showtime. A storm brews inside my being and simultaneously erupts over our destination in the middle of the perfectly clear sky. Thunder booms and lightning threads through the cloud before lashing down to make contact with the earth in and around the complex.

Rightly concerned that they might be struck down and fried - flesh, tech and all, the guards' attention is focused on the storm's rapid spread across the sky. It is empowering to know that all the technology in the world is still no match for mother nature and her minions. The guards haven't yet noted my approach.

An electro-magnetic charge, and what our ancient ancestors referred to as qi, builds within me, and with the support of the air elementals, the shockwave will travel much further. Unlike man-made nuclear-based EMP weapons, I don't need altitude to be effective. I bring the gamma and the air brings the ions, and together we produce an EMP that is low-lying, contained, high-yield and completely directional. By the time I register on the soldiers' radar, I am hosting my own seething tempest. I feel the electrifying surges from my toes to the tips of my long feral hair. I am a freak of nature and I am here to represent the 'native', organic, human path to *evolution* that has to date been completely underestimated. Before the combatants can engage weapons, I release the electro-magnetic force that has a threefold effect - a near-instantaneous powerful pulse that induces extreme voltage and overload in electrical conductors. Then a subsequent high-amplitude pulse, like a lightning strike, and a final slower and lower-amplitude waveform that feasts on long electrical conductors - similar to a mini geomagnetic storm. This lasts for several seconds as the magnetic field of existence is briefly warped. The strike rushes like a silent gust of wind over the task force before us, who drop as limbs go defunct and systems go dead. Within this task force, there are AI units that look human and transhuman - the latter are the only ones still moving. In this case, the less enhanced humans have the advantage and those who have two working legs advance towards me. Others raise any manual weapons they possess to return fire.

'With me.' I warn my invisible accomplices and with one sweeping spin, I draw down a serpent of water from the rain-laden clouds above and it coils around us like a thick donut of water.

The sight stuns the opposing force to non-action for a moment as they still have a trace of human wonder in them. But I can see the Archon riders on their backs with my third-eye vision - another of my teacher's practices passed onto me. The astral creatures squeeze the lumbar lymph nodes of their human transporters. This keeps them spiritually trapped in the primal energies of their lowest chakra, in their ego-based self, and completely cuts them off from the Inter-dweller, who is their connection to higher consciousness. It only takes a few moments for fear to override their wonder and they open fire. Bullets surging into the water shield lose momentum and sink to the ground.

'This is the most amazing water ... thingy ... phenomenon, EVER!' Annchi is clearly enjoying the show.

'This whole life is an illusion.' I repeat what my teacher taught me. 'Once you understand that, you can make of it what you wish.'

'That is a brilliant perspective.' She replies, sounding rather more subdued.

'Can we move through this water barrier safely?' Wei asks, as the enemy is growing tired of wasting ammunition and they are surely wondering the same thing.

'At present,' I inform, 'but I can also make it thick like quick-water that will hold you firm and drown you.'

'Please refrain.' Wei requests. 'Annchi, let's mop up out there.' They both charge forth through the water barrier - still invisible - and start knocking out the stragglers one by one.

After a time, one of my invisible comrades comes running back through the swirling wall of water that is still moving forward with me. 'Bugs.' Annchi informs, sounding harrowed.

'Don't worry about those. Any guards left?'

'*No, we are all clear.*'

As I allow the water shield to drop, it splashes down and recedes, leaving dead bullets everywhere. I am, from all appearances, the only one still conscious beyond the gates. '*See.*' I motion to the bug swarm sweeping towards the old Republican border to join the rest of the smart dust I dispersed from the country, back to where it came.

'*How ARE you doing that?*' She sounds like she has been waiting to ask that question for a long time.

'*I am not.*' I confess. '*Again, this is just collaborating with elementals ... air is good for so much more than keeping us alive and blowing leaves about. Everything in creation is just being, waiting to be useful.*'

'*How true is that?*' Annchi sounds mind-blown again.

At the gate, Wei has hacked into the system and the heavy metal gates slide open before us. '*So, Mr, "I can do this better on my own, but I also fry everything I touch," you wouldn't have made it past the gate. You're welcome.*'

Annchi has a giggle and is heard to clap.

The metal gates are massive, and although I could fry the lock, I would have had a hell of a time getting them open. '*I am beginning to see why the Seeker sent you.*' I cautiously move up the only road through the complex that is disturbingly quiet and abandoned. No sign of any guards around, but there are some dead drones about the place. '*This feels like an ambush.*'

'*There's nothing between us and the temple. I know because we are already there.*' Wei informs. '*That's the Naga Raja you are sensing, it is dis-ease itself. Being a native, you are more sensitive to that kind of thing.*'

'*Do you practice being patronising, or does it just come naturally?*' I increase my pace to catch them up.

'*Wei was like this before he was enhanced.*' Annchi happily ratted out her brother.

'*Whoa!*' I enter the central courtyard where the temple is located and there are several government vehicles parked here. I turn a circle to admire the two and a half thousand year-old structures, but my sights come to rest on the imposing carved columns of the Temple of the Naga Raja. 'My holy ancestors,' I utter in awe as I approach the forbidden archaeological treasure.

'*Exactly. And if we don't win the day, my father and the goon squad will knock it down and build a more sturdy container for their sub-creature.*'

The premise fuels my desire to defend my people, our history and culture, so that we don't lose all the lessons that we, as a collective, have already learnt - the president's son is quite the motivator. *'Where is everyone?'* I wonder, having no knowledge of the layout of this place. *'There is a large group of life forms in the temple sub-structure.'* Wei advises.

'If there is a subterranean chamber, any tech inside was probably shielded from the last shock wave by the earth.' I inform, as we enter the upper temple where the altar stone is located.

'Well charge up, buttercup.' Wei suggests, heading down the stairs towards the lower level. I give a silent sigh to leave behind the exquisite upper temple walls, covered in ancient Shauraseni text. *On the way out.* I comfort myself by imagining I will leave this place alive and still capable of reading, and that none of the temple will be harmed during this confrontation. The structure itself is a transient thing; it is the knowledge on the walls I aspire to save that hopefully includes the history of this place and its unearthly occupant.

There are only two guards on the upper platform that overlooks the main crypt chamber below, and they are silently taken out by my invisible companions before I reach them. But when I spot the huge, black slimy creature of darkness below, I duck down and conceal myself behind the wall that frames the platform. *'Mother of darkness.'*

'No shit.' Clearly Wei has never seen the beast either. I peer over the short wall to see the chief of state standing over the president, who is on his knees. Zhi Sumati is under guard further away, but oddly, she appears to be glowing like an angelic being, and the epicentre of the light is her heart.

'See! He has the shakes,' the chief motions to his disabled superior. 'His body rejects the technology, just like his son's did; he is useless to you. My body accommodates your enhancements with no issues and has for some time. Let me be your anointed one.'

'It's a coup.' Just something else to contend with today.

'Chief Li, a traitor?' Wei seems surprised. *'This parasite can make a turncoat out of anyone.'*

'I hope Chief kills the bastard.' The spite of the comment makes it clear Annchi isn't joking about wanting her father dead.

The creature leans close to the president, who has all sorts of nervous ticks going on. 'There is new medication, we are-' Xi Ching begins to choke and gag as the black liquid crystal is vomited from his body in the form of a long writhing snake.

Chief Li, not appearing as keen now, steps back as the parasite slithers towards him and winds itself up around his leg and body. 'I really don't think this is necessar-' The man starts to choke and gag as the deposit invades his mouth and vanishes into his form.

The sight makes me queasy. I sink behind the skirting wall to note Fangshi text carved with the same precision tool as the previous two sites. I shift out of the way to allow the light flooding from upstairs to illuminate it.

'What does it say?' Annchi has noted my distraction.

'It says; the Heart of the Naga is here. It's here! I thought it was just a myth.'

'What is the Heart?' Annchi queries.

'No one is exactly sure.' I read on. 'The Heart of the Naga is here ... and must remain until the end of the Kaundinya-'

'The what?'

'The royal family. Legend has it they were the only ones able to perceive the treasure. The last of the line is requested to return the Heart to the Mother of the Naga. Only the Heart in the hands of the true heir of the Kaundinya can control the Naga Raja, to remove the Heart is to unleash the beast from the abyss.'

According to my understanding, there hadn't been a Kaundinya on the Khmeri throne since the fifth century, but the family did rule for over seven hundred years. So is the Heart still here? Or did the last of the line return it to the Mother of the Naga long ago?

The chief has recovered, but Xi Ching is quivering more than before and Zhi Sumati appears very disturbed by the proceedings.

As I gaze at her and how she glows, like a thunderbolt it hits me that *she has the Heart*. And if she has it, she can see it, and if she can see it, she may be able to wield it. Is she aware of this?

'You will not regret this, Raja.' Chief Li bows before the creature. 'I am already negotiating with many other nations to bring together all of your deposits.'

'No, you cannot-' Both Zhi and Xi Ching, who seems to be coming to his senses, state at once.

'There are only a few guards down there, let's take them out.' Wei suggests to his sister.

In that same moment, the chief announces. 'I have brought you a sacrifice, oh great Raja.' The newly elected has no need to wave forth the guards as they are all now taking their cues from him via telepathic goo interfaced into their systems. As the guards bring forth Dr Sumati to face the creature, I take this as my cue.

I pop up and whistle for the beast's attention from the balcony.

As it spies me, it draws back like a snake affronted and judging by its squeal, I would say it is fairly repulsed. I sense its urge to strike, and imagine a cloud erupting across the ceiling of the chamber that explodes into snow!

Dr Sumati gasps. 'The Magician.'

'*She actually knows of me?*' My ego swells a moment.

'*Of course she knows you,*' Annchi silently explains. '*They tortured her daily to discover who you are.*'

My heart sinks into my gut with the knowledge that I have caused her more grief. '*I never thought they would connect us.*'

'*Get over it.*' Wei warns as I see guards suddenly drop in silence downstairs.

The beast's attack has been hindered as my snow cloud is making it rigid and subdued. I have practised this snow cloud manifestation *a lot!* Amari had informed me how much the goo hated the cold, and her tribe enjoyed the benefit of my practice during long hot afternoons. I take advantage of the break in the action to join everyone else down in the crypt, and as I arrive the last of the trans-soldiers is rendered defunct by an enviable foe. It makes me look pretty fabulous until Wei appears behind the chief and puts a gun to his head.

'Hello again.' Wei flirts with Dr Sumati.

'Hello Achiever.' She grins. 'You are looking much improved since last we met.'

The younger man grins back. 'What did you call me?'

'That is the name by which your future knows you.'

'Die you perverted, weak, murderous pig!'

We all turn to see Annchi with a gun in her father's mouth.

'No!' We all cry as Annchi splatters the president's brains all over the floor, and yet he still speaks.

'I deserve that-'

Annchi screams and stomps on his face several times, before she is riddled full of bullets by one of the guards who has regained consciousness. Wei fires a dart from a wristband and the guard falls unconscious once more. He hands me a weapon to guard the chief with and runs to Annchi. She is coughing blood, so he props her up a little.

'I told you-'

She holds a finger to his lips. 'It's ... illusion. See you ... when you wake-' She falls limp in his arms.

Wei lays her down gently and stands. His dark expression turns my way. 'Why did you tell her that?'

'Because I could not do what I do were that not the truth.' I really hope this super-bot is not about to go rogue on me, because I am really not confident I can take him down.

'Annchi set herself this task long before today.' Dr Sumati intervenes. 'She told me that damnation was a price she was glad to pay to see her father dead.'

Wei accepts that the doctor is right and so turns his anger on the chief of state - the only person left conscious to take his rage out on.

'Wei, your anger will only-' He pushes me aside to take the chief of state by the throat.

'Where is my brother?'

'I don't-' Chief Li cannot answer as he is being strangled.

As I feared, the Naga is aroused by the confrontation. Not liking that its new pawn is being harassed, it shakes off the cold and rears up again.

'You have the Heart.' It sounded like I was accusing Dr Sumati.

'How could-' She shook off the question, sensing there was no time. 'Yes.'

'Do you have any siblings, brothers?'

'No. Why?'

'Then there's a good chance you can control the Naga with the Heart.'

'What makes you think so?'

We witness the beast rise up and release what sounds like a war cry.

'The writings of Limrani.'

'You've studied her sutras?' She appears so taken by the news that my heart flutters a little.

Focus. Repay your debt in actions not words. It is Làoshi guiding me, right when I need him.

'Hold the amulet out before you and instruct the Naga to yield.' I know I am asking a great deal. 'If I could take this risk in your stead I would; however, no one can do this but you.'

The beast dives down towards Achiever.

'Naga yield!' Zhi bravely steps up.

As the Naga's attention shifts to us, Zhi holds high the Heart toward it, exhibiting the dauntless countenance that earned her the title of Mebanhcheakear. The Naga immediately withdraws to a passive position.

We all stand amazed and breathless a moment.

'Excellent,' I whisper, edging around behind Zhi carefully while keeping an eye on our dark friend. 'Tell him to liquify all his shards and take them back.'

Zhi gives the order and I release the smart dust bugs I've been holding at the borders of our nation. This is going to give the people a bit of a scare, but it will literally only take the swarm minutes to get here.

Wei is forced to back up as Chief Li hurls up liquid goo, and it slithers back to join its dark source. Smaller slug-like shards crawl out of the transhuman soldiers, and across the floor. I encourage Dr Sumati to back up with me to below where the balcony is located as a stack of smart dust comes flying into the crypt. Wei joins us in the void beneath the waterfall of bugs. 'You could have warned me.'

Through the stream, we witness the chief run into one of the sub-chambers.

'Shit!' Wei makes a move to go after him and then waves off the idea. 'There's no way out in any of the anti-chambers. He'll come running back when we turn the water on.' That's when he notices. 'Where is Annchi?'

I look to where her body had been, but only blood stains remain.

'Her lover came for her,' Zhi informs. 'Her remains are in good hands.'

'You mean she was dating an ET?' Wei doesn't know what to make of that.

'An ET who has saved your life, several times now.' Zhi points out.

'When? How?' Wei is clearly frustrated.

'They just stop time, pop in and pop out.' Zhi has such a Zen way about her that Wei is immediately calm. 'They came for a secret I hold, but didn't take it, to protect you.'

'The heart.' He worked out her secret. 'But surely they mean to protect all mankind-'

'No.' She stipulates. 'Just you. Apparently your future lover is a bit of a hotshot and they don't want to get on her bad side.'

Again, Wei is grinning like a school kid. 'I am beginning to see why they call you the Sage.'

Zhi shrugs, a little tickled by his flattery. 'I am beginning to see why they call you Achiever.'

I feel an ache in my gut that I believe might be jealousy, but on the upside, the stream of bugs seem to be thinning out.

'All I've managed to do is get my entire family killed.' Wei fobs off his part. 'You guys are the ones who've just liberated this country and the Republic of this menace in one bodacious swoop.'

Zhi and I look at each other, having not had time to consider the full implications of what just happened here.

'I never would have made it past the gate.' I quoted Wei back at him.

'And without the Magician—' Zhi began. 'I would not have known the full extent of my influence over this being.' Then she gasps in recollection and looks to me. 'You have read the teachings of Limrani?'

'In Vedic only,' I am sad to say, as I have yet to track down the original.

'Only!' She laughs. 'I guess a doctorate in ancient languages helps.'

I nod modestly, although inside I am so relieved that Dr Sumati already knows the truth about me.

Wei slaps a hand down on my shoulder. 'Dr Zeya's internship in smack addiction was entirely via the arrangement of the outgoing Khmeri Government, who were paving the way for the Republic's technological takeover.'

He had to bring that up. Still the information does confirm my previous suspicions.

'The Khmeri government didn't really stand a chance once they decided to study the goo.' Zhi silently fumes for a moment, then regains her composure. 'I guess someone leaked the news to the Republic and made us more of a target than we already were.'

Wei nods to confirm. 'Sorry.'

'I am also sorry that you were tortured because of me.' I have to get that off my chest as I feel so guilty.

She glances at the passive pile of black goo, still being coated in snow. 'Saving your life was the best decision I ever made.'

My heart wells in my chest. I had never thought to be proud of myself again, but I am deeply honoured right now. I don't notice that I am staring at Dr Sumati in the wake of the compliment.

'Shall we put this puppy to bed, and get the flock out of here?' Wei speaks up and breaks the spell.

'Yes, of course.' We both snap out of the moment.

I realise the doctor has been gazing at me too, and although it is awkward and embarrassing for us both, it is also quietly delightful to me.

'You see to putting the big guy to bed, whilst I go explain to the troops that they've all had a tech virus, and most of the world is probably infected with different strains. Fun times ahead.' He fist pumps the air a few times and heads off to do some reprogramming.

I actually really enjoy Wei's deadpan sarcasm. This to me proves that Wei is still human, and not post-human as some theorise. To artificial intelligence, sarcasm is incorrect information, and Wei certainly doesn't have any comprehension problems in that regard.

Zhi gasps and moves to a dark corner by the crypt, where some broken pieces of bone are lying. 'Tamous' statue. All the dark stone the figure was made of has returned to the creature's possession ... it must have suffocated him in stone.' She looks to the passive monster in trepidation of what it is capable of. 'At least his spirit is now free to move on.' Her voice is filled with sympathy for our holy forefather as her attention returns to me. 'How did you know I had the Heart? Can you see it?'

'No,' I suppress a smile at the implication that I might be royalty. 'I can only see the light it exudes. But the inscription on the platform up there claims that the Heart needs to stay here in the temple.'

'Don't I know it.' Zhi concurred. 'I've had disembodied doe-eyed Archons following me around for months!'

I suppress a laugh as she makes a joke of it. 'That doesn't sound very pleasant.'

'I was going to have Tamous' statue restored and place it and the Heart back on top of the crypt, but-' She shrugs, unable to carry out that plan.

'Better that the entire cluster is contained.' I spot a large earthen pot, and after turning it upside down to check it is empty, I bring it over. 'How about a nice stone one instead? It will appear less valuable.'

'It would.' She is intrigued.

At my mental request, all the bones rise up and swirl into the pot. My heart wells to see the delight on Dr Sumati's face as she witnesses the holy remains seal inside the stone jar, which morphs into a hollow statue of the monk.

'Perfect. Thank you. Amari predicted you would have great skill.' Tears well in her eyes and she gasps back her sorrow. 'I nearly had you killed. *And* ultimately, Amari was targeted because of me.' Under the burden of that belief, she begins to visibly tremble.

'Amari's death was on me.' I stress, compelled to hug her, for she has endured so much alone. She squeezes me back. 'We've been through a lot together ... apart.' I get a half-a-laugh out of her. 'I'm sure Làoshi is very proud of our efforts today.'

She pulls away to look me in the eyes. 'Làoshi was the old man who led you to the cave.'

I nod. 'Amari put us in touch.'

'Of course she did.' Zhi grins up at me, and I am completely and utterly beguiled by her.

The sound of a whistle draws our attention to Wei. 'Could we cuddle and chat later?' He motions to the creature still shivering under my cloud of snow.

With one last shy smile at each other, we look to put this dark chapter of our lives and our nation's past to rest.

Since being rediscovered, the interior of the crypt had been outfitted with a metal reinforced state-of-the-art freezer. And although the system could not freeze the creature, it did, as is presently apparent, make it very sluggish. A titanium lid sealed the system beneath the regular stone crypt lid, and Wei encoded the security lock himself.

In the process of closing the crypt, the chief of state is found cowering in the anti-chamber that houses the crypt lid when it is not engaged.

'I don't know what came over me!' He appeals to Wei as he is dragged before him.

'It was a virus.' Wei explains away all Chief Li's fears.

Chief Li will be useful to us right where he is - better a devil we could control. Hopefully this uprising diffuses the Republic's technological threat in the eyes of the world, and other nations can avoid being infected by these ancient parasites - although it is highly likely that other countries were infested already.

'I think we can all agree that Mebanhcheakear has taken back control of Khmeri. The Republic will not get back the transhuman forces they abused and experimented on without their consent.' Chief Li opened his mouth to protest when Wei turned to the troops. 'But unlike the Republic, Mebanhcheakear will not force compliance upon these warriors. So what say you, troops, who would you rather serve?'

In one synchronous movement, every soldier drops down onto one knee. 'Mebanhcheakear!'

'I rest my case.' Wei looks back to the chief, who is considering his position very carefully.

Zhi Sumati steps in to take control of the negotiations. 'Thank you, Achiever. Chief Li, I'm sure you will be president before long,' Zhi shakes the chief's hand. 'I shall look forward to discussing how best to lead both our nations toward a more sustainable future.'

Now that we have the most powerful force in the world fighting for the greater good, perhaps humanity stands a chance of leading this technological revolution in the right direction?

'Most well done, all of you.' The chief awards as he is escorted from the ruins, elated to be alive and free to go. 'You will get the peace prize for this.'

'Just peace, will do just fine.' Dr Sumati suppresses a gratified smile.

Tamous' relic is replaced on the centre of the crypt lid, and then the room is vacated so that Dr Sumati can offload her burden.

'You can both stay.' She refers to myself and Achiever before approaching the effigy where she kneels. From her pocket she retrieves the unseen treasure and appears to place it around the neck of the statue. With her hands together in front of her third eye, she bows to the relic of our forefather before rising. My heart feels like it will burst with pride as our new leader, protector of the people, steps back and places a hand over her heart. 'And now our vigil begins.' She turns to face us both.

'I have no plans.' I let the good doctor know she has my full support. In fact, I can think of nothing I should like better than to assist her to free humanity from the deceptive agendas of the current industrial revolution. Technology can also be put to good purpose - Wei is the perfect example of this and Achiever is the perfect name for him.

'Obviously you need me.' Achiever is unabashedly full of himself.

'Of course,' Zhi agrees completely. 'That goes without saying.'

Achiever looks to me. 'Let's flood this place and I'll take you to your beloved cave.'

'What cave?' The doctor is curious as she descends the stairs from the crypt lid to join us on the chamber floor.

'Your old base.' I fill her in and she frowns.

'But-' She didn't finish, and I turn to find Wei removing a finger from his lips.

He forced a grin. 'Trust me.'

Although I'd only known Wei a day, I probably had more faith in him than most I'd met since my arrest - and Dr Sumati clearly has the utmost confidence in him.

As Dr Sumati insists on accompanying us, we have some difficulty getting her new trans-guards to allow us to take off with her. So in the end, we use Wei's alien tech to just disappear from their physical sphere and radar.

Touchdown is in a clearing by a mountain range and Zhi Sumati is clapping in excitement. It is plain to see that it is not just the amazing flight that is causing her to rejoice, but being finally able to revel in her freedom. 'I know exactly where we are.' She steps off our transport and leads off through the forest. To be back on familiar ground must feel like a real homecoming for her.

I look to my cyborg friend, who appears as delighted as I do by the leader's liberation. *Actually, I did achieve something in all this.* He pursues Zhi down the track.

I follow, digging Wei's receiver out of my ear as I rather want my thoughts and brain space back.

'I can still hear you, you just can't hear me.' Wei turns back to remind me.

'Suits me fine.' I toss the earpiece back at him.

He catches it without flinching and stashes it away.

We approach a ravine with a stream running through it, and Zhi serves Wei a look of excitement. 'There doesn't appear to be much damage from out here.' Her pace speeds up.

'What does she mean ... damage?' I query, heart pounding ten to the dozen.

'I have no idea.' Wei plays innocent.

Dr Sumati gasps with joy as we enter a long cave that opens wide into the amazing cavern of script that I remember. 'Xi Ching said he blew it up.' Zhi is so excited that she is near fit to burst.

'The thing with missiles is you have to program them.' Wei replies; the rest is self-explanatory.

I front up to the closest wall to begin translating. I have read an alleged copy of these sutras, and I am dying to know if I recognise any of these writings and can confirm the ancient Vedic transcript's claims.

'Are these the teachings of Limrani?' Zhi has clearly wondered this before today herself.

'I expect so,' as the Vedic texts described this cavern to the letter.

> 'In the tongue of the Master's ancestors,
> Ziran is 'the correct self'.'

I read aloud as my company is curious too.

> 'It is to be in harmony with the as-it-isness
> and to be unaffected by artificial influences.
> Tianran is a thing of heaven
> untouched by human influence,
> A thing fully characterised by Ziran.
> It can be said that by gaining Ziran
> One draws closer to a state of Tianran.'

I drag myself away to look at the doctor and nod. 'I recognise this.'

'Sounds like I don't have a hope in hell of spiritual redemption.' Clearly Wei was affronted by the piece.

'Sorry, I didn't mean to-'

Wei waved me off. 'I'll settle for immortality.'

Our new leader is now frowning and smiling at once. 'So what did you do with the warheads, Achiever?' She very diplomatically changed the subject.

'I decommissioned them and have them stored in your old bio-lab.' He makes a beeline off toward a tunnel.

'Come, Dr Zeya, I'll show you the amazing facilities here.' Dr Sumati waves me after them.

Although I desperately want to continue the mammoth task of translating the walls, I don't want to miss the tour either. 'It's not going anywhere.' I grin, ecstatic beyond measure to finally be here. With one last twirl to take it all in, I speed up to catch my companions.

At the end of the tunnel, there is a large round metal plate in the floor.

The doctor is about to step onto the large plate when Wei pulls her back and holds her still.

'What?'

'I hear something.' I hear nothing and believe he's just really trying to push my buttons. I wondered if it was his alien makeover that made him such a handsome bastard, as you can barely tell he is transhuman. If I was a betting man, I'd stake my family jewels that he has a wee crush on our new commander-in-chief.

Wei looks at me with an innocent expression on his face, as he'd probably picked up on my thought. 'That's the pot calling the kettle black.'

'What is?' Dr Sumati is naturally curious.

Wei is still looking at me. 'Now if you'd kept the earpiece in-'

A clank of metal, like the lift engaging, shuts down our banter. Wei looks at Zhi. 'I told you I heard something.'

'But if it is not following our telepathic command, who has control of it?'

The metal plate begins to rise out of the ground.

'Has it ever done this before?' I ask, but guess not, as both my companions are backing up.

'No.' Dr Sumati replies, and Wei shakes his head to concur.

I join the retreat as I am dwarfed by the metal cylinder extending upwards before me.

'I guess that explains why the ceiling is so high in this anti-chamber.' Wei comments casually as he and I take up flanking positions on each side, and slightly in front of our new leader.

'I had no idea that there was another lift beneath ours,' she utters, watching the elevator rotate. 'And if I didn't know, no one knew.'

'So who built it originally?' Is the pertinent question.

'No one knows.' Both Wei and the doctor chime in at once.

'Well, I think we are about to find out.'

Once fully exposed, the elevator stands about two metres tall. We watch completely mesmerised as the outline of doors appear in the metal. They push forward before sliding aside over the outer casing to reveal three very tall pale beings, all dressed in white. There is one woman and two men. Their hair and skin are almost as white as their attire, making their bright blue eyes stand out all the more. From all appearances, they carry no weapons, but they are wearing some technology.

The woman of the trio steps out of the lift to look us all over, and her companions stay where they are. Stunningly beautiful to my eyes, all three of these beings appear to glow from within.

'I hear and understand you,' Wei states and all three visitors wince and fiddle with devices in their ears, while forcing smiles.

'Can you all understand me now?' A voice emanates from her, although she does not move her lips.

'Yes.' We all whisper quietly to confirm.

The visitor smiles warmly. 'No need to whisper. We have adjusted the input now. So sorry, we were not expecting to run into company. Please don't fear. I am Shankara.'

As the doctor steps forward to address the visitor, Wei and myself both bow out of the dialogue and she now understands who is in charge. 'I am Zhi Sumati, the closest thing this nation has to a leader at present.' She places her hands together at her forehead and bows to the visitor, who smiles delighted.

'I am the closest thing Agatha has to an adventurer.' She duplicates Zhi's greeting as her eyes drift back to Wei. 'You have a very intriguing energy about you.'

'This is my strategist, Achiever.' Zhi does the honours.

'I'm mostly machine,' he explains bluntly, clearly expecting her to be repulsed, but instead she whistles.

'Who's got friends in high Pleiadian places then?' She looks him over, completely enchanted.

'Creator.' One of her companions calls from the capsule.

Zhi's gasp draws all eyes to her, but she waves off her reaction as nothing. 'Apologies. Continue.'

'We are only meant to check the extent of the damage,' Shankara's subordinate appeals. 'We need to leave now in order to get back to the sub-station to report on schedule.'

'Go, report, and send the transport back for me.' She instructs.

'Is that-'

'Seeker.' The word saw him carry out her order without further question.

'You know the Seeker?' I am stunned.

'I know many Seekers.' She smiles warmly, believing she is delivering me good news.

'There are many?' I am bewildered.

'Why are you here, Shankara? Is there something we can help you with?' Dr Sumati regained control of the conversation.

'This outer earth passage had been reported damaged beyond use, so I came to assess the wreckage to find that there is none.' She is clearly happy about that.

'I prevented the destruction.' Wei stepped in. 'If your transport is so fast that some time dilation occurs in transit, then perhaps I changed circumstances while you were still in transit.'

'I like your thinking...' Shankara turns her full attention to Wei.

'Let's go and have a look at your glyphs then, shall we?' Dr Sumati suggests out of nowhere and begins leading me away. 'Read me more ...'

Wei and Shankara are clearly engrossed, until Shankara notices us leaving.

'Before you go.' She comes after us. I am aware of being spellbound by her, but the experience is not in any way alarming. 'You must forget this meeting ever took place-'

'That kind of glamour won't work on me,' Wei came up beside her, and they both observe us curiously.

'I don't need it to work on you, if you will be my accomplice here.'

'What's the agenda?'

'To keep humanity human.' She replies as the light I perceive around them intensifies. 'The timelines are shifting more rapidly now, and in our favour.'

'So we've been here before?' Wei supposes.

'I should think so.'

'Do I ever say no to a partnership with you?' Wei poses what he clearly believes is a rhetorical question.

'I should always let you decide.' Shankara smiles and looks to Wei as a light flare blurs all memory of this strange and beautiful visitation.

Chapter 12
Agartha 4133 A D
Akashi - The Fool

D rawn from my dreamtime by the sensation of being smothered in warm fuzzy feelings is the perfect awakening on any day. Yet I withdraw back into the unconscious to recall what the Inter-dweller just conveyed to me and I manage to latch back onto the message.

'In the battle of good versus evil, the war is not over until **everybody** wins...'

No, that can't be right. What kind of spiritual advice is that on today of all days? Another burst of joyful energy from Chi and I cannot withhold my giggles. 'Enough, Chi.' I open my eyes and wriggle about to encourage my constant companion to back off, lest my physical form explode from all the goodwill. Chi already knows what I have told no one else, and is excited for the day's proceedings.

Chi was my birth present from my father's Pleiadian friends, Jeroke and Gozin, who, having no children of their own, are rather like godfathers to me. Their birth gift took the form of a sphere of cosmic energy that primarily acts as a shield from any low vibratory forces - physical or etheric. This measure is hardly necessary here in Shamballa; and in fifth-dimensional Agartha it is completely redundant as no Archon presence can exist there - though the Creator begs to differ on that count. But beyond creating tranquillity everywhere we go, and filling me full of all the highest emotions constantly, Chi just floats around me and has done so my whole life. My protector is part of the family so no matter where I go from here, Chi comes too.

No other child of Shamballa has ever been given such a gift from our guardian race, or been personally tutored by the Creator and Achiever - two of the most respected minds and beings of the inner earth, and also advisors to the Council of Sophia. But I am no ordinary seven-year-old girl, as I am the cloned reincarnation of Tamous the Innocent. I have more of his DNA in me than either of my biological parents, and thus I appear far more akin to the dark-haired, dark-eyed ancient Khmer race of Kambuja, than I do to my pale Nordic cross Pleiadian, blue-eyed parents. I have been brought back to this world to disclose the secrets of the Archons to my fellow humans, as Tamous is the only human known to have endured a mind meld with the Demiurge. Unfortunately, the master was petrified in stone before he could disclose all their secrets. The Creator has been training me in past-life regression, and the fact that I am also a soothsayer, as Tamous himself was in his younger days, was a delightful surprise for everyone. The hope is that we will retrieve some of those precious insights about our adversary, discover weaknesses, and secure a better future for all organic life on earth, both inner and outer. Or at least, that was the situation yesterday, but the timelines might have altered since then, and it could be an entirely different scenario today. I seem to be the only one keeping track of the changes. Welcome to my life in the mid-planes, caught between physical time-space-history and timeless-limitless-creation. I long to go beyond Agartha and become the Inter-dweller. Tamous had also desired this, but with all the combined experience of all the chapters between he and I, we have still not figured out how to break through this simulation of existence. However, its Archontic distortion may hold a clue. It is often that which we fear that holds the answer we are seeking.

Chi floats backward as I rise to sit up and have a huge stretch. 'That's the last time I shall need sleep, ever!' I am confident of that.

The door to my room vanishes and Mother enters with a handful of clothes. 'Good morning! You are awake ... wonderful.'

'Today is the day, Mama.' I announce and stun her to a standstill.

'Today?' Her voice is suddenly hoarse with emotion. 'Are you certain, sweetheart?' She attempts composure, despite blinking tears of joy from her eyes.

'I know how excited you and everyone will be about this.' Everyone had a vested interest in my capabilities, hence my private tutors and cosmic security system. 'I would not say so in jest.'

She places the clothes aside, and taking hold of my hands, looks deep into my eyes. 'Do not rush on our account, we are all in this together.'

She is worried that I am not ready to retrieve the information I must before I shift out of this physical form that holds so much of Tamous' DNA and genetic memory - good and bad, unlike Akasha that only retains the constructive experiences. No one wants to send a child to meet the Antichrist, but the further from birth I grow, the weaker my retention of Tamous' life will be. If I do this, I can join with Sophia and return with my parents to the etheric existence of Agartha.

'The Inter-dweller and I see no need to prolong it any longer ... in fact we may have already waited too long.'

Mother kisses my cheek and hugs me tight. 'However long it takes.'

'I know, Mama.' There are certain questions needing answers that my guardians fear exposing me to. However, I am going in as an observer and therefore as emotionally detached from the experience as possible. Every night as I dream, I visit Làoshi in the Akashic library and he assists me to connect with all his chapters, including Tamous. Like them, I am eternal, so what do I have to fear from anything?

'How did you dream?' Mother brushes the hair from my face.

'Very well. I saw into an old timeline.'

'Did you?' Mother is always spooked by my timeline shifting talk, but she tries very hard to hide it.

'I saw a timeline where Father found Limrani's cave for you.'

Mother laughs - clearly she thinks my statement is a folly. 'How would that work, when I was studying the Satura Cave text before I had even met your father?' She ruffles my hair like I am being silly.

Mother heads the Surface Earth Antiquity Department at the Ancient Wisdom School in Shamballa now, but in the era and timeline I saw that was only a distant aspiration.

Okay, so we are not in that timeline anymore. I surmise.

'Everyone knows Shankara found the cave-'

'The day she met Achiever.' I finish Mother's statement. *I thought so. I dreamt this.* I suspect that Achiever has changed more timelines than Shankara or the Pleiadians. So what else has changed in this shift, I wonder?

As familiar as I am with the Department of Time at Agartha's Ancient Wisdom School, the large images of archaic surface earth cities moving slowly across the curved walls in the foyer never fail to captivate me. Today we are viewing an ancient temple that features huge statues of a snake with many snakes sprouting from its head. The sight causes a pang of recognition to pass through my entire body.

'That's a little scary.' Mother notices my eyes fixed on the image as it rolls around the foyer. 'Are you alright, sweetheart?'

'Tamous knows this place.' I guess, as I certainly couldn't have been there - no one from the inner earth went up to the surface these days.

No matter which timeline eventuated from everyone's little interferences in history, surface earth still went to hell in the late 22nd century. Zhu Sumati and Taylay Zeya established a huge awareness campaign about the risks associated with the AI goo and its technologies. They committed to print all the teachings of Tamous, and his philosophies on the inner and outer path finally saw the light of day. Many countries explored more sustainable low-tech environments to lower health risks, feed the population, and be more in flow with nature. But the countries already secretly cooperating and being controlled by the Archons continued along their destructive path. The more high tech they got, the less people they needed to feed, and once they brought all the deposits of goo together, it devoured all life on surface earth. The inner earth nations once again sealed themselves off from surface earth to avoid contamination and to protect Sophia.

'That is Boran Maon.' I turn about to see Achiever entering after us, along with my father. I run to hug them and they both squat down to my size.

'You made it!' I hug my father tight, then move onto Achiever, my teacher and best friend - next to Chi.

'Of course. We all wish to know if the Seeker initiative has had an effect on what is to come and whatever else your Inter-dweller might care to share with us.'

So that's why they think we are gathered here. That's fine, can do.

'Gosh I'd hate to think that was all for naught.' Father comments, and Mother chides him for putting extra pressure on me - which he isn't.

'This is the final exam and you are going to ace it.' Achiever has faith in me. 'Then you will *all* be free to join with Sophia and ascend back to your etheric existence.' He smiles, but I see sadness in his eyes. He will miss having us all as "physicals", as "etherics" lead very different lives.

'So no revisiting Tamous' death for me then?' I ask, and my parents both appear horrified.

'Where on earth did you get that idea?' Father asks and hugs me close again.

I glance at Achiever, who winks - not sure if it is because he is on my wavelength, or that he wishes to reassure me. I wonder if the Creator remembers why we are all really gathered here, or if I am the only one?

'Good morning, Akashi.' The Creator exits her office, smiling broadly at me.

'It certainly is.' I reply.

Shankara is wearing a physical form today, which is highly unusual for her, but the way she smiles at Achiever in greeting, I believe I understand why she has regressed. Achiever cannot ascend to be with her in Agartha, or so he fears.

'So, are we all ready for this?' Shankara poses, and my parents appear far more apprehensive than I feel.

As I have Chi and the Inter-dweller with me always, it astounds me that my elders imagine that any harm could possibly befall me. Still, I do not judge my other chapters; it took all of them to become me, our alpha and omega. Now we discover how we fared this time around. Clearly my teachers, parents, and all those around me are not as connected to the Inter-dweller as I am - in the reality of this timeline, in any case. I remember my father speaking of Làoshi when I was little, but he hasn't mentioned any personal connection to his higher self for some time now. I may have originally been created to spiritually hack into Tamous' earthly consciousness, but I had seen glimpses of the lives of all my other chapters, including those in my company now. I know the Creator's fears, but they are groundless. She is the first human soul mind to manipulate timelines, and her efforts have altered a great many things, I suspect. Shankara came back through time personally to warn the Council of Sophia that she had borne witness to an event that suggested Agartha and even Sophia were vulnerable to Archon attack. The wait that she has endured to discover whether her project has borne fruit has been excruciating! Yet she has been nothing but patient with me, everyone has been. It is my choice to deliver disclosure today.

'Where shall we go first?' I get comfortable in my recliner, eager to get started. 'Will we go straight to the future? I am sure you are all eager to learn if the worst has been avoided?'

The Creator smiles at my boldness. 'That's a bit adventurous, let's ease in.' She suggests, as all present take a seat and get comfortable.

It is clear to me that Shankara seems unsure if she wants to know if her Seeker program achieved the desired outcome. What if she failed? Could she endure another quantum leap backwards to start her crusade all over again?

'I have a question.' My father held up a finger. 'How did we find Tamous' completed verse in Taylay Zeya's Mountain of Mystery, when I know for a fact the verse was never completed?'

'An excellent paradox.' My mother nudged him affectionately, also interested to know.

'To Phnom nei Athrkambang, it is.' I close my eyes and focus on a point of light between my eyes. I go towards the light and it grows larger until I am one with the Inter-dweller and through him I enter our Akashic library.

I observe the incomplete verse on the cave wall before me and where once I stood in awe of my Master's ability to write, I now know every character. The inscription reads. 'Why man and woman? Why a dualistic universe - attraction and repulsion from the microcosm to the macrocosm?' This first part of the text was written by Tamous at the Seeker's behest, as Herodotus claimed he had read the entire verse in the future. However, the Seeker only managed to dictate half the verse to Tamous before the latter was arrested. This initial part of the verse is a complete paradox, as it cannot really be attributed to Tamous or Herodotus, only to the story itself. But having pondered the query many years, and knowing the Seeker's verse to be incomplete, I feel that I at least have an answer to the question posed here, despite who the mystery querent may have been.

'Father,' I surfaced back into the physical world to advise my company. 'I believe you already know the answer to your query.'

'Limrani.' He said surely.

I open my eyes to catch his proud smile. 'She married her general,' I inform them.

'The brother of Tamous and liberator of the Kaundinya kingdom?' My mother gasps. 'In all her writings, Limrani never mentioned that she was the Princess Soma! She was living a double life.'

'I told you I suspected that she was.' My father is vindicated, despite realising his speculation could not be accepted as fact. 'But I would not have imagined in a million years that Limrani would have married Bào Satura! They would have killed each other had I not intervened.'

Mother smiles broadly, so proud of my father's past accomplishments. 'Spirits unite to fire, by heated friction, a solar flare, creating an opportunity to love that which is objective - the non-self - and ultimately use with wisdom the form. Do you still think she was just talking about making love?' My mother nudged his shoulder.

'Was she not?' Achiever acts surprised and none the wiser.

'No.' My father looks at me and smiles adoringly. 'I now know different.'

As it seems the conversation has turned sentimental, I pose. 'Next question?'

'I have a query for your Inter-dweller.' Achiever pipes up, which is most unusual as he prides himself on knowing everything. His query must be spiritual in nature and I already know what it is. 'You wish to know if your spirit still resides with you, or if it moved on long ago.'

'Yes.' He replies frankly. 'Am I post-human?'

Achiever's celestial crystal heart centre was old Arcturian technology, for they were the procurer of these rare celestial crystals - like the Heart of the Naga. When viewed psychically, it is absolutely blinding, so not even the best seer in Agartha can discern whether a human spirit is being harboured within Achiever's transhuman form.

Shankara appears pained for him. 'Akashi won't have access to such information.'

'I am being drawn somewhere.' I politely counter the Creator's claim and relax back into my chair, wanting to help my friend solve this dilemma.

I join the Inter-dweller within the library of light, and I am immediately propelled into a rescue of one of Shankara's Seekers, who'd gone rogue in time and nearly found himself as Archon fodder.

This traumatised agent is imploring me to zap him with my taser, and when I refuse he sneezes in my face.

My perception zooms in to view a bunch of defunct devices carrying black goo as they land inside Achiever, and then reanimate.

My eyes snap open and I suppress a gasp. Achiever might be following my thoughts, so I try not to allow my awareness to resonate.

'What's wrong, angel?' Father asks, and is alarmed as Achiever rises from his seat.

'What's going on?' Shankara senses the sudden tension.

A conflict flares inside Achiever as he struggles against raising his gun arm to take aim at me. My parents and Shankara throw themselves between us, though there is no need; Chi's goodwill merges with Achiever and he is mesmerised.

'He's bugged.' I enlighten and my company are all doubly horrified.

'Oh my God!' My mother shields me as Achiever begins to cough up a cluster of bugs that are contained within Chi's sphere. Once all the offending items have been collected, the little orb drifts apart from our friend, leaving his patient in a rather euphoric state.

'Father sneezed a bunch of defunct bugs on Achiever-'

My father holds a hand over his mouth in remorse. 'So I did.'

'I believe they can reactivate when close to a power source.' I continue. 'And Achiever is the most perfect energy generator to be found anywhere. But because he radiates such huge amounts of positive energy, they've been pacified.'

'Until threatened.' Father concludes.

'Are you alright?' Shankara approaches to help stabilise Achiever in the wake of the episode.

'I adore you,' he confesses, still very woozy.

'The feeling is mutual.' She assures him as he regains his senses.

It is odd to see these two so affectionate; it warms my heart that they have found happiness with each other.

Inside Chi, the bugs calm and swarm together to meld into a smooth stone with barely detectable metal specs inside. Chi returns to me and drops the stone into my hand. My mother nearly has a heart attack.

'It's okay, Mama, it's dormant.' I place it in my pocket. 'It is safe with me and Chi.'

'How did you know Achiever had been infected?' Shankara is surely wondering if I can read a cyborg's mind now?

'I have only been made aware of twelve chapters attached to our Inter-dweller, but perhaps Achiever is a thirteenth chapter, or a whole new book?'

'How could I possibly be linked to your Inter-dweller?' Achiever approaches and kneels down before my chair.

'Chi would have had no effect on you if you were post-human.' Shankara realised, teary-eyed herself.

'That is exactly right.' I place a hand to his cheek. 'Your soul lives on just like the rest of us, Achiever.'

The news brings a tear to Achiever's human eye.

'No need to suffer physicality any longer, you will transcend along with the rest of us.'

Shankara's gasp of joy might be a little premature.

'The bugs have been holding you back.' I advise. 'Keeping your vibration in fear, and encouraging you to well ... you know.' I don't feel right disclosing his shortcomings, yet it must surface and be released for him to clear the path for his own transcendence.

'Keeping secrets, you mean?'

I nod, and his sights divert to Shankara.

'You're keeping secrets?' There is hurt in her voice - it's much easier to mask emotion in telepathic dialogue.

Achiever nods and rises. 'In my own defence, I have been bugged until now.'

'I'm listening.'

'I've been contacted by my brother.' He begins, and her gasp gives him pause a second. 'I know you wanted me to lose that connection.'

Shankara steps back, holding her palms to her cheeks. 'I dreamt of this.'

'Actually, you lived it in another timeline.' I put forward. 'But circumstances have changed dramatically since then.'

'Has Tian told you that he reached the singularity before the Archons?' Shankara recalled what she'd foreseen and put the query to Achiever. 'Does he claim to have complete control of the sentient sludge and that surface earth is now a utopia?'

Achiever is surprised. 'That is accurate.'

'You cannot believe it, surely? That's how they hacked you last time.' Shankara is incensed. 'You have compromised us...'

Chi comes to float over them and the conversation calms.

'Tian is the only sibling I have left.' Achiever appeals. 'And I thought that perhaps Akashi might be able to confirm Tian's claims today.'

'Alright then.' The Creator breathes deeply, preparing herself to face her fears. 'If Akashi is ready to look at the outcome?'

I nod, absolutely ready.

If it is at all adverse-' She adds.

'I will come straight back.' I know the drill.

'What happens if the outcome is adverse?' My father is alarmed by his train of thought. 'Do we do this all again?'

My mother gasps at the thought.

'Please,' the Creator urges, 'maintain a positive outlook.'

'Sorry, sweetheart.' My father apologises, though there is no need, I am not afraid.

'I am syncing in.' I close my eyes to join with the Inter-dweller and project our consciousness out into the future along this present timeline.

Time speeds along around me as I float high above Shamballa in a consciousness bubble, observing our beautiful city grow and prosper. Clearly this eventuality exists way beyond the time the Creator fears the Archons will invade. This does seem to indicate that by all appearances the Seeker program has been a success! But before I pronounce this, I need to investigate what is happening on the surface of the planet.

I soar up towards the surface of the physical form Sophia built around herself in order to nurture humanity. I shoot out of the dark passage and into a huge expanse crowned with tiny lights. Ribbons of light streak the sky with colour so breathtaking to my senses that the energy centre in my chest wells in appreciation and tears pool in my eyes. A huge orb reflects light onto the nightscape below me. I soar over ice, faster and faster until I hit expansive snowfields, towering mountains of ice that stretch into green valleys and waterways. There is wildlife everywhere, but no ground lighting to be seen. Had humans survived? Or had animals regained their right to rule? Where are all the Archons? Had they simply run out of food and moved on at some point? On the subject of earth history, my parents are the definitive experts, hence I know for a fact that the Archons always win out. Had we finally reached an outcome where they didn't? This would mean that the Creator's Seeker program had worked beyond expectation, but where is the goo and its minions?

It had been brought together somewhere. I ponder where I might find it, when my mind drifts to the picture in the foyer this morning that had me so fascinated. 'Boran Maon'.

I recapture the image in my mind. 'Where is this place now?'

Before me materialises a huge modern complex, yet I am flanked on both sides by the same large Naga statues that had once overseen the entrance to the temple at Boran Maon. I look around for any other indicators that I might be at the destination I had seen on the foyer wall earlier, but all other traces of the ancient temple complex are gone. I approach the building but the doors do not open for me.

An electronic eye looks down on me. 'Are you the last of the Kaundinya?'

'I am that I am.' I reply.

The modern building before me crumbles into the ruins of the old temple, which then repairs itself until it appears the very image of the reconstruction I'd seen on the foyer wall. I am swept inside the temple, past the altar open to the sky, and down the stairs to a landing where a pit of black goo sucks the souls from men, yet I am not afraid. I am eager to understand the reason behind the existence of this adverse, dark matter. I am a soothsayer; it is why I have been brought here, to know its purpose. I am led before the rippling pool of black goo as it rises up into a snake-like creature with smaller snakes protruding from the back of its head like a mane. I am in complete resonance with Tamous at this moment, in understanding that this is what I am on this earth to do. This creature must be understood and named. To be unnamed is to be eternally real. I must see past the manifestation to the mystery. Darkness is the source of all enigmas and it is a gateway that must be traversed in order to gain understanding. The monster bares down on me and

I open myself to the darkness as it closes in.

I awake with a gasp. Everyone is huddled around me. I am shivering violently, and I realise I am freezing cold.

'Oh, thank goodness. Was it horrible?' My mother is kissing me and caressing my face, trying to get me warm.

'Give her a moment, some room to breathe.' Shankara passes Mother a blanket to place over me, and the warmth is so welcome.

'Am I the last of the Kaundinya?' I ask the Creator, but it is Mother who answers.

'No baby, Tamous was not a royal.' Mother pauses as Shankara gently takes hold of her arm to advise us.

'Akashi is Kaundinya, via your bloodline, Dilan. That's why you were chosen to be Akashi's mother. It was a happy coincidence when you paired with Herodotus, who turned out to be the Seeker who ran this vital mission to retrieve her DNA. But then there are truly no coincidences.'

'What?' My mother almost chokes on the shock and excitement of it. 'I'm Kaundinya?'

'Well of course, they were staunch "natives" and so when the time came to retrieve the last of the pure humans from the surface, the descendants of Zhi Sumati were amongst them. But I hardly think Akashi will be the last of the line.' Shankara smiles to reassure me.

I smile back, knowing different.

'That explains so much.' My mother is still reeling. 'My obsession with these women, my foremothers!' She chokes up again.

Due to my mother's aforementioned obsession with the texts of these women who had both recorded the legend of the Kaundinya, I am well aware that the last of the line must return the Heart of the Archons to Sophia. If I boldly announce that I need to go to surface earth before I join with Sophia, I will be refused.

'What news of the future?' Achiever is bursting to know and so is Shankara.

'It is perfect.' I am glad to report to them, as this is the truth and what they want to hear.

'How do you mean?' Shankara is tentative.

I look to Achiever, so pleased for him. 'Everything I saw is in alignment with Tian's claims.'

I have never seen my friend smile so broadly. 'He has contained the Archon threat?'

'Are you saying there is no inner earth attack?' Shankara's eyes well up with tears of relief.

'Yes and yes.' I answer them, respectively. 'Not only is inner earth thriving way into the future, but surface earth is also thriving, like no human or machine ever existed.' *Except for the structure at Boran Maon.* 'The Seeker program is a complete success.' I confirm and I am smothered in kisses from everyone.

All the adults lose the plot, cheering and embracing each other as tears of joy are shed. I am pleased to have made them all so happy, yet Chi and I are not swept up in the excitement. I reflect on my time at one with the Archon, and dare not even think about the understanding I obtained within that void. I know what I must do.

'I am so glad you might be reunited with your brother. And I owe you an apology.' Shankara admits to Achiever. 'As I have also kept secrets.'

Achiever's adoring expression and body language remain unaltered. 'Out with it then.'

'After the dream-' She looked to me to allow. 'Or past timeline memory, I could not fully trust you with the true reason I began the Seeker program.'

'The mission was to find someone to aid us with the Archon problem.' Achiever voiced his understanding, whilst vaguely motioning to me.

'In part,' she warranted. 'But the true mission, to find the Heart of the Archons, has never been realised. Hero reported that Limrani held it once, but we don't know what became of it after that.'

'The Heart of the Naga, you mean?' Achiever corrects.

'I believe it was called that later on,' Shankara looked to Mother, who nodded to confirm.

Now Achiever is frustrated. 'I know where it is. Well, where it was anyway.'

'What?' The Creator is momentarily annoyed at herself for allowing fear to trip up her aspirations; still, she lets it go. 'Well, it would seem that the treasure is no longer required to secure our future.'

That is not entirely accurate, but I say nothing. I have stopped trembling.

'What did we miss?' Jeroke and Gozin appear.

'Only everything!' My father exclaims.

Congratulations to the cutest little physical ever! Gozin emphasises. *I won't be able to call you little physical much longer.* He pulls a sad face.

You'll just have to use her real, and perfectly wonderful name ... congratulations on your ascension day, Akashi. Jeroke added. *I look forward to seeing you all in Agartha.*

'Even Achiever will be joining us.' My father proceeds to convey all that has been revealed in my soothsaying.

'May I go to the bathroom?' I slip off the lounge and make a move towards the door, hoping they are all too engrossed to accompany me.

'Of course, sweetheart.' Mother takes a step in my direction, but before she can excuse herself, I assure her.

'I am fine by myself.' To emphasise how spritely I feel, I skip towards the door and Chi pursues. From the corridor that leads to the foyer, I glance back to see that Mother has returned to the conversation. The door to the Creator's office seals closed behind us and I head straight for the elevator.

There are several routes to surface earth, and because I have access to the Creator's memories, I know all of them. The express ride to the surface that will land me closest to my target destination is to be found in a complex deep below this establishment. It is accessed by reciting a mental code, which is picked up by the silent sensory interface of the elevator. The code is an intricate pattern you envision that flashes a certain colour sequence, and when I bring this to mind the elevator chimes back to confirm the instruction has been received. I smile at Chi floating alongside me. 'We are in.'

Chi's energy is delighted and carefree, thus we agree we are in flow with the way.

After a lengthy descent, the elevator doors part and we step out to a huge, wide corridor that leads off for vast distances in either direction. It is completely devoid of people, or life of any kind, and is unnaturally silent. Even though it probably hasn't been used by anyone since the last great human migration to inner earth, this place is pristine and well lit. If I am right, I am probably the first person here since the end of Zhi Sumati's lifetime.

Zhi and Taylay Zeya had seen the writing on the wall. Without humanity completely uniting against the immortal sentient goo, the Archons would prevail in the end. The Sage and the Magician would have been welcomed in Shamballa, but they both chose to stay on the surface and continue to seek a solution to the Archon problem and protect those innocents who had missed the migration to inner earth.

I have seen this place through the Creator's memories of the past, but I pause and go within to recall which way I proceed from here. A lift door opening startles my eyes open once again.

Achiever walks out. 'Fancy seeing you here.'

'Don't follow me, or try to stop me.' I stand my ground, not to be moved.

'I would never.' He strides right past me, turns right, waves and keeps on going.

I run after him and he slows a little so that I can catch up. 'Is this the way to Boran Maon?'

'It is.'

'You heard my thoughts, didn't you?'

'Surface earth is like no human or machine ever existed ... *except for the structure at Boran Maon.* That thought?'

'That's the one.'

'It has to be where my brother is based.'

I had not considered that the entity driving the security at Boran Maon might be Achiever's long lost brother. 'Perhaps he is personally guarding the beast and the Heart?'

'Seems logical.'

The suggestion feels true to me also.

'Shall we join forces?' Achiever suggests gallantly.

'I guess I could use a responsible adult-'

'To blame when we get busted.' Achiever teases, but he's not wrong. 'You know I don't parent, right?'

'But you do have gadgets that may come in handy,' I point out. 'Like that transporter on your back.'

Achiever nods to agree. 'It's not going to take them long to figure out where we have disappeared to, so let's speed things up a little. He retrieves the disk from his back and throwing it down, we climb on board.

The transporter makes fast work of the long distance through the tunnel, which terminates at a complex. Here there is a communication station, facilities for physicals like me, a restroom, lounge and several capsule launching platforms. These appear like ordinary lifts, but they are not.

The inner cabin of the capsule is a weighted ball that automatically rights itself no matter what trajectory the outer capsule is travelling - we could move up, down, and sideways and not notice. The floor is a light-filled flat surface, but the walls curve with the ball shape to allow for the comfortable seats that are arranged between the spaces in the four cardinal directions. These gaps are for door openings, which disappear altogether when the capsule is in motion. The passage itself feels gravity defying, like floating with no effort. I sense I am moving at great speed, yet feel no resistance to our passage.

The capsule service to the surface has several legs. We exit at a sub-station and enter another capsule to continue the ascent many times over. No one is around, not even any of our extraterrestrial or inter-dimensional friends, but Achiever is still hypervigilant regardless.

'You scared?' He queries, as the next time the doors part we shall be on the surface.

'No. You?'

Achiever is amused. 'I've been here before.'

'So have I.' I flash a cheeky grin.

'I often wonder if I am speaking with Akashi or Tamous?' Achiever glances at me sideways, sussing me out.

'I feel at one with Tamous and all my chapters.' I am honest. He doesn't have to believe me, but to his credit he mostly does.

'And you think I might be one of them? Part of your Inter-dweller's soul cluster?'

I feel that he is inspired by this prospect. 'We like to call it a story.'

'A soul story, I like that.'

'And you will be the next chapter.' I imagine. 'The chapter that takes place beyond the simulation, where the hero emerges victorious to the applause of all his nearest and dearest, for overcoming the distortion.'

'But not alone, surely?'

I laugh. 'We are all one there.'

'Where, is there, Agartha?' He queries.

'No. Beyond the simulation Sophia and the Archons created.' I voice part of my understanding, but not all, not yet.

'Shankara told you this?' He assumes.

'The Naga Raja told me.' I pull the stone from my pocket to check on it, and give it a little pat. 'You okay, little guy?'

'You connected with the Naga Raga when you were in a trance?' Achiever probes.

When I observe how concerned he appears, I have to chuckle.

'Chi and Làoshi are with me, no need to worry.'

'The Naga Raja is notorious for leading people astray, you are not to believe it.'

'I know what it is better than anyone.' I give the stone a little snuggle against my cheek and place it back in my pocket. Now Achiever appears very concerned. 'We lead by example.' I explain my actions.

'It hates love,' Achiever came over and knelt before me. 'Show it kindness and it will suck your soul from your body, or turn you into a living statue as it did Tamous.'

'I have Chi.' I remind him as I fear Achiever may break with his manifesto. 'Are you parenting right now?' People often mistake him to be my father as I appear more like him than either of my parents.

'I am friending.'

'It's okay,' I place a hand to his cheek, I so adore him. 'I have got this.'

Achiever smiles, conflicted. 'You are such a worry. You make me believe you when there is no logic to substantiate your claims.'

'That's my Chi.' I look to my guardian, floating serenely in the centre of the cabin and completely at peace with our journey.

A door appears in one of the blank spaces between seats and draws apart to expose a dimly-lit tunnel.

'Let's go.' Achiever tosses down our transport beyond the doors, and we step out into an anti-chamber that is fairly unremarkable. Achiever safely deposits me onto the transporter and before the lift disappears into the floor behind us, we are already moving at speed down through the cavern complex.

'You alerted my parents, didn't you?'

'I did.' He admits, 'they should catch up just after we get there.'

'Father will come, but not Mother.' I laugh at the thought of her even considering visiting the surface; she had always felt it far too dangerous.

As we clear the tunnel and enter the Satura cavern, with towering walls covered in the ancient text my mother had been studying for years, I know she would be thrilled to see this in person. 'Even if Mother did get this far, she'd leave this chamber.' I smile, shielding my eyes as the shafts of light leaking from outside are blinding.

'I think you underestimate a mother's determination and love.' Achiever hands me a set of goggles to wear. 'If you think the light of

Sophia is bright, wait until you see the light of Solaris!'

'The outer world sun.' I have heard much of this, and the orb I had seen in my earlier vision was the moon, which only reflected the light of Solaris. I place the glasses on my face as we enter a smaller tunnel on the far side of the cavern, at the end of which is an opening filled with golden light.

Beyond the light barrier is blinding at first, but so warm! We rise up above the canopy into a limitless, expansive sky, so unlike anything I have ever known in this lifetime. Below I glimpse forest and vast wilderness, consuming cities now occupied by animals. This is exactly as I envisioned, only now the surface is lit up a hundred times brighter and the colours are intense! My eyes water profusely as I attempt to observe the views, but I forego the opportunity as it is far more comfortable to keep my eyes closed. Clearly Mother Earth had completely recovered and had now paved the way for another round of human occupation on surface earth.

'Shoot!' Achiever veers our craft violently to the left and he grabs hold of me at the same time that I grab onto him.

I look around through squinted eyes to see a sphere of light shoot off in the direction we are moving.

'That is probably the Pleiadians.' Achiever identifies the UFO that just dropped out of subspace in front of us.

'I bet they brought Father.' I close my eyes once more and wipe the tears from my face.

'And probably Shankara too.' Achiever warrants.

'Now you're in for it.' I squint and grin sweetly up at my friend.

'I know.' Achiever dotes on me. 'I'm just your patsy.' He absolutely didn't care.

We touch down as the sun sets behind the horizon, and as the twilight is more conducive to our vision, I am able to remove my goggles.

On the stairs of the huge construction at Boran Maon, we are met by my free-floating, semi-etheric godfathers, Shankara, my father and, shockingly, my mother, who is carrying a thick coat on her arm for me - even though it is very warm.

'You had us worried, little physical.' Gozin acknowledges our arrival.

'Akashi!' Mother rushes to me, then kneels and embraces me like I've come back from the dead. 'Never do that again.'

'I won't.' I assure her.

'What were you thinking?' She pulls back to look from me to

Achiever, who is being frowned at by everyone.

'A very good question?' My father does not look happy.

'Surely you realise how dangerous this is?' Shankara appeals. 'We have finally achieved the desired outcome, and you want to risk unleashing the creature again?'

'But how did we achieve it?' Achiever wishes to know. 'And did we really, or is this just a ploy to draw humans back to the surface?'

Chi is working overtime, dashing around everyone to keep them constructive.

'Achiever is just watching out for me. This sabbatical was my idea.' I stand between my friend and his accusers.

'Good word.' Achiever, as my tutor, credits me. 'But this *sabbatical* was not your idea.' He moves me out of the firing line. 'I came to discover what happened to my brother. I have no intention of disturbing the beast. I can't speak for Akashi, however, as she claims to have conversed with it in her trance.'

'Thanks.' I look at my partner in crime, annoyed that his cyborg insensitivity just overshared with the group ... on purpose! All eyes turn to me to learn my reasons for being here.

This could be tricky. My aim is to disclose only enough to get me into the complex without alarming anyone.

'You conversed with it?' Shankara is clearly horrified.

Timelines have altered a little since they created me to join with Tamous and learn what he discovered from Naga before he died. There is no point trying to explain, it'll just confuse the issue and upset people. 'If the Archons are put down and human ego rendered redundant, then what is binding humanity to this planetary round anymore? Shouldn't humanity have ascended?'

'You think it is because the Heart has not been returned?' Mother realises my point first.

'Exactly.'

'But you may not be the last of the line, Akashi.' My mother is loath to even consider that might be the case.

'It is a choice. Don't you see? No one will be the last of the line until they decide that they are ... that we are done here.'

'I don't understand?' Tears well in my mother's eyes. 'Everything has worked out perfectly, humanity's future is finally assured in the inner and outer world.'

'If the Heart pacifies the creature and you remove it to return to Sophia,' Father adds, 'then won't you just stir up the beast, and start the destruction all over again?'

'Precisely,' I award. 'That is why we must use our advantage before we lose it.' I see Achiever heading towards the entrance of the massive building, and I follow accompanied by Chi. The last thing I want is to upset the wonderful beings who brought me back here to finally face this ancient conundrum.

'I'm lost. What are we supposed to do?' Mother appeals to Shankara and Herodotus. 'I want to get her out of here, and I certainly don't want to allow her anywhere near that creature.'

'We brought Tamous back to guide us,' Shankara defends my insistence.

'My guess is that we watch and learn.' Father suggests.

I conceal a shy smile - how wonderful it feels to be walking into this situation so supported; the last time I was here, it was a very different matter.

This complex is grossly larger than the original temple, and bland and soulless by comparison. The front doors are metal and have no visible exterior control panel to hack into.

Achiever is stumped. 'Hello?'

I reach him. 'There is this eye-'

We both jump as the small and zippy orb drone shoots out of a hidden compartment in the metal facade, and darts around sizing us up. With its camera shutter open, it looks just like an eye. 'Are you the last of the Kaundinya?' It asks in a very pleasant voice, not at all robotic.

'I am that I am.' I respond before Achiever can get a word out. 'That's how I responded in the vision.' I explain my interjection, then note that Achiever has a tear in his eye.

'Tian.' He states surely.

The eye looks to and zooms in on Achiever. 'Wei?'

'Yes.' He nearly chokes on the joy that confirmation brings him.

The huge metal doors retract to leave a double doorway-sized gap in between, and awaiting us in the foyer is a young man appearing very much like Achiever. Tian does not appear trans-human, however, nor has he aged a day in aeons.

'How?' Achiever had not taken a step towards his brother, nor had Tian taken a step towards Achiever.

'You also appear greatly improved since I last saw you.' Tian made a fair point. 'How is it that you are still hanging onto life?'

'*That would be thanks to us.*' Jeroke and Gozin float in to investigate, and Tian does not seem to register their presence. 'We had to trade in all our favours with the Arcturians to get that heart.'

'You're a hologram.' Achiever realises.

Jeroke and Gozin give him the thumbs up to confirm that. None of the technology is able to register their presence.

'It hurts less this way.' Tian explains and Achiever nods in understanding.

'No more shakes.' They both conclude at once and smile.

'I always preferred the pre-crash me,' Tian refers to his fully human projection. 'You are looking good for a hunk of junk that's a few thousand years old.'

'I had some ET friends put me back together.' Achiever explains, finally stepping over the threshold and into the building. 'I think one of them was dating Annchi, but I've yet to get a confession.'

My godfathers disappear through a wall to avoid the subject.

Tian smiles. 'I miss our sisters ... but I'm so glad you came.'

'You have the Archons contained, you said?' Achiever asks the vital question as I am joined by my parents and Shankara, who prevent me from following Achiever right away.

'I do.' Tian replies.

'How?' Achiever is now face to face with his brother, who appears completely solid and real, yet his hand passes right through. 'And why can't I connect to your network?'

'Because I trust you about as much as you trust me at this point. As far as securing the beast, I didn't have to do much. It was already hibernating here, having exhausted all its human resources, when a couple of its minions found my head and fired me up just for amusement. Once they connected me to the system, it didn't take me long to find one of the back doors we'd built into Father's network, and once I was in, I took control of everything, including this complex.'

'Like a virus.' The lovely irony is not wasted on Achiever.

'Just.'

I know that Achiever is only trying to determine whether or not his brother is lying, but the truth is, it doesn't matter. 'Do you have the Heart?' I ask.

'I cannot see it,' Tian admits, 'but I am told it is here among the other holy relics, brought here when other deposits were transported from all over the world. But if you are truly of Kaundinya descent, you will see it.'

'Goodness.' Mother took a deep breath, conflicted between wanting to leave immediately and venturing further inside to see the mysteries she'd only ever read about.

'Why gather the clusters here in the middle of the uncivilised world?' Achiever wondered.

'The Heart.' Shankara, Mother and I all answer at once as my father ventures into the foyer to look about.

'That was my conclusion also.' Tian smiles. 'When I took over, I had all the TI hardware lay itself to rest in quick dry cement.'

TI or Technical Intelligence refers to what a transhuman becomes when they physically die and are post-human, which is what I believe Tian is now. His soul is certainly not connected to this projection. Rather than a ghost in the machine, Tian is more likely a picture of his former self, which the Archons have extracted from his memory chip and are using to gain our trust.

'Would you like to see?' Tian invites us all into the crypt.

I thought he'd never ask. I gently pull away from Mother and enter the foyer, as does Shankara. I would have asked my company to wait here and proceeded alone, but there was not the slightest chance of any of them obeying me.

It is only my mother who replies to the negative about proceeding. 'This is so dangerous.'

My father grins. 'Fun, isn't it?'

'No.' Mother represses a smile.

'Are they the original walls from the old temple?' Father points to a huge glass case featuring a whole wall of ancient text.

'Yes, they are.' Tian concurs. 'It outlines the legend of the Kaundinya in several ancient scripts.'

Dilan is over the threshold in a shot. 'Holy mother!' She approaches the case reverently, staring at the contents in wonder. 'This is the account Limrani wrote about in the Satura texts?'

'Shall we come back for you?' Father calls to her as we follow Tian into a cloakroom. Mother abandons her examination and makes haste to catch us up.

But the answers she hoped to find in her pursuit of knowledge, all await in the next room in any case.

'It is extremely cold in the crypt.' Tian warns.

'Akashi.' Mother catches me up to put the coat on me, and as we move down the corridor we pass through a double set of security doors to enter a dimly-lit crypt of stadium-sized proportions.

An enormous pool of black ice sits at the centre of the complex, surrounded by tiered platforms of Archon TI's - a stark, white mosaic of horror that extends all the way to the ceiling.

'How horrible.' Mother utters, grabbing hold of me to comfort me.

'They are just machines.' Tian reminds her. 'I got them to prepare their own graves.'

I break free of my mother to approach the pool.

'No Akashi-' She tries to grab me back, but I allude her.

'It's okay, Mama, it is dormant and suffering so much.' Tears well as I sense the pain and anguish.

In the battle of good versus evil, the war is not over until everybody wins. My Inter-dweller reminds me.

'This is not winning.' I utter to myself.

'Can you see it? Can you see the Heart?' Clearly Tian is excited to finally ask the question. 'Will you be the one to free us all and take the Heart back to Sophia?'

Interesting, if Tian is an instrument of the Archons, then why is he encouraging me to take the Heart back to Sophia? I glance aside to see if Achiever has caught my thought, and as he is staring me back, I guess he has. *Because taking it away will free the Naga Raja?*

'It will enrage the Naga Raja.' Tian replies, obviously he has a silent speech interface of his own and has also picked up on my query. 'But I can hold the beast here in check until you complete your quest. This creature destroyed our family. I may not be all I once was, but I am still on the side of humanity.'

'Akashi...' Mother crouches beside me. I know she can see it as clearly as I can. 'We can leave now, you do not have to be the last-'

'But I am.' It is sad to see tears rimming my mother's eyes. Yet I feel nothing but a sense of calm resolve.

'You're just like him,' she chokes on the realisation.

She refers to Tamous. 'Walk with me?' I invite.

She kisses my cheek, squeezes me tight and rises.

We walk the length of the black ice pool, our company in tow. At the far end of the chamber, a statue of Tamous sits upon an intricate altar, with a light beaming from his chest. It is the Heart, but only Mother and I see it. Before the altar platform is a large stoneware vessel, and behind the altar platform is a tall processor that runs like a giant art installation up the height of the crypt to the steel-reinforced ceiling.

'Wait.' Achiever came forward to look over the effigy of Tamous. 'This cavity in the chest was not here before, it looks like an electronic dock for something?'

'The Heart.' Mother informs him, for we both see the set-up.

The jewel is no longer on a chain, but in a metal harness that locks into the statue.

'I believe it may be powering Tian and the security system.' She concludes, sadly.

Everyone looks to our host, who will cease to be if we take the Heart. 'It will take a good while for this pool to defrost. Plenty of time to return the Heart to Sophia.'

'No. We don't have to do this.' Achiever protests.

Then the lights go out and only the stable illumination of Chi remains. Mother and I have the additional light of the Heart to see by, and she gasps when she sees the holy treasure in my hand; she is the only one who can see I have it.

From Achiever's shoulders spring a couple of spotlights, which shed more light in the darkness.

'Thank you.' My father and Shankara are very grateful. But Tian's haloform is gone.

It doesn't take Achiever very long to figure out what has happened. 'One of you removed the relic.' He looks to Mother first, but he knows the truth. 'Why Akashi?'

The sound of ice cracking startles everyone. This is followed by another crack and another, until all that can be heard is a cacophony of shattering ice.

Achiever turns his spotlights out into the stadium. Not only is the black ice-field cracking, but all the TI soldiers, cemented into graves, are now ravenously trying to claw their way out of the ice. 'Tian lied.' He realises. 'We have to get out of here.'

Transporters are thrown down ready to make our escape, but I back away towards the defrosting pool.

'Come on, sweetheart,' Father urges me towards them, and is baffled by my refrain. 'We shall get you to Sophia.'

'The Heart was not Sophia's to give.' I advise them. 'Just as we are not Sophia's to protect.'

'No, no, no.' Achiever believes I am being manipulated by the dark stone I took out of him.

I take the dark crystal from my pocket, and now that the pool is not so cold and forbidding I have no problem returning it. 'Welcome home, little guy.' I cast it back to its cluster, and it is immediately absorbed into the melting goo.

'You need to come with us.' Achiever takes a step closer as the dark goo rises up behind me. 'Akashi, whatever it told you, it is lying. They want to keep you trapped here forever.'

'No, you have it all backwards. It is Sophia keeping us trapped here, with her beauty, abundance, adventure, and nurture. How horrid does the Demiurge have to make things before we want out of the illusion? How many more times do we go around the reincarnation loop before we realise those earthly desires we keep coming back for are the trap? Even in Agartha our spirits are still contained within the Sophia distortion we call Earth. She.' I motion back to the creature in the pit. 'Is the insurance policy released by creation to counter Sophia's defiance.'

Everyone before me gasps.

'You know I am telling the truth.' I look to the Creator, who has gone very pale.

'Ultimately, Sophia is responsible.' Shankara is unnerved to admit.

'They distort,' Achiever insists, tears of love and desperation forming in his human eye. 'You said so yourself. Please come with me.'

'Sophia is a distortion also, albeit a seemingly more pleasant one.' I feel the calm reason of Tamous and the Inter-dweller flowing through me as I speak. 'It hates love, you said, but I say how can it possibly know love, when it has no heart?'

'The Arcturians took the Heart from the Archons for a reason.' Jeroke and Gozin float into the commotion just as several of the TI soldiers break loose and come running at us.

Everything stops and my surroundings are frozen in time - except my large, floating, blue godfathers, Chi and me.

'It was because humanity could not be trusted not to misuse AI technology again that the Arcturians destroyed all the AI, and humanity was plunged into a tech-less dark age for aeons. As the protector of humanity, Sophia was given the hearts, fashioned into one jewel, for safekeeping, in the event that the beast was ever released from the abyss. But of course the Naga would mourn the loss of their connection to the creator, as would we. We all dream of going home.'

Both my godfathers appear very perplexed. 'You're supposed to be *frozen little physical.'*

'*Maybe it's the...*' Jeroke whistles as he refers to Chi flitting about.

'Are you here to see that I take the Heart back to Sophia?' After all, their father was on her council. The Pleiadians had been overseeing humanity's evolution since the conflict of which I spoke.

They both appeared offended by my suggestion. '*We are not permitted to interfere.*' Jeroke assures me.

This makes me smile as that's never stopped them before. 'Then you can let them loose, no one will be harmed. Isn't that right, Shesha?' The Naga Raja leans in close behind me, unaffected by the Pleiadians time freeze, and as passive as a puppy.

'*You know her name?*' Jeroke appears most impressed. '*You went there?*'

'I went there.' I nod, most impressed with myself for venturing into the darkness within darkness, for there lay the gateway to understanding.

'*You know what this means?*' Gozin is oddly excited.

'*Father will be·*' Jeroke notes another light anomaly, and draws our attention to the fact that Saegoi the White is manifesting in our midst.

Why is he here? Gozin sounded wary for me. *I have heard the White state that they serve Sophia.*

We protect Sophia's interests. He corrects.

I was still uncertain of the master's intent. 'Are you here to persuade me from my course?'

We are here to observe. The White looks at Jeroke. *Continue.*

Jeroke releases time, and as he does the unfrozen TI legions resume their sprint towards my parents.

'Shesha, I permit you to see your Heart!' I hold it high and all the Archon forces - machinery, etheric beings and the shapeshifting goo - stop dead and look to it. 'Humanity's gift to you for your service.' I see all the dark faces of the creature's unseen minions gazing at the Heart in absolute awe - along with the Naga Raja, who snatches the item from my grasp and swallows it.

All behind me gasp to see our one item of defence disappear down the creature's throat. But unlike when it had previously swallowed objects or people, it did not regurgitate the Heart. Instead, she began to glow from the inside. Maybe when she had swallowed Tamous, she had mistaken his sacred energy for the Heart?

Saegoi teleports himself to the Creator's side after noting

Shankara's gaze upon him.

'I thought human affairs were of no interest to you?' She queries his presence again, perhaps attempting to determine if it is a good sign or not.

We underestimated the impact your little project would have on this round, Creator. Solaris is most impressed and sends his regards.

'Solaris?' The Creator, bemused and awestruck, looks back to me and the shapeshifting entity at my back.

Shesha begins to sparkle silver through the dense blackness of her being, and all her tech units fall down defunct as etheric minions abandon their tech to join with the shining celestial presence of their source.

'What is happening?' My father is bemused, yet amazed, pulling my equally enchanted mother in close for an embrace.

One of the beast's etheric minions emerges from bathing in Shesha's energy field. Sparkling all over, the Archon takes flight to point out an ornate urn placed at the feet of the Tamous statue. *'For you.'* Shesha's tone is soothing now.

'Thank you.' I make a move toward the urn, but Achiever motions me to refrain.

I recognise that particular relic. Jeroke assures us it is harmless. *That which the Naga would not relinquish to the mighty Emperor Ashoka, they give to you now, Akashi.*

'I shall open it, all the same.' Achiever moves to the item and removes the lid, whereupon another tiny orb, the like of Chi, escapes and they dance around each other.

I clasp my hands together, feeling the orbs rejoice in their reunion.

Shesha leans in close to me, exuding the most loving energy and glistening like the celestial being we all truly are. *'All is void.'* She is pleased to declare.

'And void is everything.' There is nothing left to be done, learn, complete, fight, save, endure! But there is still much to create, love, discover, explore, and experience.

The eternal flame of spirit burns up all the activity on the plane of illusion. A quickening within my being draws into all of my individual points of awareness, heralding a release beyond any transformation endured in all our chapters on earth.

Chi and the tiny twin orb twirl to a collision and implode into a light-filled porthole, through which we are drawn into the celestial highway that leads back to the Inter-dweller.

Epilogue
The Outer-dweller

We are that beyond I am, poised to realise the potential of those transcended, formless ones who dwell in the primordial light realms of creation. We have been a dweller on the threshold between the heavenly realms and the material worlds - and within the chapters of our Akashic library each facet of the human condition has had its place.

We endured individual manifestation through the karmic cycles of time, life, death and rebirth. We have been pure of heart, abandoned, caring, and warlike. We explored the depths of our feelings, our own destructive nature and sought answers to the great mysteries to ignite our imagination. We have coveted absolute power and knowledge, worked miracles, and relinquished all we once held dear.

Through a seemingly endless process, we fathomed how to cease to make karma in the three worlds of the physical, mental, and emotional being and relinquish the physical temple imprisoning us in the desires of material matters. I merge with the spirit of the Inter-dweller on the outskirts of the great primordial light realms of creation. In mutual meditation, our vibration attunes in resonate harmony to that source from which we first came. Solaris, who holds at his core our passage back to source, sounds the joyous note of victory, and the pure frequency expands his illumination to fill the farthest reaches of the infinite night, igniting the path home for his exhausted cosmic twin and all her machinations.

References

Page 256 -   "Yet mystery and manifestation arise from the
              same source... This source is called darkness."
              Lao Tzu by *Tao Te Ching*

Page 256 -   "Darkness within darkness. The gateway to all
              understanding."
              Lao Tzu by *Tao Te Ching*

Page 262 -   "What is a good man but a bad man's teacher?
              What is a bad man but a good man's job?"
              Lao Tzu by *Tao Te Ching*

Bibliography

Tao Te Ching - Lao Tzu
By Stephen Mitchell translation.
Harper & Row, New York, USA, 1988

A Treatise on Cosmic Fire
By Alice A Bailey.
Lucas Publishing Company, New York, USA, 1925

Awakening the Heros Within
By Carol S. Pearson.
HarperCollins Publishers, New York, USA, 1991